# Praise for *A Twilight Reel*

*A Twilight Reel* is an extraordinary collection from an extraordinary writer. Grounded in place and time, Michael Amos Cody's stories are world-wise, whip-smart, and eminently readable.

—Wesley Browne, author of *Hillbilly Hustle*

A vivid portrait of a community in an age of rapid change.... Cody's is one of the most authentic and inspired voices in contemporary Appalachian fiction, addressing such subjects as AIDs, bias, troubling history, marriage, ghosts, dementia, and abiding loyalty and love. In these linked stories he speaks for both the region and the world beyond.

—Robert Morgan, author of *Chasing the North Star*

It's no accident that a character in Michael Amos Cody's *A Twilight Reel* is reading *Dubliners*, for the world of this remarkable collection—Runion, North Carolina, and the "age-rounded" Blue Ridge mountains—is pure Joycean.

Recurring characters in a dozen stories stumble toward human connection, sometimes over generations. They are shadowed by Lincolnites and Rebels, the killing ground of Shelton Laurel overlaying the cemetery where families of both factions gather in "Decoration Day." This skillful triptych of far past, reenactment of the past, and present describes the region as "a mess of allegiances." Reverend Thorn counters, "Love is the context of our lives."

Yet twilight is coming to Runion: the Good Samaritan held at knifepoint, gay neighbors treated to a burning cross, an undelivered letter, the drive-in closing, the community church turned Islamic Center, the ruin of AIDS, so many looking for love in all the wrong places.

Cody is the masterful caller of the reel, leading us into mystery, time, a little magic realism, and possibly redemption—ever mindful of the living and the dead.

—Linda Parsons, author of *Candescent* and *This Shaky Earth*

What wonderful stories these are, rooted in mountains I know so well! Cody blends traditional and modern elements, wry humor, spooky darkness, and his intimate knowledge of the region to bring us a deftly rendered Appalachian story cycle. Each of these stories sings its own song, but when read together they are even stronger, offering a symphonic, nuanced portrayal of our contemporary Southern Highlands. Expertly crafted with memorable characters and sharp-eyed details, this is a real gem.

—Leah Hampton, author of *F\*ckface*

Reminiscent of Spenser's *Shepherd's Calendar*, these twelve linked stories follow the progress of the seasons throughout a calendar year, rendering the fullness of life to be found in one Appalachian community. With its town-gown divide and its traditional and often insular residents struggling to become more inclusive, Runion, North Carolina feels both representative and one of a kind.

When a four-year-old's sucker punch ruins his mom's Valentine's Day celebration, or a hypothermic granny strips off her clothes and unloads a double-barrel shotgun at her would-be rescuer, each unexpected action is matched by the psychological drama that unfolds in its wake. And every instant of these lives makes clear the choice between intimacy and isolation. Stories this vital make me want to stand on a street corner and shout out the good news of Michael Amos Cody's talent!

—George Hovis, author of *The Skin Artist*

For those who wish to understand contemporary Appalachia—with its crazy quilt blend of past, present, and future—I cannot recommend *A Twilight Reel* highly enough! Savor each of these stories in turn and then marvel at the world they together make.

—Terry Roberts, author of *A Short Time to Stay Here*
and *That Bright Land*

Michael Amos Cody's *A Twilight Reel* avoids the old and the new stereotypes of Appalachia to present a nuanced portrait of a region learning how to understand and embrace the new while preserving the best of its traditions and letting go of what never worked in the first place. These insightful and magnificent stories make me wish for a second edition of *Writing Appalachia* so that the anthology might include one of them.

Two preachers clash over soul secrets; a widowed grandfather rekindles his passion for Marilyn Monroe; a Muslim congregation converts a failed fundamentalist church into a mosque; a small-town businessman subscribes to a gay men's magazine to help him understand a son who's come home to die of AIDS; and two flute professors, one straight and one gay, give a new look to legacy at the local state university, where in one corner of the campus once stood an ancient oak that kept secrets from the era of Daniel Boone and Bishop Asbury—all these narratives and more come to life in Cody's stories, which are both a twilight reel and the song of a new Appalachian dawn.

—Theresa Lloyd, Co-Editor, *Writing Appalachia: An Anthology*

Pisgah Press was established in 2011 to publish and promote works of quality offering original ideas and insight into the human condition and the world around us.

Copyright © 2021 Michael Amos Cody

Published by Pisgah Press, LLC
PO Box 9663, Asheville, NC 28815
www.pisgahpress.com

Book design: A. D. Reed, MyOwnEditor.com
Cover design by Jamie Reeves
Cover photo by Joey Plemmons

The following stories originally appeared in these publications:
"The Wine of Astonishment" (*Short Story*)
"Overwinter" and "The Flutist" (*Yemassee*)
"Conversion" (*Still: The Journal*)
"The Invisible World Around Them" (*The Chaffin Journal*)
"A Poster of Marilyn Monroe" (*Pisgah Review*)
"Two Floors Above the Dead" (*Tampa Review*)

Library of Congress Cataloging-in-Publication Data
Cody, Michael A.
A Twilight Reel/Michael Amos Cody
Library of Congress Control Number: 2021934473

ISBN: 978-1-942016-66-3

First Edition
May 2021
Printed in the United States of America

In memory of Jeff Rackham, who encouraged my first short story efforts.

Also by Michael Amos Cody

*Gabriel's Songbook*

A Novel

# A Twilight Reel

## Stories

## Michael Amos Cody

Pisgah Press
Asheville, NC **IP**

# Table of Contents

The Wine of Astonishment ...................................................1

The Loves of Misty Sprinkle...................................................23

Overwinter ..................................................................45

The Flutist...................................................................59

Decoration Day ..........................................................89

Conversion ............................................................ 137

The Invisible World around Them................................... 157

Grist for the Mill................................................... 181

A Poster of Marilyn Monroe........................................ 201

A Fiddle and a Twilight Reel ...................................... 219

Two Floors above the Dead ...................................... 253

Witness Tree ........................................................ 267

Acknowledgments.................................................... 294

About the Author................................................... 297

It happens that my place, the Appalachian region of America, being neither north nor south exactly, neither east nor west, but a geographical, historical, cultural, and spiritual borderland, has an interesting and complicated past (and present).

—Jim Wayne Miller, "I Have a Place"


Gravestones bear the names
of our personal history,
so many who came and went
before my time began.
In the soft voice of a mind
addressing itself, the interior
sound only I can ever hear:
"Someday you will come here
and never leave."

—Jesse Graves, "Voice"

# A Twilight Reel

# The Wine of Astonishment

One Thursday night in the dead space near the end of January, Reverend Amos Thorn stood in the kitchen of the Runion Community Church parsonage and sipped at the lukewarm dregs of his third cup of coffee. He watched his wife shake suds from her hands and rinse the last supper dishes and stand them in the drainer.

"I talked to Sam Fricker today," Thorn said. "The new dishwasher should be in sometime between now and Valentine's Day."

"That will be nice," Pamela Thorn said. "But I've kind of liked the feel of doing them by hand."

"And I could sit here all evening and watch the way you move."

She turned and smiled and flicked soapy water from her fingers at him. Then she returned to her work.

Between the swish of hot water and the clatter of plates, bowls, and silverware, he heard her soft voice, now humming, now whisper-singing snatches of a song—". . . earth stood hard as iron, water like a stone. . . ." Something in her supper of meatloaf, green beans, and baked potato quarters seemed to have affected the rims of his eyelids, making them elastic and droopy. All he wanted at that moment was to strip with her in the kitchen, to carry her in a bear hug to bed, and to fall asleep without uncoupling.

Instead he stood, thrust a hand into his trousers to tuck in his shirttail and readjust himself.

"Well, wonderful supper, honey." He set his father's old brown fedora on his head. Then he worked his way into the heavy brown overcoat the RCC congregation had given him in December of 1993 for his first Christmas as their preacher.

"I wish you didn't have to leave," Pamela said.

He could see in the set of her eyes that she felt some of the same desire he did.

"The temperature's already down to"—she leaned over the sink in an effort to see through the beads of sweat on the window— "looks like twenty or so."

He admired the shapeliness that showed through her dusty blue denim skirt as she leaned over the dishwater, admired the shading of muscle in her forearm as she braced herself with her right hand on the countertop.

*Thou art fair, my love; there is no spot in thee.*

He sighed and slipped another of her warm cinnamon buns from the cloth-covered basket on the stove top and pushed it with stubby fingers to the bottom of his cup. When he thought the bun had soaked up the last drop of coffee, he pulled it out and stuffed it whole into his mouth.

"Amos?" Pamela said, drying her hands. "What time do you think you'll be back? I don't want to have to worry about you on those icy curves any longer than I have to."

"Well," he said around the sweet wad in his mouth, "you know these mountain folk, honey. It's probably almost her bedtime right now." He stepped to the sink, sunk the cup in the dishwater, and, with a quick movement he couldn't control, caught Pamela in arms wrapped tightly around her waist.

A light sheen of perspiration lay on her forehead and her upper lip. The heat she'd drawn from the dishwater mingled with her own and rose up around his throat and face and ears.

"One yawn from the old woman or nine o'clock, whichever comes first, and I'll get out of there." He smiled. "Home by nine-thirty at the latest."

Pamela lifted the collar of his overcoat and pulled it tight around his thick neck.

"I wish you didn't have to go," she said. "What about her own pastor? Doesn't she go to church back in the hills?"

"I don't know. Granger never did say exactly. But I'm the one he asked to deliver his message." He stared for a moment into her eyes, trying again to sort the colors there—the various shades of the dominant blue, the hints of green and silver, the flecks of brown. There seemed to be in her no color of emotion or shading of personality that couldn't be found in those eyes. He leaned and kissed her. "Wait up for me, okay?" he said and raised one eyebrow and smiled again.

Pamela grinned and patted both hands on his barrel chest, chuckled, and then turned away, out of his arms.

After the warmth of the kitchen and his wife, the bitter wind outside the parsonage snapped at his flushed cheeks like a hungry animal.

He let his car warm up for a moment, then crossed the rear parking lot of the church, and turned right on Main Street. At the one light at the top of the hill he took another right onto Lonesome Mountain Drive, and with the suddenness that always surprised him when he traveled this direction at night, he lost the lights of town and moved beneath winter-wasted trees that stooped over him and shook in the icy wind.

* * *

Earlier in the day, he'd raised his eyebrows at the sudden "Afternoon, Reverend," and looked over the top of reading glasses perched on the end of his blunt nose. Beyond that he didn't move. He'd been staring at tithing pledge cards and the mail on his desk since lunch, his mind on Pamela's steady breathing in his hair and on his forehead, her sleep-warmed breasts against his cheek, her taut runner's thigh under his palm. The feel and warmth of her had surrounded him since five o'clock that morning when he was called from their bed by a choir member's sudden "heart attack," which didn't turn out to be gas and indigestion until he'd driven all the way to the hospital in Asheville.

His afternoon visitor, Granger Gosnell, filled the doorway, standing there nervously working his thick fingers around the sweat-stained brim of an old brown trilby hat. He wore heavy brown work boots. His oil-and-mud-spattered jeans hung low on his hips, their button and front belt loops hidden behind the red-and-gold-checkered flannel shirt stretched across his sagging paunch. He had a bulbous red nose and spiky white hair with shocks of black at each temple.

"Come in, Granger," Thorn said.

The big man lumbered into the room and hung his hat on one pointed shoulder of a straight-backed chair across the desk from the preacher and eased himself down onto the wooden seat.

"Well, how did your check-up go this week?"

"I keep them scratching their noggins," Gosnell said and scratched his own head. "They can't figure why I'm still kicking."

"We know the answer to that, don't we?"

"Yes, the Lord's been good," Gosnell said and cleared his throat. "But it ain't me I come to talk to you about, preacher. It's my sister I come for."

"I didn't know you had a sister. A brother, but—"

"Everybody's heard tell of Gunther, I reckon," Gosnell said and shifted in the wooden chair, his blue eyes glancing from Reverend Thorn to the books that lined the wall. "But Ollie, that's my sister, she—" He stopped and scratched the back of his head and scrunched up his face. "Well, it might be for the best that you don't know nothing about her. Most of what you might hear ain't good, but it's just mean falsehood."

"What might I hear?"

Gosnell squirmed in his seat again.

"Go on and spit it out, Granger. I was an only child, but I know it's tough dealing with siblings." Thorn released a brief thick-lipped smile and then added, "It's been that way since Cain and Abel."

"I reckon," Gosnell said and tried to smile in return. "Well, I know that for true so far as me and Gunther goes, but I ain't never known Ollie for much of a sister. She's nigh on twenty year behind me, you see. About your age, I expect. No more than a few years older, I'd say."

Thorn raised one eyebrow.

"Is she a half-sister then?"

"No. We're full-blood kin, I reckon. She just come along late in Mama's life."

Thorn took off his reading glasses and laid them on his desk. Then he leaned back in his chair and rubbed his eyes. He felt his stomach growl and peeked between his fingers at the clock, disappointed that it was still two hours before Pamela would have supper for him.

"So, what can I do for your sister?"

Gosnell rubbed a hand as big as a skillet over his short-cropped white hair and squirmed in his seat again.

"I'm hoping you'll agree to tell her about my condition."

"Granger, you told me you've known about your cancer for over five years."

"And that's right."

"In all that time you never told your own sister?"

"Well, we don't talk none." He leaned forward over the edge of Thorn's desk. "I was done and gone from the homeplace before she was born, and to her I reckon I weren't much more than a visitor that come by a lot. But when Mama took sick, she made me promise to look after the girl. 'Granger,' she said, 'you look after Ollie now, you hear?'" He leaned back again and slumped a little in the chair. "Well, the long and short of it is I ain't done it."

"Does your brother ever see her?"

"Gunther don't know who he sees half the time. His brains is so addled—" Gosnell stopped and glanced at the books again.

"He digs a fine grave," Thorn said and smiled again. "Ted Ramsey says he's never seen such precision grave digging as your brother does."

"Well, I reckon he's finally found his gift all right, but he'll probably dig my grave and never even know to think the first sad thought."

"Well, let's not get sidetracked with that here," Reverend Thorn said. He put his elbows on the desk and tented his fingers in front of his face. "Now, about your sister. Does Ollie want or need you to look after her?"

Gosnell made a frustrated swipe at the air with his right hand.

"Ah, Ollie don't want nothing but—" He paused and drew a deep breath. "You see, it's more than age that makes me and her different. Mama always said behind her hand that Ollie was something not of this earth." He paused. Then, "I don't know."

Thorn again raised an eyebrow.

"That seems like an odd thing for a mother to say about her daughter."

"Well, you ain't never seen Ollie, so you don't know." He shifted in the chair again, and his trilby hat fell to the floor. "She's got beauty and strangeness about her that's frightening to people, and there's them that call her a witch 'cause of it."

Thorn leaned forward.

"I ain't never really known her at all, you see," Gosnell said. "And I don't even know if I can get to know her. It's just that Mama's voice's been ringing in my ears the last while, and I've got to do something about my promise." He looked at the preacher. "Can you help me?"

"I'll do what I can, Granger." He leaned and pulled his briefcase up from the floor. He clenched his teeth behind closed lips and stuffed a stack of pledge cards into one of the leather pockets.

Gosnell stood up and picked up his hat from the floor. His thick fingers again began working at its narrow brim.

"I reckon maybe if you told her I was sick, she might—" He stopped and cocked his head to one side. "Reckon she might?"

"We can't know for sure," Thorn said. "The threat of a loss sometimes pulls families together." He stood up and closed his briefcase and followed the big man out of the office. "But if she does come around, she's not going to believe you're sick when she sees you. You look strong as an old bear."

"I'm strong enough yet, I reckon," Granger Gosnell said with a smile. "Excepting when it comes to dealing with the devil and females."

\* \* \*

The front tire dropped off the asphalt shoulder, and he jerked the car back into the left-hand curve. He eased his foot off the brake and coasted into the straightaway that descended toward the intersection of Lonesome Mountain Road and Highway 25-70.

Suddenly the headlights touched the broad back of a man walking some distance ahead.

The walker didn't turn around but kept striding down the middle of the right-hand lane.

Reverend Thorn eased his foot onto the brake again, and he could feel against the pedal the sudden acceleration in the pulsing rush of his blood. The man's sheer size frightened him, but he knew what would be said in town if his car were recognized as it passed by in the opposite lane and word spread that he'd offered no Christian charity on such a bitter night. Then again—he'd often thought about this—the man could be a messenger from the spiritual realm, an angel, who might have some difficult Truth to pass on or might be here as a test of his faith and his worthiness as a shepherd of God's flock.

*Be not forgetful to entertain strangers: for thereby some have entertained angels unawares.*

When Thorn's car was no more than thirty yards away, the figure suddenly seemed to lurch toward the safety of the roadside and stumbled out of sight down a small embankment.

*Now what?* Thorn thought and slowly rolled the car to a stop.

There was a movement at the edge of the light, and an old man scratched his way onto the gravel at the side of the road and stood unsteadily. He wore a heavy sheepskin coat, several sizes too big for him, its broad collar turned up around his ears. His dirty overalls dragged the ground around his feet. A high-crowned hat made of some kind of dark fur sunk low over his ears and forehead.

Thorn thought it must have been all the ill-fitting clothes that made this shrunken old man cut such a huge figure, that and some trick of shadows and reflected headlights in the clear cold mountain air. He lifted his foot from the brake and eased the car up even with the sheepish-looking fellow, touched a button, and rolled down the passenger window. The rush of cold air that entered again bit at his cheeks and nose.

The stooped old man rubbed his white whiskers and squinted at him.

"I saw you fall," Reverend Thorn said. "Are you all right?"

"Had worse falls, I reckon," the old man said, brushing leaves and twigs and bits of dirt from the front of his overalls and coat.

The voice was not the dry rustle of age the Reverend had expected but deep and rich like the low register of an old upright piano.

"Worse falls indeed," he added with a crooked, tobacco-stained grin.

"Can I give you a lift somewhere?"

The old man scrunched a little deeper into his coat and looked up toward the trees and stars.

"Well, 'tis a cold night to be a-footing it," he said. "I'm headed up to my place on Hipps Mountain. You know where that is?"

"Yes, I think so. I can take you that way as far as the Belva bridge. Come in out of the cold."

"Well, since you're asking," the old man said. He rubbed his whiskers again and flicked his tongue over his lips. Then he opened the rear passenger-side door and slid into the back seat.

"Why don't you sit up front here?" Thorn said, his voice shaking in the wave of bitter cold air that followed the old man into the car. "You'll be closer to the heat."

"I figure that place to be for your missus. I'd hate to devil it up with dirt and what all else there is about me after that fall."

"It's no problem," Thorn said as he jammed the heater and the fan to their highest settings.

But Pamela would notice. They had a trip to Asheville planned for the morning, and he knew already he wouldn't feel like stopping somewhere to clean out the old man's debris tonight. He shrugged slightly and lifted his foot from the brake and let the car roll past the stop sign and left onto Highway 25-70.

The road here was wider but no straighter. It followed the sides of the age-rounded mountains, now shouldering into a broad hollow, now swinging out into space with only the tops of pine trees peering over the guard rail. Gray pavement slid beneath him in the sudden way that sand sluices through the slim waist of an hourglass.

Reverend Thorn looked at the car's clock and saw that it was seventeen minutes after six. He glanced in the rear-view mirror. All was darkness and silence behind him—no reflection of the dashboard lights off old watery eyes or moistened lips, no whistle or aged rattle of breathing. He couldn't even distinguish an outline of the old man and thought again of his first impression when he'd seen the fellow in the road, the strange illusion of something near a giant.

*The wicked flee when no man pursueth: but the righteous are bold as a lion.*

He decided the old man was probably slumped into the sheepskin coat, maybe recovering his wits after the fall or feeling slightly embarrassed at his need for help.

The world danced and shivered in the beam of the headlights— the trees above and below, the slender brown weeds along the guard rail, the naked gray brambles of blackberry and wild rose that climbed the embankment in summer. And as if all this were not enough witness to its power over that night, the icy wind now and then swirled up dust and dead leaves into little tornados that crossed the road by fits and starts like a frightened animal.

The headlights suddenly spotted a buck at the side of the road, its grayish brown body the only still thing in the whole of the night. Its eyes glowed red in the high-beams. Long strands of winter-pale grass hung from the sides of its mouth. It didn't run or return to its eating but stood motionless on the lip of the gradient, watching as the car passed by.

"Looked about an eight pointer," said the deep voice from the back seat.

"You think so?"

"Good eating. Young and strong. Prime of life."

Where Highway 25-70 veered sharply left to cross the bridge over Big Laurel Creek and run in that direction toward Hot Springs, Thorn continued straight onto County Road 208. The narrow blacktop wound through a valley—steep dark hills on the right, the shadowed trough of Big Laurel Creek across the lane on the left. From time to time he peered into that shadow, remembering all the trout he'd pulled from those cold waters last summer. One of these, one perhaps worthy of a picture in *The Runion Record*, had broken his line without ever showing more than its darkness beneath the glittering surface.

*It was right about—*

"What's your business about this night?" The old man's breathy whisper crackled in his ear like close lightning.

Thorn jerked away and smacked the side of his head sharply against the window. The wheel turned with his sudden movement, and the car swerved toward the creek. He recovered and felt his face reddening, his palms sweating. He swallowed hard.

"Gosh, I'm sorry," he said. "I was thinking of a fish. You startled me."

Now there was nothing but the sound of the old man's breathing next to his ear. Thorn could feel the pull of the fellow's grip on the headrest and could see the arm hooked over the seat to his right.

"What's your business, sir?" the breathy voice said again.

Thorn leaned up over the wheel, straightened his coat, and slowly leaned back again.

"I'm paying a visit to the sister of a man in my congregation. I'm the pastor down at Runion Community Church."

"That so?" The whisper softened. "Sodom Laurel is it you're going to?"

"Well, yes, that's why I told you I could take you as far as the Belva bridge."

"We've not far to go to that point."

"No. I think it's just up ahead."

Around the next bend the road straightened, and the narrow old bridge came into sight. The white-and-black-striped signs that marked its sides reflected the headlights, and a red stop sign shone just beyond.

Thorn drew a sharp breath, anxious to be rid of his passenger.

"What's the name?" the old man said.

"What?"

"What's the name of the woman?"

"Miss Ollie Gosnell, I think," Thorn said. "I mean I think she's a Miss and not a Mrs." He heard a grunt at his ear. "Her brother's name is Granger. Do you know them?" He passed between the striped signs and rolled to a stop at the end of the short bridge.

There was a sudden movement close beside him, a click and a gleaming green reflection in the light of the dashboard, and then the ice-cold blade of a knife pressed firmly into a soft part of his neck.

The ragged whisper, "Hipps Mountain," bit at his ear.

Amos Thorn swallowed hard and, with the movement of his throat, felt the sharp blade impress itself a bit deeper into his skin.

"What are you doing?" he said in a shaky voice.

"Hipps Mountain."

Thorn tried to think what he could do—stomp on the gas and crash headlong into the cold dirt bank directly in front, maybe throwing the old man into the front seat where he could wrestle the knife out of the knotted grasp; throw the door open, dive out onto the cold pavement, and run; reason with him; pray. But with the knife edge sharp against his throat and a sweat breaking out on his upper lip, he only turned the steering wheel to the left and started toward Hipps Mountain.

*O God, thou hast cast us off. . . . Thou hast shewed thy people hard things: thou hast made us to drink the wine of astonishment.*

The headlights bored a culvert in the night, and he felt himself poured through it like water. The spidery arms of naked trees hung overhead, shaking, making the stars blink like eyes stung by the cold and spastic wind. Belly and wingwork flashed above as a barn owl flew over the road, hunting from tree to tree.

The old man grunted close to his ear again.

"Turn up here. Left after that mailbox."

Then they were on a wide dirt road that snaked its way up Hipps Mountain, laboring through curves packed so tightly that the end of one to the left began another to the right.

No lights stood out against the darkness.

When they were near the top of the mountain, a fork appeared in the road—the right-hand side continuing upward, the left bending sharply downward and out of sight.

"Left, preacher."

The way down was steep and no straighter than the way up had been, and he was forced to ride the brake.

He didn't realize the knife had left his throat until he noticed that its sharp green glint hung near the corner of his eye. The impression its edge had made in his skin was so deep he could feel it when he swallowed. The thought struck him that the deep red line of it might stay there forever, like a rope burn on the neck of some desperado, a man hanged but saved by his hellish gang or some wondrous miracle.

"Why—" Thorn started, but his voice failed in his dry throat.

The old man chuckled.

*Witness to him*, he thought and began racing through memorized Scripture, searching for just the right verse. But the words did not come before the knife edged against his throat again.

"Slow down now, preacher."

They passed through a narrow valley, and when the mountainside gave way on the left, the old man told him to turn again.

"Slow. Don't nose this thing into the ditch."

Thorn stopped the car with a jolt.

The headlights shot over a shadowed fissure that ran crosswise in front, between the road and a small shack. To the right, a footbridge led over the ditch to a patch of untended yard, and through this a dirt path led to a cinder-block step that lay below a lopsided porch. The shack's exterior boards were warped and gray, and the wavy glass panes in the window frame reflected the headlights like unquiet pools.

"Shut her down and get out," the old man said. "Headlamps too."

Thorn eased the gearshift into PARK and killed the engine. Then he turned off the headlights. He touched the keys but left them dangling in the ignition.

"Get out slow," the old man said as he opened the rear driver-side door and the interior light came on.

The two of them stood up out of the car as one. The old man

closed his door first, and the Reverend felt the point of the knife touch him between the shoulder blades just as he closed his own.

An absolute darkness crowded in as if the beautiful mountains of earth rising around him had rolled down from above and covered him up. This, together with the silence about the place and the biting cold, made him catch his breath at the sudden fear that this could be the very feel, and likely the very location, of his grave. . . . *and lo, an horror of great darkness fell upon me . . . even darkness which may be felt . . . darkness . . . under my feet . . . He hath led me, and brought me into darkness, but not into light.* His head fell back, and he almost cried aloud at the sight of stars clear and twinkling against the black night sky. This was not his grave. *Not yet anyway,* he thought as the pressure of the knife at his back urged him forward.

"Walk slow and take direction from the blade."

Thorn looked down and took a step forward. He wished immediately that he'd kept looking upward to the only bits of light left in his world. But it seemed his balance required that he face where he was going, even if he could see nothing, even if it felt as if he were moving back into the pitchy chaos out of which God spoke creation.

The knife pushed him to the right, then to the left, and his halting step sounded on the wooden footbridge.

"Straight now," the deep voice said from behind. "Straight to the door from here."

After what seemed a long walk, Thorn's toe stubbed against the cinder-block step, and he stumbled. And when the knife urged him on, he stumbled again over the protruding lip of the porch boards.

"Feel for the door and open it. It ain't locked."

When they were a few paces inside and the door was closed behind, the knife left his back. He felt strong hands grip his upper arms, and he was spun around and nearly fell. He heard the old man move past him, but he lost his direction in the spin and couldn't tell if the rustle of coat and thud of footsteps moved further into the room or returned to the door. Then there was the scratch and sputter of a match firing, and the old man appeared again before him, a garish bust in a burst of orange-yellow light, leaning over the opposite side of a small square table and lighting a lantern.

Apart from the table and its two small stools, one set on either side, the center of the room was bare. The weak light of the lantern revealed low walls covered with peeling brown and yellow newspaper. Against one wall stood a dusty oak chest of drawers and against the wall opposite, a small potbellied stove with its grate missing. The door they'd come through now served as the only exit, the window next to it, the old panes of which had reflected the headlights, the only visual connection to the light of the stars and the world he'd lived in no more than an hour ago.

"Sit here," the old man said, pointing down with his knife to the stool he straddled.

Amos Thorn moved around one side of the square table, and the old man moved around the other and went to the window.

Thorn looked at the old man's back for a moment and then at the door. A desperate idea entered his mind in wordless images. But then the edge of the knife held low at the old man's side glinted in the light of the lantern. He pulled out the stool and sat down.

The old man yanked at a burlap sack tacked to the top of the lightless window frame and held drawn to one side by a nail. The sack fell stiffly across the window but did not quite cover all the panes, leaving darkness to seep around its edges and into the room.

It wasn't until Thorn had been seated for a few seconds that he took notice of the cold. It seemed colder in the stillness of the shack than outside beneath the stars. He felt certain that this room had never known warmth. He felt that if he lived through this night and stopped here some summer afternoon when this old man was long dead, he might find the place as cold and the old man like a wax figure sitting on the same stool he now took across the table from him, between him and the door.

"Your cheeks is flushed," the old man said. "Fear does that to folks. That or the contrary. They either get all redded up or go plumb white." He laughed with a rumbling wheeze. "You scared, ain't you, preacher?"

"Yes," Amos Thorn said flatly and pulled his overcoat tighter around himself.

The old man stared at him across the top of the lantern but said nothing. He pulled a twist of tobacco from the pocket of his coat and laid it on the table.

The knife slid without hesitation through the twist. Then the tip of it stabbed the severed chunk and carried it to the thin-lipped mouth.

"I figured we'd talk first," the old man said around the wad of tobacco in his mouth. He stood up from the stool. "You smoke? You look like you could do with a smoke."

"No."

The old man stepped to the chest of drawers and slid the middle drawer open. He pulled out a plastic bag and turned and laid the bag on the table beside the lantern.

Reverend Thorn saw some twisted stems, some pale seeds, some dark patches where the leaves had powdered and sifted to the side the bag had lain on in the drawer.

"My gut can't take moonshine no more," the old man said, digging in the bag with a pipe he'd drawn from another coat pocket. "I'll get this here pipe loaded for you, and you smoke it."

"I wouldn't like any."

"You smoke it." He tamped the bowl with the butt of the switchblade.

"I'd prefer not to."

"You smoke it while you've yet a throat to pass it through," the old man said, holding the loaded pipe toward him with one hand and moving the knife toward him with the other. "While you've yet breath to draw it with."

Thorn took the pipe and stuck it between his teeth, picked up one of the matches from the table and struck it.

As the dry weed in the bowl began to glow red and crackle and the sweet smell rose into his nose, his mind flashed back to his last years in Hendersonville, the time after he felt he'd grown too old for Sunday School lessons and hymns and prayers and his father's sermons. He'd smoked marijuana then, smoked it with his teammates on Friday nights after football games as they cruised back and forth between town and the Interstate. Sometimes he'd smoked it alone in the barn after his evening chores. Those nights he would drive around for an hour or two afterwards on some made-up errand, thinking he could feel the pavement beneath his tires as plainly as if he were walking on it barefoot.

"What's your name, preacher?"

Thorn looked at him for a moment, not sure that he'd spoken.

"Speak up now," the old man said. "Let's come to know one another a bit."

"Thorn. David Amos Thorn." He swallowed against the dryness in his throat.

The old man spat at a wall and drew the back of one hand across his stained lips.

"Harry, some calls me."

Thorn set the empty pipe on the table and rubbed his forehead and cheeks hard with one hand. Then he drew a deep breath and squinted at the face on the other side of the lantern.

"Do you believe in God, Harry?"

The old man didn't answer. He grunted and laid the knife on the table and spat this time into the darkness of the stove's belly.

"Give me that pipe here, preacher."

Reverend Thorn handed him the pipe, watched him beat the ashes onto the table, and fill the bowl from the bag again.

"Please, no more."

"Smoke," the old man said.

And now as he pulled the smoke into his lungs, without thinking that the old man might not make him inhale or know if he did, he remembered particularly one night when his father was away at the side of a dying deacon, and he'd smoked a bowlful in the barn before he realized the family's only car was gone. He went back to the house. His mother asked him to sit with her at the kitchen table while he did his homework and she went through the contents of some old shoe boxes full of sepia photographs and yellowed letters. From where he sat, he could see the faces and bodies of two people as close together as they could get, and although he could read nothing of the letters, he noticed the writing was in a bold script, somehow still dark in spite of the yellowed paper. The only things he could tell for certain were that the man in the pictures was not his father and that the letters weren't written in his hand. He remembered nothing of what he and his mother said that rare hour or two they sat together, but try as he might— and he was never sure if it were the reality or the high—he never forgot the look of her eyes as she gently fingered the pictures and papers. That evening he thought of her green eyes as mossy plugs in a dam, holding back something savage and seething. And later that night, and on many nights until she died suddenly at the age of forty-six, he lay awake long hours, imagining with both fear and desire that the savage and seething thing behind those green eyes might escape. When one morning after her death he recognized above the pure white shaving cream on his face the same look in his own green eyes, he began to pray again.

Thorn drew the second bowl to ashes and returned the pipe to the old man.

"How about you, preacher, do you believe in God?" The old man dug the pipe into the bag to fill it again.

Thorn lowered his gaze and didn't answer. He watched his cold red hands twitch on the tabletop as if a book lay there and they flipped through its pages, first this way toward the front, then that way toward the back.

"You're in a muddle, preacher," the old man said and chuckled. "Do you believe in God when you're in a muddle like I got you in?"

Reverend Thorn's hands fell still.

"Well, I reckon preaching and praying ain't what they used to be whenever I was doing them," the old man said. "That's all I got to say for it."

Thorn's mouth hung slightly open. He raised his drooping eyelids and looked at the grizzled face.

The old man chuckled.

"This is powerful smoke, ain't it?" He tapped the ball of his forefinger on the bowl to pack it. "Them town boys got it doctored with something or other." He struck a match. "I'll take this one for myself, I will. It helps the arthritis." He drew on the pipe. "Yes, preaching and praying ain't what they used to be, Reverend Thorn. You got yourself an office in the back of the meeting house and a little place thrown in for you and the missus, I'll warrant."

Thorn stared.

"In my day a preacher worked of a week like any other man, paid his way and found his shelter like any other man. I worked six days a week at the bandsaw mill in Runion."

"You were a preacher?" Thorn finally said.

"I held a little church at the head of Sodom Laurel. Rode a pale gray mare there early of a Sunday morning and come back to the house late of a Sunday night. Went back to work at sunup Monday and worked till sunset Saturday. It took a strong man to do all I done." He licked his lips. "Why, preacher, if our places was turned about and it was back then, I'd have done and whipped your ass six ways from Sunday by now and be down on my knees praying for the strength to start over again." He drew on the pipe and spoke through the smoke. "You probably preach standing behind a fancy box, I reckon."

Thorn nodded.

"I preached all over the house. Up and down the aisles. Over the pews to get in the face of a sinner the spirit was calling. I could see it in the face. And when the spirit got hold of me, it knocked me to the floor, and I begun to roll." He drew on the pipe again and after a moment released the smoke in a slow cloud. "But the body wearies and worries the spirit until all you got is flesh a-rolling around. I felt the stove when I rolled up against it. I felt a woman when I rolled up against her. And when I rolled up against that gal you fetched yourself out to see tonight, my preaching and praying days seen their end a-coming."

Thorn stared.

"That's right. The Gosnells was members of my church. That Ollie was a wild child of fourteen, the most beautiful creature on earth, and done a woman in body. I took her under me that very afternoon in a field below the church. Twenty-eight year ago, that was."

"Ollie Gosnell?"

"I preached just regular as you please that night, and she sat there looking like a preacher's wife except for them eyes of hers. They'd a wildness she couldn't never hide. Green as any you ever seen." He drew on the pipe, pulled it out of his mouth, and looked at it. "Well, I preached the next Sunday and the next after that and on and on until it got found out somehow. She weren't pregnant so far as I know of, but come the middle of one week, Gunther Gosnell up and caught me outside the mill at quitting time. His brother that goes to your church stopped him within a blow of sending me to my reward." The old man chuckled. "Crazy son of a bitch, that Gunther Gosnell." He tapped the pipe on the table and filled it again from the bag. "There's them that say Ollie's a witch and them that say she's a harlot. Them that say she's both." He chuckled again and reached the pipe toward Thorn. "Now, preacher, when you've had another smoke, you can drop your breeches and drawers in yon corner and let this here blade save you from such sin as what ruined me."

Thorn swallowed hard and blinked. He watched the old man's knuckles knot around the bowl of the pipe and thought the stained fingernails grew black and long. The old man's face seemed to thin and grow gaunt with shadows and, at the same time, the body to swell into the clothes until, still sitting, he towered above the table. The pipe turned in the gnarled hand and came toward him. The stem pecked against his clenched teeth.

He glanced from the door to the knife that now lay on the edge of the tabletop next to the old man's swollen belly. Then, in his struggle to keep the pipe from passing his lips, his knee came up and jarred the small table, lifting his side of it off the floor as the old man's weight pushed down on the other side.

The old man fell back, fumbling to get his stool under him, and the knife rolled off the table and clattered on the board floor.

Thorn lashed out at the lantern, backhanding it into the lap of his once more shriveled and coat-swallowed enemy. Like the offensive guard he'd been for the Hendersonville High Bearcats almost twenty years before, sweating out his salt behind the blocking sled during Monday afternoon practices, he powered his weight into the table, churning his stocky legs, driving the old man off his stool and hard into the wall beside the window. He yanked the door open and flew out into the clear cold darkness, leaving the old man clambering and howling behind him.

He fell off the edge of the porch and sprawled face down onto the stiff grass and the frozen ground, scrambled to his feet and stumbled blindly across the short yard. But when his stride stretched into too much air, he knew he'd missed the bridge. And then he was on his knees in the ditch with the thin stream of ice popping beneath him and his trouser legs soaking up freezing water. He clawed and scratched his way up the opposite bank and cracked a knee hard against the bumper of his dark car and fell sprawling again, this time onto the cold hood. He rolled over and lay breathless, listening for the tramp of the old man's boots on the footbridge.

Then, as if in answer to his thoughts, footsteps pounded somewhere on old wood.

The stars shone above him again, cold in the black sky, dancing to the beat of his heart, swimming and dissolving as his eyes filled with tears.

"Damn you, preacher," the old man wheezed in the darkness.

Thorn judged that the voice came from just in front of the car, near where he still lay on his back. He drew his knees to his chest, feeling the water already beginning to stiffen in his trouser legs.

"God damn you, preacher," Thorn said and drove both feet at the darkness. "God damn you to hell, you—" He choked and coughed and blindly rolled from the hood, opened the door of the car, and fell into the driver's seat, expecting every moment to be stabbed in the back or to have his throat slit. He cranked the engine and yanked the gear shift down into reverse, turning on the headlights at the same time.

The old man stood staring directly at him from across the black ditch. His eyes glittered from the massive folds of the coat. The towering fur hat was gone, and his bald head hunched low beneath the high collar as if he were simply carried in the pocket or pouch of a thing much bigger than himself.

Behind him the orange light of a fire flickered in the open door of the house and danced in the window, its movements strange in the wavy rectangles of glass at the edges of the glowing burlap sack. Thorn stomped on the gas pedal and slung gravel and dirt behind him through the sharp curves that snaked up the backside of Hipps Mountain.

He passed the fork and finally reached the stop sign at the main road. He braked the car with a jolt, rammed the gear shift to PARK, threw open his door, and dove out. On all fours in the cold dust, he vomited until the first wave of convulsions subsided, and he stood up into freezing night air. At the edge of the road, he retched again above the weeds. He tasted only an acidic bitterness and knew in that moment he would never be sick like this again without feeling the knife against his throat and the dizziness in his head or seeing the old man standing across the footbridge with his staring eyes glittering in the headlights.

He found a napkin in his pocket and dabbed the tears brought on by the retching and the cold wind. Then he wiped his nose and mouth and tossed the crumpled napkin into the weeds.

\* \* \*

He drove slowly, with the same sense of the unreal he'd felt in coming this way only an hour before. Then when the Belva bridge was coming up on his right, he brought the car to an uncertain stop in the middle of the road.

He sat and rubbed his eyes with his knuckles.

His throat burned from the pot smoke and the vomit. When he swallowed, the saliva seemed to sizzle on the back of his tongue like water drops on a hot frying pan.

*Water,* he thought. *Just a cup of water.*

Pamela and the parsonage waited to the right some seven or eight miles, some twenty minutes' drive through the mountains. She didn't expect him home for another two hours. She would be reading or maybe talking to her mother on the telephone. He knew she would take him into her arms and hold him, fix him hot chamomile tea, put him in a warm bath, and wait for him in bed.

Ollie Gosnell waited half a mile ahead, just around the next bend and up into a dark hollow to the left. She didn't wait for him, but he felt somehow she would be there, waiting and alone. She might be watching *Jeopardy* or might—

He didn't know what she might be doing. He imagined her coming to the door and pulling it open without wondering or asking who knocked, without flinching at the frigid air that rushed around him to meet her where she stood in a faded calico nightgown. He saw the piercing green eyes look coolly at him— somehow knowing him for a preacher—as he shivered in the darkness on her porch. He heard his first words to her stuttered through chattering teeth: "Can I have a cup of cold water?" He imagined her motioning him into the house and silently taking his hat and coat. She would settle him into a stuffed and ragged rocker with an afghan tossed over it and go outside without a coat or a scarf or a word. And when she returned she would have a dented tin ladle full of cold water from her spring. "I broke the ice with my fist to get it," she would say as she lifted the ladle to his lips because she'd seen with another chilly and penetrating glance of her green eyes how his hands trembled. And when he'd drunk and swished the icy water against the bitterness in his mouth and swallowed it, she would dip a corner of her apron into the cup to soak up the dregs and with that cold damp cloth dab away the blood dried on his cheek where he'd cut it when he fell.

* * *

The car waited in the middle of the road, its lights on, its exhaust billowing and red-lit. The engine murmured in the stillness, mingling its breathy rhythm with the muttering of the shallow rocky creek beside the road and the shrieking hiss of a barn owl in a dead pine partway up the mountainside. Then the brake lights dimmed, and with the same uncertainty with which it'd come to a stop, the dark car rolled slowly forward toward the Belva bridge.

# The Loves of Misty Sprinkle

The call had come that morning, a Friday, while she sat filing her nails in the back room at Eliza's. She had two fingers to go and hoped to finish them before her eleven o'clock shampoo and set showed up. The morning had been typical February bluster. Snow had fallen much of the previous evening and part of the night. First light found more flakes dancing in the air but not much additional accumulation. Preschool had been called off, so she'd dropped two boys off at her mother's instead of the usual one. But since she'd been at work, the morning had alternated—sometimes with surprising speed—between sunshine and clouds, with sparse snow flurries passing by the salon's big front window all the while.

*Her husband'll get her here*, she thought and filed faster.

"Dead engine yard on a dead-end street," Eliza Tanner sang from the salon's main room as she danced away from Betty Oakley's perm-in-progress and turned up the stereo. A perm-rod-and-comb became her microphone, as Betty Oakley shook her half-rolled head and laughed. "He's a-rebuilding cars and ignoring your needs, Arlene."

The telephone rang, and she picked the cordless up from the table in front of her, reached a toe to close the backroom door, hit the TALK button, and said, "Eliza's."

"Misty, it's me."

"Me who?"

"Jimmy."

"I know who you are, Jimmy Shetley," she said with a grin she hoped he could hear.

"Why'd you ask for?"

"I'm just playing." She looked at the nails of her left hand. "Where are you?"

"I'm at Mother's," he said. "What're you up to?"

"About a hundred and forty-five," she said. "So don't buy me no candy for Valentine's Day."

"I ain't planning on it," he said. "Who said I's buying you anything for Valentine's anyway?"

*I hear it in your voice,* she wanted to say but didn't. "I'm just playing with you, honey," she said instead.

"Well."

"How's your mother?" Misty asked. "I heard she was in the hospital a few weeks ago. She all right?"

"Yeah, she's fine. Had a knee replaced, but she's up and around pretty good with a walker now."

"I'm glad." She looked at her nails again, then at the clock, then at the front door where her shampoo and set stood unbundling by the coat rack.

"Shit, my eleven o'clock's here, Jimmy. Was there anything you wanted?"

The sound of a cigarette lighter scraping up a flame came through the line, followed by the pause of a smoker's first drag.

"I's just wondering if I could drop by the house this evening," he said.

"It's y'all's house," she said. "I reckon we'll be there."

"You and the boys?"

"Who else?"

"I'll come 'round when I get Mother settled after supper."

"I gotta go, Jimmy," Misty said, holding her voice even. "My eleven o'clock's here."

\* \* \*

As soon as she heard the key scratch in the lock, she was up off the couch and smoothing and patting her hair and skirt as she trotted to meet him. When the door swung open with its high-pitched creak, she covered him like honey, pulling him into as much contact—knees to cheeks—as she could. And when he felt restless in her arms, she released him so that he could greet her boys, wondering for a split second what they thought of this man who kept charging into and retreating from their lives.

Her older son Randy, a four-year-old from her second marriage, yelled and attacked, punching him in the groin with a tiny fist.

Jimmy's knees buckled, and he fell, hitting his cheek hard on the corner of the foyer table as he thundered down but miraculously managing to settle the 12-pack of Michelob bottles—tied up with a Valentine's bow—to the floor with only the lightest clinks.

Her two-year-old JJ startled at Jimmy's crash and began to scream.

*   *   *

Three hours later the man lay still and quiet on his back beside her and held a washcloth full of ice to his face.

She lay naked, propped up on her left elbow, looking at him, smiling and waiting, but satisfied for now.

The left cheek had swollen and closed the eye. His other eye stared at the ceiling.

"So, where you been since November?" she said.

He didn't turn to look at her.

"Nowheres much." He rubbed his belly with his right hand. "I got Mother through the surgery and Christmas and then went to my cousin's in High Point and stayed there a while looking for a job."

"Is he the cousin married to the girl that sweats?"

"Yeah, but he got her a operation to fix it. O' course, they's separated for now."

Misty took over the belly-rubbing for him, and he dropped his hand to his side.

"Guess you didn't find nothing?"

"Nothing I wanted."

She pinched his nipple lightly and saw his chest spasm.

"Well," she said with a small laugh, "what is it you want, Jimmy?"

"Hell if I know."

She leaned down and licked where she'd pinched him and felt the tremor with her tongue. Then with a smacking kiss she raised up again and looked at his swollen face.

"You didn't bring me any chocolates."

He blinked his one good eye and turned his head towards her.

"You said you didn't want none."

She laughed her I'm-gonna-get-you laugh and climbed on top of him again.

\* \* \*

He was asleep almost before she dismounted, and his stuttered snoring kept her more or less awake until she couldn't stand it any longer.

In the kitchen, the glowing clock on the microwave read 2:14.

She smiled at those numbers together and opened the refrigerator and took out a Diet Pepsi, then reached into the pantry and grabbed the box of Valentine candy she'd bought and stashed away with the intentions of giving it to him in bed the next night. She tore off the cellophane wrapping and carried the soda and the heart-shaped box to the living room, found the remote and her favorite chair, settled down with the open candy box in her lap, put the cold can on a coaster, and turned on the television. Just as the screen was warming to life, she popped a mystery piece in her mouth, and her jaw almost locked in the ecstatic rush of rich chocolate, caramel, and flakes of toffee.

The television was still on 13 WLOS, where before going to bed she and Jimmy had watched the local weather and the scores from area high school basketball tournaments. At this hour the station had turned its programming over to a home shopping network. She fingered the chocolates, looking especially for those that didn't yield under the pressure she applied, and inspected a dazzling garnet ring that glittered in a close-up shot as the hosts talked about the piece with a caller. In one corner of the screen, a timer counted down the minutes and seconds left if she wanted to purchase the ring, and beneath it a counter tallied up the many being sold while she sat eating chocolates and watching.

"A lot of idiots awake at this time of night," she said aloud around the double-chocolate piece in her mouth. She pointed the remote and surfed through several channels, stopping next on a sports network because the announcer looked familiar.

He was talking professional basketball, giving scores and commenting on highlights. The New York Knicks had beaten the Chicago Bulls, which she knew would disappoint all of Runion's Michael Jordan fans—like Eliza, who had met the basketball star the previous summer at the First Baptist Church over in Mars Hill. His college roommate and teammate had married a Madison County girl, and Jordan had been the best man. Eliza had done hair in Asheville for the groom's mother and sister for years, and they'd hired her to fix up the wedding party. In addition to what she got paid, she got a picture of herself with Michael Jordan. But it almost didn't look like him, Misty had decided, so much darker he looked in the photo beside Eliza than he ever did on TV. Maybe the fact that the Charlotte Hornets had beaten Miami would make up for Chicago's loss. The Boston Celtics had won too, which would've made her father happy.

*Roger Gunter*, Misty thought, and she couldn't believe it took her more than ten seconds to realize that the sports announcer looked familiar because of her first husband. The man on the television didn't look like Roger had ever looked in life but rather like Roger might've looked if he hadn't turned into a filthy gutter drunk before they reached their first anniversary. She'd married him on June 11th ten years ago, when she was just two weeks out of high school. He had good looks and a wildness in his blue eyes that promised she'd never be bored. But his looks fell apart through all the late-night weather, and the wildness in his eyes turned into wilderness and then bleary bewilderment. They stayed together a little over four years, through cleaning up and breaking up and making up and cleaning up and breaking up and on and on. Two years after they split for good, he'd shot his girlfriend in the ear and himself in the roof of his mouth. Every time Misty thought of him now, she thanked God that somehow Roger Gunter hadn't knocked her up like the other two had.

*Thank you, God.*

Without thinking, she picked up a chocolate she hadn't inspected, and a fruity goop nearly gagged her before she spit it back into its little brown paper nest. She swished a quick mouthful of Diet Pepsi to foam and swallowed. Her left hand again took up the search through the chocolates, and her right hand the channel surfing. While the room flashed on and off around her, she discovered a round piece that resisted her candy-pressing finger, picked it up, and popped it in her mouth—a piece rich and slightly nutty.

Two women wrestled to the roar of a crowd. One was a slender white with long and wavy auburn hair. She wore a white leotard and silver leather booties that came up to just above her ankles. The woman she wrestled was black and pretty in a big-cat-print leotard and black leather lace-up boots that rose to the middle of her calves. The white woman seemed to be winning. She charged across the ring at the other and in acrobatic moves too fast to be followed on the screen she wound up sitting on her opponent's shoulders, legs astride the dazed woman's neck. The woman in white then pitched forward over the other's head and forced the two of them together into a half somersault that ended with the white woman sitting on the ring floor with the black woman lying back-to-the-mat before her, head held and squeezed between white thighs.

The camera switched for a moment to Peter Falk at ringside, obviously amazed by what just happened, and then switched back to the wrestling.

Colette France once held her like that. Both of them were between marriages, Colette between her first and second, Misty between her second and third. One Friday, as Colette sat in the styling chair and Misty circled her, they'd decided on a girls' night out at an Asheville bar called 45 Cherry, where they would drink away their grievances over ex-husbands, overbearing mothers, mothers-in-law, and loneliness.

At the club, Colette and Misty drank and danced together, rejected all advances from the club males and drank some more. During the break after the band's second set, they realized that neither of them should be driving and decided they'd get a nearby room and sleep it off.

"You don't have work in the morning, do you?" Colette asked.

"Not tomorrow," Misty said. "The lady I usually do ain't getting home from Bermuda until Sunday. I'm doing her Monday morning."

"Oh, that's great," Colette said. "Bermuda."

A dreamy beer pause hung between them for a moment.

"The bitch," Misty said, and Colette laughed.

Later, in a motel just across I-240 from the club, still giddy from the band's finale and the bar's last call, the two of them danced and stripped to their own singing. Somehow as they stumbled through "You Shook Me All Night Long," the singing and dancing together turned to giggling and wrestling, and they fell into the middle of the king-sized bed. They rolled around until the giggling gave way to grunts and heavy breathing. Then Misty found herself in the same position as the black wrestler in the movie, her head squeezed between Colette's thighs. Muscles under soft skin pressed hard against her sweaty cheeks and heated her ears. The muscles flexed and relaxed, flexed and relaxed, but Colette wouldn't release her. After a time Misty stopped trying to pull herself free from those thighs. Instead she began to try to turn, to face into Colette's body and not away from it. Little by little Colette allowed her to make the turn, still without releasing her. When Misty lay on her belly and could raise her eyes to look up past the fleshy swell of Colette's breasts to her face, their eyes met for one clear moment before Colette shifted her legs in some way that forced Misty's face deeper into her crotch, where her panties were wet and smelled vaguely of some exotic musk fruit. Misty briefly struggled again but then relaxed. Colette lay back and, having taken hold of Misty's wrists, pulled the captive's arms forward alongside her hips and guided the trembling hands to her breasts.

Another fruity mistake among the chocolates gagged Misty and brought her back to the moment.

The movie was still on, and now four women—two blacks in big-cat prints and two whites in white—wrestled toward a frenzied climax that saw the white women win to great hoopla. The black women and their black manager turned out to be good sports, and Peter Falk and the brunette turned out to be in love.

A breathless thrill ached in Misty's chest and throat. Her stomach spun. She swallowed hard and leaned forward and set the candy box on the floor. When she sat back, she moved a fingertip to turn the volume down a little further and accidentally changed the channel to Miss Cleo and the Psychic Readers Network.

Two months after their night together, months that saw a handful of attempted reenactments, Colette married her second husband and disappeared west, to Knoxville, maybe, or to Dallas. Misty realized that she now had no idea which, and as she sipped the last of her Diet Pepsi, she pictured Colette asleep in her bed instead of Jimmy and wondered if Miss Cleo could help them reconnect in some way.

With a deep and tremulous inhalation and release, she wandered away through the channels until she stopped on one of the cable news networks. Colette and Cleo and Jimmy left her mind as she followed a retrospective report on a six-year-old event and watched the grainy security camera footage of two nameless ten-year-old boys leading a two-year-old named James away from his unsuspecting mother, who was shopping in a mall somewhere in England. The story ended badly, as Misty knew it would.

Footsteps upstairs—Jimmy sleepwalking to pee—startled her out of her horrified trance. She turned the television off and waited until she heard first the flush and then the footsteps return to the bed. Her nerves on edge, she gave him a few more minutes to get back to sleep, her mind in the darkness a tangle of images from the television, her memories, and her fears. After a while, she crept upstairs, went into the boys' room and took JJ from his crib. She carried him to the spare room, where she turned down the covers and crawled into the bed without putting him down. She wrapped herself around him, and in the darkness the tangle of images returned for a moment but was softened and then dissipated by her baby's steady breathing and his sweet-smelling warmth.

\* \* \*

She took the boys to her mother's in a cold gray morning that smelled of more snow, then came home to find Jimmy still asleep, and showered for her Saturday appointments. After going through her closet with a flashlight, she took her clothes and her hair-styling basket downstairs to the kitchen. She was bent almost double, drying her hair with her head hanging upside down, when she saw between her spread legs Jimmy reach the foot of the stairs and turn toward her.

He was barefoot. His blue jeans were wrinkled from lying all night bunched up on the floor, and his shirt seemed to hang upward out of one front pocket. His hips and sides were narrow, making his belly paunch more pronounced. Seen upside down, his chest had details but no definition—the nipples that seemed painted on his ribcage, despite the muscles her lips had felt shiver the night before, and the scant patch of hair between them. Further downward his swollen eye looked somewhat better, and his good eye was staring at her ass.

She let him get a little closer and look a little longer, but then she quickly unbent, throwing her hair up over her head so that it settled around her shoulders with a couple of slow-motion bounces.

"Morning, sleepy head," she said without turning as she unplugged the hairdryer and laid it on the table.

"Morning," he said, wrapping his arms around her from behind and pulling her to him. "I missed you when I woke up."

She could feel him swelling against her already and bent forward and shook her hair a couple of times, twisting her hips slightly with each shake.

"Don't start that," she said. "I'm gonna be late for work as it is."

He didn't let go.

She dragged him behind her toward the coffee pot.

"You want a cup?"

"You know what I want."

"I reckon I do, Jimmy, but you're going to have to settle for your second choice." She turned in his arms and brought her own up around his neck. "Now, what's your second choice? Coffee or a kiss?"

"Hmm," Jimmy said. "What if it ain't neither?"

"Well, it's your choice, whatever it is," she said, turning again in his arms so that she could get at the cups in the cupboard. "But you ain't gonna get your first choice."

"Where's the boys?"

"I took them to Mama's already."

"How 'bout if my second choice is this," Jimmy said. "Let's leave Randy and JJ at your mama's house while you and me go off somewheres tonight and tomorrow night."

"What kind of somewheres?" she said.

"I don't know. Anywheres from Hot Springs west to Nashville, I reckon."

"What about east?"

"I done been thataway."

"You got any money?" she said. "You better have, 'cause I don't."

"I've got co-sign on Mother's checking account."

"We can't take her money for going off and sinning." She turned sideways to him and poured coffee into the mug she'd been holding in her hand.

"She don't mind," he said, taking his arms from around her and standing there next to her in the kitchen. "She knows we're sinning right here in the house."

Misty knew when he dropped his hands to his sides and didn't put them in his pockets his quick temper was about to flare.

"Well, my mama don't know, and she will mind," she said, trying to move the conversation away from the touchy subject of his mother. "She has the boys Tuesday through Saturday, and she don't need them Sunday and Monday too."

"How 'bout if I pay her?"

"With your mother's check?" Misty said. "I don't think so, Jimmy Shetley."

"Aw, shit," he said, reaching for her again. "Come on."

She pushed his arms away, not hard, and moved toward the

kitchen table where her brushes and combs and makeup waited.

"Besides," she said as she pulled the chair back, "I was hoping that you'd go to church with me tomorrow."

Jimmy blew a chuckle out his nose and wrapped his hand around the cup of coffee she'd poured for him.

"Since when do you go to church, Misty?"

She began to tease out her hair before she answered, working it with short strokes of her long-tail comb.

"I don't much." She blasted a section of her hair with hairspray. "But it's an idea that came to me in the middle of the night to be thankful for the things I love. Besides, it's Valentine's Day tomorrow."

This time Jimmy laughed out loud.

"People go to church on Christmas and Easter," he said. "They don't go 'cause it's fucking Valentine's."

"Well, maybe I do." She blasted another section into place. "And if you want to see me tomorrow, that's where you'll have to go too."

"Shit, girl, that ain't gonna be no fun. Let's go somewheres."

He had to step back away from the cloud of her final all-over spraying.

"I am going somewhere," she said. "And I'm going at eleven o'clock tomorrow morning."

"All right, all right. Have it your own fucking way," he said. "Which one of them joints you going to?"

She was refilling her hair-styling basket and glanced at the clock.

"I'm gonna be late," she said and picked up her stuff and started for the stairs.

"Which one, goddammit?"

"The Runion Community at Main Street and Mill. Used to be the First Southern Missionary?" She turned at the foot of the stairs and started up.

"I'm still gonna spend the night again tonight," he called after her.

\* \* \*

A man met her at the door, took her hand, and shook it, saying, "It's good to have you all join us this morning." His hair—thick and iron gray, parted on the left and combed back away from his forehead—didn't flinch in the cold February wind. His teeth—somewhat coffee stained but perfectly straight in his smile—didn't chatter. He wore a red tie and a gray wool suit. The lapels of his jacket bore on the right a rose bud and on the left a nametag that said in large letters, "GREETER," and beneath in smaller letters, "Ted Ramsey."

Misty knew who he was, although she'd never really talked to him. She always found it hard to figure out what to say to a man who owned a funeral home, so if she said anything at all, it tended to be about the weather or his wife, Anne, who kept a standing appointment with Eliza every week.

"It's chilly," Misty said, shifting JJ to her right arm and putting her left hand on the top of Randy's head to hold him steady so the man could shake his hand. She didn't want him attacking Mr. Ramsey the way he'd attacked Jimmy two nights before.

"You've got a strong little handshake," Mr. Ramsey said to Randy and then straightened up and took hold of JJ's chubby arm. "If you'll go down the steps just inside to your right," he said to Misty, "you can take these boys to the nursery." Still holding JJ's arm, he looked down at Randy again. "Although this little man with the strong hands might prefer our children's church."

"Okay, thanks," Misty said and stepped past him as he turned to greet somebody coming up the steps behind her.

Randy dove easily into the noisy play going on in the room for children's church. JJ screamed and cried when she left him with the two young women in the nursery. Misty stood out of sight outside the door to make sure he calmed down. He did so quickly, just like she knew he would.

Upstairs, at the doors leading into the sanctuary, a teenage boy she didn't recognize handed her a program and a red rose.

"Happy Valentine's Day," he said and reached into a box for another flower.

Just inside the doors a tall man in a gray short-sleeved knit shirt held her elbow, smiled and pointed out spaces where she might sit. She followed his direction around to the left side of the congregation and found a seat on the outside end of a pew. She wished for a moment that Jimmy had decided to come with her. But once she was seated with the program and the rose in her lap and shyly returning the smiles and waves of people she knew from town, mostly from the salon, she was glad he wasn't there.

As the organ began to play, she looked out the spotless window that offered a view across the cemetery to Mill Street where it ran along the backside of the Runion State campus. Among the few other churches she'd been in over the years, she couldn't call to mind another that had clear windows. She remembered the church she attended sometimes growing up, when her father was still alive, and how its windows were made of bumpy amber-colored glass through which she could see light and movement and shapes outside but nothing clearly. The church where she'd married Roger Gunter had frosted windows that let in only a pearly light. She'd married Joe Romaine in a church that seemed made mostly of stained-glass windows, and she remembered feeling her vows went unnoticed while all around her colorful saints went about their holy business. Gonzalo Rodriguez married her illegally one night in a Gatlinburg wedding chapel, and she couldn't remember now if the place had windows or not.

The organ moved beyond its crescendo to a contemplative ending.

Misty turned away from the window and then quickly back to it, her attention now caught by a familiar car parked near the intersection of Mill and Back Street—Jimmy Shetley's car.

Jimmy sat behind the wheel with his window rolled down, looking her way through a pair of binoculars. He waved.

"Oh, Lord," she said aloud just at the moment the organ fell silent.

From behind, a small bird-light hand squeezed her shoulder. A ragged whisper said, "Bless her heart," and the hand withdrew.

\* \* \*

When Reverend Amos Thorn came to the pulpit, he took for his scripture a passage Joe Romaine had requested—insisted—that Father York read at Misty's second marriage—"If I speak in the tongues of men and of angels, but have not love, I am only a resounding gong or a clanging cymbal. . . ."

Misty listened as Reverend Thorn continued to read in his raspy voice—*He kind of sounds like President Clinton*, she thought. Her gaze wandered from the man at the pulpit to a woman in the first row of the choir behind him, and she wondered what it would be like to be Pamela Thorn and married to such a man. Ever since the Thorns had moved to Runion, she'd always thought him handsome—rich black hair, deep green eyes set in a strong tanned face, broad shoulders and barrel chest and solid belly, meaty and strong hands. She could imagine it. She could imagine herself sitting there looking at the wide back her arms so often wrapped around or watching his familiar hand gestures or gazing out at the congregation and seeing that girl who works with Eliza—Misty, yes—in church today and sitting back there by the window.

"Context," Reverend Thorn said, bringing Misty back to herself. He presented a dictionary definition of "context" and then began interpreting the passage he'd just finished reading. "A resounding gong," he said. "What's the point? We don't use gongs much these days, but the doorbell or the church bell or the dinner bell or that little beep that's going to sound from some of your watches at noon are our gongs. Gongs announce something—a visitor, the time, the beginning or end of some event. But for a gong to be struck apart from one of these contexts is meaningless." He paused and looked back and forth across the congregation. "Just noise."

Misty felt flushed as his gaze stalled on her for a moment—curious—before moving on.

"Are you with me?" he asked. "Read Paul's 'clanging cymbal' the same way. Put that cymbal in a marching band or an orchestra, give it to Don Henley of The Eagles, and it makes sense. But for it to clang at us without music or rhythm is just as meaningless as the gong that sounds out of place." He picked up a handkerchief from the top of the pulpit and wiped the corners of his mouth. "The gong and the cymbal gotta have their contexts. Otherwise they're just noise."

Misty turned to the window and for a moment stared back at Jimmy and his binoculars, but she was listening to the preacher.

"So, what's this got to do with love, preacher? Some of you are asking that right now. Some of you might already know." He turned toward his wife and the choir and then back to the congregation. "Love is the context of our lives. And God's love is the context of our love. Without us knowing God's love, we wouldn't know how to love one another. All the big and little acts of love you can name are only imperfect reflections of God's love." He wiped his mouth again. "What did Paul say?" He looked down to read. "Now we see but a poor reflection as in a mirror; then we shall see face to face. Now I know in part; then I shall know fully, even as I am fully known." When he looked up, his face was flushed, his green eyes bright. "Outside the context of love, of God's love, all the motherly or fatherly acts of love, all the acts of love between husband and wife or boyfriend and girlfriend, are hopeless and meaningless. Some even sinful."

The last word crashed into her like a wave suddenly breaking over her from behind. Submerged, she was all flailing limbs and confusion, not knowing in which direction she would gulp sand or air. Salt stung her eyes. Life blurred around her, a darkness cut here and there by shafts of light from a source she couldn't guess. But then she saw the moving bubbles of light and followed them to the surface, gasping as she strained upward into the air and her feet found the sand beneath.

People close around her turned at the gasp, and for a moment the hand lit on her shoulder again.

She felt her face heat up and turned once more to the window.

Jimmy's car still sat there, but now he leaned back in the shadow of the roof and tinted windshield, smoking something. Puffs of blue-gray rose through his open window and disappeared in the breeze.

"Think of the things you love," Reverend Thorn said as

Misty turned away from the window again. He was looking in her direction but seemed not to have taken notice of her gasp. "Think of the things you love, the things that make your life rich. Start with your five senses. Now, don't think of these things in the meaningless context of your own pleasure but in the context of God's love and the wonderful experience of his creation." He took up the handkerchief and wiped his forehead and the corners of his mouth. "This is the interactive part of the sermon, so I'll call the sense and then we'll say those things that we love."

The congregation shifted uneasily for a moment and settled down again. Somebody's watch beeped.

"That beep was full of meaning," Reverend Thorn said with a smile, and the congregation laughed. "So, we'll save the things we've tasted and loved till last." He paused. "Sight," he said.

A quiet hung over the congregation.

"A rainbow," Reverend Thorn said.

Misty pictured the best rainbow she'd seen in her life. She and Gonzalo Rodriguez and little Randy Romaine had been traveling down Old Fort Mountain on I-40, heading for a Tina Turner concert in Greensboro. It was February then, too, just a few weeks before her divorce from Joe Romaine became final and just a few months before Gonzalo married her while still having a wife somewhere in Mexico. She remembered how the hilly piedmont rolled away beneath them, how a storm that had passed through Asheville was moving east toward Morganton and Hickory, how the sun over the mountain behind them struck the storm clouds in front, how she held Gonzalo's hand and thrilled at the double bands of color that stood out as if in a child's drawing with each end of each bow descending all the way to the horizon.

"A sunrise," Reverend Thorn said.

"A sunset," somebody behind her said in a shaky voice.

Misty tried to think of something to say but couldn't say the things she thought of. Beneath the dual rainbows in her mind, she saw Roger Gunter's wild blue eyes, Colette's hair reflected in colored stage lights, her breasts, Joe Romaine's olive skin, Gonzalo Rodriguez's white smile, his strong hands that were never clean.

"Smell," the preacher said.

"Biscuits baking," a man on the other side of the sanctuary said.

"That makes me as hungry as talking about taste," another man said, and the congregation laughed.

As voices around the room murmured or sang out, Misty's mind flashed with images and phrases—*Colette's perfume, baby JJ all clean after his bath, this rose, hot chocolate, my daddy's cigarettes, fingernail poli*—

"Sound."

*Randy's little laugh. Tina Turner's voice. Gonzalo's crazy Spanish in the middle of sex. That one song of Gabriel Tanner's that I can never remember the name of. This preacher's voice.*

"Touch," Reverend Thorn said. "Something felt."

*Jimmy's heartbeat*, she thought, but couldn't decide if that should go with the sense of hearing or touch. *Colette's*—

"A trout on the end of my line," Reverend Thorn said.

"Biscuit dough," a familiar voice said.

"Oh, come on," another said. "Lay off the biscuits."

The congregation laughed.

"I'll bet he ain't never had his hands in biscuit dough," a woman's voice said, and the congregation laughed yet again.

"Here we go," Reverend Thorn said. "Taste."

"Biscuits," the familiar voice said again, and the congregation seemed to breathe together. "With butter and strawberry preserves," he said, and several men moaned.

"Popcorn."

"Fried chicken."

"Anything from Sam and Sharon's kitchen."

"Milkshakes."

*Chocolate. Cold beer in July. The salty sweat on Colette's skin. JJ's fingers covered with birthday cake. Mama's pumpkin pie.*

"My wife's kiss," a man near the front said.

"Well that's done us all in," Reverend Thorn said to more laughter. He stood at the pulpit and waited for stillness. Then, "Our lives are rich, but keep in mind the context of your acts and experiences of love as you go through this week. Love it all in the context of God's love." He paused a moment and then turned to his wife and handed her a rose he pulled from somewhere beneath the pulpit top. "Happy Valentine's Day," he said as she took it and smiled. He turned then to the congregation and spread his arms, saying, "Amen and amen."

"Amen and amen," the people repeated, and then as the organ played and the choir sang the part of the service called "Sending Forth," all began to stand and gather their things.

*   *   *

"Come back and see us again," Reverend Thorn said, holding her hand and looking directly at her.

She wanted to stand there like that for a while, but she worried about the way she talked and the way she looked, about the boys' behavior, about the people waiting in line behind her.

"Thanks," she said and started down the steps. Then she turned back. "I liked your preaching."

He held another hand but turned to look at her.

"Thank you."

By the time she got the boys in their seats, the church's parking lot was almost empty. She heard the car pull up behind her and the door open and close.

"Hey, Misty," Jimmy said. "How was church?"

She turned to face him and his blackened left eye.

"Couldn't you tell through them binoculars? Maybe you should have had the place bugged or tuned the service in on the radio."

"It wasn't on the radio," he said. "WHMM had on its own preachers this morning."

"That's not the point, Jimmy Shetley," she said. "What do you mean sitting out there staring at me through them things?"

"Aw, come on, Misty, you said if I's going to see you today I had to come to church. Besides, you know I can't keep my eyes off of you."

"So you say," she said. "But if that's the case, how come you disappear for so long? Or how come you can't come to church like a normal person on Valentine's Day and sit beside me?" She opened her door and heard JJ screaming. She looked in at him and then at Randy, who looked innocent enough, and decided that the baby just needed his lunch and his nap.

Jimmy had hold of the door.

"Come on, Misty, let's go away somewheres, just for the night." He paused. Then, "We can even take the boys with us if you want to."

She pulled on the door, but he held it open.

"Let go of the door, Jimmy."

"Ain't you going to at least invite me over for a Valentine's lunch?"

"If your mother don't mind you coming over, then I reckon I don't either." She knew that was too far and tried to stop herself but couldn't. "The house is your mother's anyway."

She saw Jimmy Shetley's hands drop to his sides, saw his jaws redden and work. She closed the door and braced herself.

"It's my fucking house," he shouted. "And I fucking want you and them little bastards the hell out of it."

Misty felt the few people still crossing the parking lot either look or not look at Jimmy and her. She knew she was on her own.

Jimmy must have felt their attention too but just stood there looking at her through the window.

She glanced in the rearview mirror.

JJ's face hung ready to wail again, as if he was holding his breath and gathering strength, waiting to be certain of what he had to cry about. Randy looked toward Jimmy without expression.

"I can't do this anymore," Misty said to the rose in her lap. She felt sorry for JJ, and she felt afraid for Randy. She pressed the button to lock the doors and started the engine. Then she realized that she couldn't move her car until Jimmy moved his, and she could feel him still standing there looking at her. She pressed another button and rolled the window down enough for Jimmy to hear her. "Would you please move your car?"

"I want you out of my fucking house," he said.

She turned to look at him. And then she looked beyond him.

Pamela Thorn stood in the middle of the section of parking lot between the back of the church and a house that stood under the trees beyond the rear lot. She stood in the cold wind, looking either at Misty and Jimmy or at the back of her husband who, in fedora and billowing overcoat, was striding toward them.

Jimmy turned to follow Misty's gaze and stood for a moment looking toward the man approaching or the woman behind him. Then he turned back to Misty.

"Get out of my house by the end of the month," he said and turned and walked to his car. Then, "I fucking mean it, Misty."

She winced at hearing her name said like that within earshot of the preacher.

Reverend Thorn had stopped when Jimmy moved away from Misty's window, but he stood watching, apparently waiting to see that this was the end of the ordeal.

As Jimmy dropped into his car, he said something to the preacher or Misty or the Runion wind, but she couldn't make out what it was. Then he slammed his door and squealed his tires and left the parking lot.

The preacher didn't come any closer.

Misty could see the green eyes under the brim of his hat, but she couldn't read the look in them. His gaze reminded her more of Colette's than of Roger's or Joe's or Gonzalo's or Jimmy's. She rolled up the window and turned away from him, put the car in reverse, backed up and then followed Jimmy's path out of the lot.

\* \* \*

At home, she fed the boys, put JJ down for a nap and let Randy go to his room to play. In the quiet aftermath, she sat again in her favorite chair with the remote in her hand, but the TV remained off. She half expected to hear Jimmy's key scratch in the lock, but all remained still except for periodic small musical sounds coming from some toy in Randy's room.

She liked the house and wondered if Jimmy's mother would sell it to her, then wondered if she could afford it. If not, where would she and the boys go? Their fathers wouldn't or couldn't take them in. Her mother would, but with such sighing and stomping that none of them would rest under that roof, just as she herself had never rested there after her father died. No, she decided, she couldn't—wouldn't—leave.

*Jimmy'll get over it*, she thought. *I'll stay right here, and he'll come and go again and again until he's dead.* She took a deep breath. *Or until I'm gone like Colette. Sudden and for good.*

She heard the heat pump kick on and felt the way the air in the room changed. She could feel it in her hair, the hair on her head and the down on her arms. She could feel it on her lips. It somehow made her think of the warm breath of God. Of love and the context of love the Reverend Amos Thorn had talked about that morning. And she tried to think of how the loves in her life fit in the context of love from a loving God. Randy and JJ were easy, even if the loves that brought them into this world and left them in her care had died achingly complicated deaths. Her love for her dead father, maybe the closest thing to a god that she understood, had gone quietly unrequited. Her love for her mother clung to the back of her mind like some kind of nest woven from strands of envy and admiration and gratitude and guilt. Her love for Eliza was also easy, although it too had its complications to do with her enviable talent with hair, with her husband Gabriel, and somehow with what had happened between Colette and herself.

She heard the heat pump cut off, and it unnerved her that in the quiet coming and going of that warm breath and the absence of a comforting uncomplicated love, she would spend Valentine's Day, her favorite holiday, alone. In her mind, the loves of men and women became a tangled knot without one end visible to begin the unraveling.

"Amen and amen," she said.

She turned on the TV and, without any dangerous surfing, entered the number for a channel she remembered as having advertised back-to-back romantic movies for this Valentine's Sunday afternoon. Then she nestled the remote between her thighs and pulled her fingernail stuff—a lap desk and a basket of emery boards and little bottles of polish—from under the coffee table. She opened a bottle of red, took a deep breath, and sat painting her nails in the stillness.

# Overwinter

Snow has got the road to Asheville blocked," she said after hanging the receiver in its cradle on the kitchen wall. She leaned her forehead into a trembling white hand, then left her bags by the door and went to bed without looking at him.

The power went off soon after.

He felt his way to the catch-all drawer in the kitchen and found the flashlight and a few candle halves left over from some hurriedly eaten romantic dinner.

He dug to the back of the closet beneath the stairs where the kerosene heater stood buried among junk. He set the flashlight between his teeth, then picked up the bulky heater and the red can next to it, shaking both to hear how much fuel sloshed inside.

The flashlight died in his mouth just as he kicked the closet door shut. When he gurgled a curse, his teeth lost their grip on the cylinder. The bulb flickered when the flashlight hit the floor but fell dark again.

Working cautiously by candlelight, he set up the heater in the bedroom where she hid under the thick layers of a comforter, two fuzzy blankets, and a double wedding ring quilt. He glanced at the bed now and then, but the lump never moved. With the heater rattling away he set one candle in its own wax on the bedside table and left the room.

He stood by a front window and cooled down from the struggle with the heater and then kept getting colder along with the cabin. Numbness oozed from his mind and fell to fill his shoes and gloves, his shins and forearms. His heaviest coat—denim lined with something intended to look like sheepskin—hung on a peg between the window and the front door, so he put it on over his sweatshirt and sweater and began to pace the room, passing back and forth in front of a fireplace that yawned empty and dark. Now and then he clapped his hands together or stomped his feet on the board floor. In the quiet spaces between he could hear the furious hush of snow pelting glass and wood. He lit a cigarette with the shivery flame of a candle he'd set on the mantel and didn't care if she smelled the smoke.

In the darkest part of the night he gathered all her decorative and aromatic candles from the mantel, the china cabinet, the bookshelves, the knickknack rack. He covered the kitchen table with them and lit every one. Then he took the afghan from the back of the couch, wrapped his legs in it, and read stories from *Dubliners* until the bluing at the windows and the keening in the wind brought him back to the storm.

A drift collapsed into the room when he opened the door and stood with a yardstick in his hand.

The snow lay fifteen inches deep, and the darkness of the woods was lost in the swirl of the blizzard. Above, white noise roared in the tops of the trees beneath a sky that hung low and unreadable.

He jabbed the yardstick to the ground in a level place a short distance from the cabin but close enough to read the numbers from the front window.

The wind swept low, and the snow stung his eyes and face.

He stumbled into his tool shed and found his woodworking goggles, then made his way up behind the cabin and inside the tree line. He adjusted the goggles and looked up the hill and started high-stepping through the snow along the path. Gusts in the tops of the trees showered him with powder. He stopped at the sudden crack and crackle of a tree blowing down somewhere along the windward ridge. Others around him creaked in the quiet that followed. He started again and quickened his pace.

The first thing he noticed when he could see the old woman's house through the naked trees was that no smoke rose from the chimney. He waded through the drift of yard, stopping only to glance into her shadowed woodshed, where he saw about a quarter cord of wood.

Mrs. Jenkins's silver-haired head looked too small for the body wrapped in layers of clothing beneath it. Her eyes shone clear behind small round glasses and her smile. The toes of thick leather boots stuck out from under hems of three different colored skirts of different lengths.

"Come in, boy," she said. "Worse than '27 out there this morning."

"Thought I'd come see if you needed anything," he said.

"Lord, no. I'm fine. A little chilly is all."

A candle burned on the table beside her chair.

"I think you could do with a bigger fire," he said.

She followed his gaze, and a start of surprise twitched in her neck at the sight of the empty fireplace. A trembling hand went to her lips, and when she turned back toward him a timid, toothless smile worked at the corners of her mouth and tears stretched in her eyes. "You'd think a body my age would've taken notice."

"Let me get some wood and build one up for you."

"I'm afraid of sparks catching on the roof."

He smiled at her a moment. Then, "The snow up there's way too deep for that."

When the fire caught, he moved her chair closer to the hearth, lifted the candle and pulled the small table up alongside her chair and set the candle down again. On the floor where the table had stood lay an open tin box full of folded pieces of yellowed paper. He picked it up and laid it on the table beside the candle.

He carried an armload up from the woodshed and piled it into the box beside the door. Then he found the past week's *Runion Record* and opened it on the floor beside her, opposite the table, and laid three smaller pieces of wood on top of it.

"If your fire gets too low to keep you warm, lay one of these on it. But be careful not to let sparks and cinders get beyond the hearth." He patted her on the shoulder. "I'll come back up this afternoon, okay?"

"How's my girl?" Mrs. Jenkins said.

He reached for the doorknob.

"Fine, I reckon. Haven't seen her out from under the covers since I got home last night."

"Tell her to come see me quick as she can."

"I'll tell her. You take care."

\* \* \*

"So, how did you fall in with this guy?" he'd asked.

She stood by the telephone, rubbing both temples with the tips of her long white fingers. She held her eyes shut.

"He built some cabinets in the kitchen at work," she said after a moment of silence.

"Has he been here?"

"No, never here. I gave him directions, but he's snowed in up the river at Stegner's Diner." She turned toward the bedroom. "I thought you'd be late at that faculty thing."

\* \* \*

The yardstick measured the snow at nineteen inches.

He shoveled around his front door and down to the edge of Genesis Road.

The road scraper had passed while he was up on the hill, but the blacktop still lay under an inch or two of packed snow.

Back in the house and quiet after stomping powder off his feet and legs and squirming out of his heavy coat, he heard her on the telephone in the bedroom, the melody and cadence of her murmur the echo of a memory—when he was the man on the other end of the line. He waited for her to finish and then went into the bedroom.

The kerosene heater had died, so he refilled it from the red can and fired it up again. He grabbed the telephone and sat down at the foot of the bed next to the heater and called French Broad Electric.

The woman said she guessed it might be Monday or Tuesday before electricity could be restored to much of the area. Twisted and broken trees were still piling up on the roads and downed lines.

He returned the telephone to the bedside table and changed his jeans and started back to the front room.

A muffled word came from the bed.

He stopped.

"John?" she said. But that was all.

He stood again at a front window and lit another cigarette.

The road scraper passed an hour later. It sent a high spray of snow into the air and left a low jumbled bank of it like a roadblock at the end of his driveway.

Midday passed with no shift in the light, no ebb of the wind, no end to the snow.

\* \* \*

"Mrs. Jenkins?" he called and knocked again. He stepped backward into the yard and looked up but couldn't detect a trace of smoke.

The doorknob squeaked, and the door opened enough to see half of her face. The skin of her cheek looked pale and rubbery. Dark brown tobacco stains pulled the corners of her toothless mouth into a frown. Her nose was red and swollen, and her eyes squinted against the wind and the whiteness.

"Eldred?" she said. "Is that you?"

"It's John, Mrs. Jenkins." He hesitated. "You've let your fire go out."

She turned away into the darkness of her house. She'd changed her outer skirt or maybe added another, white and antique. The tight bun at the back of her head was loosening and escaped strands of silver-gray hair floated around her ears and the back of her neck. She sat down in her chair and laid her right hand on the pile of folded yellow papers on the small table next to her.

"Why didn't you throw a stick or two on the fire before it died?" he said as he stepped in and closed the door. "It's too cold in here."

"Bet you're colder in Montana," she said. "I just bet you are."

He shook his head and from the box by the door loaded a

sizeable log and some sticks of firewood in the crook of one arm and picked up a few chips of kindling in his other hand. He walked past her chair and sat down on the edge of the hearth.

She leaned toward him but kept her gaze on the floor. The corners of her mouth twitched at intervals—now a strange smile, now a tragic frown. "Would you like to take my place?" she said. "I'm about wore out."

He arranged the last bit of kindling under the firewood and turned to look at her.

"Mrs. Jenkins, you're going to be fine. You'll make it through this." He reached up onto the mantel and felt around for a match. "The cabin is plenty big enough for me."

She smiled.

"It's cool for this time of year, don't you think, sir? But I declare I'm burning up all of a sudden."

"As soon as this fire gets going good you'll be able to shed a layer or two of clothes. You're probably just feeling a bit smothered."

"I do believe I'm all out of breath," she said.

"Just relax. It's starting to warm up already."

The flames swelled, and the wood began to pop and hiss.

He didn't want to get too warm without the promise of staying warm, so he stood up and moved away from the hearth.

She turned her face from him.

"Senator Jenkins never cared at all for the look of a woman's bare arm, much less for me in my ragged hand-me-down of Eve's first dress."

He looked down at her.

Her left hand pushed at the wiry gray strands of hair around her face and then moved to the back of her head where the fingers danced around the unraveling bun. Her right hand still lay on the folded yellow papers, and she rubbed a corner of one between her thumb and forefinger like a young girl with a red satin ribbon.

"I'm going to get some more wood and put it right in front of you on the hearth," he said and stepped outside.

The snow blinded him, but he felt better in the light. He piled wood into his arms and decided he was confusing her or had somehow hurt her feelings with his talk about the fire.

"Now," he said when he'd stacked the wood on the hearth. "Whenever you feel like it, all you have to do is lean over and grab a stick and toss it onto the fire. Just about any old way it lands will be fine." He put a hand on her shoulder. "But why don't you plan to come stay with us in the cabin tonight?"

"It's going to be long winter ahead."

"Why, Mrs. Jenkins, I'll bet you by this time next week it'll be warm as the first of May."

"Leave me here. But come back like you promised."

\* \* \*

The road scraper again moved down Genesis Road toward Highway 251, the jangle of its chains and the rumble of its engine muted by the snow and wind. Behind the spray and wake of its passing the roadbed still lay white and forbidding.

The snow now wrapped itself around the yardstick's twenty-two-inch mark.

She'd been out of bed while he checked on Mrs. Jenkins. An open box of Corn Flakes sat on the table among the remains of her candles. A few milk-logged flakes floated in the bowl of leftover milk she'd set in the sink beside the emptied ashtray.

He used the telephone on the kitchen wall to call the sheriff's office.

"Deputy Boyce, here." The voice was a deep purr.

"Deputy, this is John Riddle from up on Genesis Road."

"Yes, Dr. Riddle. You folks holding out okay there?"

"Well sir, I'm calling about Mrs. Jenny Jenkins from up the hill behind us. I'm worried that she's not doing too well through all this." He paused.

"Go ahead on, Dr. Riddle," the deputy said.

"She's cold. She won't keep her fire going. I've been up there twice today and got it burning for her. But I'm afraid she's just going to let it die again."

"Has she got wood enough to last?"

"She has plenty of wood, but she won't use it. I bring it in for her and it just stays where I leave it."

"Well, let me see." There was the scrape of whiskers on the other end of the line, a sharp deep breath and a slow release. "Dr. Riddle, I've got a couple of men around that the sheriff deputized for this emergency. I'll send one out on the next road scraper, and you go up the hill with him. See if she won't come out with you."

"I've already asked her, and she wouldn't do it."

"Well, maybe by the time our man gets there she'll think better of the idea. We'll put a badge on him and make him look official."

"Do you know Mrs. Jenkins, Deputy?"

"Yessir. Had her for a teacher in third grade. Acquainted most with the flat of her hand back then. She whipped my ass every day for three months or so."

"I'm sure you deserved it," John said and paused. When Deputy Boyce didn't laugh, he continued. "Maybe she'd feel better if you come out yourself. She seemed a little disoriented just now when I was up there."

"Tell you what, Mr. Riddle, if she don't come out with you and our man, I'll see what I can do." A buzz sounded in the background. "I've got another call coming in, Dr. Riddle. Anything else real quick?"

"How are the main roads?"

"Not much better off than yours. The county crew's behind but catching up a little here and there. The Tennessee side's still pretty bad yet from what I hear. Asheville's all but shut down. Supposed to come a change in a couple of hours."

He went into the bedroom and refueled the heater. He took some dry clothes from the closet and stripped. For a few moments he stood naked and let the heat draw some of the cold damp numbness from his legs.

"Hannah?" he said. "I'm a little worried about Mrs. Jenkins. Maybe you could get up and go see her for a little while."

One edge of the mass on the bed lifted slightly. "What did the deputy say about the roads?"

He pulled on the dry clothes and left the room.

Through the rest of the afternoon, the wind subsided to short fitful gusts and then died away. For a while the snow fell thick and straight in large flakes, then thinned and grew fine and stopped at twenty-five inches. The clouds lifted from the western mountains and the clearing seemed on its way.

He sat by the window in the increasing light and read a short Yasunari Kawabata novel he'd picked up at a used book store.

The road scraper made two more passes but didn't stop to let off the expected deputy.

When the blue rim of sky on the horizon began to take on a hint of gold, he called the sheriff's office again.

A woman answered and said she was the sheriff's wife. She told him everybody was busy with a small fire at the Runion Pizzeria and took his name and number.

He bundled up and shoveled a deep path from the front door down to the road. Then he took an old sled and some rope from the shed and started up the hill again.

As the sun settled into the space between the low clouds and the mountains, the white woods reflected its gold in dazzling sparkles.

He stood for several minutes and watched this display and breathed the cold air deep into his lungs. A tingle began to awaken parts of him numbed by the storm. He felt light-headed and imagined that beneath this golden cocoon of snow his world lay chrysalid and ready to be made new.

Hints of crimson softened the gold and warned him back to his mission.

Only a slight wisp of smoke rose from Mrs. Jenkins's chimney. "Hello?" he called and knocked.

This time she was quick to answer in a voice cracked and dry. "Who are you? What are you about?"

"It's John, Mrs. Jenkins. John Riddle. I've come to take you to the cabin for the night."

"Go away," she said. Her voice sounded close on the other side of the wooden door. "You've got no claim on me now. Get from here."

"Mrs. Jenkins, the storm's stopped but it's going to get mighty cold tonight if the sky clears."

"Get away, I say. You left me here too long, and I'll not be taking up with you again."

He moved away from the door to a window where he could see her.

She stood slightly crouched the length of her shotgun's double barrels from the door. Her head nodded and shook with small quick motions. Her gray hair had finally freed itself from the bun and flowed wildly down the full curve of her back. She was naked except for a pair of red wool socks.

"My God," he said and ran back to the door and stood to one side of it and knocked lightly and pulled his hand away. "Mrs. Jenkins, you've got to let me in. Put the gun down, okay?"

The shotgun blast ripped through the door, and the sound of it died in the snow-muffled woods.

He dropped down and bellied back to the window and peeped in again.

She picked herself up from the floor and used the gun as a walking stick until she was steady. By the light of the tiny remains of her fire and the candle on the table beside her chair, her skin looked translucent. She put a quivering hand to the right side of her head and stooped as if to peer through the ragged hole in her door.

He watched for her face to relax and then rapped sharply on the window.

She turned to the fireplace first and then toward him. Her eyes were wide and shiny, and her chin was lined with tobacco juice. Gray hair hid all but the movements of her breasts. The bulge of her belly sloped down into a wedge as dark as youth.

"Mrs. Jenkins, it's me, John," he said and waved.

She hoisted the shotgun into the pit of her arm.

He fell backwards just as the second blast shattered three of the window panes and sprayed him with bits of glass. He rolled onto his stomach and then stood up quickly with his back to the house. He looked at the depressions he made in the deep snow and saw no blood. He heard the chink as she broke down the gun to reload.

"Eldred?" she called.

"Mrs. Jenkins, it's John Riddle from the cabin."

"Eldred? Are you killed?" Her voice was closer to the window.

"I've got Hannah with me, Mrs. Jenkins. She's come to see you like you wanted. We brought a sled for you to ride down the hill to visit with us."

"I ain't going with you. I don't want to see you, and I sure as hell don't want to see no woman you brung here."

"If you won't let me in at least take the wood I carried for you and build up your fire. It's still there on the hearth."

"Get from here."

He swung away from the house at an angle between the door and the window and escaped into the blue woods.

When he came out of the trees and into his own yard, Deputy Boyce's squad car was just pushing through another wall of snow the road scraper had deposited in front of the driveway.

The deputy listened to the breathless report of the old naked woman and her shotgun.

"Well, no use us going back up there to give her more target practice. Let me see if I can get hold of one or another of her kin. Your phone still working?" He made two or three calls and accepted two or three more.

John sat down on the hearth and lit a cigarette and stared at the empty space by the door.

The bags were gone.

"I guess the river road must be passable by now," he said.

"Yes, but barely. Only for emergency pretty much. They'll probably close it down after it's full dark."

The telephone rang again, and the deputy answered, spoke for a few moments, and hung up.

"There's a niece near about Trust township. She's coming, but it'll be nigh on an hour before she can get here. In the meantime, I suggest you get some dry clothes on and warm up." He walked over and picked at the rainbow melting of the candles hardened on the table. "Mrs. Riddle asleep?"

"I don't know," John said and went into the bedroom and

closed the door behind him.

He found no hint of goodbye other than the fact she'd turned off the heater. He poured the last of the kerosene in and carried it to the front room and started it up again. Through the window he saw Deputy Boyce bending down and shining his flashlight on the yardstick stuck in the snow. He went back to his bedroom and felt in the closet for more clothes. The numbness ached in his shins and thighs and crotch and arms. He again stood naked at the foot of the tousled bed and tried to imagine how cold Mrs. Jenkins must be.

*   *   *

The niece arrived sooner than expected, and the little rescue party made its way up the woods path by the glow of Deputy Boyce's flashlight. They reached the edge of the yard and the house stood dark in front of them.

"Give her a yoo-hoo," Deputy Boyce said to the niece.

"Aunt Jenny," the niece called through cupped hands. "This is Delsie. Your niece, Delsie."

The snow soaked up her voice.

No answer returned from the silent house.

"You folks keep behind me," the deputy said and started across the yard. He went to the window first and held the flashlight at arm's length and looked in. "She's in the chair in front of the fireplace. I don't see no shotgun."

The front door was unlocked, and they went in.

Mrs. Jenkins sat with her back straight and her head leaned over on her left shoulder. Her hands lay folded in her naked lap.

Deputy Boyce put two fingers to the old woman's neck. He shifted his touch for a moment and then shook his head.

"Oh, Aunt Jenny," the niece said and started to cry.

"There's nothing we can do here," the deputy said and began guiding the woman toward the door. "I can't get anybody up here till the morning. We'll just have to leave her."

"You go on," John said. "If you don't mind my handling her, I'll lay her out straight before she stiffens up like this."

"I'm sure Mr. Ramsey and the folks at his funeral home will be obliged," Deputy Boyce said.

The niece's sobs and the low purr of the deputy's voice faded into the woods.

He took the logs he'd stacked earlier that afternoon and quickly got a fire going in the hope that it would keep the old woman's body warm long enough for him to get her straightened out.

He lit a candle and found the bedroom and made the bed ready for her.

He returned with a double wedding ring quilt and spread it flat on the floor and lifted the old woman's body and laid it out in the center. He folded the cold hands upon the sternum and heard a crinkling sound.

A corner of yellowed paper was now visible beneath the fall of gray hair that covered her left breast.

He pulled the paper free and saw that it was a letter and laid it on the hearth. Then he tossed both sides of the quilt across the body and lifted it and carried it into the bedroom.

The fire blazed in the fireplace, and its heat was drawn out into the room by the draft between the shotgun holes in the door and the window.

He sat down on the floor and scooted as near to the flames as he could tolerate. He stretched his legs and felt the tingling sensation again as the numbness began to melt from him.

The heated air fluttered the brittle letter on the hearth.

He picked it up and looked at it in the light of the fire.

*13 April 1927*

*My dearest Jenny,*

*Sad news! I have just this morning seen your Senator disembark from the Asheville train, a full two days early in his return from the session in Raleigh!*

*If I knew you were ready, I should fetch you posthaste, and we would away to Montana this instant.*

*But, with him in the area, at our departure, there is no way we could flee beyond his jealous grasp, especially with no place yet to run.*

*So, forgive me, pretty one, but I must leave thee.*

*I shall make Montana as quickly as possible, and, once there, procure us such a piece of land as might be large as all Madison County. There, the building of some small shelter, in which to overwinter, and the surveying of our heaven, shall occupy the remainder of the coming summer. And the next, that of '28, shall see the founding of our empire, and our future. When I have spent yet one more winter there, to be sure your palace is strong against the cold, I shall return.*

*Meet me, then, only a little more than two years hence, around that Maypole, where I received your first gentle smile, and felt the first touch of your silken hand when you gave me your ribbon.*

*Now, destroy this letter, and keep yourself safe, until we meet again.*

*Faithfully,*

*E—*

He folded the letter and started to put it back with the pile on the table but stood up and tossed it into the fire instead. He found the sled he'd left behind when the late afternoon shooting started and piled it high with Mrs. Jenkins's wood. He filled his arms with kindling and started down the path.

He staggered to a stop halfway down the hill and waited.

The first chill came like the sudden smell of something burning, and then the cold surrounded him like smoke. The numbness and the ache followed like soot and ash.

He drew a sharp breath and hugged the splintery kindling closer to his chest and stumbled on beneath the naked trees that webbed a winter sky still aching with snow.

# The Flutist

W hen Dr. Brian Anderson used up his last breath on a moderately difficult ascending passage in Gaubert's *Nocturne and Allegro Scherzando* and fell over dead on stage during his annual Ides of March recital, the Department of Music at Runion State University—for the first time in forty-one years—faced the task of finding a new Professor of Flute. The pressure was on. Because of Dr. Anderson's longstanding reputation as a teacher and an artist, RSU was a favorite destination for area flutists transitioning from high school to college. Applicants were many and acceptances restricted, and the music department, jealously guarding one of its most significant claims to prestige, wanted to move quickly so as to lose as few of these recruits as possible. In the name of decency, however, the department chair and university administration agreed that the search for Dr. Anderson's replacement would not officially begin until after his on-campus memorial service was held on the last Saturday in March.

But Anderson had been dead less than thirty-six hours when Dr. Joanna Whitmire, Chair of Runion State's Department of Music and Professor of Clarinet, put her Executive Aide to work gathering the addresses of department chairs and graduate directors at the nation's best music schools, focusing particularly on those east of the Mississippi River and, for the most part, south of the Mason-Dixon Line. Meanwhile, Dr. Whitmire created the Search Committee, wrote the job description and submitted paperwork for the "Request to Advertise." At three o'clock in the afternoon, with the collected email addresses entered and waiting, she finished drafting and revising the communiqué to be sent along with the job description. All was prepared, pending the approval of Human Resources and the arrival of the Monday after the memorial service, still a dozen days away.

Dr. Whitmire sat for a moment in her high-backed black office chair, looking from the computer screen to the clock on the wall.

"What the hell," she said, clicked SEND and left the office for her three-thirty hair appointment at Eliza's.

\*   \*   \*

The harried and hurried Search Committee wanted a woman, having for so long had a man in the position. During the two-week period when the search was open, a surprising twenty-one applications arrived. Dr. Whitmire, with her committee's email approval, disqualified twelve of these immediately—five had neither work completed toward a doctorate nor professional experience to be considered equivalent; three fell prey to nasty, knife-in-the-back letters of recommendation; three more doctoral degrees had gone cold, having been in hand for more than five years while the candidates moved almost yearly from one adjunct position to the next; one sent application materials apparently intended, or previously used, for another position at another university.

With nine viable candidates remaining in the files, six women and three men, the Search Committee met on a Wednesday afternoon in the middle of April to reduce the nine to five. Those remaining would be interviewed by telephone, after which two survivors would be invited to visit campus. The overheated faculty lounge became a sweat lodge as rain poured down outside the closed windows and the custodial crew buffed the hallway outside the closed door. The committee read and reread the candidates' credentials and listened to audition recordings, listened again and reread recommendation letters and teaching statements. As rain continued outside, conference calls babbled on both ends, and then arguments for or against one candidate or another roared or hissed from committee members. Finally, the new green leaves and pink petals beyond the windows darkened, as the day shifted to its relative minor key, and only two files remained on a coffee table littered with stained Styrofoam cups and half-eaten donuts. The committee escaped into the approaching night, and the head custodian propped open the lounge door and raised the windows to clear the air of the odors of sweat and stale breath.

\* \* \*

Dr. Julia Baker was the favorite and the first to be scheduled for a campus interview. At gray dusk on the last Monday of the month, she arrived at the airport in Asheville, shaky and pale and somewhat drunk after a storm-tossed journey from Tallahassee, which included a three-hour layover in Charlotte.

"I'm going to be sick in all kinds of ways, and I have to find a restroom," she said to Dr. Whitmire and Dr. Boz McWilliams, Professor of Percussion, when they met her at the gate. "Would you mind getting my luggage? It's Seminole garnet and gold. You can't miss it."

When the three of them, along with Dr. Baker's bags, were settled in Dr. McWilliams's minivan, Dr. Whitmire leaned forward between the front seats.

"We thought we'd take you to dinner—"

"Oh, Jesus, no," Dr. Baker said. "I couldn't eat a bite." She dropped her head back on the headrest and closed her eyes. "Just take me to my hotel."

Beyond the east end of the Smoky Park Bridge, Dr. McWilliams eased the minivan off the four-lane and descended to the winding two-lane river road. His glance at the rearview mirror met the question in Dr. Whitmire's eyes. He raised an eyebrow and smiled. When she smiled back, he accelerated into the near dark of the old, all-but-abandoned route that twisted alongside the French Broad River between Asheville and Runion.

Less than forty-eight hours later, Wednesday, following a full day of interview and social events on Tuesday, every member of the Search Committee—claiming doctor or dentist appointments, class meetings or makeup lessons—bowed out of the final luncheon with the tall, blond and red-lipped Dr. Baker. A disappointed Dr.

Whitmire paid a commuting student from Asheville $20 to drop off the candidate and her garnet-and-gold luggage at the airport and went home early with a headache that took half a bottle of wine to mask.

* * *

The second candidate, Mr. Jubal Kincaid, ABD, arrived the following evening from Ann Arbor, Michigan. Stocky and somewhat short, with close-cropped hair and beard and an easy smile, Kincaid shook hands with Dr. Whitmire, Dr. McWilliams, and Dr. Geoff Warmack, Professor of Bassoon and Double Reeds. In the brief silence that followed the introductions, he stood with the heavy bag on his shoulder and looked from one to the other. He knew that his eyes were sparkling, as they always sparkled when he was excited.

"You can't help being elfish," Chuck had told him at the airport in Detroit that afternoon. "But think more Lothlórien, less Santa's Workshop, okay?"

"Should we go pick up your other luggage?" Dr. Whitmire said.

"No, thanks," Kincaid said. "I just have this one bag."

"Well then," Dr. McWilliams said. "Let's get going."

"We thought we'd take you to dinner somewhere," Dr. Whitmire said. "If you're hungry."

"I can always eat," Kincaid said. "As you can tell."

At Magnolia's in downtown Asheville, they sat at a table for four, their food ordered, their drinks arriving. Conversation moved smoothly between the professional and the personal—Mr. Kincaid's hometown of Chicago, his work with Amy Porter at the University of Michigan, his lecture-recital on the flute music of Katherine Hoover, places he'd lived and visited, when he'd begun to play the flute, his teaching experiences. They talked through beers and glasses of wine and their different entrees. As their desserts and coffees arrived, Dr. Whitmore asked a question she liked to ask, a question that others would ask throughout the interview day to follow.

"Do you have anything you want to ask us?"

Jubal Kincaid took a tentative sip of his coffee, forked a bite of cheesecake, and sat with his hand hovering halfway between his plate and his mouth.

"Okay," he said after a moment. "What can you tell me about the man I would be replacing?"

The Search Committee members seemed briefly thrown off by this unexpected question. They shifted in their seats and looked at one another.

"Well," Dr. McWilliams said after a moment. "You probably already know that his name was Brian Anderson. He'd been teaching at RSU for—what, Joanna—three decades?"

"A little over four actually," Dr. Whitmire said.

Dr. Anderson had been stationed in Europe in the early 1950s, and while there he'd fallen in love with an Amsterdam woman who taught him to play the flute. For many years, according to Ms. Judy Robertson, adjunct professor of French Horn, who boasted the next longest experience in the department, he spent part of each summer in Amsterdam. But some twenty years or so before his death, the summer trips stopped, and as far as anybody knew, he'd rarely left Runion since.

"He learned flute from a lover?" Kincaid said and stopped. He looked down and forked the last bite of his cheesecake. "I bet they never dreaded his lessons." He laughed, nervously and alone for a moment, but the beer and wine consumed around the table—and the common experience of having, at one time or another, dreaded giving or taking a music lesson—set the others to laughing with him.

As they waited for the check and then the return of the department credit card, Dr. Whitmire told Kincaid what she knew of Brian Anderson's history at Runion State—how in 1958 he had begun to teach flute there without a degree; how by the late '70s he'd earned degrees at Mars Hill College, Western Carolina University, and the University of South Carolina; how he'd developed a strong program for high school students, including a summer flute camp; how he'd become regionally famous for his annual Ides of March concerts; how he'd died at the last one.

"I played my final dissertation recital at Michigan that same night," Kincaid said.

"That's kind of creepy," Dr. Warmack said and, after a few quiet moments, seemed ready to say something else but didn't.

"Gentlemen," Dr. Whitmire said as she signed for the meal. "Mr. Kincaid has a long day tomorrow, so I think we ought to get him to his bed now."

Outside Magnolia's they climbed into the van, and Dr. McWilliams drove them the straightest way home.

\* \* \*

The evening before he died, Brian Anderson played randomly in Taffanel and Gaubert's *Complete Method*, cleaned his flute, put his music in order for the recital, and poured himself a glass of red wine. He stood in his sunroom and looked out at a twilight that struggled to darken a back yard still knee-deep in snow. When he'd been without power during the height of the blizzard, Saturday afternoon as the snow and wind continued and he lay dozing on the couch under layers of blankets, he dreamed vividly, for the first time in a long time, of Anna and Amsterdam—the feel and smell of her, the look of her carrying a bag of groceries down her street or undressing by the streetlight falling through the window, the music in her movements and voice and soul. Still haunted by that dreaming, he swallowed the last of his wine and left the darkening sunroom and went to a closet in the den. He took down a large box, set it on the floor beside the coffee table and lay aside the dusty lid. For a moment he sat and looked into it, his hands clasped between his knees, his elbows on his thighs, the house perfectly still around him and quiet except for his breath and the ticking of the clock on the mantel.

The first item out of the box was the flute she'd given him over forty years before. A 19th-century instrument by French maker Louis Lot, it had belonged to her father, Wrestling Poliander Kirkhoven—a "descendent of English Leyden," as she described him, a man whose beautiful, musical soul and tremendous, undeniable gift were bound and controlled by layers of Puritan severity and sternness. The anger and shame he felt at making his living by so frivolous a means as music drove him to levels of emotional intensity and technical proficiency that no other in all of Amsterdam could match. He held first chair in the city's Concertgebouw Orchestra. He became a sought-after chamber player, known from Paris to Vienna. In the downstairs parlor, he thundered and stomped away his last years, a feared teacher whose lessons only the best students could survive. He'd hated himself from the moment he discovered his gift, and he hated his instrument, even as it gave him life. But both deserved love, Anna said. Depending on her mood, she'd moved between her own flute and her father's in the years since his death, and she seemed glad to pass the instrument on to somebody who could not feel or hear the pain in its tones as she could. She would love her father and his gift, as she'd always done, if Anderson, as she called him, would love this instrument.

And love it he had, playing it every day from the moment she handed it to him, a soldier twenty-one years old, until that summer day in 1979 when he—now a flute professor forty-eight years of age—arrived in Amsterdam on his annual pilgrimage to find her rooms occupied by two young men, strangers, who nevertheless told him where he could find her grave. Even though paying for lodging nearly drained his savings account back in Runion, he stayed in Amsterdam the entire six weeks as planned. Every day he visited her at lunchtime, and for many days after his arrival and discovery, spent the afternoons visiting music shops in search of a new flute. He thought he might find hers somewhere, but he didn't. Instead he purchased a flute by a Japanese maker he'd never heard of, a flute he found he could make sing with a tone to match his mood. Her father's flute he carried home with him and stored away in this box with all the other pieces of her and their life together and their lives apart.

He took the pieces from the case and gently fit them together. After checking the key alignment and making an adjustment, he brought the lip plate against his lower lip. But the breath he drew to play stuck like a bone in his throat at the sensation of having caught, he thought, the aroma of her breath rising like a sigh from the embouchure hole. Her lips and fingers on this flute, her lips on his lips, her fingers intertwined with his, her body in naked ecstasy above him and below him, the flute lying on the pillow beside them as if watching this part of his lesson—a sudden burst of such images blinded him and left him kneeling in the middle of the floor and clutching the flute to his chest, his breath returning in great ragged gasps.

*    *    *

Sometime between three and four o'clock in the morning, Anderson woke up sweating, his mind feverishly hung up on an almost inconsequential passage in the Fauré *Fantasy*. He threw off his comforter and electric blanket, rolled slowly out of bed and moved stiffly to the window, which he unlocked and raised a few inches for air and the sound of the creek that sang over rock falls beside his house. He bowed his head and noticed the gleam of sweaty skin beneath the gray hair on his belly. He wondered why he'd felt the need to set the blanket on seven when he'd never been able to stand it any higher than three, even on the coldest of nights. And why, after years of seemingly dreamless sleep, he'd suddenly begun to dream again, especially of Anna. He wondered why the inanest thoughts and snippets of music swirled around and around in his sleeping brain until he awoke. He sighed as the music of the creek slowly took the Fauré passage down among its smooth stones and washed it away.

With the Fauré silenced for the time being and the sweat dried on his chest and belly, he lay down again but couldn't go back to sleep. Across the valley, where an extended family of hunting mountaineers lived in a train of doublewide mobile homes, a chorus of dogs had begun to bark in maddeningly different rhythms and pitches. This racket was beyond the power of the creek, so he got up, closed the window, and turned on the loud exhaust fan in the bathroom. But the barking cut easily through his walls and the white noise. He tried earplugs, which quieted the dogs but replaced their cacophony of yelps and howls with the rhythmic thump and whoosh of his working heart. In some way that he refused to try and put his finger on, this sound was the most disturbing of all, and before long the earplugs were back in the drawer of the nightstand.

So, at some minutes before five o'clock in the morning on the day that he died, Dr. Brian Anderson stood open-robed and sock-footed in his kitchen, thick black-rimmed glasses riding low on his nose, their ever-present clip-on shades flipped up, his thick white hair sticking out in all directions. After a couple of deep breaths, the second of which ended with a stretch that seemed unable to stretch far enough, he turned on his countertop television, turned to The Weather Channel and proceeded to whip up an elaborate and buttery breakfast for one.

*  *  *

Jubal Kincaid stirred just as the sky began to gray above the campus lampposts and streetlights. His upstairs room in the Faculty House took shape around him as he dozed—the starched white pillowcase, the handmade quilt with its intricate pattern of stars, the nightstand and lamp, a small desk and chair, a bureau and mirror. His bag lay mostly empty between the bureau and a corner closet door, and in the closet's darkness hung a clean white shirt and red tie on one hanger, blue jeans and his one sport coat, black, on another. Yesterday's traveling clothes lay in a heap on the seat of an overstuffed chair by the window. That window—the tree branches, building top, mountain top and glowing sky it framed—was the first thing he saw when he finally opened his eyes.

He lay still for a moment, remembering where he was, and then threw back the covers and sat up on the edge of the bed. Naked except for black briefs, he sat rubbing himself with both hands—rubbing knees, thighs, belly, chest, shoulders, neck and head. As his hands came away from his face, he looked at the stubby fingers and wondered, as he did almost every morning, how these graceless-looking things of bone and flesh could dance like ballerinas and flamenco masters upon the keys of a flute.

He arose and walked to the window and, with one hand

braced on the frame and the other still slowly rubbing his belly and chest, stood looking out at the campus. In the dawn mix of natural and electric light, he saw the backs of buildings of various designs and heights, trees greening and flowering, concrete and brick walkways that wound between the trees and the buildings. He sensed an open central quad not far away and began to notice his first Runion folk in the early twilight—two runners, a girl on a bicycle, a man in a small utility vehicle that stopped at every trash receptacle along the various walkways. When this groundskeeper seemed to notice him standing in the window, Kincaid lingered for one more moment and then moved away, pulled on athletic socks and sweatpants, a sweatshirt, a wool cap and walking shoes. He checked his watch, put it in his pocket with the keys to the Faculty House and his room, went quietly downstairs, and stepped out into the late April morning.

He wound his way through the small campus until he found the quad he'd sensed was there. Picking up his pace, he walked a couple of laps around this, looking at the buildings and reading their signs, nodding a smile to the few people he met and trying to guess if they were students or staff or faculty. He noticed as he walked that, although the day was growing brighter and the lights topping the lampposts were flickering off, no direct sunlight gilded the tops of the buildings or trees. He looked up and saw the mountain rising east of campus and decided that the sun might be a long while climbing from behind it. He pulled out his watch—plenty of time before his 8:30 breakfast with Dr. Whitmire. He got his bearings and turned toward the western edge of campus and the town of Runion.

He paused on the corner of Mill and Main, marching in place to keep his muscles warm, and took in the surroundings so different from his native Chicago. His reflection in the large windows of Rio Burrito caught his eye, and he wished he would lose a little weight. Across Mill stood a church, and beyond the church stood a house. Just as the thought about his weight was leaving his mind, he saw a man of almost his exact build walking from the house toward the back of the church. The man saw him as well and threw up a hand, and Kincaid waved back. He looked both ways on Main Street and crossed, noticing, down the hill to his left, the Stonehouse Café, where he would eat breakfast in a little over an hour. He saw men going into and coming out of the place, and his stomach growled. On the corner in front of Eliza's, a hair salon, and the offices of a chiropractor and a dentist, he turned north on Main Street. He walked and looked at buildings and read signs as he'd done on the Runion State quad—an old theater, a department store, the public library, Radio Shack.

Outside the hardware store, a pick-up truck sat parked with its engine running and three men inside. The smoke of their cigarettes and breath rose from the open windows.

Kincaid felt a twist of tension in his stomach and a sudden urge to laugh at the only movement in the cab of the truck. The two passengers' heads—balanced on thick necks and broad shoulders—made a slow and simultaneous swivel, following him, while the thin man behind the wheel stared straight ahead. The moment passed quietly, but he could hear the words as if the men had spat them out the window at him—"stranger," "city boy," "damn Yankee," "fuckin' queer." He wondered if what he heard in his mind's ear was dialogue from some film he'd seen or some book he'd read. Just moments before, he'd experienced the exhilaration of a quick affection for this little mountain town and the job and life that it might hold for him. As he tried to recover that feeling, he couldn't shake the echo of those imagined words or the image of the three—the two big passengers impossibly twisted around and watching through the misty back windshield, the man behind the wheel still appearing to stare straight ahead but watching, he guessed, in the rearview mirror.

He wrestled his mind back into focus on the town, on Runion— its grocery store, funeral home, pharmacy, health clinic, jail, and pizzeria. He passed the offices of the *Runion Record* and made a mental note to pick up a copy before he left for Michigan the next day. Outside Two Rivers Books & Music, he recrossed the street, casting one last glance at the parked truck and its occupants, and hurried along Lonesome Mountain Drive to the entrance of the Runion State campus.

When he returned to his room at the Faculty House, he quickly
wrote in his planner "Mountain Homes Realty" and "Fredricks
Agency (insurance + real estate)," then took his toiletries and
interview clothes, minus the tie and sport coat, to the shower at
the end of the hall.

\* \* \*

At two o'clock that afternoon—having survived breakfast at the
Stonehouse Café, an informal gathering of faculty and students
in the music department's lounge, back-to-back meetings with
Human Resources and the Dean of the College of Arts and
Sciences, and lunch at the university cafeteria—Kincaid stood
flute in hand beside Dr. Whitmire at center stage in the small
recital space inside Bryant Hall.

"I want to thank you all for being here on a Friday afternoon,"
Dr. Whitmire said to the twenty-seven faculty and students who
sat scattered through the 120 seats. "For those of you who haven't
met him yet, this is Mr. Jubal Kincaid, who comes to us from
the University of Michigan. He's soon to be Dr. Kincaid when
he finishes his oral exams"—she turned to Kincaid—"which I
believe you said would be next Friday. Is that right?"

"That's right," Kincaid said.

"Okay," Dr. Whitmire said. "Y'all know the way we usually do
this. We have three of our flute students here. Each of them will
play a short piece for Mr. Kincaid, and he'll give them and us a
mini master class. Then he'll play a couple of pieces himself, and
we'll follow that up with some questions and answers."

"Let's hope there's no blood this time," Dr. David Grobian
said, and several of those in attendance either laughed or groaned.

"Hush, Dr. Grobian," Dr. Whitmire said with a grin, as she
took a seat in the front row.

Kincaid stared for a moment at Grobian, Professor of Trumpet
and Band.

"If you're ready, Mr. Kincaid," Dr. Whitmire said. She nodded
at a young man in t-shirt, shorts and sandals. When he stood up
with his flute and music, she said, "I'll let the students introduce

themselves."

Kincaid motioned the young man to the music stand.

"What's your name?"

"Danny Green," the young man said as he set his music on the stand.

"What year are you, Danny?"

"I'm just finishing my freshman year."

"All right, good. What are you going to play today?"

"The last thing me and Dr. Anderson worked on was Telemann's Fantasia number twelve, so I'm gonna play the Rondeau from that."

After his military service ended in the mid-1940s, Jubal Kincaid's father had moved to Chicago from Swanpond, Kentucky, bringing his accent with him. He married a Chicago girl who worked in the same factory, and twice a year he took his wife—and later his wife and children—"home" to Swanpond on vacation. Having an ear for his father's voice, always searching it closely for tones of praise or anger, Kincaid had little problem understanding his southern grandparents, aunts, uncles, and cousins. His own accent—thanks to his mother's side of the family—was almost pure Chicago, but his ear for interpreting the speech of Swanpond became well known at the Jewel-Osco supermarket where he worked during summer vacations. Sometimes when a delivery truck arrived from the South, he would be paged to go to the loading dock. "Kincaid, come over here," his manager would say, "we need a translator."

"Good, I know that one well," he said to Danny Green. "Begin whenever you're ready."

The young man blew into his flute to warm its body, set his feet, and set his lower lip on the embouchure piece. With a visible count of "one-two-one-two" tipping the end of his nose, he jumped into the presto tempo with decent technique in both fingering and breathing. With few halting passages in which fingers or tongue stumbled, he sprinted through the piece, repeats and all, and arrived breathlessly at the end in under three minutes.

"G minor is a good key for you," Kincaid said. "You got through that fairly well."

"Yessir," Danny said. "Thanks."

Kincaid stepped around the music stand and stood at the young man's left side. He looked at the music, leaned closer for a moment, and then pointed to a passage on the second page.

"Would you mind replaying the section from measure"—he leaned closer again—"seventeen to thirty-six. And I want you to try a couple of things for me." He took a pencil from his pocket and jotted some notes on the score as he spoke. "Jean-Pierre Rampal has done minimal editing on this particular piece, so let's help him out a little bit. Rather than keep that presto pace throughout, I want you to pull back a bit at seventeen. Maybe think allegretto through this line. Then at the start of the next line, bump it up a notch to allegro and hold on to that through the remainder of the section." He took a step back. "Now, look it over. Think it through. And when you're ready, take another run at it."

After a moment of staring and then another count with the tip of his nose, Danny played the passage through again.

"Good," Kincaid said when the young man stopped. "Good. Did you hear how the changes right there where the key shifts add some depth to the emotional range of the piece?"

"I think so," Danny said.

"Now, next time do the same tempo pattern in measures thirty-seven to fifty-six, and when you go into that final section, jump back to your presto. Okay?"

"Yessir," Danny Green said.

A junior named Laurie Babb came forward with her flute and music. Short and stocky, she wore faded blue jeans that seemed tighter than skin and a yellow short-sleeved knit top with a neckline swung low enough to reveal that she had little self-consciousness, perhaps little modesty. Her face was round and smiling and blessed with alluring dimples. Her hazel eyes were bright behind blue cat-eye glasses, and she wore her dark brown hair in a curly bob.

*A pixie to my elf*, Kincaid thought.

"And what have you been working on, Laurie?" he said.

Her smile somehow turned both whimsical and wistful.

"Dr. Anderson had just got me started on Debussy," she said.

"One of my all-time favorite solo pieces," Kincaid said, curious as to how the contrast between his first take on her demeanor and his idea of Debussy's *Syrinx* would play out.

Whenever he performed the piece, he imagined the monster Pan pacing absent-mindedly among the dark trunks just inside the tree line of a thick forest. Beyond the shadows, a rolling meadow stretches to the base of a wild mountain capped with rock and snow. Nearer at hand, the sun glints off the troubled surface of a pond, from the edge of which he's just taken a reed and made a flute. He plays to an empty, echoing forest and a longing heart. The shadows that envelop him obscure a face lit only by the irregular liquid flashes of sunlight that the pond casts into the darkness. His arms and chest and belly are cut with muscles beneath skin strangely alive with gooseflesh. Kincaid's hand freezes as it reaches toward the beautiful monster, and he can neither touch nor recoil. His longing for contact with that powerful torso and his repulsion at the god's goat hips and legs and hoofs become embodied in the dark melody and rushing rhythms of the flute.

But as Laurie Babb played for him, the forest brightened like a stage in the first scene of a pastoral masque. A bright and bubbly waterfall appeared in the background over Pan's right shoulder. A crown of dainty white flowers appeared on his heavy brow. Although her performance was far from technical perfection, it was bright and rhythmic, conjuring into the forest—from behind the trees or up out of the melting shadows—a company of dancing nymphs. These circled Pan with alternating looks of adoration and menace, crowding Kincaid into the background scenery, and as the piece ended, Pan closed his eyes and disappeared downward into their circle.

When Laurie ran out of breath and the last low D-flat trembled to nothing, she pulled the flute away from her lip and the pixie smile snapped back into place.

Kincaid smiled in response.

"An interesting interpretation," he said. "I'd never given much thought to *Syrinx* as a dance piece."

"I think it's fun."

Kincaid cringed behind his smile.

"It's fun in a way," he said as he again moved around the music stand. "If we get a chance to work together, we'll work on some of the more interpretive elements, but let's address a couple of mechanical issues quickly here." He turned toward her. "Okay, face me and raise your flute and get set to play." When she did so, he raised his hands and said, "Freeze."

She froze, but not before her eyebrows arched in surprise.

Kincaid felt the dampness in his armpits and hoped that it wouldn't become visible through his sport coat. At the same time, he felt his forehead becoming glazed with perspiration. He blinked and then smiled at the young woman frozen before him.

"Can you feel that your embouchure is pulled slightly to the left? Like this?" He raised his own flute and mimicked her. When he was sure that she'd seen what he wanted her to see, he lowered his flute and let it hang in a hand at his side. "This isn't a bad thing. You've got a full upper lip, but you keep it high so that you're still using the most sensitive portion. That's good." He wiped the heel of his free hand through his right eyebrow. "Just be careful not to pull any further to the left, because you'll have problems when the air begins entering the flute at an angle."

"I'll remember that," Laurie said. "Thank you very much." She took her music from the stand and returned to her seat.

The final student approached the music stand with fluid movements. Her complexion was pale and clear, and startling green eyes shone behind wire-rimmed glasses. Her hair was a reddish brown, full and straight, less than shoulder-length and parted on one side. At the stand she stood still, slim and tall, easily three or four inches taller than Kincaid and not drooping in the shoulders and back as many tall girls do in an attempt to appear shorter.

"And you are?" he said, dazzled by the green of her eyes. Even filtered through her glasses and somewhat obscured by the reflection of the overhead lights, their depth and the sparkling green rivaled the eyes of the most beautiful person he'd ever seen.

Kincaid remembered being eight or nine years old at the time. His parents had gone on a trip his father won at work and left him in Chicago for a week with his mother's folks. While he was there, his grandparents threw some sort of neighborhood party, and he was standing between them in the kitchen when a newly arrived guest entered in search of a beer. The man turned partially toward Kincaid's grandparents and smiled and said their names. His hair was thick and black, short on the sides and at the back and wavy on top. He wore a black suit with a white shirt and black tie. The cut of the suit revealed a powerful triangular upper body, its points the shoulders and the waist. He opened the refrigerator and grabbed a brown bottle, popped the top, and drank. When the bottle came away from his face, Kincaid saw the strong dimpled chin and the eyes—deep green and practically glowing like those of some powerful beast in the jungle.

The man began talking with Kincaid's grandparents, and Kincaid stood yanking on the sleeve of his grandfather's brown suit coat.

"I want to wrestle that man, Grampa," he said two or three times before his grandmother told him to hush and the green-eyed man looked directly at him. He lost his voice then, his ears burned, and his body became light.

Kincaid couldn't remember ever having thought much about wrestling. He'd watched it on television with his father and both grandfathers, and he'd wrestled with his cousins down south. He remembered knowing only that he must get his dancing hands on the man, that he needed to get his puzzled young body as close to the man's as possible, and wrestling came to mind.

Later, away from his grandparents, he found the man in the dining room talking to a woman. Kincaid squirmed in between them and stood looking up across the broad chest to the dimpled chin.

The green gaze drifted down to meet his.

"You wrestle, mister?"

The man smiled broadly, looked at the woman and, recomposing a serious expression, back down at the boy.

"Sometimes," he said. "I've been known to."

"Do you know who I want to wrestle?" Kincaid said.

"Tiffany Drouillard," the green-eyed girl looming over him said.

Kincaid snapped back to the moment, blinked, and cleared his throat.

"All right, Tiffany, I'm guessing that you're a senior flute major."

"Yes, I am."

"Are you going to be moving on to continue studying flute somewhere?"

"Yes, I am," she said again. "I've been accepted into the master of music program at West Virginia University."

"Good for you," Kincaid said. "Good for you." He paused and felt the weight of the flute in his hand and, in his mind's eye, glanced back over the road Tiffany Drouillard would soon be traveling. "So, what were you working on with Dr. Anderson?"

No sooner was "Anderson" out of his mouth than the corners of her lips and eyes turned downward. Her eyebrows lowered and pulled her forehead and hairline down with them. Her face reddened and glistened with sudden tears. Her tight mouth broke open in a strained wail, and she made an ungainly run for the door.

This all happened like close lightning, thunder, and downpour, and Kincaid stood like stone and stared after her, the smile of wishing her well still on his face but the blood of good humor completely drained from it. His left eyelid spasmed as a drop of sweat slithered down from his forehead and into the corner of his eye.

The room was quiet and still while the siren of Tiffany Drouillard's distress faded down the hallway.

"No blood this time," Dr. David Grobian said. "But some sweat and tears."

* * *

At three-thirty in the afternoon, just a little more than five hours before he would draw his final breath and deliver it—or part of it—into his flute, Dr. Brian Anderson met Tiffany Drouillard at the door of his office. Normally he didn't like to play at all on the day of a big performance, but over the years he'd learned that the students he sometimes involved in an evening's program needed the reassurance of a final afternoon rehearsal.

"Nervous?" he said as he dug in the pocket of his overcoat to get his keys.

"Yes, I am," Tiffany said and stood quietly above him, waiting.

"Don't be," he said as he unlocked the door. "You'll do just fine."

And he believed she would. Tiffany Drouillard was one of the best flutists he'd taught. She was better than she knew, and he was looking forward to performing with her and showing her off to his audience of old community faithfuls and hopeful students. He'd scheduled their duet—Briccialdi's *Duo Concertant No. 2*, a work for two flutes alone—right after the intermission.

Five years before, when she was a junior in high school, Tiffany had been one of the hopefuls in his audience. She was there with her mother Catherine, a single parent who desperately wanted her talented daughter to receive one of the scholarships he could offer. Following that concert, the two Drouillards were on campus often, in his office often, during the months before the scholarship recipients were announced. Catherine shared a similar physicality with his lost Anna, and so Anderson found it both easy and difficult to be in her presence. For a while he entertained the idea that he would ask her to include a dinner with him when she visited Runion to see her daughter, but after Tiffany became one of the chosen, the mother drifted away.

Near the end of the third or fourth lesson early in her freshman year, he noticed how much Tiffany began to look like her mother and, in a way, like Anna, but she was only a child then. A comfortable familiarity grew between them over their four years of lessons together. Sometimes they took lunch together and talked about her technique or her preparations for graduate study. Sometimes, if in a bright mood, she enveloped him in a hug on campus or at the end of her private lessons. He was initially uncomfortable with her girlish embraces, but eventually grew accustomed to them, realizing that in the absence of a father and in his role as mentor he was an important part of her life. Now she was a senior, and she had turned twenty-two in February, about the same age Anna was when they met.

He'd been stationed at Ramstein Air Base and was on a weekend furlough in Amsterdam, sightseeing and buying cigarettes to sell on the Kaiserslautern black market. Walking in amazement and some discomfort out of the Red Light District, first moving south on Spuistraat and then drifting eastward, he found himself in the neighborhood of Rembrandtplein, where he heard her flute before he saw her under the trees that lined the sidewalk. As her audience came and went over the next thirty minutes, he stood still and listened and looked, infatuated and excited, easily drawn to her beauty and strangely drawn to her music. She finished with the seventh of Telemann's *Fantasias*, and he emptied his pockets of change in appreciation and spoke to her. She thanked him in English, and he asked if she would have a drink with him. Together they crossed the street and settled at a table in Café Schiller, where they ate and drank and talked until *hoogste tijd*. Before dawn that Saturday morning they were deep in an exhausted sleep in her flat across the bridge on Amstel, and when they awoke, his flute lessons began.

"West Virginia offered me a graduate assistantship," Tiffany said, her voice coming to him as if from the other side of a door nearly closed.

Dr. Anderson returned to her and the room around him, to the music on the stand and the flute in his hands. He looked at her and smiled and spread his arms to meet the embrace he saw in her eyes.

"I can't thank you enough for everything," she said, her arms around his shoulders, her lips close to his ear, her breath warm against his neck.

With his eyes closed, he completed the embrace, his flute still held in his left hand and pressed against her back, his right hand patting her softly until he felt the pressure of her pulling away.

Then her lips were on his, and his face was cupped and lifted in her upturned palms. Her kisses were warm and dry and so rapid and light that he became dizzy and the breath seemed taken from him. He tried to speak, to tell her that he was old and afraid and alone, but so deeply submerged had he been in his memory of Anna that, with eyes still closed, he slid beneath the surface with her again.

\* \* \*

Jubal Kincaid stood behind the storm door of the Faculty House and watched the April rain splash down in the front yard, the parking area, and the street. He expected lightning and thunder, but the darkening sky gave only rain. He felt glad to be in a mood not easily dampened by the weather. Despite a couple of odd moments, the interview process, he thought, seemed to be going smoothly. Two out of the three student sessions in the afternoon went well, and he'd nearly convinced himself that Tiffany Drouillard's breakdown and flight hadn't been about him. Despite his being flustered after his encounter with her, his own performance for the faculty and students present—Bach's *Partita in A Minor*, Hoover's *Kokopeli*, and, by request, his own interpretation of Debussy's *Syrinx*, from memory—had been well received. Echoes of the Debussy piece still lingered in his mind and mingled with the sounds of the rain beyond the glass of the storm door.

"This campus is beautiful in the rain," a voice behind him said, and he turned to meet the serious expression of a Faculty House student worker passing through the living room and up the stairs.

As he turned back to the scene outside, thinking that an unusual comment for a student to make, Dr. Warmack pulled into the parking area and honked his horn.

Kincaid splashed out to the car but then stood waiting in the rain while Warmack finished removing sheets of music and granola bar wrappers from the passenger seat.

"So, how long have you been here?" Kincaid asked as Dr. Warmack wheeled the car through a U-turn.

"At Runion State? This is my sixth year."

"You must be ready for promotion."

"Yeah," Warmack said and seemed about to say something else but didn't.

They exited campus on the south side, turned right on Back Street, left on Lonesome Mountain Drive, and right again on Main Street, which quickly left town and became River Road, following the French Broad River in a westerly direction toward Hot Springs.

They were on their way to the home of Dr. Teresa Marchioni, Professor of Piano, for an evening meal with the Search Committee and some few other members of the department.

"So, you've been here for six years," Kincaid said. "You must like it."

"Well enough. I came close to being stuck in permanent adjunct limbo before I came here, so I know the value of a tenure-track position."

While Warmack negotiated a series of tight curves, Kincaid stole a glance at him—wiry body, blond hair, thick eyeglasses that enlarged plain blue eyes.

"Do you live in Runion?" Kincaid asked.

"God no. I live in Asheville. Not a big city, but it's a city. Cool vibe there. Lots of different people and cool places moving in."

"Really?"

"A lot of RSU people live there. It's an easy drive."

Warmack slowed the car and turned right into a driveway between a small house and a doublewide mobile home. Gravel spurs led to the back of each dwelling, but the driveway itself continued straight ahead until one deep curve to the left and then another to the right led to a large house in a secluded hollow.

The front of the house was mostly glass, and the interior was brightly lit against the hollow's shade.

Warmack parked the car alongside several others in a spot where the driveway widened in front of the house.

"Music at Runion State must pay well," Kincaid said, as he and Warmack walked up a set of concrete steps that brought them to the main level of the front yard.

Warmack grunted and blew air through his nose.

"Don't I wish," he said. As they walked across a stone path toward the deck and the entrance, he added, "I think they came here with money," and then again grunted and blew air.

Inside, several members of Runion State's Department of Music mingled with drinks and appetizers. A heavyset man with thick silver hair and a green apron over a white dress shirt and red tie was stocking the dining room table with bowls of pasta and salad, boards of bread and bottles of wine. After a few minutes, he took off the apron, replaced it with a sports coat and called the guests to the table.

"Compared to all the formal stuff today, this is a social event," Dr. Joanna Whitmire said, looking at Jubal Kincaid. "We're still kind of interviewing you, but we'll all just relax and have a good time." She paused and then went on, her wine glass raised. "Al Marchioni, this meal looks amazing."

*  *  *

Dr. Brian Anderson couldn't eat his last meal. He'd driven into Runion that morning between piles of dirty snow, strolled the sidewalks downtown, and then bought all the ingredients of his ritual pre-recital meal at Whitson's Green Grocer. Now the greens seemed rotten, the bread stale, the dressing too oily, the tea too weak. And he felt old—older than he actually was, he thought—and confused and afraid. He'd crossed the line with a student, that last lesson with Tiffany a perversion of his first lesson with Anna years before. An unsteady hand brought fork or bread or glass near his mouth, and the shaking fingers smelled like that young woman. When he stopped trying to eat, his upper lip smelled like her, and his breath smelled like hers. He pushed all the food away and moved unsteadily into the bathroom to splash water on his face.

The old man in the mirror frightened him. His complexion was off in color and tone, something different from pale and too deeply lined. He couldn't meet his reflection's weak and watery gaze.

*Butterflies*, he thought when he became aware of the strange sensation in his gut. *No. Hunger.*

Then he turned to the toilet and vomited.

"God, Anna," he said as he flushed, "help me," then wretched again so intensely that he felt as if something deep within him must either rip or snap.

\* \* \*

"You want to know about the blood, right?" Dr. Grobian said as they sat waiting for Al Marchioni to serve dessert.

"Not at the table, David, please," Teresa Marchioni said.

"The blood I mentioned at your teaching performance today?" he said, ignoring her.

"I wondered," Kincaid said, staring at him again.

"It was your competition," Grobian said. "I won't tell you her name." He glanced around the table, playing to the smiles and ignoring the rolling eyes. "Her nose started bleeding about midway through her teaching performance. Somebody said she picked it, but I didn't see it. My guess is that she needs to lay off the cocaine." He smiled and winked at Dr. Whitmire. "I thought she was going to bleed to death right there in front of us."

"You are so inappropriate, David," Dr. Whitmire said.

"Well, we never did get to hear her play," he said.

At that moment, Mr. Marchioni came out of the kitchen with a coffee pot, which his wife took and began serving in the upturned cups while he retrieved a tray of tiramisu from the server.

Jubal Kincaid swallowed his first bite of dessert, took a sip of coffee, and cleared his throat.

"Let me ask what you don't like about Runion State or living in Runion?" he said.

For a moment the table froze in tableau—forks of tiramisu, cups of coffee or napkins at the mouths sitting around him.

"I mean," he said, "Dr. Anderson apparently lived here for years and years, so everything must be okay. But I remember Swanpond, Kentucky, where my dad was from. It was a mean place"—an image of that morning's three men in the pickup truck glowed in his mind—"and my mother said she always felt like an outsider there except with just a few of Dad's family."

He stopped talking and wondered if he'd just asked the worst question he could ask.

"Well," Dr. Whitmire said, "I'll tackle the Runion State question." She placed her fork on her dessert plate as if the two bites she had taken were all she could eat. "We have too many damned administrators who take too damned much of the money. Sometimes they get into squabbles among themselves and we get caught in the middle. And they pass down all these evaluation programs and processes that're supposed to improve what we do, but it's all just bullshit. And if they had to do the evaluations and reports themselves, they'd know that. We haven't had a raise in three years, and merit pay has gone the way of AM radio." She picked up her fork again and cut away another bite of tiramisu. "As for the department, we get along fairly well. Better than some, I'd say, not as good as others. You know how, according to the Department of Biology, the first thing that develops in humans is the anus? Well, we've got a couple of folks"—she raised her fork as if to toast Dr. David Grobian—"who never outgrew that stage of development."

The crowd around the table had grown quiet and seemed somewhat nervous when Dr. Whitmire began this speech, but they all broke into relieved laughter at the end of it.

"To our chair," Dr. Grobian said, raising his cup of coffee, and most around the table followed suit.

"This is Appalachia, Jubal," Boz McWilliams said. "It's a place kind of stranded in time, I think, between a very old and scary world and a very new and scary world. And it tries to play nice in the middle. I want to say that the nice is all an act, but I don't think it is. It's at least strong enough to cover a lot of violence and meanness—again, both old and new violence and meanness. And when I say 'meanness' I'm thinking of more than one meaning. It's mean as in bad attitude and dangerous, and it's mean as in poor and deprived. Deprived and depraved—"

Dr. Bailey Everett, Professor of Low Brass, interrupted.

"Now, Boz, it's not all that bad," he said. "What you see as just a veneer of sanctimonious posturing I see as a sincere attempt to get along and go along."

"That's the view from your gated community, Bailey?" Boz McWilliams said.

"I grew up not far from here," Dr. Everett said. "I—"

"You grew up wealthy," Dr. McWilliams said. "You—"

"You grew up behind a gate," Dr. Grobian said. "Even if that gate was just the family name and the family business."

"Now, gentlemen," Dr. Whitmire said, "you're about to make a bad impression on Mr. Kincaid." Her eyes moved quickly from Everett to Grobian to McWilliams. To Kincaid she said, "Runion is like any other place and unlike any other place, if that makes sense. It's an old community with lots of old prejudices. And it's a college town where in spite of the dumbasses at the top, the college promotes a lot of new ideas and brings in a lot of new things. We're a little uncomfortable with the community sometimes, and they're uncomfortable with us a lot. But mostly we all get along pretty well."

Eased by the resurgence of the wine that followed on the heels of the coffee, the remainder of the evening went smoothly. As was fitting for the participants, the conversation was mostly about music—composers and movements and anecdotes from history and the classroom.

Kincaid knew they were, each in her or his own way, feeling him out, trying to get a sense of him as somebody they wouldn't mind bumping into in the mailroom every morning for years to come, as somebody worthy of the position of Dr. Brian Anderson, whom they all seemed to admire and miss. He felt the tensions between them. While these seemed largely benign, he could imagine their being easily susceptible to situations in which they might be blown out of proportion. Still, this group of the faculty seemed to accept the tensions and manage them or cover them. He saw that they could argue, but the fact that they could also laugh before, during, and after the argument struck him as promising.

He could live in this community, he thought. Making a home here would have its challenges, but he knew of no place where that wouldn't be true. He couldn't find out everything about these people and this place from one visit. They couldn't find out everything about him. All the things he was couldn't, in two days, be rubbed up against all the things this place was to learn what living here would be like. The work was the one element that was

certain. He could do the work, that he knew, if the opportunity
came his way.

* * *

With Wrestling Poliander Kirkhoven's Louis Lot flute in his hands,
Dr. Brian Anderson paced up and down near the stage door in
Bryant Hall, while Ms. Glenda Šedá, the Department of Music's
longtime staff accompanist, stood absolutely still in her black
concert dress and stared at the door as if waiting for the slightest
opening that would allow her to squeeze through and go to the
piano.

"Is my tie straight?" Anderson asked her on one of his passes,
and Šedá looked away from the door long enough to tell him that
it was.

The day had been one of the longest he could remember, and
when he'd stood in front of the mirror in the dressing room, he
could see that in his face and feel it in his hands as he tried to tie
his bow. The stress of the weather over the past few days—the
blizzard—had become transfigured into the stress of memory and
longing and guilt.

"Come back to the States with me, Anna," he'd said near the
end of his time in Amsterdam, summer of 1963. "Marry me."

She laughed.

"No, my darling, no, I cannot live in that place. The New
World." She took his right hand between both of hers. "And we
are already married. You know this."

He knew. They'd talked about it before, but his will and his
understanding of their lives together and apart always broke down
in the last few hours before his return home.

She released his hand and reached up to adjust the tie he'd put
on for his flight.

"From the moment we met, we have been each other's forever.
I will die with you in my heart." She handed him the flute that had
been her father's and also hers, to put last into the suitcase he was
packing. "And you will die with your lips on mine or on this flute.
I know this." She'd cupped his face in her hands, her palms warm

and dry. "We will find one another in the next world and then be together always."

He ended his pacing at the stage door and looked through the small square window into the Bryant Hall recital space.

Despite the weekend's blizzard and roads that were still dangerous, the hall appeared—from what he could see—to be nearly full. Several of his colleagues were scattered through the seats, which he thought unusual. Most had wandered away from this event years ago, having heard him play, having ever more bustling lives and pugilistic egos. Clusters of students appeared here and there in their blue jeans and hooded sweatshirts. Tiffany Drouillard sat gowned and erect in an aisle seat on the front row, her flute case and music on her lap, her mother Catherine in the seat beside her.

He was trying to read the expression on the mother's face when the lights inside went down. He took a deep but stuttered breath as somebody began pushing the stage door open and Glenda Šedá disappeared, seemingly sucked through the opening like black smoke.

Dr. Brian Anderson followed to great applause.

* * *

"What did you say?" Chuck asked when Kincaid called him from the airport in Asheville.

"I said yes." Jubal felt again the tightness of excitement in his throat and belly.

He had a job. His mentors at UM had told him that, being male and white and forty-one, among other things, he ought not expect to find a tenure-track position. His degree would always allow him adjunct work in most any music department in most any place he wanted to live, and a good life could be made of that, albeit piecemeal. But now, against all odds, he had a job.

Quiet on the line.

"Honeybear?" Kincaid said.

"I'm here," Chuck said. "I'm just trying to find this place again in the atlas. Is it spelled r-e-u-n—"

"No, it isn't Reunion, it's Runion. Without the e."

More quiet.

"I don't see it," Chuck said.

"What state are you looking in?"

"South Carolina."

"Try North Carolina."

The airport in Asheville was nearly empty, and Kincaid could hear Chuck's breathing and the pages of the atlas being turned.

"Look, we'll go over it all again when I get back to Ann Arbor. Okay?"

"Okay," Chuck said. "Ten o'clock, right?"

"Yes. US Airways." He looked at his ticket. "Flight 1606."

"All right," Chuck said. "I close the store tonight, but I'll be there in time."

"I'm going to get a snack before takeoff," Kincaid said. "I love you."

"I love you too," Chuck said. "Hurry home."

After going through security and stopping at a vending area, he sat at Gate 4—his carry-on bag in the seat beside him, his flute case in his lap—and ate a honey bun and drank a cup of coffee. He looked across the tarmac to the tree line, beyond which rose a small mountain dotted with palatial houses. A break in the near ridge line to the north revealed more distant blue ridges layered ever higher to the ragged horizon.

*Home was a loaded word to use*, he thought. They'd met in the lowlands of Michigan, and Chuck had never lived anywhere else. *He'll never get used to all this ground thrown up in the air.* They'd talked about the possibility of a move, but the tone in Chuck's voice on the telephone revealed that he hadn't believed it would happen. *Hadn't believed that he'd really have to move?* he thought. *Or hadn't believed that I'd ever get a job?*

A white jet suddenly descended against the hazy blue backdrop of mountains and settled down on the landing strip, visibly braking.

He would promise to look for position openings in Michigan and the upper Midwest, but he knew he could neither assure Chuck that positions would be available nor that he could get any

he might apply for. Besides, already he felt the potential for home
in these mountains and among the people he'd met so far, already
wondered about living in Runion or commuting from Asheville.

Airline personnel announced boarding for his flight, and he
exited the gate and walked across the tarmac with his fellow
passengers. Beside him to his right walked an older man who
reminded him of Dr. Brian Anderson as he appeared in the
departmental photo that hung in the main office of Runion
State's Department of Music—not tall, tending toward stocky,
handsomely weathered features, beautiful blue eyes, white whiskers
on his chin and upper lip, rich white hair on the verge of misrule.

Every summer for years this Dr. Anderson had left Runion and
his life, probably walked across this same stretch of tarmac, to lose
himself for weeks in the world of a woman in Amsterdam. And
she waited for him there, waited for years until all waiting was over.

Chuck and he fell in love the first night they met, a story that
must have been similar to that of Dr. Anderson and his lover. But
if Chuck couldn't leave Ann Arbor with him, then Jubal doubted
that either of them possessed the same constancy as Anderson
and the woman who'd taught him to play the flute. Not to mention
that Ann Arbor was not Amsterdam.

He put his bag in the overhead bin and settled into his window
seat, aware that the handsome man who strolled so easily across
the tarmac beside him sat one row up and in the opposite aisle
seat. Jubal could put away all concerns about moving and Chuck
and relish the man's profile all the way to Charlotte. But he pulled
his gaze away and leaned back against the headrest as the jet roared
down the runway.

And then he was lifted into the air and they were climbing
steeply, the mountains dropping away beneath him.

# Decoration Day

The Rebels held the barn, the corncrib, and the house behind. Hiding as best they could, they waited in the close air that felt more like August than May, sweating in their wool and homespun, trying to keep still amid the wasps and flies and hovering dust.

Across the grassy field that sloped downward from barn and corncrib, the Lincolnites moved freely inside the tree line, out of range and mostly out of sight.

The Rebels envied them their movement and the free air beneath the trees. But not their position. The high ground, they knew, is always best.

Yet one young soldier in the corncrib seemed unable to stand the tension and heat any longer.

"Come on up here, Yank, I got some salt for ya." Then he sneezed.

As if this were their cue, a wave of Lincolnites burst from the trees and into the field. A second wave followed close behind. These were flanked by men in blue on horseback.

Gray riders came from around the far side of the barn to engage.

"Shoot that big'n'," a panicked voice sang out from somewhere.

Many men in the two Lincolnite waves already lay still or writhing in the tall grass, while those yet on their feet moved steadily forward up the gentle grade.

"Fall back," one of the Lincolnite cavalrymen cried out from the far side of the battle. "Back to the trees!"

Infantry in the middle of the field stumbled ahead a few steps, struggling to check the momentum of their charge, then tottered in place for a breath. Two more of them crashed to the ground as the rest turned and ran, firing over shoulders and around hips toward barn and corncrib, one last stuttered volley to cover their retreat.

"Oh, Gawd!" screamed a Rebel as he staggered from shadow into sunlight and collapsed to the dirt in front of the big barn door.

The last reports from rifle and pistol faded into the woods, and bodies of blue smoke floated away over the field like the departing souls of men who lay still in the grass.

A few seconds of breathless quiet passed, and then the dead and wounded rose to light but appreciative applause.

\* \* \*

A half mile away as the crow flies across the French Broad River and the hills of Piney Ridge, but a two-mile drive from Runion along snaky North Carolina Highway 209-A, thirty-seven people and a preacher exited cars and trucks parked on a gravel pull-off and wove their way through the pines to Anderson Cemetery. On their left as they passed beneath the arched, wrought-iron entrance, a quintet of musicians—playing a mandolin, two fiddles, and two guitars—stood together in the shade of a white oak that grew outside the cemetery's boundary and played "Am I a Soldier of the Cross?" The men among the thirty-seven carried paper grocery bags of food and coolers of more food and drink. They set these on a table made from 2x8s and sawhorses that stood in a clear space a few paces inside the cemetery entrance. The women carried bouquets and bundles of flowers in green plastic vases and here and there a small box holding some toy or trinket. They directed the men in arranging the elements of the meal and then led the way as all spread out along the short ridge to clump around headstones in different family sections—the Andersons, Metcalfs, Ramseys, Smiths, and others.

The singers sang.

*Sure I must fight if I would reign;*
*Increase my courage, Lord;*
*I'll bear the toil, endure the pain,*
*Supported by Thy Word.*

Miss Gussie Guthrie set down a brown paper bag nearly full of dinner rolls and fried chicken and, beside it, a Tupperware cake carrier protecting her famous German chocolate. She pulled yellow silk flowers and a small ceramic rooster from the top of the bag and angled left along the ridge toward one wide granite headstone with SMITH chiseled into it and a surrounding cluster of low grave markers. She stopped and stood above two flat stones to the right of the central one.

The old stones she'd helped care for since she was a girl had been replaced by the cemetery association five years before. The replacements were holding up well, although both showed new lichen spotting them like the beginning of a rain.

*Or like tears*, she thought.

Somebody recently—not earlier that morning or that weekend but certainly in the past couple of weeks—had remounded the graves according to old tradition, removing the grass from the length and width of each and mounding fresh soil on both so that, together with the replacement stones, they looked almost new. That same somebody—or somebody else since the previous year's Decoration Day—had left a string-gathered bundle of pink plastic flowers between the two stones.

The singers sang.

*The saints in all this glorious war*
*Shall conquer, though they die;*
*They see the triumph from afar,*
*By faith's discerning eye.*

Gussie knelt in the passageway of close-clipped grass between the mounds of dirt and lay her grave decorations on the ground beside her. She leaned one way and then the other and with the palms of her hands wiped bits of loose leaves and grass straw from each stone in turn.

To the right—

**MARTHA MATILDA
GILBERT SMITH
MAY 18, 1823
FEB. 10, 1905**

And to the left—

**EPHRAIM GEVER SMITH
JUNE 24, 1820
JAN. 16, 1897**

*Why two stones?* she wondered as she situated her silk flowers in an arrangement incorporating the pink plastic bundle. *Y'all's choice together, or Matilda's, or them that bought the stones?*

Her fingers found the little rooster in the grass, and she lifted it up and studied it for a moment, turning it in the late morning light—its comb and face and wattle a vivid red; its hackle bright yellow and splayed around its neck and across its saddle like the hair of a rock-'n'-roll singer or a TV wrestler; the black feathers of its breast and wing and tail highlighted with tints of coral and turquoise. She rubbed it between her hands like a magic lamp and then set it carefully on Ephraim Smith's grave marker, as her mother and grandmother had done before her, wondering about the hundred or so other roosters left here over the past century, wondering what they meant and where they went from year to year. Then she gently touched each stone and rose slowly, certain not to shock her knees with too quick a movement from kneeling to standing.

The singers sang.

> *When that illustrious day shall rise,*
> *And all Thy armies shine*
> *In robes of vict'ry through the skies,*
> *The glory*—

A sudden clanging from near the cemetery entrance drowned out the end of the song, and Gussie turned to see Dorothy Anderson Metcalf bouncing a clangor around inside a triangle dinner bell. At

Dorothy's "Y'all come," Gussie moved back along the ridge, joining others who moved in the same direction and noticing, sidelong, those who remained aloof. She stopped on the edge of the crowd, the waist-high headstone of Donald T. and Diane B. Anderson and the tables of food and drink between herself and Dorothy.

"We're so glad to see all of y'all here today," Dorothy said. "It's so good when we can gather as family and friends to remember and respect those who've gone on before us, especially those that gave their lives in whole or in part to fight to protect the freedoms we all enjoy."

At this, Trent Metcalf, Dorothy's son, gathered up an armful of 12x18 American flags on sticks and began decorating the graves of veterans, his wife Cindy guiding him with a list and a map as his mother continued.

"We're grateful to Wayne Metcalf, Burch Anderson, Christine Anderson Phelps, and Lady Nan Smith Anderson for the general sprucing up they've done the past couple of weekends."

The gathered applauded.

"And we appreciate our musicians who've played so beautifully and Pastor Donald Roy from the Lonesome Mountain American Christian Church who'll bring us a message in just a few moments."

The gathered applauded again.

"As those of you who've been here before already know, our oldest below-ground citizen is Andrew Jackson Anderson, my great-great-grandfather, known as AJ in the life he lived from 1818 to 1897. You'll find his grave directly ahead at the end of the ridge, where tradition tells us he was buried at the front door of his cabin." She paused and looked directly at Gussie Guthrie before looking away and continuing. "Not much changes in a place like this from year to year, but just after the blizzard in March we lost my cousin Brian Anderson, Dr. Brian Anderson, who was a veteran and an amazing musician and taught flute over at the college since 1958. He's buried just to my right, your left, next to his parents, my Uncle Cecil and Aunt Ruby."

Several attendees turned toward the shiny black granite stone near the fence, but Gussie turned the other way, to where Donald

Roy and the musicians stood waiting in the shade of the white oak.

The mandolin player was a Goforth, distantly related in some way, she thought, to her old friend Delbert Gunter. A Davis played one of the guitars and a Penland the other.

*Lord, I'm getting so forgetful of names.*

One of the fiddlers looked a bit like Sheila Kay Adams but was too young to be her. The other fiddler, the one standing close beside Roy, didn't look familiar at all.

"We'll begin our formal program now," Dorothy said. She stepped to the food table and lifted a pan of cornbread that was doubling as a paperweight, took a thin stack of paper from beneath it, and turned back to the gathered. "Our kind group of musicians will now lead us in a couple of the old hymns, and I've got the words printed on these sheets." She divided the sheaf and handed the halves to Trent and Cindy, who began to circulate among the people with them. "Y'all'll notice that at the bottom of your song sheet is an address for sending your money to the cemetery association, if you don't happen to have cash or checkbook with you when the hat is passed around."

Pastor Donald and his leather-bound Bible appeared beside Dorothy, and to Gussie's left the musicians stepped from the shade of the tree and began to play quietly as the Penland man spoke.

"We run across this song sometime back of this and thought it'd be perfect for today," he said. "It's a song that was written for the ladies of the South that lost their men in the War for Southern Independence." He stopped and fingered a few chords with the rest of the instrumentalists. "Y'all ain't likely to've heard this before, so Janie Gentry is gonna teach you the refrain."

The young woman Gussie hadn't seen before lowered her fiddle into the crook of her arm, turned her head slightly to the left and closed her eyes, then turned back to the gathered and sang.

> *Kneel where our loves are sleeping;*
> *They lost but still were good and true.*
> *Our fathers, brothers fell still fighting.*
> *We weep, 'tis all that we can do.*

She sang it through again, and first one and then another of the gathered joined her.

When the Sheila-Kay-looking fiddler stepped up to harmonize with Janie's lead on the first verse, Gussie began to drift back toward the Smith corner of the cemetery but stopped halfway to stand detached between the graves of her parents. They'd held her so in life as well—aloof with them, secure between them.

After three solos—guitar, mandolin, and guitar again—the fiddlers harmonized through the second verse.

> *Here we find our noble dead,*
> *Their spirits soar'd to him above.*
> *Rest they now about his throne,*
> *For God is mercy, God is love.*
> *Then let us pray that we may live*
> *As pure and good as they have been,*
> *That dying we may ask of him*
> *To open the gate and let us in.*

Gussie now looked across the cemetery to Brian Anderson's tombstone. Maudlin as were the words of this war hymn and sensational but unheroic as was her distant cousin's death, onstage during his March flute concert, she imagined herself at that gate, asking him finally to let her in.

*We weep, 'tis all that we can do.*

\* \* \*

Ephraim Smith blew meager warmth into the hard palms of his hands. From where he stood somewhat camouflaged against the laurel thicket at his back, he looked downward through budding trees and watched the comings and goings down by the river below Runion. He did not shiver, cold as the May morning was for the threadbare coat he'd worn through more than half the winters of his life. As a child he'd hoped to grow up to live somewhere warm, but he was now a man, son of a father and mother buried over at Jewel Hill, in its Methodist Cemetery, a husband and father himself, a struggling provider. He was rooted in place and used to the cold.

*The day'll warm.*

Off to his right, the village that had begun growing up around the Laurels Institute and the sawmill stood with its back to him, but he could picture its main street and storefronts. He saw beyond the village buildings the tops of trees that sheltered the grounds of what was now Laurels Presbyterian College, where he once thought his journey to somewhere warm might begin. Recently, from another vantage point, he'd spied on the college, watching the vermin of the occupying Rebel detachment profane the campus's central green with their ignorant presence and profane themselves with liquor and whoring and gambling on eye-gouging fights. He'd thought what delicious devilment to be atop Mashburn Hall with a crate of the Ketchum grenades.

He shut down these pleasant imaginings and focused his attention on the Drovers' Trail below.

A herd of hogs, down from Tennessee or Kentucky, minced and jostled its way south toward Barnard, Marshall, Alexander, Asheville.

Smith reckoned the herd around 500 head and wondered when the smell would reach him.

The cacophony of snorting and squealing intensified every few seconds as three Rebel privates—Oliver Davis, Bird Treadway, and Solomon Wells—culled beasts under the direction of 2nd Sgt. Madison Guffy, to become requisitioned pork for North Carolina's 64th Infantry Regiment. The privates stumbled and slid in the mud and shit, herding the hogs they claimed into a small holding pen.

Smith shook his head and chuckled to himself, took one last look at the brightening spring sky beyond the greening trees and started down the hill.

"Private," Guffy yelled when Smith appeared at the edge of the Trail. "Help them boys with them hogs."

\* \* \*

## Scene Four

*A day of breezes, blue sky, and cumulus congestus clouds. After the rains of Thursday night and Friday morning, the air is clear, the ground somewhat muddy but solid. Grass and trees are bright new green. In front of the split-rail fence beneath the maple tree stands a uniformed man in his fifties. That is, the actor is in his fifties even though the man he portrays, 3rd Sgt. James L. Brown, would actually be in his late twenties. He wears a gray shell jacket with seven gold buttons down the front; the top one is unbuttoned, exposing curly white chest hair, and the three at his belly are under considerable stress. His gray pants are a few shades darker than the jacket. A canteen hangs from his belt by a leather strap and rests against his right hip; its mottled and faded gray canvas cover has CSA stenciled on it. From down the hill to his right, from beyond the edge of the woods there, comes the sound of gunfire. He pulls a pocket watch from inside his jacket, looks at it, snaps it closed, and returns it to the inside pocket. He looks this direction through silver-plated wire-frame eyeglasses and strokes his full white beard three times before he speaks.*

BROWN: My name is James Brown, and I am a 3rd Sergeant in Company C of the North Carolina 64th Infantry Regiment, under the command of Colonel Lawrence Allen. When I learnt that North Carolina had seceded from the Union in May 1861, I figured I'd sign up. So, I enlisted on the Confederate side come the 4th of July. The stencil on my canteen, CSA, can be taken as signifying either the Confederate States of America or the Confederate States Army. Works for both. (*He looks up and nods to another uniformed man who passes on horseback.*) The 64th holds most of Madison County pretty firmly in hand, even though probably three quarters of the population has Union sympathies. We hold the towns anyway. I spend much of my time in a camp on the river flat down below Runion.

*(A rooster crows from somewhere near the corncrib just a few yards away on the other side of the fence behind 3rd Sgt. Brown.)*

I was born in 1835 and grow'd up near Mars Hill, the second son of seven gifted to Caney and Robbie Brown. I got a brother of thirty-two, Aubrey, who is Second Lieutenant in E Company. His middle name is Levi, so we call him Al instead of Aubrey. The string of boys was interrupted early on by a girl—between Al and me. Evoleta married Daniel Anderson in 1851 and then later loaned him to the Confederates. Dan's a Confederate States Army Captain in B Company down in Henderson County. After me come Handsome H., who died of scarlet fever when he was but seven years old. Still miss that boy. Joe was born in 1839, and he signed up with me and serves as a private in Company C, where I can keep an eye on him for Mama and Daddy. The next two, Increase and Amos, have gone missing, and we fear they're running with the so-called Home Circle men and Union-lovers over yonder in Tennessee. *(He pauses and swallows before continuing.)* I don't know what to think about that.

*(The rooster crows again; 3rd Sgt. Brown again pulls out his watch, looks at it, and stows it away.)*

Now the least one is Will, who ain't but seventeen. You might say that he's precious to Daddy and Mama like Joseph—he of the coat-of-many-colors fame—was to Israel and Rachel. *(Glances to his left. Does a double take.)* Well, I'll be. Here comes Will now.

*(Enter seventeen-year-old Will Brown. He is fair-haired and slight of build. He wears a white shirt and apron-front overalls of a dark green cotton corduroy. On his feet are dusty, gray, pegged brogans. He tries to keep his eyes on his brother as he approaches, but he seems unable to stop glancing around with excitement.)*

BROWN: Will, what in the world are you doing here?

WILL: Hey, Jimmy! *(He stops speaking and stops in his tracks.)* Sergeant Brown, I mean. *(He stands in front of his brother and runs the fingers of his right hand through his hair.)* Daddy sent me.

BROWN *(eyes narrowing)*: Daddy sent you where?

WILL: Here to you, where do you think?

BROWN: Daddy sent you.

WILL: Yessir.

BROWN: What for?

WILL: I come to enlist, Jimmy . . . Sergeant.

BROWN: Now, Will, boy, I can't hardly believe that. If Daddy did send you, he sure as hell ain't sent you to enlist.

WILL *(toeing the ground)*: Well . . .

BROWN: Will?

WILL: Jimmy, it's hard times at home. It's lonesome—
BROWN: Will?
WILL: All right, all right. Daddy sent me to Mallie Reeves's place to borrow some plow traces.
BROWN: Then what the hell are you doing here?
WILL: Like I said, I come to enlist.
BROWN: Little brother, you'll break the hearts of Daddy and Mama with such foolishness. And with all the rest of us gone, Daddy needs you to help out—like fetching plow traces from Mr. Reeves. *(As Will's face falls into a frown, his brother's voice softens.)* Besides, Will, you wouldn't like life in this army. *(He pauses for a moment and strokes his beard once.)* Hell, I don't even like it.
*(Rooster crows.)*
You think you had it bad when Mama moved you out of her and Daddy's room and up into the attic with Joe and Ink and Amos? Well, that's gonna be like heaven when you find yourself bedding down in a six-man tent with ten or twelve nasty, stinking rascals, half of 'em sick and all of 'em mean.
*(He shudders. Gunfire sounds from somewhere behind Sgt. Brown— beyond the corncrib, near the barn or in the woods. Will, his eyes alight, raises up on his toes and cranes his neck to see where it's coming from.)*
Pay attention, little brother.
*(Will settles back on his heels but glances every few seconds toward the hidden source of the gunfire.)*
You ain't heard the like of snoring nor smelled the like of farting. Ink and Amos picked on you unmercifully at times, but these fellers'll beat hell out of you every chance they get just to stop being bored for a few minutes.
WILL: I can fight. *(He squares up in a boxing stance.)*
BROWN: *(Quickly grabbing Will's fists and pushing them down.)* This ain't fighting I'm talking about, Will. This's meanness and brutality to no more purpose than kicking a rock down the road.
*(Cpl. J.W. Glance, in his mid-twenties, appears in the background, meandering back and forth, trying to tie the back of his trousers and button the back of his suspenders.)*
And the food, Will—Dear God, the food is horrible. You don't

get none of Mama Brown's biscuits and gravy. Don't hardly get no meat and milk, and don't never get it fresh. *(He spits to his right.)* Even living the highlife here in Runion mostly what you get is hardtack, which'll come without bugs more often than not in camp, but that ain't the case on a march—

GLANCE *(Coming up from behind on Brown's right)*: Sergeant Brown, can you fix me in the back?

BROWN *(Turning away from Will)*: Darn it, Corporal Glance, can't you see I'm in the middle of something here?

> *(Will, glancing between his brother and the area from where the shots sounded earlier, begins to tiptoe away toward the corncrib.)*

GLANCE: Sorry, Sergeant, it's just that Maria usually dresses me, and I never can seem to get my fingers to work right backwards.

BROWN: All right, turn around. *(He begins to tie up the back of Glance's trousers.)*

> *(In the background, Will picks up his pace and disappears behind the corncrib.)*

GLANCE *(Turning his head to speak over his shoulder)*: Maria always gives me some sugar when she has me fixed.

BROWN *(Stopping in the midst of buttoning the suspenders; holding the pause, then pushing Glance away, playfully but somewhat hard)*: You're on your own. *(He begins to turn back toward where his brother had stood.)* There, Will, you see the kind of fool—

> *(Brown turns in a full circle, then stretches his neck, looking here and there over the heads of the audience.)*

Will?

\* \* \*

"Will you not say with me that you're happy to be a simple man? A simple mountain man?" Pastor Donald Roy said. "I'm happy." He spread wide his arms, revealing dark blue crescents of sweat hanging beneath his armpits. The index finger of his right hand remained between the pages of the Bible he held, marking Romans 13:1-7. "For I hold it better to be a simple mountain man and have Jesus than to be like them professors that teach at the college over in Runion, a college that begun as a religious place, even if it was

Presbyterians that started it."

Sniggers popped and hissed here and there among the listeners but cowered to quiet beneath guttural amens.

"They got nothing but bootless learnin', as I heard Granny Roy say many a time."

Caught in the pull of the cemetery community as it drew closer to hear Donald Roy, Gussie returned to where she'd stood earlier. She took a tissue from the pocket of her light blue, red-poppy-print dress and sat down on the extended base of the largest Anderson headstone, her back to the preacher and the small group of congregants around him, the length of the stone between her and them. She planted her feet side by side in the dirt, adjusted her dress over her knees, and leaned forward with her right forearm across her thighs, her left elbow on top of that, and her chin in the palm of her left hand. In her right hand, she worked the tissue into a ball.

She'd known Eula Roy to be the most ignorant and meanest woman to step through the doors of a little mountain church, a woman who'd presided over at least three church splits, whose iron intolerance, sharp tongue, and dull understanding had ruined many individual Christian lives, especially Christian women's lives. Hearing the same tones of ignorance and meanness in Eula's grandson pained Gussie and caused her to work the tissue into a tighter ball.

"This here is a Christian nation," Pastor Donald said. "Always has been. And its army is God's army, with Jesus at the head of it. Its leaders—" He stopped, let his Bible fall open in his hands and looked at it for several seconds. "Well, I don't know why God give Bill Clinton power over us. Brothers and sisters, it's hard to look at that man and hear the words of Romans: 'Whosoever therefore resisteth the power, resisteth the ordinance of God: and they that resist shall receive to themselves damnation.'"

The most guttural of voices from the amen cluster growled something low and garbled, the only word of which Gussie made out was *queers.*

"That may be, Brother Campbell," Pastor Donald said. "But this reign of witches'll pass over. God's displeasure with his people, with his favored nation, will end soon. If we turn back to his ways, the so-called homosexuals will be turned or be destroyed, and he'll bless us again and put the whole world under our feet. He'll make us great again. Amen?"

Again, the guttural response.

"Think of all them soldiers of good, clean hearts and minds and bodies that lay at rest all around us here in this graveyard, like Ms. Dot said. Just look at the beautiful little flags that wave over their graves—"

"They ought to be Confederate flags."

"That may be, Brother Campbell," Pastor Donald said again. "That very well may be. But we ought to all be little flags walking around in the county and over yonder in Runion. A man's patriotism and his religion ought to be bound up together just like the red and white stripes on them flags or like the stars and bars that Brother Campbell says ought to be there. Them that don't respect them that've fallen in our wars, them at the college that teach our young people to disrespect soldiers right here with us that died to defend their confederated country in the recent rebellion, they disgust me and earn for themselves the utter contempt of Jesus Christ."

"Amen, Brother Donald."

"Lord, God, listen to him."

*Ignorant damned savages.*

Gussie's feet sprang up like startled cats and plopped down again with little puffs of dust. She covered her mouth with both hands as if those words actually had come out of her in the voice of her father, Elder Metcalf Guthrie. His words ricocheted hither and thither and yon through her mind, and she kept her lips pressed tight together and covered, fearing at any moment they might find an escape route and blast—in her own voice—into the heated air of Anderson Cemetery.

*Andrew Campbell's great-great-great-uncle deserted the Rebels up in Virginia,* her father continued to speak her mind. *He freed a Yankee prisoner of war and escaped with him, going north into the wilds of the new West Virginia. Remember, Gus? I told you this story on Decoration Day in 1963.*

She heard nothing else the preacher said and couldn't tell how long she struggled to control her clamoring mind. At last, without turning her head toward the preacher and his congregants, she opened her eyes and scanned the few faces she could see.

One of the fiddlers, the young woman named Janie Gentry, gazed back at her, her right eyebrow slightly raised, the opposite corner of her mouth pulled back in a half smile.

Pastor Donald closed with prayer that ended with a blessing for the coming meal, and his listeners amened with him.

"Amen, and thank you for that, Pastor Donald," Dorothy said as she again centered herself in front of the gathered. "Now, as y'all know, this cemetery doesn't just appear here every Decoration like Brigadoon." She smiled and looked at the faces around her. Then she sighed. "I reckon I'm gonna have to drop that reference, as I can see that few if any know the movie." She blinked and smiled at the light laughter. "Anyway, this hallowed place lies here in weather the year 'round, and it needs year-round care. The Anderson Cemetery Association takes on this care and pays for it with your donations. Mowing, brush removal, headstone repair and replacement—your generosity funds this work." She turned and nodded to her son. "We're gonna eat in a few minutes, and then throughout the afternoon you can enjoy this place and share the company of friends and family both above and below ground. Trent is passing the proverbial hat. But this one is special, as it's the actual kepi worn by Confederate States Army Captain Daniel W. Anderson, who served in Company B of the North Carolina Infantry's Sixty-fourth Regiment. He and his wife Evoleta are buried over there near AJ Anderson." She paused to watch people admire the hat and contribute. Then she cleared her throat and said, "While Captain Anderson's kepi goes all around the cemetery, we'll have one more song from our wonderful musicians." She turned toward the quintet. "How about something we all know, maybe something both religious and patriotic?"

"Y'all play 'Dixie'," a loud voice called from somewhere behind Gussie.

*Ignorant white trash.*

Elder Guthrie's voice thundered in his daughter's mind. But he'd been soliloquizing and grousing in there since his first explosive *Ignorant damned savages*. He no longer startled her. She now enjoyed hearing that beloved voice again, speaking her very thoughts.

The musicians turned to each other and then, with confused looks, huddled for a moment before beginning an initially tentative but then rousing version of "God Bless America."

\* \* \*

Smith lay with eyes closed and listened to muted sobs and the rhythmic rustling of masturbation, waiting for sleep to take these rancid men and boys polluting the stifling atmosphere of the tent with their mouth-breathing and flatulence.

Faces and bodies—images real and imagined—scuffled before his mind's eye.

Matilda in tears, leaning heavily against him in the weak light of late January.... Their youngest Martha—and something of a surprise to Matilda and him in early middle age—with the doll her cousin Jim gave her that Christmas, child and toy ghost-like on the cabin floor, while the small fire in the hearth touched them with the ruddy glow of life.... Jim Metcalf dead, his mouth agape and filled with dirt, eyes and skin blanched and flecked with decaying leaves and more dirt, an ear lost to rooting feral hogs.... He and Jim laughing and waltzing Matilda across the cabin yard, that full moon summer solstice in '53.... Jim skin-to-skin with him as they shivered by the swimming hole they'd troubled muddy as boys.... Jim coming home along the creek after walking away from the madness that almost enlisted him in the Confederate Army last Fourth of July, Martha and Matilda running to meet him.... Shelton Laurel women beaten for information about their husbands and sons.... thirteen old men and boys rounded up by suspicion and marched a while and then, in a clearing in the woods, made to kneel for execution.... Sergeant Nicholas B. D. Jay, a Virginian, standing atop the massacred and piled and barely covered in a too-small mass grave, saying, "Pat Juba for me, while I dance these damned scoundrels down to and then down through hell."

In spite of her love and the lingering sorrow she'd been unable
to shake since Jim's violent death, Matilda had begged Ephraim
to disobey the Rebel conscription order. But he'd sworn to avenge
the death of her cousin and his friend, and the way to do it was
from the other side, from the inside. He wanted Lieutenant Colonel
James Keith, the evil man who'd ordered the murders, but he'd
resigned from the Confederate States Army and disappeared. He
knew others had either gladly or reluctantly pulled their triggers on
the unarmed old men and boys who knelt before the firing squad in
batches of five, five, and three, but he could muster only small ire
against them. Jay's "Pat Juba for me," however, drove him toward
madness, and Jay was the one he would kill this night if he could.

Yet more than his tentmates' wakefulness kept him pinned to his
bunk in the stenchy dark. He grieved the images of Jim Metcalf that
haunted his mind, images of such a physical presence that he felt
he could reach out and touch the living friend of his youth, reach
out and touch the man living and the man dead. He grieved the loss
of whatever once lived within himself that wouldn't have allowed
him to prowl through the darkness, knife in hand. He grieved the
bad luck or ineptitude that would lead to failure, to the loss of his
freedom, to the loss of his life, to the loss of Matilda and the older
children and Martha, to their loss of him. He grieved the fear that
unmanned him in the dark, the fear of looking into Jay's face when
he realized the blade was at his heart, the fear of such success as
much as of failure, the fear of dying in the presence of mountains
and a river that would not alter in the least at his passing, the fear
of getting away and running away as a stranger into familiar woods
and soon feeling the relentless pursuit of Cherokee troops borrowed
from Thomas's Legion specifically to capture him.

Waves of grief and fear lifted him up through the breathless
desperation of the last image and set him on his feet in a dark tent
finally stilled. When his breathing evened, he managed to make
his way to the opening, not with the grace of a seasoned killer but
with seemingly little more caution than that of a soldier going out
to relieve himself under no threat worse than the indignation of
his nasty brothers in arms if he should wake them. He stooped

through the opening and stood up in the cool outside. The rush of fresh air dizzied him, as it did every time he came out at night, and he reached up to touch the taut edge of the tent's roof and steady himself. When his mind cleared and the dizziness passed, he moved left along the alleyway between the rows of facing tents and into trees that secluded the latrine area. Alone there, he lifted his gaze to the glistening night sky and listened.

The river flowed with an easy murmur and wash to the left. To the right, over near the sleeping town, a dog barked, and then another, farther along in the same direction, responded. To his rear, deeper in the trees, beyond the latrine, awkward and clandestine thuds and grunts sounded just on the edge of hearing.

*Some buggery most likely.*

To his fore, from the officers' quarters, probably from their mess, came a snatch of drunken song. He recognized the tones of Sergeants Nick Jay and James Brown's singing to Lieutenant Obadiah Ramsey's banjo, and although he couldn't make out the words, he knew them from the tune.

> *Our women forever, God bless them, Huzza!*
> *With their smiles and their favors, they aid us in war.*
> *In the tent and on the battlefield, the boys remember them*
> *And cheer forth the daughters of freedom!*

While the singing continued, he crept left and took an oblique approach toward the five spacious tents that made up the officers' quarters. The voices of river and men masked his movements. The odors of river mud, moldy canvas, and worse from the camp gave way for a moment to the aroma of honeysuckle somewhere close by, and he stopped to snuffle the air before he lost the scent and listened again.

The singing stopped. The river babbled like a brook along the shore line but from out in its center offered a deep, unmeasured chant to the quiet mountains standing darkly against the silent stars. Then up through this ancient music rose the drone of men in conversation.

Two lanterns hung above the officers sitting around a round-top table in straight-backed chairs of wood and wicker. Lieutenant Charlie Candler sat facing the darkness that hid Smith and the river. Brown and Jay faced each other from the left and right, and Ramsey sat facing Candler, his back to the nearer lantern, to Smith and the darkness beyond, his banjo standing beside him, butt on the ground and neck leaned against the edge of the table. Now and then, Candler, Brown, or Jay raised a tin cup to his lips and drank. Now and then, Ramsey turned his head to the right and spat a dark stream in the direction of the tents in which the enlisted men lay asleep or not. And all the while, the officers talked.

Smith wasn't yet close enough to distinguish their words, so he crept farther forward until he was within earshot.

"... backcountry ranks have lost a passel of sick and deserted," Candler was saying, "since Keith's ill-advised actions of January last."

Brown voiced a wordless yawn, at the end of which he drew a quick breath and said, "From our own we lost Green Anderson somewhere in Laurel in February and Rizi Oliver in March, same area."

"Might as well add Solomon Carter to that list, too," Jay said. "He went home sick about the time Private Roy went missing and ain't come back yet."

Candler sipped from his cup and then set it on the table and held it between his palms.

"Tomorrow I want you to pick a detail from amongst our trustworthy youngsters," he said. "Maybe at least one of 'em that knows Carter. Go to Carter's daddy's place to check on him." He tilted back his head and scratched beneath his beard. "Tell 'em to keep their ears open for any news or sign that might be floating around the hollers and any word on either Higgins or Roy or the damned Home Circle in general. If we get nothing, we'll bring in some of Thomas's Cherokee."

"Yessir," Jay and Brown said.

A shiver ran along Smith's spine.

Ramsey leaned over the table and said something Smith couldn't hear.

"I don't give a goddamn," Candler said, as Ramsey leaned back away from him and Jay and Brown straightened in their chairs. The lieutenant took a breath and swiveled his neck. "Hell, I know there's them that says it ain't right for a white man to be hunted down by redskins, but if they was true whites, they wouldn't've run off like they done." He sipped from his tin cup, dashed the remainder on the ground, and stood. "I'm gonna bed down."

Ramsey and Brown rose as well, leaving Jay, the junior officer, to clear the table.

Smith watched the men disappear through their tent flaps.

Jay gathered the cups and carried them to a rough-hewn sideboard. He brushed the tabletop with a cupped left hand into the palm of his right and flung crumbs into the darkness. Then he doused the lantern that hung above the table and lifted the other from its stand and carried it in front of him as he walked toward the river.

Smith froze for a moment, then lowered his face and backed slowly toward the water's edge. His hand found the handle of the knife inside his coat, and he imagined the deed from Jay's perspective—glint of a blade out of the darkness, blur of a man following it. But just as he felt the ground beneath his feet declining toward the water and drew the knife, Jay stopped, held the lantern up in his right hand, wrestled his penis from his trousers with his left, and pissed. Smith could smell the urine pooling between them. With his face still lowered, he watched Jay jiggle himself back into his trousers, turn and walk to his tent, stop and take one quick glance toward Runion, and then disappear through the flap.

He released the breath he held and moved to his right, where he was out of the path of the pungent urine if it ran to the river.

Jay's hazy shadow moved on the tent's near wall, alternately larger and smaller, as he stripped and folded his clothes one item at a time and stacked them on something near where the lantern sat. Then he doused the light and sneezed once in the darkness.

Smith hunkered down on one ham—the river to his left, Jay's tent to his right—and waited while his eyes adjusted fully to the dark and Jay drifted off into his last living sleep.

\* \* \*

Three men in nineteenth-century military garb stood smoking in the breezeway between the corncrib and the barn. Jesse Scott "J. S." Benjamin, a personal tax accountant in Runion, served as 2nd Sergeant of the 64th North Carolina CSA Reenactors and for this event played 3rd Sergeant James Brown. Lucas Welch, manager of Runion's Stonehouse Café, played Rebel J. C. Lowry, the 64th's Quartermaster-Sergeant. Dewey Lipscomb, a deputy jailer in Runion, played Hiram "Harm" Deliverance Waugh, Chaplain. Welch and Lipscomb doubled as cavalry and had horses stabled on-site, just on the other side of the barn wall they stood beside and smoked.

The rooster shouted so close by that the three men startled and ash broke from Benjamin's cigarette. They grinned, and Lipscomb held up a finger for the others to listen.

"Dang me if I don't get that rooster before suppertime," Rick Gentry said on the other side of the corncrib. A Christian Life coach in Runion, he played the part of mess cook Davey Barnett. "I'll teach him to desert his women folk."

The rooster crowed again and again startled the men, and through the slats of the corncrib they could see the cook make a show of searching for it. "Oh, he's a brazen one," they heard him say and heard his audience laugh in response.

"Did you eat roosters?" an older woman's voice called out in a northern accent.

"Well, I'm a-comin' to that in a bit, ma'am, if you'll just have patience," Rick Gentry said in his Davey Barnett voice. "Y'all Northerners get a mite agog," he said and the audience laughed.

"I'm from Florida," the woman said, and again the audience laughed.

"Well, your voice ain't," Gentry's Barnett said, and the laughter grew louder for a moment. Then, "I'm just funnin' you, ma'am."

Benjamin, Welch, and Lipscomb flicked the burning ends from their cigarettes, toed out the embers in the dirt, and dropped their butts in a trash can that stood at the end of the breezeway. They made their way across the grounds of the Stackhouse-Putnam

State Historic Site, and each entered his tent.

These made up the end of a row at the southern edge of the Confederate camp, across a strip of yard from the back porch of Putnam House and near the fence line that ran alongside Genesis Road. Lipscomb's tent, smaller than the other two, stood shaded by an oak growing at the edge of the road. He kept its front flaps closed. The tents of Benjamin and Welch were taller and wider, their canvas whiter in the sunlight. Like Lipscomb, Welch kept the front flaps of his tent closed, but Benjamin kept his entrance open, the flaps rolled back and tied at the eaves.

After a few moments the three emerged stripped of coats and canteens and weapons. They sat on wooden boxes with rope handles and began rolling period-appropriate cigarettes.

Colonel Robert K. Byrd, played by Dr. Rex Peters, chiropractor and proprietor of French Broad Chiropractic on Main Street in Runion, rounded the corner of Putnam House, clean and authentic in white shirtsleeves, dress blue vest and trousers, and black boots with knee flaps. The brim of his spotless Hardee hat nodded at the men on their wooden boxes and then turned toward the Putnam House kitchen door, where a man stood with a small blue camera pointed at the yard, its fire pit, and the tents. Peters stopped and struck a pose, tin coffee cup in hand, and then continued toward the Visitor Center.

"King Prick," Lipscomb said.

"Mm-hmm," the other two agreed.

They sat smoking and watching the civilian visitors and their fellow reenactors who moved through the grounds or clumped together in one place or another.

"Look yonder," Benjamin said, pointing with his cigarette hand toward a space just left of the area where Rex Peters had assumed a position in front of the crowd still seated at the tables beneath the trees and Rick Gentry was bowing and waving his way out.

The other two turned in that direction.

"What are we looking at?" Welch asked.

"Here comes Rick," Lipscomb said.

"That Jeep," Benjamin said.

A shiny blue Jeep Wrangler sat with its rear hatch window up and two of its four doors open.

"Looks good," Welch said.

"Look who's looking at it," Benjamin said.

Two young men stood facing the Jeep, their backs to the three watching them. The white one was dressed in blue trousers and a blue shirt with the sleeves rolled up. He wore a dark blue kepi pushed back on his head, and white suspenders hung in a jumble around his legs. The black one wore a bright red windbreaker and tan corduroy pants. They turned their faces toward one another periodically, apparently making admiring or critical comments about the vehicle.

"Well, ain't that a picture," Welch said.

"Something you'd've never seen back in the day," Benjamin said.

"Probably Runion State boys," Welch said.

"Mm-hmm," Lipscomb agreed.

Rick Gentry came out of his tent with a wooden folding chair and set it up facing the three on their boxes.

"Rick," they said.

He nodded and opened a bottle of water and drank deeply from it.

"Did you get that rooster?" Lipscomb asked. "Or did you get that Florida woman?"

All laughed.

"Lord, I never got so many questions," Gentry said. "A couple more, and that rooster's neck might've been safer than hers." He drank again. "But I think I got 'em all answered to her satisfaction."

"You never can tell what can of worms people like that are gonna open up on us," Benjamin said.

"Mm-hmm," the other three agreed.

They fell to smoking and spitting and talking about the history they were reenacting, their fellow reenactors, the day's audience.

"Has anybody heard from the Carter boys since that hissy fit they pitched last year?" Lipscomb asked.

"Now that was about the worst I've seen," Benjamin said. "And a prime example of what I said about a can of worms."

"You'd think everybody in our organizations would understand that these mountains were a mess of allegiances," Welch said. "We simplify it quite a bit."

"Consider the source," Brown said. "You've got folks like the Carters and, for that matter, that Frisby boy and his folks. They've gone through years' worth of Confederate flag t-shirts, listening to the worst of the Charlie Daniels Band and Hank Jr." He huffed a chuck and spit in the grass between his boots. "Acting out a bunch of ignorance and calling it heritage."

"Now, J.S.," Gentry said. "That's a mite harsh, don't you think?"

"Could be, I reckon," Benjamin said. "But that don't make it less true."

"The Frisbys come to church sometimes," Gentry said. "They're rough-and-tumble, for sure, but lots of folks are around here."

"And lots of folks ain't," Welch said.

"Well, if that history teacher from the college hadn't come around to stir things up," Gentry said. "What was his name?"

"Dr. Rowe," Welch said. "Caldwell Rowe, I think. He's in the café a couple times a week." He reached in his pocket for rolling papers. "Seems like a nice enough fellow. Definitely not rough-and-tumble."

"He was probably just excited about the information he'd found," Benjamin said. "Thought the Carters would share that excitement."

"Oh, they got excited all right," Lipscomb said, and the other three laughed. "How long was it he was in the hospital?"

All four shifted in their seats.

"The innocence of the academic," Benjamin said after a moment. "Never considered what the rebel flags or the Hank Jr. might mean." He stood up and brushed ashes from the belly of his shirt and the knees of his pants and sat down again. "You just can't go around telling folks like them that their beloved ancestors were Union sympathizers or outright Lincolnites."

"Mm-hmm," the other three agreed.

All got up and moved around, stretched, went into their tents and came out again, hawked and spat and farted, visited the porta potty, returned, and in a few minutes were settled down again with bottles of water, tobacco and papers, and candy bars.

"Where's Janie and her fiddle today, Rick?" Welch asked.

Gentry sat with head bowed, scratching at something in his right palm, and then looked up.

"She's with her bluegrass group and Pastor Donald over at the Anderson Cemetery's Decoration Day."

"Well, I guess that's good for those folks," Welch said. "But tell her she can't do that next year. We need her here."

Gentry chuckled and went to work on his palm again.

"Yeah, that's not really the kind of thing she hears very well," he said.

The other three shifted in their seats.

Lipscomb rubbed his palms back and forth across the tops of his thighs and cleared his throat.

"You know, Rick," he said and stopped.

Gentry looked up again.

"What?"

Lipscomb's jaw muscles flexed twice.

"You hear things in a jail," he said. "See some things too, in the cells and out on the streets of Runion." His hands gripped the tops of his thighs. "I ain't saying no particulars, but I don't think Donald Roy is the man y'all think he is." He paused and looked toward the back porch of Putnam House. "And I don't think you should let your pretty wife go around with him so much."

Gentry's hands drooped between his knees and then balled up into fists.

"What?" he said again. "Dewey, if you got something to say, just come out with it."

Benjamin and Welch looked at each other and then back at their companions.

Lipscomb stood up.

"All right, you know what I'm saying, Rick," he said. "Janie's puttin' out for that son of—'"

Gentry rocketed from his chair and shouldered into Lipscomb's midsection, and the two tumbled into the grass, wrestling and rolling in the direction of the firepit.

Benjamin and Welch struggled up, looked at each other, and then turned back to the two on the ground as if they couldn't understand what they were seeing.

Lipscomb and Gentry rolled, one on top and then the other. They jabbed punches at close quarters. Sharp breaths hissed in and exploded out in grunts and curses.

Benjamin took three steps forward.

"Now come on, boys," he said. He reached back and took Welch by the upper arm and pulled him forward.

The scuffle in the grass tightened and intensified.

"Guys," Welch finally said. "There's people watching."

Lipscomb's face was dark red as he settled in quick, terse movements atop Gentry, who had ended up on his back, his shirt up into his armpits, his white belly, pink-striped, heaving at the blue sky. The hard and strong deputy jailer lay across the Life Coach's chest and tightened his headlock.

"Okay," Gentry wheezed, but with the spittled submission the hold choked him out and his arms and legs collapsed to the ground.

Rex Peters and three Union cohorts came sprinting toward the brawl just as Lipscomb rolled away and lay on his back in the grass next to his unconscious friend.

* * *

"Goodness, Gussie Guthrie," Dorothy said. "Your fried chicken tastes just like—well, I don't know. It's like perfection. Like the way God meant fried chicken to taste like."

Gussie toed the dirt beneath her feet.

"Oh, Dottie, you say that every year."

"Well, I can't help it, 'cause it's true every year."

These distant cousins rarely spoke to or saw each other in the intervening time between Decorations. Even though that wasn't the case this year, both of them having been here a few weeks earlier for the graveside service of Dr. Brian Anderson, their cousin-in-common, they kept their usual distance from each other until after lunch. Now they sat side by side in metal folding chairs. Forgetting the annual awkward first moments of standoffishness, they talked easily together, watching the milling groups of relatives who were friends and relatives who were strangers.

"Perfection is still not the way to describe it," Dorothy said. "It's got something to do with memory. The best memories."

"Well now, I like that description," Gussie said. "I guess I sort of think about it that way, too, 'cause it comes from way back in our family, the way I do the chicken." She stopped and laughed. "Part of what comes from back yonder in the past is that those chickens I fried up were clucking around the yard day before yesterday."

"Oh, Lord," Dorothy said. "I forgot about that. You didn't wring their necks yourself, did you?" She paused and heard her answer in another of Gussie's laughs. "Well, that freshness has got to be a big part of it," she said. "And the very reason I'll never be able to provide such a treat to these people." She patted the nearer of Gussie's knees. "Between the fried chicken and the German chocolate cake, the men around here don't know what they've missed, letting you stay single all your life."

Gussie laughed through a blush.

"Now, I've had something to say about that myself, you know."

"Yes," Dorothy said. "Yes, you have." She smoothed the lap of her dress and let her gaze drift away from Gussie's face and come to rest on the gleaming black granite headstone of her first cousin, Brian, who'd died in the breathless hush of days between the worst blizzard since '93 and the first bud-signs of one of the most beautiful springs in memory. As his next of kin, she'd picked out and designed the stone herself.

Etched musical notations—in quarters and eighths and sixteenths—descended like angels from the stone's rounded top corners, with Brian's name—followed by D.M.A.—and dates of birth and death centered between the notes. Beneath these, he arose—chest, arms, shoulders, and head, playing his flute—above a bed of clouds. And beneath the clouds, she'd had etched a quote from Victor Hugo found on Brian's desk—"Music expresses that which cannot be said and on which it is impossible to be silent."

*Lord, he would hate it,* Dorothy thought again now. *But he doesn't have to look at it.* She smiled at that.

Gussie sat gazing toward the black stone as well and startled when her cousin spoke.

"What would you have said if Brian had asked?"

"Asked what?"

"You to marry him."

"There never was a danger of that, Dottie. So, I never considered it."

"Now, I don't believe that for a second."

Gussie turned her gaze back to the stone.

"All right then, I never considered it for longer than the sigh such a thought brought on." She turned back, glanced from under her eyelashes at Dorothy, then blushed at the ground. "Besides, we were cousins."

"Not that close," Dorothy said. "Third cousins or something. Not close enough to worry about."

"There was the woman in Amsterdam."

"Yes," Dorothy said. "There was always the mysterious woman in Amsterdam." She straightened in the metal chair, feeling on the verge of sliding off of it, then found herself looking toward the deep left corner of Anderson Cemetery—the Smith section—and at Pastor Donald, who stood in the shade there with one of the female musicians.

"I saw you decorating graves down in the Smith section," she said. "Was that Ephraim Smith and his wife?"

"Yes," Gussie said, raising her gaze to the same section of the cemetery. "Ephraim and Matilda. They were my great-great-grandparents on my father's side. And it was their daughter Martha that married into the Anderson line and made us cousins."

"Do you know when that was, when Martha married Levi Anderson?"

"Yes, I believe it was eighteen and eighty-two when they married. And they had my granny Polly in eighty-six."

"You know," Dorothy said. "I always heard that Ephraim Smith was a double agent in the Civil War, but it's just something people've said. I don't remember a story about it."

Gussie waved a fly away from her face and settled her hands, left over right, in her lap. She stared a moment at the brightly colored rooster she'd set on Ephraim Smith's grave marker.

"Well," she said. "I don't reckon I know too much more than that myself. Like you say, it's just been a thing that was said and not a story told." She wondered briefly if some hint to this family mystery might be keyed to that ceramic rooster, but she couldn't make a connection. "My father was once telling a story about his grandmother's chicken 'n' dumplings. About how that was the only time she cooked rooster. And he said something about Ephraim Smith that sounded from the war." She paused and looked in the direction of Brian Anderson's grave, her brow and lips bunching for a moment. "You remember how Daddy talked. He said his great-grandfather's engagement with both sides of the Civil War was personal 'stead of ideological." She heard these words in her father's voice. "That just sounds like the way the war was for everybody around here, so I don't know what bearing it has on the notion of him being a double agent." She laughed. "Nor do I know what it had to do with Great-Granny Anderson's chicken 'n' dumplings or Ephraim Smith's rooster."

                              *  *  *

A fish or some other creature splashed in a backwater on the Piney Ridge side of the river, and something moved in the darkness surrounding Jay's tent. The night became more visible around Smith as his mind returned from some violent realm beyond to find him squatted on his hams between river and camp.

He stared at the tent, straining to see who or what moved there.

Nothing. Everything still all around except the water heard behind him.

He knew that if a clear and wary mind were there in the dark he was already seen, silhouetted as he was against the pale gleam of the starlit river.

*But a mind fogged with fear?* he wondered. *Or desire?*

He blinked slowly, and as his eyelids closed, he breathed in and exhaled and opened a relaxed gaze slightly directed toward Brown's tent, taking in the night scene as a page instead of as a word. Then he saw quick movement, and a small figure—a woman or maybe a boy—dissolved into Jay's tent.

*Damn.*

He slid backward down his calves to sit cross-legged in the sandy grass. After a moment, he leaned forward, rose to hands and knees, and crawled toward the lesser dark of Jay's near tent wall. Just short of it, he rocked back again and listened.

Indecipherable whispered words. Light metal clink. Hurried rustle of cloth against cloth and skin. A wheezy laugh choked short, then a gasp, a whimper. The stir and stick of bodies. A sucking sound and a panting.

He felt a pulsing pressure in his groin and stood slowly, tightening his grip on the knife in his left hand and watching for any shadow he might cast on the tent. He snaked a quiet right hand into his trousers and took hold of himself but then, with a sudden ache along the inside of his thighs, released his grip. He smelled his own funk as the reluctant hand rose out of his smallclothes and trousers, and he quickly stepped backwards, away from the noses in the tent, and passed the knife from his left hand to his right and gripped it tightly.

Two grunts and a gagging. A sound like a snore. Whispered gibberish. A growl. Slaps of moist skin against moist skin. A hoarsely whispered "my will" or "thy will."

He couldn't tell which.

Then Jay's voice rose just above a whisper.

"You've damned us both to hell," he said. "I've a good mind to slit your fuckin' throat."

A light laugh from the other as the rustle of cloth began again.

"I go into the Laurels tomorrow to hunt down deserters," Jay said. "But as soon as you see me back, be here that very night."

Smith heard a hurried whisper and movement quicker than those before.

"Wha—"

A wet sound like a slurp and a gulp stopped Jay's voice, and the quiet darkness inside the tent erupted with a momentary wild thrashing that stilled to two quick breathings, Smith's own and one inside the tent.

He expected to hear Jay curse and to see the tent of Brown or Ramsey or Candler light up, but everything remained quiet and dark. And atop the fading smell of his funk and the pervasive aromas of the night and the river, he picked up the unexpected stench of blood iron and shit.

He sensed movement in Jay's tent but heard nothing for a moment. Then a light tapping, a patting of skin on skin that crescendoed to a rhythmic slapping that accompanied a breathy singing, itself more rhythmic than melodic.

> *Juba!*
> *Juba!*
> *Juba this and juba that, and juba killed a yellow cat*
> *And get over double trouble juba!*

Light bloomed in Brown's tent.

The slapping faded to patting but didn't break rhythm, and the voice whispered through the same words again. Then again everything but the river stilled.

"Sergeant Brown?" a voice called from one of the darkened tents.

*Ramsey.*

Smith heard a quick rustling and then saw the small figure, ghosted by Brown's glowing tent, flee across the officer's mess and disappear into the darkness in the direction of Runion.

"Strange sounds from Sergeant Jay's tent, sir," Brown called back.

Smith's right hand cramped, and he tried to open his fingers to drop the knife. But he held tightly to it and began backing toward the river's edge.

Ramsey's tent now glowed with light as well, but still neither Brown nor he made a move toward the darkness that held Jay.

Smith stepped one foot down into the water, and its chill

caused his breath to catch. But he continued to step backwards, his eyes fixed on Jay's tent and the darkness beyond, into which the woman or boy had disappeared.

Nothing moved except himself and the water around him.

When he stood immersed to his thighs, when he saw both Sgt. Brown and Lt. Ramsey follow lanterns from their tents, he drew in a deep breath and lay back into a flow startlingly cold for May, the marvel of bright and distant stars blurring in the wash of his tears as the current bore him slowly spinning toward Mountain Island, Lover's Leap, and Warm Springs.

*  *  *

Rick Gentry sat on Dewey Lipscomb's wooden box, elbow planted on knee, forehead bowed into hand. Lipscomb sat beside him in the folding chair, an arm draped loosely across Gentry's shoulders, a hand carrying a filterless Camel to and away from his lips. J.S. Benjamin stood on the other side of Gentry, staring off in the direction Welch had disappeared to retrieve beer to be smuggled into camp for the final night's festivities.

Rex Peters paced back and forth in the grass between the three men and the fire pit.

"Goddammit, boys," he said. "Goddammit."

Of the three, only Benjamin cut his eyes at Peters, but in the space of a blink he was staring after Welch again.

"What in the hell's wrong with y'all? Getting in a brawl in broad daylight? At a family event?" He stopped and looked toward the tables around which people were gathering for the final Q & A. "I wouldn't be surprised if they cancelled our October encampment and got somebody else for next May." He shook his head and started across the grass toward the gathered. "Goddammit."

Somewhere a bugler rehearsed "Taps," and the director of the Stackhouse-Putnam State Historic Site stood a moment and listened as he watched Rex Peters approach. Then he turned away and scanned the faces of the reenactment attendees seated beneath the site's oldest white oak. When Peters joined him, the director cleared his throat and began.

"I'm Dr. Wallace Murphy, and I'm an historian and the director here at Stackhouse-Putnam. Before we begin this last information session, I'd like to thank you for joining us today. I hope you've had a good time." He turned toward Peters. "I'd also like to express my appreciation to Mr. Rex Peters, Captain of the 64th North Carolina CSA Reenactors, for another fine event full of history and entertainment. He and his troupe do a great job every year."

The two men shook hands.

"Thank you, Dr. Murphy," Peters said. "We enjoy ourselves at these events and look forward to next time." He turned to the small audience. "You folks come back to our encampment here October the twenty-second to the twenty-fourth, when we'll have lots more demonstrations and period relics on display. There'll be a special mock battle for children, and we hope you'll all come back and bring your family and friends." He paused and smiled. "In the meantime, if you're in need of chiropracty, come see me in my civilian life. I'm on Main Street in Runion." He reached up and adjusted the hat on his head. "Now, if you'll excuse me, I'll go muster my troops for the pass and review." He then bowed, came to attention, performed about face, and walked away from the light applause.

"Thank you, Captain," Dr. Murphy said.

The gathered group sat quietly while another rehearsal of "Taps" faded beneath the murmur of movement as, on the other side of the fence behind the director, the cast members in their blue and gray made their way behind Peters down the slope toward the field's lower edge.

"Now, you've already heard enough about how we all welcome your support, so no more about that except to say that you'll find donation forms and volunteer applications on the table as you exit." He paused and looked at his watch. "The final pass and review will take place in about ten minutes. Between now and then you have the opportunity to ask any final questions you might have about the site here or the period the 64th has reenacted."

The rooster crowed.

"That's Gilbert, by the way," Murphy said. "We named him after the most recent patriarch of the Stackhouse family."

"Is he a retard or something?" a boy asked. He stood off to the left with two other middle-school-aged boys who tried to hide their snickering behind their hands. "I mean, the sun come up a long time ago," the boy added.

Dr. Murphy stared at him for a moment. His eyes narrowed, and he took a quick breath as if to speak but seemed to think better of it and let the young man's comment hang in the air for a moment.

"No, Gilbert's not confused," Murphy said at last. "It's a misconception that roosters crow only at sunrise. They're territorial animals, and Gilbert's the alpha male among the Stackhouse-Putnam fowl population. He's just reminding everybody that this is his farm." He paused and looked again at the group of boys. "Although I take issue with your wording, it's a good question, as I'm sure a lot of people have been wondering about all the crowing."

"Yeah, cock-a-doodle-do," the young spokesman said as his compatriots continued snickering behind their hands.

The audience turned back to Murphy with a variety of shakes of the head and rolls of the eyes.

"That cook never did tell me about eating rooster," the Florida woman said.

"Well, he and a couple of today's other characters were supposed to have been out here with Mr. Peters," Dr. Murphy said. "But we had a little misunderstanding earlier over in the Confederate camp." He looked at his watch again. "You'll just have to come back next year for that answer, I suppose, but we have time for another question or two before the pass and review."

A man wearing an orange sweatshirt and standing at the back of the gathered group raised his hand.

"Yes, sir," Murphy said.

"Yes, Dr. Murphy, we drove down this morning from east Tennessee and took the scenic route from Wolf Laurel. And not long before we got here to Runion, we saw a historical marker commemorating the Shelton Laurel Massacre. Could you tell us something about that?"

Murphy nodded his head and rubbed the palms of his hands

over the hips of his dress slacks.

"Yes, well, the massacre," he said. "It's one of the reasons that Madison County has long been known throughout the state by the nickname Bloody Madison."

"What happened?" the Florida woman said.

"Yes, well, I'm afraid we won't have time to go into much detail about it, but I can give you a little more than you'll find on the marker, which basically just says that Confederate soldiers killed thirteen local men and boys suspected of Unionism at a site not far from here in January of 1863." He crossed his arms and seemed to settle them atop his belly. "First let me say that allegiances in these mountains weren't nearly as clear cut as Mr. Peters and our reenactors necessarily have to portray them. Quite frankly, they were a complicated and violent mess." He glanced again at the group of boys, who stood in a giggling huddle. "The area you drove through—the Laurels, particularly Shelton Laurel—was the site of a sort of feud between the 64th North Carolina and the folks who lived back in there, folks whose loyalties were largely to themselves and their way of life rather than to the causes of either the South or the North. If pressed on the matter, Shelton Laurel would probably have claimed to be Republican to the bone—not republican as in today's political party of Reagan and the Bushes but as in 'to the Republic for which it stands.' The official Confederate stance was that the mountaineers were disloyal, a bunch of bushwhackers and deserters—'Tories,' the smarter ones sometimes called them." He paused as if for a comment and then continued. "Salt was life in those days of subsistence farming before refrigeration. A group of men—ironically, made up mostly of the many, many deserters from the 64th—came down out of the Laurels and pinched a significant portion of the salt the Confederates had stockpiled in Marshall." He grinned and looked around, then continued. "After a few days, the Confederate leaders—Colonel Lawrence Allen and Lieutenant Colonel James Keith—took their desertion-reduced 64th on a revenge raid into Shelton Laurel."

He paused and glanced to the left.

The middle school boys were gone.

He unfolded his arms, put his hands in his pockets, and began pacing.

"Allen and Keith brought their regiment into the valley from different directions. They picked up a few men and a boy or two about the age of the little gang that was here a few minutes ago and tortured some women for information on their menfolk."

"Tortured how?" the Florida woman asked.

"Well, it wasn't pretty. They beat them with hickory rods. They hung them until they were nearly dead. They beat a girl named Mary—a mentally handicapped child by all accounts—and tied her to a tree with the rope across her neck and left her like that all day. They hung and whipped eighty-five-year-old Mrs. Unus Riddle."

"Dear God," the Florida woman said, while those around her stared down at the table or toward camp off to one side of the corncrib and barn or toward the mustering reenactors down to the other.

"Eyewitness accounts that have come down to us from both the Shelton Laurel folks and some members of the 64th tell us that the tortured women gave up no information."

"Good for th—"

Drums down at the tree line launched into the rattle and rhythm of "Army 6/8," and every head turned in that direction.

Dr. Murray raised his voice to invite people to the fence line to enjoy the pass and review and to let them know that he would be available afterwards to discuss any lingering questions.

The fife and drum ensemble marched up the slope first. Just before it reached the waiting audience, the two drummers shifted the rhythm and the three winds—one period fife and two piccolos—screeched out "Battle Cry of Freedom." Once past the audience on one side and the corncrib on the other, the ensemble made an awkward but successful maneuver out of the main avenue for the pass and review. The players took up the tune of "Tramp, Tramp, Tramp" as the Confederate infantry reenactors advanced, their marching as out of step as their uniforms were unmatching. Welch and Lipscomb followed as Rebel cavalry, their horses shying slightly from the strident music. Then came the larger number of

well-dressed and well-disciplined Union infantry, followed by Rex
Peters, outfitted in full captain's uniform, and himself followed
by three Union cavalry reenactors—all to the final tune of the
medley, "Battle Hymn of the Republic."

As the audience's appreciative applause faded, a young man
holding a period bugle and wearing a Union uniform appeared
beside the fife and drum ensemble. With a series of crisp, smooth
motions, he stood straight as a flagpole, his left arm held close to
his side, his right hand holding the bugle to his lips, his eyes staring
straight ahead.

The Stackhouse-Putnam grounds fell quiet, and "Taps" began.

In the ninth measure, scuffling and bumping noises arose inside
the corncrib, and by the beginning of the tenth measure, three boyish
screams crescendoed to a dissonant pitch. Then the three screaming
middle schoolers burst in a line from the corncrib's doorway. Blood
ran down the right thigh and knee of the first. The red face of the
second contorted with terrified tears. The third, the spokesman of the
group, ran screaming and ducking his head away from the flogging
wings of the rooster latched to his shoulders.

When the crowd laughed and applauded, Gilbert released the
boy and flapped away into the middle of the day's battlefield.

Unflustered and without even breaking his fixed stare, the
young bugler concluded "Taps" as the rooster crowed three times,
triumphant but out of tune and out of rhythm.

\* \* \*

Anderson Cemetery lay in blue shadow. The surrounding trees
stood quiet, empty of birds and breezes and watching over the dead.

Miss Gussie Guthrie had always liked being the last to leave,
liked—when finally alone beneath the darkening boughs and the
deepening blue of the sky—to stand on her plot and close her eyes
and listen to how the world above would sound when she joined the
rank and file of the buried. She pictured poor Gunther Gosnell on
his backhoe, digging a near perfect grave and talking to ghosts while
she lay in state at Ramsey's. She imagined her graveside service,
who would be there and what they would say, how they would

look, and how they would sing her chosen hymns—"In the Sweet Bye and Bye" and "Come, Thou Fount." She always expected that Brian would be there with his flute, playing something elegant and hallowed, something in a minor key that would have a hopeful— maybe even triumphant—turn at the end.

But none of that would happen now. Since Brian's death in March and his burial on the opposite side of the cemetery, some nine or ten plots away from hers, she'd decided to return the one beside her parents—the one they'd bought for her under the assumption that she would never marry—to the Anderson Cemetery Association and be cremated instead. She knew her father, radically minded as he was, wouldn't approve of her blowing or floating away as ash to who knew where in the world. And as for that, she didn't know who would carry her ashes to scatter somewhere on wind or water. She could ask Dorothy to take care of her, but she didn't want to. She wondered how much Ramsey's would charge to lug her off to somewhere meaningful, if she could figure out where that might be, or, if she couldn't think of a place, to dump her gently in either the French Broad or the Laurel, off the edge of Stackhouse Park. Then she thought—with a sudden thrill in her throat—that she could arrange the paperwork with Ramsey's in such a way that her ashes could be turned over to somebody trustworthy but unscrupulous, who would bring her here some new moon night and spread her thickly over Brian's grave.

She laughed aloud at that and then shook with a sudden violent chill at the uncouth sound of laughter in the lonely cemetery, where the dead far outnumbered her. She stepped off the plot no longer her own, picked up the paper grocery bag with the empty Tupperware, passed beneath the wrought iron archway, and walked quickly through the twilight trees to the roadside where she'd parked.

Her car wasn't the only one still waiting. Some twenty yards to the right, at the Spring Creek end of the gravel pull-off and facing that way, a large maroon car sat silent and apparently empty.

*Maybe car trouble*, she thought. *Or maybe some folks've gone for supper together and left this one to get later.*

She noticed the quiet and felt a tingling uneasiness around her ears and at the back of her scalp. She heard nothing but the stones clicking and crunching beneath her feet—no sigh of river or wind, no call of crow or mockingbird, no hum of motor and tires from either direction. The quiet felt like the pressure of altitude deep inside her ear canals.

At her car, she unlocked and opened the trunk, checked that her purse still lay where she'd left it, and set down her Tupperware. Then she drew back one fold of the blanket she kept in the corner of the trunk and removed a thing wrapped in white paper. She unwound the wrapping and stuffed it in the grocery bag, closed the trunk, and stood holding in her hand another small ceramic statue.

She returned to the path and passed along that—through a darkness more visible beneath the trees—into the cemetery again. She circled around to the right, slowly following the wrought iron fence and touching each spearhead finial as she went. In her mind's eye, she saw herself and thought she looked girlish and shy.

*And silly.*

As she came alongside the foot of Brian Anderson's mounded grave, the melody of an old Elvis song bubbled up in her mind, and she found herself humming it, slowing the tempo to her walking pace and changing the lyrics as they came to mind.

> *Well, I've got a guy, he's as cute as he can be;*
> *He's a distant cousin, but he's not too distant with me.*
> *We'll kiss all night.*
> *I'll squeeze him tight.*
> *We'll be kissin' cousins—that'll make it all—*

Her breath suddenly caught in her throat and stopped her humming.

"I'm sorry, Brian," she said and startled at the sound of her voice. "So sorry," she said again, more quietly. She moved to the head of his grave and stood beside the gaudy stone, reached across and set the little statue in the middle of its glossy black top.

Her ceramic boy sat on a low split-rail fence—the fence, his jacket, and hair all painted the same reddish brown. He wore a broad-brimmed straw hat perched on the crown of his head, a white shirt with a blue bowtie, dark brown shorts, and white socks with a gold stripe around their tops. He wore black shoes—the heel of his right resting on the lower rail of the fence, the left planted in green grass. His eyes were closed, and long lashes lay on his cheeks. He lifted a dark wooden flute toward a red mouth drawn up like a bow.

"A new tradition, Brian," she said. "I don't have anybody to pass it on to, so it'll just be for a few years. I hope you won't hate it as much as I'm sure you hate this tombstone Dottie bought." She took a step back and looked at the statue and stone together. "And at least we'll all know what this little decoration means." She chuckled and hummed again for a moment, then broke into a softly sung line.

*. . . a distant cousin, but he's not too dis—*

A shuddering shriek sounded from somewhere in the woods on the other side of the cemetery.

Gussie collapsed to hands and knees at the side of the grave. For a moment all she heard was a rushing sound in her ears and then the pounding of her heart. Just as these calmed, she heard the cry again—different this time, more human than beast, more pained laugh than shriek, which didn't startle her as the first had but somehow made her more uneasy. She looked up to the patch of sky above the cemetery. Although the tops of the trees were already in shadow, she knew from the light in the sky that it must still be at least an hour before sunset. She leaned forward onto her hands and slowly made her way back up to standing.

*Why linger here?*

Her father's voice again.

*Leave this place, Gus.*

She glanced from Brian's stone to her father's, then to the darkening woods.

"Yes," she said quietly to herself. "That's a good idea, you old fool."

As she walked, hurried but quiet as she could, through the trees and toward the parking area, a guttural moan froze her to listening stillness. The same sound again. Then something more like a growl and then a whimper.

She listened a moment longer and then stepped slowly in the direction of a laurel thicket that stood right of the path, thinking the sounds seemed to come from within the thicket or somewhere on the other side of it. Edging quietly toward the thicket's thinner left side, she walked carefully on the carpet of long-dead brown pine needles. She knew from old memories that a small hollow lay beneath the other side of the thicket and a steep rise on the other side of that. As she approached the thinning, she began rising to her toes and craning her neck to see through laurel blossoms and leaves. Then she froze again as movement caught her eye. Through a roughly diamond-shaped opening framed by blossoms of pink and white with maroon streaks, she watched the movement of something in the gloaming almost the same color as the petaled frame.

Without leaving its frame, the thing stayed in almost constant rhythmic motion.

She cocked her head left and then right, and when she heard again the growl and a whimpering giggle, she knew that what she was watching was a man's naked buttocks.

*Ass.*

She gasped at her father's voice and her own intertwined, then covered her mouth, certain she'd been heard.

But the motion in the frame of petals—with now and then a second body glimpsed—and the noises of the coupling continued steadily.

She thought she might throw up or faint or go blind—or all three at once. But she kept her dinner down and stayed on her feet and watched until the movement locked in place and the noises crescendoed before shuddering to quiet. The bodies stayed together so that she couldn't see their faces, and now that their minds were regaining human consciousness or returning from wherever they'd been wandering, she feared moving forward and risking discovery.

She steadily and deliberately walked backwards, losing sight of the bodies as she went, until she found herself on the path again. Then she turned and hurried stealthily out of the trees.

When she found herself on the edge of the gravel, she stopped and listened. No sounds came from the direction of the laurel thicket, so she walked straight across the gravel with as little noise as she could and stepped onto the blacktop. She stopped and listened again, then turned to her right and almost ran to the maroon Buick still sitting there facing Spring Creek. She slowed as she approached it and hunkered down a little to see through the back windshield.

*Nobody in it.*

When she came alongside the back door, she stopped and looked in.

Her own face loomed down out of the clear, late afternoon sky, which shocked her for a moment. Her short, gray-brown hair sprung wildly from her head and framed an alien expression. Her mouth hung open and drawn down at the corners. Her eyebrows hung at mid rise beneath a crowded brow and above shadowed eyes that seemed drawn back in fear of the abyss that fell away toward the evening blue.

She closed her mouth with a thunk and blinked her expression back to familiar. Then she looked through herself at a leather-bound Bible and a fiddle case that lay together on the gray-on-black back seat of the Buick.

\* \* \*

Ephraim and Matilda Smith left their home on Big Laurel Creek—to which they'd returned earlier in the spring after nearly a decade of hiding and tenant farming in the vicinity of Camp Creek in Greene County, Tennessee—and walked through most of the warming morning. Their journey took them across Cutshall Branch and Johnson Branch and through woods and fields before, between, and beyond these streams. Near noon they crossed a footbridge over Shelton Laurel Creek and in another fifteen minutes reached their destination. They joined their oldest daughter Julina, her husband Mallie Reeves, and their grandchildren Maggie, Mollie,

Woodard, and Joe, and spread their blanket and unpacked their lunch and sat and ate among some forty others gathered beneath the trees at a respectful distance from the ground where their kinsmen were massacred nine winters before.

When the gathered had eaten and rested, Joshua Goforth came by with his fiddle and collected Ephraim's son-in-law, and the two of them went to stand beneath a white oak to one side of the horrible and hallowed scene of the massacre. Goforth struck up a mournful melody, and the people on the ground fell quiet to listen. None looked at another as the melody intensified but sat with eyes lowered to the ground, raised to the trees and sky, or closed.

Mallie Reeves turned his face up to green leaves and thin white clouds and sang.

> *Come, O Thou Traveler unknown,*
> *Whom still I hold, but cannot see!*
> *My company before is gone,*
> *And I am left alone with Thee;*
> *With Thee all night I mean to stay,*
> *And wrestle till the break of day.*

As Goforth swelled the interlude, Reeves bent down and picked up his son Woodard, who'd tottered out of reach of his mother and grandparents as they listened to the hymn.

Reeves sang.

> *In vain Thou strugglest to get free,*
> *I never will unloose my hold!*
> *Art Thou the Man that died for me?*
> *The secret of Thy love unfold;*
> *Wrestling, I will not let Thee go,*
> *Till I Thy name, Thy nature know.*

At this, Reverend Waldo Hathorne Cooper rose from the blanket where he'd shared lunch with his wife and two members of his former charge, Antioch Methodist Church in Hot Springs. With his black hat hanging from his left hand and his right hand latched to his jacket's lapel, he walked slowly among the gathered, his eyes cast down and his lips moving.

Reeves shifted Woodard across his chest, from right arm to left, and sang his last verse.

> *I know Thee, Savior, who Thou art.*
> *Jesus, the feeble sinner's friend;*
> *Nor wilt Thou with the night depart.*
> *But stay and love me to the end,*
> *Thy mercies never shall remove;*
> *Thy nature and Thy Name is Love.*

"Thank you, Brother Reeves, Brother Goforth," Reverend Cooper said when the last note of the fiddle had faded. "A touching song from the sainted Charles Wesley." He continued a slow pacing in the open space between where the gathered sat watching him and the space where their loved ones had once been dumped into a mass grave.

"Brothers and sisters," he said at last. "This new observance known as Decoration Day is made for cemeteries. Where we gather today is not a cemetery but a place of murder." He looked at his audience for the first time. "Here are no flower-decked, well-mounded graves. The bodies of those whose lives were taken here were taken from here long ago and interred in more hallowed grounds, but I think it is fit that we come just once so that we might feel the pervasive horror of this place. We should not gather here again, not for this purpose."

A kingfisher chittered somewhere above Shelton Laurel Creek.

"None of you, I fear, will approve of all I say in the next brief while. But none should detest all I say either. The late war left deep scars, yet in these scars lie deep meanings. We must not shrink from the tedious and painful process of probing our scars for these."

He paused, and his gaze flitted across each face before he continued.

"I see in attendance those who fought on one side and those who fought on the other. And some, I think, who played the middle against both ends. And I see in attendance the mothers and widows and orphans of men who did the same. We see around us here, in Runion and Hot Springs, in Marshall and Mars Hill, men who were once whole and strong now made of stumps. We see across these sacred mountains and along the French Broad River farms from which everything was taken in the name of man's war and farmers who returned—and the families of those who didn't—deep in debt and destitute."

Ephraim Smith looked down at his hands, clean but callused. Since returning to his homeplace from Tennessee, he'd tried to find a team of mules to help in the work of reclaiming his farm. Even one mule would help. But the best he'd accomplished was to walk one milk cow back from Camp Creek and to accept the charity of a rooster and two laying hens from his son-in-law's family over in Jewel Hill. He knew he wasn't alone in these bitter struggles. Matilda struggled with him, although this felt as much like reproach as help.

"This Decoration Day, here, in this place, is a dark celebration," Reverend Cooper said. "We have, on the one side, a desire to focus on the bravery, the heroism, of both sides equally, as if no difference existed between what spurred them to fight. And if the war were thus reduced to its individual participants, we would indeed find on both sides courage and loyalty to applaud till kingdom come." He drew a yellow bandana from the inside breast pocket of his jacket and wiped his mouth and forehead. Then he tucked the bandana into the crown of the hat and continued. "But such praise would only salve the scars and yet not touch the deeper meanings."

Crows raised a ruckus to the north, in the direction of Billy Knob. Reverend Cooper stood still and listened, then visibly shuddered.

"It freezes me," he said. "It freezes me to imagine a horde of crows settling on the murdered men and boys barely buried just yonder." He pointed toward the nearby clearing, the center of which was, by design or mystery, still bald. "It freezes me to know of thirteen dead men and boys—fathers, brothers, husbands, sons, uncles, cousins, friends. Regardless of their allegiances, regardless of what they did or did not do in Marshall or elsewhere in the days before their horrible murders here, they were men and boys of these mountains, sharers of the lives we have here, and their ghosts accuse any Confederate, any secessionist, any rebel who would lay claim to or be celebrated for courage and heroism." He took the bandana from inside his hat and wiped his face again, then held it in his hand instead of returning it to the hat. "I'm sorry," he said and stopped but scanned the gathered with a glare fierce and unapologetic.

Several people shifted on their blankets. Others lowered their own gazes to the ground between their blankets and the minister's boots. One man, with a black beard that lay on a thin chest, stood up and cleared his throat, but he didn't speak.

Two imagined images haunted the darker byways in Ephraim Smith's mind, images striking enough to have haunted him through the Tennessee years and to have disturbed his sleep as recently as a quarter past three o'clock this morning. In one, a roughhewn pine box lay across sawhorses by an open grave in the churchyard at Piney Grove. Inside and unseen lay the naked body of Jim Metcalf, covered with streams of dried blood to which stuck bits of leaves and dirt. Jim's lower jaw hung open more than a natural man's could, and a black tongue lurked within the mouth. His eyes, unseen and unseeing, stared always at Matilda, whether she draped her weeping body over the coffin or stood aside holding Ephraim's hand. In the other image, a tent rose in front of him, and from it came the choking and gurgling sounds of Nick Jay's death throes. Blood seeped through the canvas walls and pooled there, and the muted impression of a face pushed toward him from the inside.

The crows cawed to each other again, sounding somewhat nearer.

"I'm sorry that I don't have greater words of comfort, but we all know that this war isn't over. That it hasn't been over in these seven years since it is said to have ended up in Virginia. And won't be over for any currently foreseeable time. And so, as our Lord Himself says in Matthew 10:34, 'Think not that I am come to send peace on earth: I came not to send peace, but a sword.' Those who would still defend the rebels and those who still persecute them that made the mistake of rebellion will not allow for nor welcome peace, and a false peace does none of us any good." He wiped his face again and continued speaking even as he still dabbed at his eyes. "Make no mistake," he said and returned the bandana to the inside breast pocket of his jacket. "Make no mistake in thinking that this will be healed in forgetfulness. Perhaps it might have been, if all the horrors like that that happened here hadn't been driven by a rebellion intending death to the republic. All the courage of the Confederate, all the fire of the secessionist, all the daring of the rebel is swallowed up in its dark dedication to that one horrible purpose." He paused and took a deep breath and closed his eyes. "God forgive us, and God help us," he said. "Amen."

He settled the black hat on his head and stepped forward with his hand extended to his wife, who took it and rose, and together they walked into the trees and disappeared.

Without much talk or much sound of packing up, the gathered prepared to leave. Some breaths huffed in wordless anger, and others caught to control tears. Group by group they turned away from the spot and departed like puffs of black smoke.

At the near side of Shelton Laurel Creek, Ephraim and Matilda bid goodbye to Julina and her family. Both hugged their daughter, and Matilda gathered the grandchildren in her arms while Ephraim shook hands with Mallie, then helped him lift the little ones into the wagon, which then rumbled away—Mallie at the reins—along the creek road. Matilda waved them out of sight, while Ephraim stood still beside her.

When they were alone again, they turned their backs on the woods that sheltered the killing ground and crossed the foot bridge, Matilda in front and Ephraim behind. They could feel the late spring chill that rose from the clear and shallow water below, sparkling and singing on its journey toward Runion and the French Broad River. Matilda waited at the far end of the foot bridge, and when Ephraim looked up from the water and stepped down, they set off homeward, their rough and warm hands clasped together, fingers interlocked, tethering their ghosts between them.

# Conversion

The old woman and the girl, her great-granddaughter, sat on the covered porch of a weathered board-and-batten farmhouse and watched a group of men work around the prefab church building across Lonesome Mountain Road. Both munched on salted slices of raw potato and looked on without speaking. The northeast breeze danced the girl's long blond hair across her face and quivered kinky iron-gray escapees from the old woman's bun. Both squinted against the late-morning glare that fell straight down beyond the shade of the porch's cover and bathed the activity around the opposite gray-and-white building.

The men filled the clear air with the thump and snarl and screech of hammer and saw and crowbar, the angry whines of handheld electric tools. One group tore down a storage shed at the far end of one dusty gravel parking area, and at the opposite end another group took apart a small, stand-alone structure designed to look like an old-fashioned well with a bell in place of the bucket. A third group near the front entrance unboxed a variety of lighting fixtures and unwrapped doors inset with colorful glass, then disappeared into the building with these. Two men removed three white crosses that stood in the south yard and laid them on a tarp spread on the white gravel in the same order as they'd stood—short, tall, short. Stained glass windows—white doves in their top corners, white lilies in their bottom corners, and red crosses in their centers—winged the doors in the façade, and these they carefully pried from their frames and laid on the tarp with the crosses. At the near edge of the north yard, two men lowered and folded the faded and frayed American flag, then pushed and pulled to loosen its naked white pole, dug around it, and lifted it free, dirt flaking from its rough concrete cone of root. Another man, young and lithe, climbed a ladder and scrambled onto the roof of the prefab building. He dropped the white nylon rope he carried loosely coiled around his left shoulder and without hesitation shinnied up the spire to detach the cross. Down on the roof again, he disassembled the spire and used the rope to lower the pieces to hands waiting below. Then he secured his end of the rope to the spire's base, which he left in place, and flowed back down the ladder to the ground.

Between the sounds of careful destruction and construction, the old woman and the girl heard strange accents and unknown tongues as the working men called out to one another. They were all young—of the old woman's daughter's and granddaughter's generations. And they were healthy—not a fat man among them. Their work clothes seemed from the "Men's Workwear" section in one of the mail-order catalogues that used to appear in the old woman's tilting mailbox. Sweat glistened on various shades of brown faces and forearms, and sawdust and small splinters speckled the black hair of those working with saw and crowbar.

The girl turned to look at the old woman, who looked back with a raised eyebrow. The girl shrugged and turned again just as a new man arrived in a shiny green Nissan pickup with a large U-Haul cargo trailer in tow.

He drove the truck into the yard where the crosses had stood, stopped and waited while two workers unhitched the U-Haul, and then wheeled the truck back into the parking lot, where he stopped again, killed the engine, and opened the door. He stood tall after he unfolded from the cab. His skin was the same brown as that of several others, but his beard, with no overarching moustache, and his hair, thinning and parted on the left side, were a blend of white and gray, striking in contrast to his complexion. He wore round, silver-rimmed glasses, green surgical scrubs, and brown sandals.

His entire face smiled when he looked across the road and up the embankment at the old woman and the girl. Although they didn't respond in kind, his smile didn't dim as he turned and joined his colleagues, who gathered around him with their own brilliant smiles and obvious deference. He handed a key ring to one man and pointed toward the doors of the church and to the tarp, then gestured to the cargo trailer. As the men busied themselves with their assigned tasks, he turned and strode across the road, where he stood for a moment and looked at the brambles of blackberry and honeysuckle on the low, graded embankment and then up at the old woman and the girl.

"Assalamualykum, sister," he said, smiling and bowing slightly. "I am Dr. Muhammad Baddour. Please allow me to apologize for the disruption of your peace this fine day."

The old woman munched on potato and nodded.

Behind Dr. Baddour, a brawny man ducked into the U-Haul and began handing out rolled rugs of varying sizes, and two others carried each of these into the building.

The girl turned toward her great-grandmother, and when the old woman nodded again without looking down at her, she turned back to the man and brushed blond hair from her face.

"Our noisy work is almost finished," Dr. Baddour said. "And now we must remove all that the former occupants have so far neglected to claim."

Men emerged from the church as if on cue, carrying pieces of a sound system—speakers, speaker stands, microphone stands, mixing board, boxes brimming with cables, and cases of microphones. Each handed his burden to the big man stooped inside the cargo trailer, who disappeared for a moment and then came back empty-handed to take another piece.

"We wish to be good neighbors," Dr. Baddour said. "Please speak to us at any time, if we may do anything to assist you."

Three men carried the crosses to the U-Haul, and the packer inside took them out of sight.

Behind the old woman and to her left, the screen door screeched open, and her grandson stepped out onto the deck and stood there, heavy-bearded and thickset and shirtless, wearing only faded, mud-spattered blue jeans and unlaced brogans. Short dark hair tilted in several directions on his head and swirled in patterns across the bulk of his tanned torso.

Dr. Baddour offered a diminished smile and a terse nod in recognition of the new arrival.

"Where's Pastor Donald and his people got to?" the grandson asked.

"They are none of my concern," Dr. Baddour said, turning for a moment to look over his shoulder at the work carrying on behind him.

"They know what y'all're doing?"

"They had some recent trouble, I think." Dr. Baddour lifted his chin. "As for what we are doing today, it is ours to do. The building now belongs to our community."

Again the girl and the old woman exchanged a glance for a nod, and again the girl turned back to the man.

"Y'all Indian or something?" the grandson asked.

"Yes, some of us are Indian, brother," Dr. Baddour said. "Some of us—"

"Cherokee?"

The men who'd been carefully wrapping the stained-glass windows, the spire, and its cross in canvass, delivered them to the man in the cargo trailer, who motioned them aside to make room for the oak pulpit two others were just wrestling through the double doors.

Dr. Baddour blew a breath through his nose, and his eyelids flared wider for a moment.

"Ah, no, I see," he said. "Those of us who are Indian are generally from the north central regions of India, on the other side of the world." He paused again and drew another breath. "And those of us from the many nations of Africa arrived directly from those nations and do not descend from your American slaves."

The pieces from the roof and the bell now went into the U-Haul.

The grandson grunted and turned and disappeared into the house, letting the screen door slam at his heels.

Dr. Baddour stood staring at the empty doorway, his lower jaw slightly offset.

"Very well then," he said as his smile reappeared. He raised his hand. "Assalamualykum, sister. Peace be upon you." Then he bowed slightly and turned and strode back across the road, where he directed his attention and that of his carpenters to dismantling the signage.

They turned first to the sign that stood close beside the road and read, "Lonesome Mountain American Christian Church." This the workers carefully detached from its two stout posts and leaned against the side of the trailer, leaving the posts themselves planted. Above the double doors of the entrance, a second sign hung in the gable, this one a large slab of rough-hewn wood with the words burned into it.

**LONESOME MOUNTAIN AMERICAN CHRISTIAN CHURCH**
**Resolute in Teaching Biblical Principles That Sustain Liberty**
**A Tabernacle of the Living God the Father of Jesus Christ**
**And the Author of the Holy King James Bible**
**PASTOR: DONALD ROY**

When this was unbolted and lowered, it and the roadside sign were wrapped in blankets and loaded into the trailer.

Then the same young man again climbed the ladder to the roof, followed this time by two others.

The old woman stood up and brushed the palms of her hands down the bodice of her brown dress and the lap of her navy-blue apron.

"It's lunchtime, Livvy," she said and disappeared into the house.

Livvy stood and, for a moment, watched as the stoutest man on the roof began hoisting a small green dome the size of a soap-boiling kettle upwards from the hands of two men on the ground. Then she turned and disappeared through the screen door without a sound.

\* \* \*

By the time the old woman and Livvy returned to the porch and took their seats, the ribbed green dome the girl had seen being raised was mounted on the absent spire's base, and rising from its apex, a slender golden stem ended in a golden moon shaped at a stage something less than a quarter. The trailer had been closed and reattached to Dr. Baddour's truck.

The men stood in the gravel front lot of the building, looking up at the dome and crescent moon—many in fresh clothes, wood chips and sawdust mostly gone from their black hair. Seemingly satisfied with what they saw on the roof, they milled around and settled into small groups, some clean and smiling and laughing, others gathering into tighter, quieter knots that at random directed unreadable glances toward the road and across it to Livvy and her great-grandmother and their weathered house.

The building's double doors stood open, revealing an interior floor that appeared a reddish confusion of colors and patterns, and somewhere inside a man began to sing indecipherable words in a voice both tremulous and strong, sliding through intervals odd to the ears of those on the farmhouse porch, who watched as the men quieted and Dr. Baddour, with wordless handshakes and pats on shoulders, shepherded all into the building. Then with his back to the activity inside and his smile beaming at the watchers across Lonesome Mountain Road, he disappeared behind closed double doors.

Livvy stared a few moments at the inanimate scene and then turned to look up at her great-grandmother, who shrugged, spat off the side of the porch, picked up the faded overalls she'd been patching before all the activity began that morning, and set to work again. Livvy turned back to watch a black Chevy Silverado roll slowly past the building in the direction of Runion, its driver invisible beyond tinted windows.

"I'd say this day won't end without some spot of trouble," her great-grandmother said when the truck noise faded.

Livvy turned again just as the old woman pulled the pile of blue jean cloth against herself, beneath her slumping breasts, to protect it from spatter off the stream of tobacco juice she jetted into the sparse grass of the side yard.

"Don't know what it'll be," the old woman said. "But it'll be something—"

"Big Granny," her grandson yelled from inside the house. "Where's them other overalls that was on the door in here?"

Big Granny's hands collapsed into her lap, and she sat still a moment, except for the slight lift of her body with the deep breath she drew.

Livvy turned back toward the road and the building on the other side of it.

"Big Granny," her grandson yelled again.

"I'm patching them," she said no louder than if he were standing on the porch beside her chair.

"I was gonna wear those," he said through the screen door, where he suddenly stood in only his white briefs and white socks.

"You've got other britches," she said. "Get some on." She lifted her hands and began working again to patch the crotch of the overalls. "Or you can wait on these if you'll not stand there naked for all the world to gawk at."

"I ain't naked and ain't nobody gawking," he said and turned back toward the dark interior of the farmhouse. "And I can't wait on you."

Big Granny didn't respond other than to shake her head and continue her needlework.

Livvy suddenly stood and hopped down the steps to the yard. She swiveled to look at Big Granny for a moment and then hopped across the side yard and into the woods toward the spring house.

"Leave them lizards where they be," Big Granny called after her.

"What?" her grandson yelled from somewhere inside the house.

\* \* \*

Dr. Baddour and a crew of three spent the midafternoon at work around the front of the building. They first installed windows and blinds where the two stained-glass pieces had been. They turned next to the two posts left standing after the removal of the

previous occupants' signage and spent nearly an hour attaching a
new sign to the posts.

# السلام عليكم

## Islamic Center
## Muslim Community of Western North Carolina
## 916 Lonesome Mountain Road

Then the stoutest man among them backed a small blue pickup
near the posts and lowered the tailgate to reveal a bed partially
piled with stones—most of them rectangular in shape and of
varying sizes, most of them dark in color, tending toward the red
spectrum. Over the next two hours Dr. Baddour and the other two
handed the stout man stone after stone as he raised a monument
to frame the sign along the bottom and up each side.

"That big'n' lays mighty fine stone," Big Granny said.

Livvy didn't turn but nodded her head as two oversized
pickup trucks—a red Dodge Ram and the same black Silverado,
each coming from a different direction on Lonesome Mountain
Road—rolled to a dust-raising stop in the gravel lot.

Dr. Baddour and his coworkers straightened up and glanced at
each other, then waited, looking from truck to truck.

Invisible drivers shut off engines, and the trucks stood quiet
for a moment. Then all doors opened at once, and four men
stepped down onto the gravel. Ranging in age from early thirties
to sixties, they wore loafers of black or brown, dress slacks of
blue or brown or maroon, short-sleeved white shirts, and neckties
of various somber colors. One wore this uniform draped over an
enervated thinness, and the other three pushed hard at buttons
and seams with bellies and hips and thighs.

"Greetings, gentlemen," Dr. Baddour said. "Welcome."

The new arrivals stood hitching up the waistlines and shaking
down the legs of their slacks. The two Ram men lipped cigarettes
from packs pulled from their shirt pockets.

"Dr. Baddour," the driver of the Silverado said at last.

"Mr. Johnny Anderson, you appear to have lost some weight,"
Dr. Baddour said with a smile. "How have you been sleeping since

our last meeting?"

"Better, doctor," Anderson said. "Much better with that CPAP machine." With his right forefinger inside his key ring, he swung the keys in three full circles and then tossed them onto the seat of his truck and shut the door. "At least I was until all this mess got started."

The Ram men nodded their heads and blew clouds from their nostrils. The driver of the Ram stepped around to the front of his truck.

Dr. Baddour glanced at him and then turned back to Anderson. "To what mess do you refer?"

"This mess right here," the Ram driver said with a jerk of his arm. "You devils taking apart our house of worship to do God-knows-what unholy business in it."

Big Granny grunted, and Livvy turned to look up at her.

"Don't need to hear what that Andy Campbell's saying to know it ain't good." Big Granny stopped, then rearranged the overalls in her lap.

Livvy's eyes lingered on Big Granny for a moment, and then she turned back around.

"Begging your pardon, my friend," Dr. Baddour said. "Whatever we do is ours to do, as this property is now held by the Muslim Community of Western North Carolina." He partially extended his arms with hands open and palms up. "It is no longer your business, but please let me assure you that nothing we do here shall be unholy."

"Bullshit," the second Ram man said.

Campbell turned to look at the thin man with greasy, golden brown hair and eyeglasses that were thick-rimmed and thick-lensed.

"Now, Bruce," he said. "Brother Wallin. Pastor Donald wouldn't want you to use such language in defending him."

"And what's the difference, Andy," Johnny Anderson said, "between Bruce's BS and you calling the doctor and these men devils?"

The other Silverado man huffed.

"Donald Roy's all but ruined this church, anyway," he said. "Along with a bunch of lives."

"Hey, Gentry," Wallin said. "We know what you think he done, but a bunch of us don't believe he done it."

"And even if he done it," Campbell said, "which I don't think he done, it don't ruin him, Rick. All King David done to get hold of Bathsheba didn't ruin him for God, did it?"

"And you're still alive," Wallin said with a narrow grin. "Not dead like Uriah."

"My friends," Dr. Baddour said, his arms opening again. "Please, let us talk together about why we are here." He paused a moment. Then, turning to the Silverado men, "Why you are here, I should say, where as friends you are welcome but where otherwise you have no business."

The spring hinge on the back door of the farmhouse screeched, and then the door slammed. In a moment, an engine grumbled to life and gravel began to pop under tires. Big Granny and Livvy watched their old Ford pickup come from out back and nose up to Lonesome Mountain Road, then pull out to the left and chug toward Runion.

"No telling when we'll see your uncle again," Big Granny said and sighed.

Just as the sound of the pickup faded, three cars arrived to join the scene across the road. A LaSabre up from town pulled into the parking area behind the Silverado just as a Taurus down from Lonesome Mountain stopped behind the Ram. The third, a BMW M3, also up from town, parked alongside the road, in front of the newly erected signage. From these cars, six women and a child emerged—two, dark-skinned and black-haired, from the M3 parked in front of the sign; two from the LeSabre; two and the child—a girl of six or seven years old—from the Taurus. All gravitated toward the closest group of men.

"Assalamualykum, sisters," Dr. Baddour said to the women who stood on the other side of the sign from him and his work crew.

"Wa Alykum Assalam," the older of the women said, while the younger modestly bowed.

Dr. Baddour smiled at them just as one of the newly-arrived Taurus women huffed.

"If y'all are gonna talk in front of me," she said, "you talk American."

"Amen to that, sister Doris," Andy Campbell and Bruce Wallin said.

"Sounds like a bunch of jibber-jabber, amen," Doris said.

"It is a simple greeting," the stout layer of stone said, squaring himself to the Ram. "Peace be unto you."

"I don't give a flip what it means," Doris said. "It's offensive in my hearing."

The stonemason stared at her through narrowed eyes but said nothing more.

Big Granny blew another sigh from her nose, and Livvy turned and looked up, brushing away strands of blond hair that had again blown across her face.

"Such acting up," Big Granny said with a shake of her head. "And from them that got every cause to act better."

Livvy nodded and turned back around. She stretched her bare legs out in front of her, bent and grabbed her toes, held and then released, planted the small feet on the second step below her, planted an elbow on a knee and her chin in her palm.

"Lord, forgive them that think you'd've acted thataway," Big Granny said.

The young girl in the scene playing out across the road stood between Bruce Wallin and the driver of the Taurus, attempting to get the attention of one and then the other, tugging at pantleg and skirt and peering up into their faces—his flushed, hers pale. But Wallin kept his eyes locked on the stonemason, while her mother seemed trying to see all the faces present but repeatedly glanced with a look like confusion or fear at the younger of the two M3 women.

"Muslims live in these mountains," one of the younger men with Dr. Baddour said with a sweeping gesture of his arm. "We have needed a mosque for our brothers and sisters in Mitchell and Yancey and Haywood. Many of them do not wish to confront the traffic in Asheville to attend the overcrowded mosque there."

"Yeah, but this ain't a mosque," Johnny Anderson said. "This is a church."

Dr. Baddour raised a hand.

"In its essence, this is only a building," he said. "Neither Christian nor Islamic." He paused and looked at the faces surrounding him. "My friends, if I may," he said with a tight smile. "Let us begin again." He pressed a palm against his chest, drew a sharp breath that seemed to widen his eyes, and exhaled with force. Then, "I am Muhammad Baddour, and I am a family physician. Your friend Mr. Johnny Anderson is my patient." He indicated the stonemason with a hand to the man's shoulder. "And this is Dr. Jamil Salim, who is Professor of Engineering at Runion State University." With a wave of his other hand, he presented the two younger men. "These Nigerian brothers are the twins Moosa and Najeeb Yakubu, university engineering students." Finally, he extended his arms in front of him as if for an embrace. "These are my wife, Anne, and Dr. Kanta Sidhu, who is a pediatrician in Runion."

"Molly, be still," Wallin said without turning away from those caught in the middle of this gathering.

Rick Gentry lurched forward from the passenger side of the Silverado.

"Look, I was here when we dedicated the building," he said. "Janie and me was both—" He stopped and stood, and his head bowed.

Everybody looked at him for a long moment. Andy Campbell shifted gravel with the toe of a loafer.

"We were all here," Anderson said at last. "Seems to me like if it was dedicated to God then it's got to be undedicated or something before it can be turned into anything that's not a God-fearing church."

"And who's going to do that?" the LeSabre woman said. "Our preacher's taken all our money and gone off God knows where."

"Why, he ain't neither, Rose," Doris said. "He's just over in Burnsville."

"And he's holding the money as our pastor," Campbell said.

"He's trying to find us a new place."

"Do you really believe that, Andy?" Rose said. "Doris Johnson, do you really believe that?"

"I do," Campbell said.

Doris stood with her right palm pressed just below the hollow of her throat, her fingertips lightly tapping her collarbone.

"I've got faith in Pastor Donald," she said.

Gentry looked up at them.

"And is Donald Roy holding my wife over in Burnsville, too?" he said and waited a moment. Then, "And paying her way with the congregation's money?"

Everybody stared, but nobody moved until Molly broke away from her parents and in three strides stood in front of Dr. Kanta Sidhu, holding the hand her pediatrician had extended at her sudden approach.

"Hey, Dr. K," Molly said. "Do you know me?"

"Molly, get back here," Wallin said.

Dr. Sidhu smiled and lowered herself into her skirt until she was at eye level with the girl.

"I know you, Molly, of course," she said. "But I can hardly believe how much you have grown since your last appointment."

"I turned six on April the 18th," Molly said and smiled.

"Well, you look healthy and happy and almost big enough to be seven already."

Molly laughed and drew herself up to her full height.

Everybody watched, but nobody spoke.

"Are you out of school for the summer, Molly?"

"Yes, ma'am, and I was supposed to be in bible school today but they ain't having it so we're going fishing when we leave here and fish 'til it's dark."

"Molly," Wallin said, "Get back over here, now."

But his daughter seemed not to hear.

"You know, Molly, I have never been fishing," Dr. Sidhu said.

"Oh, it's fun! We take a picnic, and I like to splash in the water and try to skip rocks and lots of other things."

The pediatrician smiled.

"Do you catch many fish?"

Molly stood still for a moment and looked in the direction of the old woman and the girl sitting on the porch across the road.

"Not really, I guess," she said and turned back to her pediatrician. "But even when I do, I make Daddy let them go."

"Well, Molly, you be careful and have fun, whether you catch anything or not, okay?"

"Okay!"

"And I will see you before school begins again, yes?"

"Okay."

"Very good, Molly," Dr. Sidhu said and rose. "Many of my children bring me pictures they make in Miss Barnett's art class. I hope you will bring me one of yours."

"Oh, I will, Dr. K, I promise!" At that Molly turned and bolted back to where her parents still stood and took each by a hand.

"Do you know her?" Big Granny asked, pointing with her chin toward the little family across the road.

Livvy turned and shook her head.

"Well, she's awful bright and shiny to come from them two," Big Granny said.

Livvy looked at Big Granny a moment longer and then turned back to the scene across the road.

"We've seen miracles right on these premises," Andy Campbell said.

"Amen," Doris Johnson said.

"Remember when old Pastor Rash held his revival here?" Campbell said. "How he lit that torch and then petted the flame like it was a kitten?"

"And not a burn," Rose said.

"Not a burn," Doris echoed, pushing up her glasses and dabbing her eyes with a tissue.

"Those were blessed days," Anderson said and turned away from the group gathered in the circular drive and looked down the road in the direction of Runion.

In a moment, a car rounded the near curve and rolled carefully into the parking area. Then two more arrived and found places.

Soon the two dirt-and-gravel lots were full, and more cars lined the roadsides.

The Silverado and Ram people bunched closer together, except for Rick Gentry, who remained apart.

Many of the workers present in the morning now returned with women and children. More arrived besides these and surrounded the group surrounding Dr. Baddour. One lanky, white-turbaned man passed through the throng around the roadside sign, the Ram, and the Silverado and disappeared into the building, leaving the double doors standing open.

"And just what's going on here?" Doris said. "What are all these people?"

"It is almost time for Asr," Dr. Baddour said. "Our late afternoon prayer." He smiled and looked around at the people gathered. "We will not always come at this time in such numbers, but it is our first day here as a congregation."

"Congregation, my foot!" Doris shrilled. "Congregations are for Christians."

Everybody turned to stare at her.

She clamped a tremulous right hand over her mouth for a moment and hugged her belly with her left arm. Then uncovered her mouth and again began tapping her collarbone with her fingertips.

"This looks more like one of them gang riots, amen," she said in a shaking voice.

"Good Lord, Doris," Rose said. "What's got into you?"

"What's got into you, Rose?" She let both arms fall to her sides, fists clenched.

Somewhere inside the building, a man began singing.

Molly's mother gasped and covered her mouth with her fingers, and Doris Johnson covered her ears with both hands.

"My God, what is that noise?" she bleated.

"Do not be ridiculous," Dr. Baddour snapped and stopped, then drew and released a quick breath. "This is our traditional call to prayer, and so, as we are also God-fearing people, we must go."

The recent arrivals, who'd been standing and listening and

glancing at each other, began to flow toward the open doors.

Rose and the second LeSabre woman turned away toward their vehicle.

"Look, y'all," Anderson said. "We're just here for our church, and it looks like all we got left of it is to make sure our crosses and such are handled proper." He rubbed his right cheek with the palm of his hand. "Everything looks on the up-and-up to me."

"There ain't no church without Pastor Donald," Campbell said and lipped another cigarette from his pack.

"No church without Pastor Donald," Doris said.

"Don't you mean no church without Jesus?" Rick Gentry said.

Doris looked directly at him for a moment and then at Dr. Baddour.

"No church without Pastor Donald," she said, spreading wide the fingers of both hands and dropping a balled-up tissue to the gravel.

Livvy suddenly stood up, and several of those across the road looked in her direction, as if the brightness of her had caught in the corners of their eyes. She stood staring back at them, and the surrounding woods seemed to go quiet.

"Livvy," Big Granny said.

The girl didn't turn. Her hair blew across her face, and her toes wriggled over the edge of the step.

"Livvy, darling," Big Granny said. "Just leave them be."

At this, Livvy turned—eyes narrowed, lips pressed together, chin jutted.

"It'll be all right, Livvy," Big Granny said. "Don't you get riled."

After a moment, the girl's face relaxed, and she turned and again sat down.

Dr. Baddour now stood loose-limbed and lanky, his smile once more the one bright spot in the center of the withering scene. He motioned the stonemason and the Nigerian twins toward the entrance, where they hovered, watchful, in the double doorway. Then he turned to Rick Gentry.

"Your Jesus, peace and blessings be upon him, brought beautiful messages of loving thy neighbor and welcoming the stranger."

"Pastor Donald preaches that means love thy American neighbor," Doris Johnson said, an edge of tears in her voice.

Andy Campbell drew on the last of his cigarette and nodded.

"And welcome the legal stranger," he said through smoke that blew from his mouth and nostrils.

"I am sorry for your loss and the pain you feel," Dr. Baddour said to Gentry. "You are welcome to this mosque at any time." Then his smile reappeared. "And I'm also accepting new patients."

With that, he turned, strode to the doorway as his friends went inside. He turned again, and, with the same smile as before at the old woman and girl across Lonesome Mountain Road, closed the doors.

Big Granny chuckled.

"Now that there's a man," she said. "I don't care what."

Livvy nodded but didn't turn.

The people in the parking area stood a few moments and stared at the closed doors, not even turning when the LeSabre, its tires grinding and popping across the gravel, backed out onto the blacktop and then sped toward Runion. The sound of it faded, leaving only the returning sounds of birds and bugs and the hum of indecipherable voices from inside the mosque.

"Well, if that don't beat all," Andy Campbell said.

Doris Johnson huffed.

"You gonna turn Arab now, Ricky?" she said and crossed her arms over her breasts.

"Muslim," Gentry said.

"What?"

"Never mind."

Johnny Anderson stepped around the front of the Silverado, opened the driver's door, and raised up on the step bar.

"Rick, let's go," he said. Then he turned back to the Ram people. "Y'all tell Donald that I'll have Dr. Baddour deliver the church's stuff to my house. He can come get it there if he's of a mind to." He started to duck down into the seat but popped back up. "You coming, Rick?"

"Yeah, I reckon," Gentry said. He turned toward the Silverado's passenger side but then kept turning until he'd circled to face the

Ram and Taurus people again. "No, wait now. What's the difference between me turning away from Jesus and going Muslim and y'all turning away from Jesus to worship the likes of Donald Roy?" He then turned again and opened the Silverado's front passenger door.

"Why, there's a world of—" Campbell started.

"Ain't no difference, Andy," Gentry said and stepped up into the truck. "No difference at all that I can see."

"Ricky Gentry, you're gonna burn in hell," Doris Johnson half shrieked and half cackled. "And I'm just gonna sit up there with Abraham and Lazarus and laugh my ass off."

"Watch your language, Sister Doris, there's people praying in yonder," Gentry said, dropped down into the shotgun seat, and shut the door.

When the Silverado had backed out of the lot and disappeared in the direction of Runion, the remaining members of Donald Roy's church stood quietly and seemed to look everywhere except at each other.

Finally, Doris Johnson stooped over, picked up a handful of gravel, and threw it at the closed doors of the mosque.

"Doris!" Molly's mother said.

The hum of voices from inside continued unbroken.

"Pastor Donald is gonna get an earful about these Arabs and Ricky Gentry," Doris said, her weak chin trembling her words.

Bruce Wallin awkwardly stooped and picked up Molly.

"Brother Campbell," he said. "Can you put give Sister Doris a ride back up the mountain?" He reached out a hand to his wife, and she dropped her ring of keys into it. "We're gonna get this little girl down to the river and try to do some fishing before it gets too dark."

\* \* \*

Big Granny and Livvy sat on the porch and watched the sky change as the sun set over the mountain behind them. They shared a love of the softly fading light and the gentle cooling of the day. The eastern sky had darkened enough to reveal its brightest stars but still remained light enough to silhouette the mountain ridges. The temperature had already dropped twenty degrees from its high, and both porch-sitters draped their shoulders with sweaters they'd brought out with them after supper.

"Did you like your fish?"

Livvy nodded.

"With all that talk about fishing this afternoon, I'm glad we had them that your uncle brought home over the weekend." She folded the overalls she'd finished with the last of the good light and laid them aside. "Too bad he didn't get none, but that's just his luck, I reckon."

Livvy nodded again. She huddled herself forward to warm her arms between chest and thighs. Then she was still, her head turtling up just over her knees to look across the road.

One lone security light, partially blocked by the high limbs of trees to the left, lit the silent and still mosque and parking area, washing out all the color of the building and sign and stone, the leaves of trees and grass.

The two people of the Ram had left only minutes after the Wallins left in the Taurus, and the congregants at the mosque then came out to find themselves alone on the property at last. They stood briefly and talked quietly together. And then they'd gone too.

"Livvy, it's going on 9:30, so let's go in and close up for the night." Big Granny picked up the folded overalls and held them in her lap again. "After you brush your teeth, you go on up and get in the bed. And be sure to pray that the meanness we seen over yonder today don't get in your dreams, or you'll shake the place off its foundation."

Livvy pulled her left arm from under her chest and extended it to point toward the darkening eastern horizon.

"What is it?"

The girl didn't raise up but pulled her right arm free, reached back, and beckoned Big Granny with three quick crooks of her index finger.

"Well, if I get down there, you'll likely have to help me get back up," Big Granny said with a grunt as she stood.

The girl again pointed at a spot on the horizon.

Once seated a step below Livvy, Big Granny lay her left forearm along the step behind the girl's back and leaned so that they were cheek to cheek. Before she tried to see what Livvy was showing her, she turned and tenderly kissed the girl's temple. Then she settled in again and looked.

The mosque's crescent moon rose just above the dark mountain ridges and hung silhouetted against the dusky blue heavens. It lay on its back above the skyline and seemed as if extending arms to reach for the zenith except that its points turned slightly towards each other. From the vantage point of the step-sitters, the moon's arms held a pulsing white star in their silhouette-black embrace.

"Well, ain't that something," Big Granny said, then turned to look in the girl's face. "Reckon what it might mean, Livvy?"

# The Invisible World around Them

Gene Fredericks sat up wide awake and sweating at 3:13. His wife Catherine—a furnace beside him under the sheet and comforter but not the larger cause of his sweating—lay still with her back to him, snoring lightly, undisturbed by his sudden rise out of sleep and then out of bed. He shaved and showered and dressed and drove to his Main Street office through patchy fog and muggy dark. This journey from bed to the Fredericks Agency sapped his energy but not his wakefulness, and he flopped like a wrung-out dishrag into a chair in the waiting room. From there he stared blankly through the large front window as Main Street transitioned from street light to twilight to morning light.

He thought of sissies, boys he remembered from elementary school, maybe fourth or fifth or sixth grade. They talked like the girls and hovered near the girls, joining in their gossip and tittering behind their hands like the girls, and didn't do any of the things the other boys did. They didn't play football in fall or basketball in winter or baseball in spring and summer. They didn't wrestle in the playground grass or cuss and fight behind the schoolhouse. They didn't ride bikes on the highway or walk along the railroad tracks or circle up in the woods to smoke menthol cigarettes stolen from their mothers' purses. As he remembered Frankie Wilson and Bruce Chandler in particular, he recalled how their girlish natures had puzzled him beyond words and how he'd joined with his friends in teasing and shunning them. But sissies were just sissies to his friends and him, and any sexual connotations or implications that might have swirled around their behavior were lost on grade-school boys.

Early-rising townsfolk began to pass along the sidewalk, crossing his field of vision framed by the window. Pam Thorn, the preacher's wife, jogged by. Sheldon Dean ambled in the direction of the Stonehouse Café. Ben Frisby pulled his pick-up to the opposite curb and sat waiting, his two grown sons in the seat beside him.

He thought of queers, who were different from sissies and came later. He remembered talk about these in high school. Although a sissy at Runion High might have been called a queer for playing clarinet or taking cosmetology, cooking or typing, that was just teenage meanness. Real queers were grown men of shadowy rumor, whiskered and feral. Real queers were monsters in the closet. They were supposed to drive the mountains in windowless vans or in pick-ups with nasty mattresses in the truck bed. They lurked in dark places—riverside picnic areas and dead-end dirt back roads—and whispered offers of beer and reefer to senior football stars and sophomore wrestlers, never revealing what they really wanted until it was too late to resist. They were ridiculed in daylight's bravado and feared at night. Still, while the sexual element attached to *queer* was threatening, it was but little understood by high school boys.

Daylight grew broader and bolder in the window frame, and in the businesses across the street—Whitson's Green Grocer and Fricker's Hardware & Appliances—front doors were unlocked and "Closed" signs turned to "Open." Ben Frisby went into Fricker's, and the son in the middle scooted over behind the wheel, dropped the pick-up into gear, and roared away.

To his knowledge, Gene hadn't met an actual homosexual until he was in his mid-thirties, when he met the Jacks. One Jack was the brother of Catherine's brother's ex-wife, and he and the other Jack had stopped in Runion once in the 1970s on their way from Michigan to Florida. Gene and Catherine had allowed them to set up their camper in the lower yard and stay the night there. That afternoon the Jacks had gone to Whitson's and returned with two bags of groceries that they used to make the most amazing meal Gene had ever eaten. Afterwards, they all sat on the porch until nearly eleven o'clock and talked and laughed under the yellow light bulb. Gene remembered feeling slightly sinful due to this proximity to sin, but he had a good time. The Jacks were sissies and queer, he knew, but not in a bad way. When they retired to their camper that night, he made love to Catherine—lights on—and tried to imagine the Jacks as being just men traveling together like Granger Gosnell and he were when they used to go on hunting trips to Maine or Montana.

But being gay was now the thing, as far as he could tell. Rock Hudson and Raymond Burr had turned up gay. So, he'd heard, had Jerry Smith and Glenn Burke. The Fredericks family had once laughed together at the fake gay gags in *Three's Company*. Last year Catherine and he chuckled by themselves at a new show called *Will & Grace*, in which the gays were supposed to be real, not just pretending in order to rent an apartment with female roommates. States from Massachusetts to Wisconsin to Arizona had put gay men in Congress. In some Christian congregations gays were strongly preached against, but others welcomed them with reluctantly open arms. Gays regularly held noisy parades of pride and protest in cities all across America, even up the river in Asheville.

But given the few sissies he'd grown up with, the widespread rumors of evil queers and the not-so-bad homosexuals like the Jacks, Gene had never known anybody living in Runion who was actually and openly gay. He knew some that other folks claimed were gay, but no one had ever confessed this about themselves. Certainly not to him. A few of the faculty at the college, he'd heard, were gay. But that was to be expected, as was the fact that they mostly lived in Asheville and weren't really part of Runion.

What had awakened him in the middle of the night and driven him from his house and into these thoughts of sissies and queers and gays was knowledge he still found difficult to believe and, so far, impossible to accept—that Runion's first gay son was his son. He'd learned this within half an hour of Mike's arrival at home the previous afternoon. His son's confession had ripped a hole in the fabric of Gene's life. But this was not all. When he'd seen Mike's car pull into the driveway unannounced, he thought his son had come home to celebrate his thirty-ninth birthday. But five minutes after learning that Mike was gay, Gene learned that he'd come home, not to celebrate his birthday or even to come out of the closet, but to die, and the fabric of his life was in that moment torn to shreds.

Everybody called him Mikey when he was growing up in Runion. A stout and sturdy lad from birth into his middle teens, he made good grades and stood out as catcher on his Little League team, the Runion Braves. He took karate and participated in 4-H and Boy Scouts. He sang well and often performed solos in Christmas and Easter musicals at the First Southern Missionary Church. And when he was eleven years old and the breakfast cereal called Life released a popular TV commercial featuring a little boy named Mikey, Runion's Mikey, his Mikey, displayed his seemingly endless good nature as he endured the trio of one-liners his classmates and the community adapted from the commercial and repeated over and over for years afterwards—"Let's get Mikey!" and "He won't eat it, he hates everything!" and "He likes it! Hey, Mikey!"

Taking after Catherine's father, he very early tinkered with musical instruments, particularly piano and guitar, and when this musical grandfather died in June 1973, a month before Mikey turned thirteen, he left the boy his fiddle. Later that summer, when the Little League season ended, and, with it, Mikey's last year before he was to be bumped up to the Babe Ruth League, he put down his mitt and picked up his inheritance. Within two years he was fronting his own trio at local events, and within two years more the trio was playing regionally on many weekends and much of the summer and Mikey won the junior division competition at Fiddler's Grove.

During these years the sturdy and stout boy he'd been trimmed down to a lean and muscled young man. He suffered braces on his teeth and traveled—first with his mother and then on his own—to Asheville every three weeks to have his hair cut in a salon there. He dated a series of beautiful girls from Runion High and other area high schools, seeing each for some three months at a time— fall, winter, spring—but always remaining without romantic entanglements for the three months of summer when the trio made most of its out-of-town trips.

Gene had always thought this was smart, but as he sat now in the waiting room thinking back on Mike's high school days and the beginning of his impressive accomplishments in music, he held the boy in his mind and compared him to the sissies he'd known in his own school days, looking for similarities. He looked for signs that Catherine and he might have missed. He saw neither similarities nor signs beyond the fact that Mike played music instead of football, but he believed that to be more his own prejudice than sign. And then he wondered if the bodybuilding and hair were signs and he'd been the only one to miss them. Maybe Catherine knew or suspected. When Mike's revelations of yesterday had ended and they learned they were losing their son to something they couldn't understand, Catherine and he hadn't found the heart to speak before bedtime. And when they found their bed together, still lost in separate experiences of their common pain, they were too dumbfounded and exhausted to talk.

He heard a key in the back door of the Fredericks Agency, and before he could stir himself out of his maze of thought, Hannah Henderson walked quickly down the hallway past his office door. He was trying to stand against the stiffness of his joints when she swept into the waiting room and, at the sight of him, gasped and stumbled back against the hallway door frame.

"Jesus, Gene," she said. "You scared the daylights out of me." She paused for a breath, a hand to her chest, as he finally got fully upright. "What're you doing sitting here with the lights off?"

"Sorry, girl," he said, pulling back his shoulders. "I was just watching the people go up and down the street."

"Watching the people," she said. She put her purse down on her desk and went to the front door. "Watching the people." She unlocked the door, turned over the "Open" sign and checked the thermostat. "See anybody interesting?"

"Not really," he said, rubbing the back of his neck. "Same ol', same ol'."

"Same ol', same ol'," she said. She took a hairbrush from her purse and stood in front of the waiting room mirror and touched up a head of layered hair that was just as big and golden as it had been when she was in high school with Mike in the late 1970s.

Gene watched her dumbly, thinking how she'd been one of the only girls Mike had gone steady with more than once. Although she'd married somebody else right out of high school, a marriage now over for several years, he felt sure that she hoped for another chance with his son. He once liked the idea, thrilled at the possibility that she could bring Mike home once and for all, and even though the same thrill shook him now, it lasted only a breath before it gave way to gut-wrenching emptiness.

"What?" she said, stopping in mid stroke and finger-flicking some loose hairs into the wastebasket by her desk.

His throat clenched, and he couldn't speak for a moment. He turned to the window and its view of the street. "Nothing," he managed at last and cleared his throat behind the word. He suddenly felt desperate to get out of the office. Hannah always knew when Mike was home, even though his trips these last years had been so short and so far between, and he was certain she knew now.

"What appointments have I got today?" he asked, hoping to distract her before she said anything about Mike.

"Let's see," she said and plopped into the chair behind her desk. "Looks like you've got that ten o'clock closing on the Simms house. Then you're having lunch with Granger and talking about his life insurance. And then—"

"Call Granger and tell him I'll just meet him at his place at one o'clock. I don't think I'll be up to eating lunch today."

"Well, all right," she said. "Are you feeling okay?"

"Yeah, I think something didn't agree with me yesterday, so I'm gonna go easy for a meal or two."

"I bet it's this heat."

"Probably." He started to turn toward the hallway and the back door but stopped. "Seems like there was something else."

"At two o'clock you're meeting Dr. Kincaid to go look at rental property. He's a new professor in the music department at the college."

"That's right," Fredericks said. "Did you print out that list of places I gave you?"

"Sure did," she said and handed him a manila folder. "I added a couple of listings that came in since you set up the meeting. And you might want to pick up a couple of bottles of water to share while y'all are riding around. It'll probably be hitting ninety degrees about then."

"Thanks, girl," he said. "You're a jewel." He started down the hall toward the back door. "I'll look these over and be back here by two."

"Oh—"

*Here it comes*, he thought.

"—when did Mike get in?"

He stood a moment with his hand on the handle of the back door.

"Late yesterday afternoon," he said at last.

"Home to celebrate his birthday?"

"Yeah, that's right," he said. "He's thirty-nine tomorrow."

"Well, tell him to call me."

"Sure," he said and escaped into the bright sunshine of the parking lot on Back Street.

\* \* \*

He was surprised when he knocked at the back door of Granger Gosnell's house and Granger's sister Ollie suddenly stood on the other side of the screen. He stepped backwards down the steps when she pushed the screen door open to let him in.

"Come in, Mr. Fredericks," she said and turned away into the kitchen.

He followed her, holding a hand behind his back to keep the screen door from slamming and noticing as she turned toward him again that she was several months pregnant.

"How are you, Ollie?" he said.

"Reckon you can see for yourself," she said and flourished her left hand over her swollen belly in the same way that the pretty women on game shows did to point out the prizes to be won. Her tight knit top concealed neither the belly nor the large breasts.

He noticed that her left hand bore no ring, but he wasn't sure that meant anything these days.

"Who's the lucky guy?" he asked.

"Ain't no lucky guy," she said. "I just call it immaculate conception and let well enough alone."

He didn't know how to respond to that, so he stood awkwardly before her, trying to remember how much older she was than Mike.

*Only a couple of years,* he thought. *Early forties.*

"You want to see Granger, I expect," she said, sounding already weary of his presence.

"How is he?"

"He's mighty poorly," she said. "When I started coming around to see him again back in the winter, he seemed like his old self. Maybe a little lighter. Then along about middle of April the cancer come back strong and been raging ever since." She cupped her left hand under her belly and grimaced slightly. "I'm afraid he won't see out the summer."

"I hate to hear that, Ollie," he said. "You know Granger and me been hunting and fishing buddies for many years."

"So I heard," she said and opened the refrigerator. "Would you like a drink of homemade iced water? I chilled it myself."

Again, he didn't know how to respond except to say "Sure" and then "Thanks" when she handed him the glass she poured.

*Yeah, about forty or so,* he thought again. He tried to remember stories he'd heard about Ollie Gosnell, stories Granger had told him on one or another of their expeditions, stories Catherine or Hannah had told him at home or office, stories he'd overheard on the street or in the grocery store. She lived alone, he seemed to remember, in a one-room cabin in a dark Laurel hollow near the Belva bridge. Some stories had her a recluse, leaving the cabin only in the darkest hours of the night to go "God-knows-where" and do "God-knows-what." Others had her a wild child who went on tour as concubine with some 1980s country-rock band, following them all over the world for years. He bit his lip when he remembered that he used to wonder if Mike had women like her following him around. Regardless of the truth, in any story he'd heard, except those Granger told, she was at least a drug addict if not a witch. He could remember the hurt in Granger's voice when he talked about her, the sense that the big man felt as if he'd broken a promise to his mother and failed Ollie.

She was on her tiptoes, looking for something in the freezer, and with her back bowed somewhat, the extent of her condition was easy to see.

Gene guessed that she was nearer her time than not, probably less than two months to go.

"How long since you seen Granger?" she asked as she shut the freezer and turned toward him with a box of frozen peas in her hand.

"Too long, I know," he said. "I think it might have been Easter."

"Well, you'd best prepare yourself for a shock, I reckon. He's lost a lot of weight and a lot of strength since then." She pointed toward a doorway. "He's in the front room, when you're ready."

Granger Gosnell sat in a wheelchair with his back to the doorway, his once powerful frame frail and silhouetted against the near side of the room's large picture window. Most of the rolling fields beyond the window was Gosnell land, and Gene knew that Granger must ache to be out there warring against half a summer's worth of overgrowth.

"Come," Granger said in a weak voice, motioning briefly with a hand toward a ladderback chair placed to his left.

Before moving to sit, Gene came forward to stand a moment beside Granger's wheelchair and take the sick man's large hand in his own. He felt a slight return pressure and release, then let go and sat down.

Ollie's warning had been understated.

Gene felt more than shock as he took in Granger's sallow-gray complexion and caved-in body. Actual pain closed his hands into fists, and an ache shuddered from his chest down into his groin. A stutter shook his breath, and his eyes dimmed for a moment.

"I'm right puny," Granger said in a hoarse voice, and although the old smile flashed briefly from his watery eyes, it wasn't strong enough to lift the corners of his mouth.

"It's all right, Granger," he said and wondered why he said it. *What the hell's all right about it?* he thought. A memory surfaced of a fishing trip to a remote lake in Canada, and he saw Granger in his mid-fifties. The two of them sat in a boat at the mouth of a cove, densely wooded shoreline and hills on three sides and a great expanse of glassy water at their backs. The fishing hadn't been good that day, but their beer had stayed cold in spite of the heat. When the mosquitoes suddenly got worse, Granger stood up and began shedding his shirt and shorts, and Gene remembered his friend somehow looking bigger naked than with his clothes on. They were drunk and laughing when Granger belly-flopped into the water at the side of the boat, and the echo of the smack came back from several different directions. Gene's head swam for a moment in an effort to connect that man, thick in thigh and belly and chest, with the man folded like a cardboard cutout into this wheelchair.

"I want you to do a couple of things for me," Granger said.

Gene listened to the ragged breaths, waiting.

"Anything I can do," he said after a moment.

"Two things," Granger said. "I want you to make sure that my life insurance is in order and that this place goes to Ollie, free and clear."

Gene processed this for a moment. He'd sold Granger and Carrie the life insurance policies over thirty years before and helped make sure all went smoothly when Carrie died in an automobile accident a few years later. He knew that the policy was in good order, with Ollie as beneficiary because Granger and Carrie had no children.

"I can vouch for the insurance," he said. "All that will go to Ollie. But the stuff about the farm needs a lawyer, I reckon, and a will." He stopped and turned to look out the window. "Is Ollie executor of your estate?"

"That's you, if you're willing," Granger said. "I set it up with Bob Robinson down at the courthouse back in the winter."

"I'll try to see him tomorrow," Gene said, feeling as if something was missing from their conversation.

"I reckon to get better when cooler weather comes," Granger said. "If I can just make it through August I might make it to another winter."

Gene didn't know how to respond to that either. He wondered if Mike's disease would reduce him to this or something like it, and he felt his throat close at the thought. He couldn't imagine, and as he pushed from his mind the shadowy image of Mike in a wheelchair by a window, he grabbed hold of what was missing here in this moment.

"What about Gunther?"

Granger sat and looked out the window, his eyes darting back and forth as if seeking something that he couldn't find.

"I ain't forgot about him," he said. "But I can't leave him nothing straight out, 'cause he wouldn't know what it was or what to do with it." He paused to breathe. "Ollie'll see he's taken care of."

Gene wished Carrie were still alive. She'd been a strong, level-headed woman, who kept Granger from going the ways of Gunther and Ollie. He had no doubt that if she were here she would see Granger and his brother and sister through what was coming. He wasn't sure that Ollie was up to the task of taking care of herself and her coming child, much less Gunther and the Gosnell farm. But Granger seemed as calm as if Carrie were with him, standing just behind the wheelchair and in control.

When Gene had assured his friend that he would take care of things with his insurance company and confer with the attorney, they sat quietly together looking out the picture window as if they'd made their casts and set their reels and now waited for that first thrilling tug from the invisible world around them.

\* \* \*

He returned to the office twenty minutes late for his two o'clock meeting and found Hannah at her desk and the clients in waiting room chairs, the three of them talking and laughing.

"Gene," Hannah said, "this is Dr. Jubal Kincaid, who's gonna start teaching flute at the college next month, and this one is Chuck Leggett. They're moving down here from Michigan."

Gene tried to shrug off the sadness of his son's homecoming and his meeting with Granger Gosnell and shook hands with each man in turn. They were much alike, he thought, both just under six feet tall and stocky, both with short-cropped hair and beards—Kincaid's salt-and-pepper, Leggett's ginger—and both in sandals, shorts and baggy shirts.

"Well," Gene said, "has culture shock set in?"

At the same time, Kincaid said, "No," and Leggett said, "Yes!"

"Where's your stuff?" Gene asked.

"It's parked at a motel in Mars Hill," Kincaid said. "We drove the car from there this morning and had lunch at the Stonehouse Café."

"Well, that's as good a place to start as any in Runion," Gene said. "But let's get to it. I've got a list of places picked out for us to look at. Any changes in your preferences since we talked last?"

"We're probably going to have just the one car," Kincaid said. "Chuck's died just before we left up north. Do you have any places that are close enough so that I can walk to campus?"

"There's two or three that might work," Gene said.

"Yeah, two or three that might work," Hannah said. "Gene, did you get some bottles of water?"

"That's it," he said. "I knew I was forgetting something."

"At least you still know when you're forgetting something," Hannah said. "There's some back in the fridge."

"She's a jewel," Gene said to Kincaid and Leggett.

As the three were stepping out the door to the parking lot on Back Street, Hannah called, "Gene?" from the front room.

"Excuse me," Gene said. "Mine's the dark green Explorer there. It's unlocked." He handed Kincaid the keys. "Go ahead and start it to get the AC going again."

Hannah craned her neck to be sure that the clients had stepped outside.

"They're queer," she said as she turned back around. "You sure you want to rent to them?" When Gene didn't respond, she added,

"You can't show them just any ol' place on your list."

"What do you mean?" Gene asked.

"What do I mean?" she said. "What do I mean?" She craned her neck to look down the hall toward the back door again and lowered her voice. "I mean there's some places around here that might be dangerous for them to live in. Runion don't know how to act around queers. And some folks around here might be scared of them."

"Why would you say that?"

"Well, first, there's just the fact that they ain't used to queers." She lowered her voice. "And then there's AIDS."

In his grief and confusion over his son's returning to die, he had yet to give much thought to how the community might react to Mike or how that reaction might affect his business in Runion. He'd seen newspaper stories and TV news segments about how communities in other places—Florida was one, he thought—had responded to the sudden presence of AIDS in their midst, and most times he hadn't blamed them for those responses, except when children were involved. He thought there had been a bombing in Florida related to school children with AIDS, but the kids were hemophiliacs and not gay.

"My first husband was queer," Hannah said. "We both found out about it too late." She paused for a moment. "Anyway, I've studied up on it a little bit, and I've got an eye for it now."

"I didn't know that about your ex," Gene said, wanting to add that she apparently hadn't seen it in Mike.

"There's not many that does know that," Hannah said. "I've known you well enough to tell you for a while, but the subject never came up. "

"All right, thanks," he said, not knowing what he was thanking her for. "I'll give some thought to the places I show them." He turned toward the hallway again but stopped. "Is that it?"

"Yeah, that's it," Hannah said. "Don't forget the water, and don't drink after them."

Outside, he found Kincaid and Leggett standing beside the Explorer. Something in the way they stood made him think they were arguing, and he wondered if they'd somehow heard Hannah call them queers.

"Ready to go?" he asked.

"Sure," Kincaid said. "Can we stop by our car out front? We need to get a couple of things out of there."

Gene drove to the end of Back Street, turned right on Mill and right again on Main. Then he pulled into a parking space just behind an old Honda Civic with Michigan plates.

"Actually," Kincaid said, "do you mind if we drive our car and just follow you? We need to get used to driving on these roads."

"Well," Gene said, wondering again if the two had overheard Hannah and were upset or if they needed to continue the argument they seemed to be having on Back Street. "You'll miss all the juicy details I like to pass on about the people and places we see, but sure, that'll be okay, I reckon."

The two got out of the Explorer and settled into the Civic, Kincaid driving.

Gene pulled up alongside and rolled down his window. Kincaid rolled his down as well.

"I'll take her slow," he said. "Here we go." He slipped his foot off the brake and slowly rolled up Main, making sure they were coming up behind him. Already in his rearview mirror, he could see them talking, but they didn't seem to be arguing at the moment. He accelerated slightly past the end of town and descended toward Big Laurel River. Just before the bridge, he turned right on Riverview Trail and followed it alongside the Big Laurel for a quarter of a mile to the first house he wanted them to see—a two-story, three-bedroom, two-and-a-half-bath place on a clean corner lot. He pulled up at the curb and turned off his engine, glancing at the rearview again as they parked behind him.

He walked them through the house—a living room, half bath, kitchen and master suite with full bath downstairs; two bedrooms and a full bath upstairs. The place sat nearly against the hillside that rose behind and looked across Riverview Trail to the Big Laurel. He could tell that the two of them liked this house, but he hadn't told them the rent yet and worried that, at just beyond their upper limit, it would be too much.

"This place is about a hundred dollars north of your price range," he said when they were outside by their vehicles again, "but you'll save some of that on gas." He pointed out the cross street that formed the corner lot. "You walk right up that hill to Lonesome Mountain Drive, and the main entrance to the college is just a couple hundred yards to your right. Downtown is just a little walk beyond that."

"It's cool inside," Leggett said. "Cool as in temperature, I mean."

"Well," Gene said, "it's an old house with thick walls, and here under the hill and the trees it stays shady most all the time."

"What about heating and cooling?" Kincaid said.

Gene shoved his hands into his back pockets and looked at the house.

"There's an oil furnace in the basement. No air-conditioning, but a couple of small window units, one downstairs and one up, ought to take care of that if you need it. But you notice that it's cool even in this heat."

"Wait, there's a basement?" Leggett said.

"You access it around the other side there. It's just dirt and the furnace down there, and some shelves for canned goods."

"Any water problems?" Kincaid asked.

"No, you'd think it might with all the shade and the hill in back, but the folks that built it did some wondrous job on the drainage. It stays pretty dry. And there's no mice and no snakes, and that's kind of unusual for a place this close to the river."

Kincaid opened the trunk of their car and removed a small case, a collapsible metal music stand and, after a moment of rummaging through a box, a piece of music.

"I need to play in there," he said. "You're welcome to come in, or we'll be right back out. This will just take a few minutes."

"I'll wait for you here," Gene said.

He stood by the open trunk and watched through the windows of the house as the pair moved from room to room. He heard a piece of music begin, the flute singing clearly for a few seconds.

Then a second piece of music. The two pieces were repeated as the two of them tried the various rooms, Kincaid playing and Leggett standing and looking out a window.

When they moved to one of the upstairs bedrooms, Gene lowered his gaze to the trunk of the car. It held a couple of boxes, one of which was filled with books of music and another filled with jumper cables and other pieces of hardware. Some magazines lay scattered around the trunk, apparently once in a pile but having now slid all over.

His eyes moved over these magazines without really seeing them at first. And then he began to notice details—the title *RFD*, dates that included seasons and years, colorful images on the covers. Some were drawings or paintings, and others were photographs. The title reminded him of farms and his mailing address when he was a child, but he could not reconcile that with the covers, which were strange in color and image, strange in some way he couldn't quite identify. A couple of them were paintings of dark-skinned men oddly drawn, with eyes and jungle images all around one and profuse vines and flowers wound around the other. One photograph portrayed a group of men somewhere in the woods, all in a circle, holding the edges of a kind of trampoline and tossing a shirtless man into the air. The image that held his attention longest depicted two angels all in white. One was young with dark hair and beard, and he was kneeling or sitting and holding in his arms an old angel, bald with a white beard, who appeared to be dying in the shelter of the younger one's outspread wings. Beneath the picture were printed the words, "The 25th Year: A Celebration of Our Elders."

He heard the flute play again somewhere in the house and stop and one of his clients laughing, but he did not look up from the trunk.

Then he realized what it was about the covers that he could not identify before. All the images were of men, no women or children. And then he began to see other details emerge from the pictures—a naked butt among the men around the trampoline, a drawing of an uncircumcised penis clearly visible among the flowers and vines.

He reached into the trunk and picked up the magazine with the angels on the cover. He looked more closely at the image for a moment and then began to leaf through the pages.

"I hope that's not a problem," Kincaid said as he and Leggett suddenly appeared standing in the road beside their car.

"What?" Gene said, awkwardly slapping the magazine closed.

Kincaid stepped forward and lay his music stand in the trunk. "Is it a problem that we're gay?" he said. "Because we really like this house."

"This is a magazine for queers?" Gene said and stopped. "For gays, I mean."

"It is," Kincaid said. "I hope that's not a problem."

Gene looked down at the magazine in his hand and then gently laid it in the trunk among the rest. He scanned the covers spread before him again and tried to make connections between his Mike and these covers—Mike as the man in the air above the trampoline, as the handsome young angel, as the withered and dying angel. His vision blurred for a moment, and he blinked it clear.

"Mr. Fredericks?" Kincaid said.

"Hmm?" Gene said, turning to the two of them standing there in front of him.

"This won't keep us from renting the house, will it?"

"No, I don't think so. No. It'll be all right." He looked back down at the magazines and then at the house again. "It'll be all right."

"I know we shouldn't take the first thing we see," Kincaid said, "but we're going to anyway if you can work it out for us."

"Well, the owners live in California, so I have say as to who rents. I'll just tell them you teach at the college. That should be enough to vouch for you." He paused to recall what he should say. "Take the weekend to think about it. If you're still sure on Monday, you can just come by the office sometime and we'll take care of the paperwork. It'll be all right."

He could forego his fee for managing this place in order to drop the figure nearer to what these men felt comfortable paying. As proctor for the absentee landlords, he could insert himself into these men's lives with the hope of learning more about them and, at the same time, perhaps learning more about his son. Maybe he could find out why Mike was dying and they weren't. Maybe he could learn from them about what Mike would face, figuring that they'd done some research on a subject so close to them—maybe they'd even had friends die in the same way. He could introduce Mike to Dr. Kincaid, and maybe they could become friends and talk about being musicians and being gay and being sick.

"It'll be all right," he said again and then paused, cleared his throat and looked toward the house. "My son is gay."

\* \* \*

He noticed the quiet as soon as he was in the back door of the Fredericks Agency. Hannah's car was in the parking lot, so he thought she must be running an errand up or down Main Street. But as he walked down the hallway he could feel her presence, and when he stepped into the front room he found her at her desk, bent over with her forehead on the desk blotter, her shoulders shaking with quiet sobs. He stood a moment beside the desk and looked through the front window at the sunny street, the shadows different from this morning, and the Runion folk moving slowly in the late afternoon heat.

"Hannah, what's wrong?" he said at last.

She didn't respond.

"Are you okay, girl?" He knew that was a stupid question, but his mind was running on limited resources. And he felt he already knew why she was crying.

"Hannah—"

"It's too late!" she said, jerking herself upright so violently that he took a step backwards.

"Too late for what?"

She snuffled hard and then covered her face with her hands.

"Oh, Gene, I'm so sorry," she said. "Too late to turn Mike. I could have turned him if he'd given me the chance. I know I could."

He didn't know if that was true or not. He doubted it, given that she hadn't turned her first husband. He'd never given homosexuality much thought before yesterday. He knew his heart would explode if it turned out to be true, that somebody could have done something or said something to make Mike normal and healthy.

"You go on home now, girl," he said. "Try to have yourself a good weekend."

She yanked up a tissue and blew her nose, and before she could say anything else, he stepped into his office and closed the door.

He sat at his desk and listened while Hannah shut down her computer, locked the front door, blew her nose again, got her things together, and finally left through the back. When all was quiet he turned to his computer, logged in and opened up the Internet. He searched for *RFD*, and in a few minutes he had a telephone number. He dialed it twice and hung up both times before anybody answered. The third time he made himself stay on the line. He stammered and cleared his throat and stammered some more until he finally got subscription information for a year. Then, after he gave his credit card number, he froze when the woman on the other end of the line asked him for a delivery address.

*Can't have it sent to the house*, he thought. The idea struck him that he could hang up and next week rent a PO box in Weaverville or Asheville. But the news about Mike wouldn't be kept secret, especially now that Hannah knew. *She won't tell many people, but them she tells will tell many people.*

"Your issues will arrive in a plain brown wrapper," the woman at *RFD* said. "If that helps."

"Okay," Gene said. When the next moment of panic subsided, he cleared his throat and gave her his business address. "I can explain it to Hannah," he said.

"Excuse me?" the woman said.

"Sorry, ma'am," he said. "I'm just talking to myself."

"That's okay, sir," she said. "I hear that a lot."

\*   \*   \*

Catherine would have supper on the table in a few minutes, but he didn't feel like going home. He wanted to collapse into the waiting room chair again and watch daylight fade to dark. And yet he knew he must go home and begin learning to live with what awaited him there. Tomorrow he might know better how to begin taking the difficult steps forward. But on second thought that seemed unlikely. Tomorrow was Mike's thirty-ninth birthday, and he might not see forty.

When he pulled in the driveway, he saw his son sitting in a rocker on the porch, waiting for him like he did when he was a young boy. For the first time, Gene sobbed aloud, one outburst that escaped before he could choke it down as he had all those before it. He rolled to a stop and sat for a few moments, breathing heavily and loudly through his nose and pretending to be gathering important stuff from the passenger seat and floorboard, as if he would bring it in the house. But when he got out of the Explorer, he left the neat pile of pads and pens and property detail sheets in the passenger seat, locked the doors and walked up the yard.

"Supper about ready?" he said as he arrived at the top of the porch steps.

"It's ready," Mike said.

"What did Mama fix?" Gene asked as he eased himself down into the other rocker.

"Mama's gone to bed with a headache."

"Well, she shouldn't have cooked anything if she was feeling bad."

"She didn't," Mike said. "I cooked for us."

The queer Jacks flashed through Gene's mind, followed closely by a vague uneasiness with the idea of eating something prepared by a sick man. His gaze dropped to Mike's hands. They hung still as stone off the ends of the rocker's armrests.

"It's okay," Mike said. "I wore gloves."

"What?" Gene said, his gaze returning to his son's lean face. "What did you fix?"

"I fired up the grill and did some fish in foil pouches with cherry tomatoes, some pesto and some other stuff. And I grilled some corn on the cob."

"Sounds good, fancy," Gene said and rocked up to his feet. "I'd better check on your mama and then wash up."

"How's Hannah?" Mike asked.

"Hmm?"

"When I went to Whitson's I stopped by your office, and I told her."

Gene sat back down and leaned forward with his elbows on his thighs and his hands clasped together between his knees. "She was crying pretty hard when I got back," he said. "I sent her home."

Mike's only response was to fold his arms across his chest and turn his eyes to the wooded slopes on the opposite side of Baylor Run Road.

Gene followed his son's thousand-yard stare and let his own gaze move slowly over the rounded hills and the trees slightly sharpening in look and color now that the mountain evening was taking the edge off the heat. He wondered what moved or sat still in that canopy or beneath it—birds of many kinds and sizes, squirrels, deer, maybe even coyote or bear or bobcat. He thought of them there like fish unseen in the murky depths of a mountain lake.

"Dad," Mike said. "I am so sorry about this." His voice sounded tight and shook through the long vowels with audible sorrow. "Maybe I shouldn't have come back."

Gene wasn't sure how to respond to that, but he knew that he couldn't sit quiet.

"Of course you should've come home, son," he said. Then before he could think better of it, he added, "You should've come home a long time ago."

Mike closed his eyes and drew a deep breath, but he didn't say anything.

"You should've never left," Gene said and felt himself on the verge of losing control, on the verge of a pointless lecture to a grown son. He drew a deep breath as well, closed his eyes and pressed a palm to his forehead. "I'm sorry," he said.

"Don't be."

They sat rocking almost imperceptibly, their eyes open again and staring again at the hillside and the sky across the road.

"Sometime when this isn't so raw," Mike said, "I'll tell you and

Mama about it." He stopped for a moment. Then, "About my life. If you want to know."

Gene wanted to know but didn't want to hear. Maybe Mike was right, he thought. Later the hearing might be bearable.

"It's your birthday tomorrow," Gene said. "Is there anything you want?"

"I've actually thought about that today, and if you're not working, I'd like for you and me and Mama to go driving in the mountains for the day. Maybe take a picnic to eat somewhere."

"We can do that," Gene said. "Let's hope Mama feels better."

They rose to their feet together and turned toward the door.

"I better check on her," Gene said. "I left before she was awake this morning."

"I'll get the table set," Mike said. "Tea to drink?"

"Tea will be fine," Gene said and followed his son into the coolness of the house.

* * *

Sometime in the night—he didn't turn to look at the clock—Gene awoke to find himself still lying on his back, his fingers laced together behind his head. He lay naked beneath only a sheet that covered his right leg, his groin, and belly. He felt the chill of the air conditioning on his exposed skin and thought that must have awakened him.

Catherine had joined Mike and him later in the evening. Her headache was almost gone, but it had taken a lot out of her, leaving dark rings under eyes red from obvious tears that none of them mentioned. The idea of the birthday drive pleased her, so she'd gone back to bed with plans to get up early and prepare the picnic lunch. Now she lay asleep beside him, curled and lightly snoring beneath the mounded comforter, the edges of which he gently picked and pulled at until he had enough of its fluffy softness, warmed by her body heat, to cover himself.

He lay in the dark, his head turned toward a window that framed a handful of stars hanging above the hills between their home and Runion. He listened to Catherine breathe, to the breathy whir of the ceiling fan, to the almost imperceptible hum of the air conditioner. His own breath was shallow and trembled in his chest as it rose and fell. Beneath his breath, he felt his heart beat, something he couldn't recall noticing before. His breath sharpened with an edge of fear, and the movement of his heart quickened. Without forethought or warning, he drew a sudden deep breath like a man just breaking the surface of some body of water, and as he exhaled, he calmed. And as he calmed, he turned his thoughts away from breath and blood to think about the plan for his son's birthday.

They'd begin by taking Lonesome Mountain Drive into Laurel. From there they would travel the mountain road over into Tennessee—to Flag Pond, Erwin, Unicoi, Johnson City, Elizabethton. Then 19E to the village of Roan Mountain and 143 up and up to the mountain itself. They'd picnic there, on the bald if Mike felt like walking. After lunch they'd drop back down the North Carolina side into Glen Ayre and Bakersville, then to Spruce Pine, Burnsville, Mars Hill, Marshall, Jewel Hill, and Runion.

Just as he brought them home in his mind, he heard Mike's fiddle. He couldn't tell where it came from—the boy's old room, the kitchen table, the front porch, maybe the yard or the edge of the woods. He didn't know the tune, but it was slow and sweet and clear, to be hushed as it was. He listened sleepily to the melody pushing against the quiet night like light pushing against darkness, like life pushing against the horrors of blood and body. Tears stung and then warmed his eyes. The music swirled around him like wind, lifted him, carried him down Baylor Run and through the night-lit and deserted streets of Runion. He floated on it across the dark French Broad River and passed through the murky woods up and up the far mountainside toward Piney Ridge. Invisible to all the sleeping world, an owl watched him pass by, and a fox, weaving its way through the underbrush, stopped in mid stride and lifted its head to sniff the night. The wave of music paused when it reached the churchyard behind Piney Ridge Holiness Tabernacle. There it became a swirl of rich red light and ebbed among the headstones until it lingered and steadily pulsed above the graves of Catherine's parents. Then like the sudden passion of anger or love it rose and carried him through the star-dusted night sky to Granger Gosnell's place, where it calmed again and swirled and slowly wrapped itself around the house. He saw Granger still sitting in the wheelchair at the window, his head leaned back on a pillow, his mouth open for ragged breaths, and Ollie at the table in the brightly lit kitchen, a book in front of her and one hand laid flat on her belly. In the space of a heartbeat, he found himself back on the Runion side of the river, where the light hovered, curious, around the empty house on Riverview Trail that still echoed with a kindred spirit. A magenta tone pulsed steadily at its heart in the moment before the light rose again, like flame bursting through the roof of a burning house, rising above the silver and dark campus and town, above ancient, haze-shawled Lonesome Mountain, finally leaving Gene Fredericks floating helplessly in its black wake, until he lost sight of that light in the roseate brilliance of a yet distant morning.

# Grist for the Mill

I'll bet you yonder man's part of that Witness Protection Plan the government runs, you know?" Pearl shot a sidelong glance at Nell and Betty as the three sat drinking iced tea on Nell's front porch. "I seen a TV movie on it last night."

"Oh, I watched that too," Nell said in her quiet, short-of-breath voice. "But I fell asleep before the end."

Pearl put a hand to the ropy flesh at her throat.

"Well, I'll tell you what happened. The crooks found out where the government hid that Londono fellow. Some of them hit men come to get him and shot the neighborhood up good. But he got away with that school teacher he got sweet on, and at the end they was on the run from the government and the crooks, too."

The porch slowly filled with heat, and each woman fanned herself with a different section of the *Runion Record*.

Two houses up and across Mill Street, the subject of their morning's conversation walked stoically back and forth, mowing his yard in the midday heat of a Wednesday in the gut of August.

Pearl sipped her tea and narrowed her eyes.

"I reckon that there fellow must've been some gangster or drug dealer, you know?"

"Why," Betty said, "he don't look like either one to me."

The other two looked at her.

"I mean, good Lord, he's almost y'all's age." At forty-eight Betty was twenty years younger than either of her friends. "And besides, he don't look like a foreigner, and Sanders don't sound like any gangster name I ever heard of. And if you two weren't

afraid to get up close, you'd see he's a nice looking man, too." She
stopped and took a quick swallow of tea.

Pearl heaved a heavy, impatient sigh and turned her gaze back
up the street to where Carl Sanders continued mowing.

"Honey, they change the name, you know? What kind of
protection would it be if they didn't change the name? His name
could be anything. And almost anybody looks American these
days." She sloshed the ice in her glass. "You know, Betty, that
house was up for sale near two year, and hardly nobody never
looked at it." She took another sip of tea. "I was ready to buy it
so's I could rent it out to somebody nice when all of a sudden
like he's moving in. Burns me up, you know? He oughtn't have
been allowed." She fanned herself harder with her section of the
weekly—mostly obituaries and legal notices.

"Well," Nell said, "the other morning, Ruthie came by to take
me to the doctor, and when we crossed the bridge over the Big
Laurel—going toward Hot Springs, of course—that man was
standing there in the fog. Ruthie was driving and didn't notice him
much more than to make sure she didn't hit him, but there he
stood in that leather jacket he wears, with a foot on the railing and
smoking a cigarette and staring down at the water." She stopped
and reached for the beaded pitcher. "More tea?"

When the glasses were refilled and already sweating again in the
humidity, all three women sipped and fanned.

"You remember how glad we were the day the Tweeds moved
out of that house?" Nell said. "So much yelling and loud music
and ball playing. I swear I don't know what gets into people."

"Who'd've knowed then that we'd end up with a hardened
criminal in place of that bunch?" Pearl said. "At least with them
Tweeds, we never had to worry about a shoot-out giving us all the
heart attack in the middle of the night. Why, I believe I'd rather
have all that fuss going on than—"

Betty was about to stand up and scream the Ninth
Commandment at Pearl when Mill Street suddenly fell quiet.
Deathly quiet. As if all sound had gone out of the world. She
could feel the pressure of the quiet on her ears, and it seemed to

steal her breath for a moment.

But then, as if from far away, Nell's canary whistled through the open living room window, and slowly the neighborhood seemed to come to life again as the pressing quiet slowly released her. The sprinklers hissed in Mr. Tipton's yard next door. A telephone rang at either the Nortons' or the Goforths' house across the street. Pearl breathed with a wheeze.

Betty discovered the mock silence had come when Sanders cut off his mower, and the absence of its roar hushed the two women on the porch with her.

The three watched the shirtless man push the silent mower across the yard, pick up the gas can sitting on the walk, and head for the rear of the house.

Just as he stepped out of sight, the sound of a motor revving made Pearl and Nell and Betty look left toward town. A long black sedan pulled out of Back Street and started up Mill. It rolled slowly past Pearl's house and then crawled past Nell's porch. The three women fell open-mouthed-speechless at their own reflections in the darkly tinted windows gliding by. It rolled slowly past Mr. Tipton's, where a quick shot of water from the poorly placed sprinkler danced on its shiny darkness with a sound like a distant toy machine gun. The car swayed toward the left-hand side of the street, slowed when it reached the front of Sanders's property, then inched along the entire length of the chain link fence that separated yard from sidewalk. At the end of the lot, the lightless apparition pulled to the curb and stopped, silently blocking the driveway.

"My God, it's them," Pearl whispered.

Betty heard the whir of a small motor. Then she saw Sanders come around the near back corner of his house with a weed trimmer and begin to clean along the foundation under his bedroom window, working toward the front of the house.

She suddenly thought the noise might wake George, who was still sleeping off his graveyard watch at Haywood Milling Company. The bedroom of their house was just across a strip of lawn divided by another stretch of chain link fence, within twenty feet of Sanders and his buzzing weed trimmer. She pictured

George's eyes snapping open, his lips immediately bunching and paling with anger, his puffy face reddening. Then she realized the air-conditioner in their bedroom window was set on high, and George wouldn't hear a thing.

She turned her attention back to Carl Sanders and saw that by the time he got to the section under the den he would be in full view of the watchers waiting in that car. She wanted to run toward him, screaming and waving her arms. But she sat like Pearl and Nell—frozen.

Just at the moment she dreaded but felt powerless to stop—Sanders trimming serenely under the den window, out in the open and unprotected—the black sedan lurched forward with a squeal of rubber and quickly disappeared around the elbow curve that marked the end of the neighborhood.

\* \* \*

Later, in the sweating darkness, Pearl lay listening for the gunplay she was sure would eventually begin at the old Tweed place and spread from house to house until it reached her room.

*Betty'll see one of these nights.*

She suddenly missed Bill, missed the restless heaviness of him that had for almost two decades driven her crazy and made her slap him in his sleep. Whenever she worked herself into such tense moments, she wished she hadn't run him off all those years ago.

In the living room next door, Nell sat asleep in Don's recliner. She still had her own on the other side of the telephone table, but she felt closer to him in his. The snowy blur of Channel 13 reflected off her glasses, and its dead-air hiss filled the room. Her knitting lay in her lap. The muscles in her neck and legs and fingers twitched from time to time as she dreamed that Don stood on the porch, wearing a leather jacket and banging on the storm door with the butt of a pistol.

One house up and across the street, Betty shuddered and gasped under the warm weight and gentle thrust of Carl Sanders.

\* \* \*

Betty's husband, George Oakley, worked as the night watchman at Haywood Milling Company, thirty-five miles away in Asheville. He had been with the mill forty years, spending the first fifteen slowly working his way up to the next fifteen that he spent as manager of the eleven-to-seven graveyard shift. Then, ten years ago, cutbacks had to be made, and his shift became the first thing to go. The company offered him a position as night watchman, and, considering his pension there and his prospects elsewhere, he accepted. He was given five roomy uniforms and a gun. As the years passed, constant cleaning kept the gun looking new, but he and the uniforms slowly fell apart.

Betty did what she could for him. She cooked and mended. She watched as the belt of his pants—carrying the holster and the heavy gun that as far as she knew had never been fired—sank lower and lower, and she replaced all the buttons that popped off as his belly grew big and round with the inactivity of sitting all night, coming home and eating, and going straight to bed.

She'd been seventeen when she met him. He was thirty-two. She worked that summer in the concession booth at Stackhouse Park. George captained the First Southern Missionary Church's softball team. It was 1968, and most of the boys Betty had dreamed of marrying had either married somebody else or gone to Vietnam. George was a live wire on the softball field and everywhere else around the park. He was slim then, slim and tan and handsome, always in jeans and a tight, white, sleeveless t-shirt.

At some point, he started talking to her between games. Then between innings. Soon he was waving to her from his position at second base and winking at her when he walked up to bat.

She had plans to go to college in the fall, but that summer she fell in love with George and forgot them.

Now he'd become a quiet man. The only time she heard much out of him was when he watched sports. With an arsenal of remote controls—one for the VCR, one for the television, and one for the satellite dish—he would lie on the couch in his underwear, watching every sports program he could find, drinking glass after glass of the pineapple juice he thought would help him lose weight. He watched baseball, football, and basketball in season. He watched golf, racing, tennis, and boxing. Every Saturday he watched, between these other sports, countless wrestling shows from all over the world. When his man or his team was winning, George would suddenly bolt upright and say, "Godamighty! Did you see that?" But not to Betty, just to himself. When things went badly for his favorites, he would pick up the heavy wooden magazine rack sitting at the end of his couch and pound it on the floor. "Godamighty damn!" Then he would stomp off to the kitchen for more juice. The only sport he watched in peace, besides golf perhaps, was fishing. Sundays Betty would come home from church and find him up, sleepily watching some country boy's fishing lesson to pass the time until baseball or football or basketball came on.

* * *

She awoke with a start when George was suddenly standing over her. She glanced at his side of the bed. The pillow was empty and smooth with no depression or telltale hairs, and the covers were pulled up as if her solitary sleep were all that had disturbed them. She drew a deep breath and squinted against the early light that fell in lines through the blinds. This grillwork of brightness and shadow spread across the bed and rose to bend around George's thighs and straining zipper, his pistol and that belly. Beyond the dust-bright shafts George's face hung dark and unreadable.

"Are you home early?" she asked, the words rounded by a yawn and strained by stretching.

"Why, hell no." George's face bent into the bars of light and came alive with anger. "Godamighty, woman, it's damn eight o'clock already. I need my breakfast and my bed."

"Oh!" Betty threw off the covers and swung her feet quickly to the floor. But then her momentum faltered, and she sat frozen on the bed's edge.

She was naked.

The air in the room tensed and locked like a muscle cramping.

She sat with her back toward him, her face in her hands, peeping down through her fingers at her body. Although George didn't say anything, she could feel his angry eyes on her.

"It was so hot last night," she said at last. "Don't you think it was awfully hot?" Answered with silence, she tried to divert his attention. "Oh, George, I am so sorry. I must've stayed up way too late." She jumped to her feet and slung on her robe. "What do you wan—"

"Biscuits and gravy, tenderloin, eggs, coffee, and pineapple juice."

Two minutes later, she had the coffee perking, juice and a glass waiting on the counter, and tenderloin thawing in the microwave. She stood over her end of the tabletop and mixed flour with butter and milk for the biscuits.

George, already stripped to his underwear, leaned against the frame of the door leading from the kitchen to the living room, now watching Betty work, now watching a satellite sports channel.

She strewed more flour over the tabletop.

"Was everything quiet at the mill last night?" she asked without looking up as she dumped the lump of biscuit dough onto the floured surface.

"Yeah, maybe too quiet, I reckon," he said.

"What do you mean by that?" She looked up at him now but didn't stop working the dough with the rolling pin.

"Something's going on down there." He walked to his end of the table and sat down, leaving the television blaring baseball scores from the night before and the schedule of upcoming games.

Betty finished cutting the biscuits and put them in the oven. She filled two cups with coffee and gave one to George. Then she took the thawed tenderloin from the microwave and dropped it into the waiting frying pan.

The first loud sizzling and popping subsided to a bubbling hiss of hot grease. The yellow and white kitchen began to fill with the blended aroma of coffee, frying tenderloin, and baking biscuits.

She stood quiet and let the food ready itself a little without her help. Staring out the window into the back yard, she wondered if Carl was awake yet. He'd fallen asleep with her, she knew that much. She remembered looking at the clock at a quarter past five, and he was still there, breathing heavily beside her. She'd set the alarm for half past six, but either he turned it off or she didn't hear it. She shuddered, picturing him slipping out the back just as George barged in the front. Suddenly her attention snapped back to the last words George had said.

"Something like what?"

"What?"

"You said, 'Something's going on down there.' Something like what?"

"Oh hell, I don't know. There was just a strange feeling about the place. Offices locked that usually ain't. Lights left on in the storage rooms. Some of the machinery looked like it hadn't been used much yesterday."

"Are there a lot of folks on vacation or something?"

"Damn if I know. I don't see nobody no more except for the cleaners and a few of the early-shift boys."

When the tenderloin and biscuits and gravy were ready, Betty fixed George's plate and set it in front of him, refilled his coffee and juice, and told him she was going to dress and go for a walk.

\* \* \*

Forty-five minutes later she returned to the house to find the bedroom door shut and the television still blaring. On the end table beside the couch sat an open box of cereal and half a bowl of yellowed milk. She went into the kitchen and found George's breakfast plate sitting just as she'd served it to him, except that now two raw eggs lay broken in the middle of it.

*Oh my Lord,* she thought. *I forgot his eggs.*

With guilt weighing on her as palpably as Carl's tanned body had in the sweltering middle of the night, she released a tremulous sigh and washed the dishes.

\* \* \*

"I wonder where Betty is," Nell said. "I saw her out walking earlier."

"Well," Pearl said, "if she comes by, I hope she's not near jumpy as she was yesterday."

"Yes, she did seem on edge, didn't she?" Nell sipped her iced tea and nibbled on a saltine cracker. "Actually, I feel a little jittery myself this morning after the way I dreamed last night. Such crazy dreams of Don and guns."

"I tell you, it's that Sanders fellow doing that to us. I thought of Bill last night for the first time in I don't know when. I reckon I just wanted somebody there with me. Just in case something was to happen, you know?"

"Oh, imagine how Betty must feel, living right next door to the man. And George always gone or sleeping." She reached and touched Pearl's forearm with the cool dry fingers of her left hand. "Pearl, I think if she doesn't make it over this morning, I'll go over there later and tell her that she can stay the night at my house anytime she wants to."

"I was thinking the same thing." Pearl looked up the street through the slow motion of Nell's newspaper fan. "You seen Sanders today?"

"Oh, that's what I was sitting here trying to remember to tell you," Nell said. "I fell asleep in my chair last night and didn't wake up until a little before six this morning." She quieted her voice and leaned toward Pearl. "Well. I stepped out on the porch to get some of the cool air and pick up the Asheville paper, and I saw that man come out to get his own paper."

"Gets up early, does he?"

"I suppose so, but there was something that struck me as mighty odd."

"For heaven's sake, Nell, spit it out."

"Well, when I saw him it was still pretty dark, and he was coming from out back of his place. He walked right up between Betty's house and his. He just had his pants on, but he was carrying his shirt and shoes. Then after he got his paper, he went back in the front door. Don't you think that's odd?"

Pearl took a long sip of tea and didn't answer.

\* \* \*

When the plates and cups and pans were stacked in the drainer and covered with a clean cloth, Betty sat down at the table instead of going across Mill Street to Nell's. She thought she'd better stay home until she felt less shaky. She sat as still as she could and avoided looking toward her laundry room window and the view it offered of Carl's house.

Under the influence of Pearl's anger and fear, she'd watched him from the day he moved in. She watched for the first morning movements beyond the gossamer curtains of his bedroom. She watched him throw back his head and laugh at the television late at night. He was a tall man, easily over six feet, she guessed. He was not thin, but he carried his weight as if comfortable with it. Not like George, whose heaviness looked abnormal, suffocating. And George was so pale. Carl worked outdoors a lot, wearing only a baseball cap and cutoff jeans. His skin was so deeply tanned she thought his hair was snow white until the day she saw him wearing a white cap and knew his hair was a light gray. He wore one thick gold chain around his neck and no rings.

Something struck her as strange about him, although she could not put her finger on it for a long time. One day she watched him go from room to room in his house while she stood in the kitchen and talked to Nell on the telephone. They were in the middle of planning for the church bake sale when it hit her. The strange thing about Carl Sanders was that he never talked on the telephone. In the six weeks since he'd moved in, she never heard or saw him say one word to anybody over the telephone. She never heard his telephone ring, even though it had been a hot summer and the windows in both her house and his were open day and night. Knowing how talk with her friends helped fill her life, she was overwhelmed with a sudden sense of how lonely he must be. She couldn't answer when Nell asked why she was crying.

She shook her head and tried to think of George—of the day they bought this house and the first feast she prepared in it; of visits to Shiloh and Appomattox and Kitty Hawk; of drives to Atlanta once or twice every summer to watch the Braves play a Sunday doubleheader; of Saturday nights at ringside in Asheville, watching

Johnny Weaver wrestle; of Friday mornings she remembered when George would come home from the mill and wake her with kisses and caresses and make love to her before he slid his folded paycheck between her breasts and fell asleep. But these few thoughts still held him young—the wiry, smiling softball captain of those summer days in Stackhouse Park.

"What are you going to do now, Betty Boop?" she said and stood up.

The morning's cooking, badly as it turned out, had put her in the mood for more. She'd always loved to cook, and she was good at it. And once she got started, it always took her mind away.

"A feast for one for lunch," she said.

She decided on chicken cordon bleu, scalloped potatoes, fresh green beans, and homemade bread with garlic butter. It would be only for herself, but she would make enough for two. George could have the leftovers if he wanted.

In the garden the dew was quickly drying in the hot morning sun. She passed through the three short rows of late beans, pulling from the vines only those that seemed at that moment perfect and dropping them into the large pockets of her red apron. She stopped every few steps and stood breathing, smelling the dry clodded dirt beneath her feet, the ripe green tangle of the garden, and the fresh clipped grass of Carl's yard.

"Good morning," he called from behind her.

She turned and smiled.

"Good morning, yourself," she said.

"That garden looks awfully healthy for this hot weather," he said.

Their conversation across the fence was as simple and neighborly and innocent as the first time they'd spoken almost three weeks before. That day, too, they'd talked about the garden and the heat. That night, after she'd taken the supper leftovers out to her little compost heap at the end of the bean rows, she left on the light that lit the back of the house. And Carl had knocked on the back door nearly at the same moment George left the driveway on his way to work. They didn't seek her bed that night, nor any night over the next three before the weekend. They sat at opposite ends of the kitchen table and drank coffee and talked until after two o'clock in the morning—not about themselves, but just about the day as some couples do in the evening. It was the next week, after George's Saturday and Sunday on the couch with the television blaring, that her neighbor had come back, had moved his chair around to the corner of the table, had sat at her elbow.

Now, for the first time, he came in daylight, just as she laid two place settings for the feast that had changed from hers to theirs.

"You're sure it's all right?" he said as he set down the pitcher of tea she'd asked him to get from the refrigerator.

"Yes," she said. "It's all right. He has the air conditioner going full blast in there. He doesn't even get up to go to the bathroom." She smiled and sat down in her place. "He has a jar by the bed, and all he does is roll over to the edge to do his business."

"He must be accurate."

Betty laughed.

"No, he's not that accurate, not now nor even when he used the toilet. He picks up the jar and holds it to himself."

Carl seemed to think about that a moment, and then he pulled out the chair at the opposite end of the table and sat down.

They ate.

She heard no knock. Nor did she hear the door open. She didn't know the women were in the house until she heard Nell's "Whooooo?" as she and Pearl passed through the living room.

Betty thought she would sputter and choke, wondering, even as she pictured herself doing so, if Carl knew the Heimlich maneuver. But when the two women were suddenly in the kitchen with them, she didn't choke. Her face flushed, but she only wiped her mouth with her napkin and smiled.

"Come to lunch, girls," she said.

"Yes, come to lunch," Carl echoed. He'd risen in the calm quick way an older gentleman automatically rises at the sudden presence of ladies he doesn't know. He stepped toward them and a little to the side. "I think we left enough."

Pearl and Nell, dumb and staring, attempted an open-mouthed

retreat, but their rumps jammed in the doorway.

Nell recovered first.

"We weren't expecting—" she started and then stopped.

"No, we just come over—" Pearl followed and then stopped too.

"Come in, come in," Betty said and stood up. "We were just finishing."

The two women still stood wedged in the doorway.

"Pearl Roberts, Nell Freeman," Betty said, walking toward them now, "this is my neighbor, Carl Sanders."

\*   \*   \*

Pearl and Nell jellied off the front porch and scurried diagonally across Betty's front yard. They stayed close together, almost arm in arm, across the street and onto the sidewalk in front of Nell's house. There they parted without breaking stride or saying a word to each other, but Pearl's telephone began to ring before she'd yet struggled halfway up her front steps.

"Oh, I thought I might die right soon as he shook my hand," Nell said when the other lifted the receiver from its wall cradle in her kitchen.

"He's got something on her," Pearl said. "Don't you think she looked strained in the face?"

They talked for almost two and a half hours, each in a kitchen chair, in kitchens that were only some twenty feet apart. The first few minutes they tried to decide what they might have done differently, what they must do now. Then they settled into reliving their visit, going over every movement and glance and word of the meeting, every shudder of their hearts, every detail of the nearly empty plates and bowls and glasses. Each new angle they took to recount events and observations ended with "and George sleeping right in the next room" from one or the other of them.

They finally stopped talking and hung up without deciding on anything apart from not yet calling the Sheriff's Department. Then each moved nervously around her own kitchen, preparing a small supper that could be ready and on a tray before the television in time for *Oprah Winfrey*, the five o'clock news from Asheville, and the game shows.

* * *

That night after she saw George out the front door and welcomed Carl in the back, Betty made blackberry waffles.

They'd talked while she cooked, Carl helping in whatever way she would let him, but now they sat side by side at the table, eating and murmuring their sounds of pleasure over the waffles smothered in butter and a pecan praline syrup she'd been given last Christmas by a friend she saw at Eliza's beauty shop every Friday morning.

At last Betty got up to refill their coffees. She leaned over his shoulder to pick up his cup and stopped with her hand on the saucer and the coffeepot poised above his head.

"Pearl and Nell think you're some kind of fugitive being hid by the government."

Carl looked up at her, bowed and laughed silently, and looked at her again.

"You aren't, are you?" she said and smiled and poured the coffee.

He cleared his throat and stood up, gathered the dirty dishes from the table and carried them to the sink. He turned on the hot water tap and held his fingers under the stream, waiting. When the water began to warm, he plugged the drain and opened the cabinet under the sink and brought out the golden dishwashing liquid.

He could feel her watching his back, could picture how she stood beside the table—an arm crossed over her breasts, the fresh cup of coffee raised halfway to her lips. He could hear what she might say next—"I don't know a thing about you"—so clearly in his mind that he suddenly couldn't be sure that she hadn't actually said it.

He turned off the water.

"I grew up in Chicago," he said and looked at the double reflection of his face in the window above the sink. "Mount Prospect, really. But I spent most of my adult life in Atlanta. That's where Paula was from. I went to Emory and met her there. We eventually got married, even though her parents didn't approve of her marrying a Yankee. I guess giving them grandchildren might've softened them up, but it was always just the two of us." He slowly wiped at a plate hidden beneath the suds. "We drove through these mountains every autumn for thirty-two years. Runion seemed so quaint and untouched. Atlanta was growing up around our ears. We'd made plans and saved for a move to this area when we finished work." He heard her sit down. "After Paula died, I worked hard for another five years and retired. My parents were long dead already, and because I traveled so much with work, I had no close friends anywhere to speak of. So I came here like we'd planned. That's really all there is to it. Thirty-seven years of work. Thirty-two of marriage. No children. No pets." He fell silent.

Betty crossed to the light switch. She turned it off and came to him at the sink.

He leaned down into her arms. Then he straightened and pulled her to his chest with wet, sudsy hands.

They stood in the darkness like that and watched his house, waiting for the electric timers to turn off the lamp and the television in his front room.

*  *  *

When the sports segment of the eleven o'clock news came on at eleven-twenty, Pearl turned off the television and all her lights, picked up her cordless telephone, and stepped onto her porch. She dialed Nell's number and let it ring until her neighbor woke up and answered in a confused voice.

"Turn off your TV and bring your phone out on the porch," Pearl said. "Don't turn the outside light on."

Nell wrapped a shawl around her shoulders and did as she was told, even though she'd been dreaming that dream again and feared meeting Don at the front door with his pistol and his leather jacket.

They stood in the darkness of their porches and watched George lumber across the yard to his car and leave at eleven-

twenty-five. They saw the door that he hadn't closed close behind
him and then the lights go out in the living room.

Pearl whispered into the receiver.

"The lights are still on in Sanders's front room."

"Betty's kitchen light is on too," Nell whispered.

They each took chairs and watched.

"Pearl?" Nell called across the darkened space of yard between
them.

"Quiet," Pearl hissed and held up her handset, pointing at it
with exaggerated motions.

"Pearl?" Nell whispered into her telephone. "What are we
doing?"

"We're just watching, you know?" After a moment she added,
"Tonight's *Matlock* got me to suspecting something."

"Oh, I saw that—" Nell started and then suddenly fell silent
and looked through the darkness at her friend on the other porch.
At last she said into the receiver, "Honestly, Pearl, you don't
think—" and stopped again.

"Yeah, I do think," Pearl snapped.

"Oh, Pearl." Nell shook her head and after a few more minutes
of sitting in the quiet darkness she said she had to go to the
bathroom. She turned off her telephone and went inside her
house and didn't come back out.

Pearl kept watch, hardly noticing Nell's defection.

After what seemed a long time, the light in Sanders's front
room went dark.

She listened, thinking she might hear something—the jangling
rattle of a chain link fence being climbed over, or perhaps the
bang of a back screen door slipping out of a desire-shaken hand.

She nodded and roused and nodded again, dreaming that she
rose lightly from the rocking chair and triple-locked her front door
and went to bed. But still she sat on her porch in the tepid August
night, her cordless telephone in her lap, her hands gripping the
arms of the rocker, her fleshy chins stacked upon her breast.

No longer watching. No longer listening. Dreaming that she
lay sleeping in her bed. Dreaming that as she lay sleeping in her

bed, she dreamed she stood naked in Betty's kitchen before a Carl Sanders that looked like her long-gone Bill. But she knew it wasn't Bill. She knew it was the stranger, and her lack of fear scared her.

No longer watching. No longer listening. Dreaming that she lay sleeping in her bed dreaming herself naked with Sanders in Betty's kitchen, she didn't see the lights of the car that came around the elbow curve and rolled down Mill Street, didn't hear its motor humming clearly in the still and heavy night. She didn't see it stop at the curb and then darken, didn't hear its motor die and the door open and close when the man got out.

But she heard the shot. Or what she thought was a shot. It was hard to tell the way the sharp pop echoed among the Mill Street houses and the near hills and her fleeing dreams. In one motion her chins unfolded from her breast and her eyes saw Betty's house ablaze with light and her hands found the telephone in her lap. She rocked forward and pushed herself up with her right hand as the thumb of her left found the preset 911 button.

\*   \*   \*

Fifteen minutes later, she stood at the front of a small crowd in Betty's yard and held Nell's hand. She squinted against the lights that glared from the picture window and the open door and from the bulb on the ceiling of the porch. She swayed a little in her weakness and fear and the dizzying swirl of blue and red lights from the two patrol cars, the rescue squad vehicle, and the fire truck.

She could see Sheriff Greene, Deputy Boyce, and two paramedics inside. Sheriff and deputy moved back and forth in the directions of Betty and George's bedroom and the kitchen. The paramedics stood in the living room and smoked.

She hadn't seen Betty or George. She knew George was in the house because she'd watched him leave for work and now his car sat at the curb behind her.

Nor had she seen Carl Sanders. Except in her mind's eye. She pictured the bedroom spattered with blood, pictured Betty and him lying on the stripped bed, them naked, contorted, bloodied, and still. She pictured George sitting in the kitchen, his elbows on the table, his head held in his hands, his hair fallen over his chubby fingers in thin oily strands. She pictured the gun lying in a plastic freezer bag on the table's other end, its deadly blackness stark against the yellow tabletop. She'd seen it all on television a thousand times.

Deputy Boyce came out of the kitchen, passed through the living room, and stepped out to the lip of the porch.

"Where's Betty, Deputy?" Pearl called. "Is she dead?"

The lawman didn't answer.

"Is she dying?" Pearl said. "Is she gone too far to get her off to the hospital?"

"No, she ain't dying, Miss Pearl," Deputy Boyce said. "You calm yourself now. She'll be all right."

Disappointed, Pearl stopped squinting and swaying and imagining. She heaved a heavy sigh.

"Y'all go on home now," the deputy said. "Don't none of you look like you could lose out on any beauty rest."

"What is it?" Jesse Goforth said. "What's happened in there?"

The deputy stood still another moment, as if considering whether or not to answer.

"It's George Oakley," he said and without another word turned and walked back into the house, closing the door behind him.

\*   \*   \*

Three weeks later, Pearl and Nell sat on Nell's front porch, each with a section of the *Runion Record* opened and spread on her lap, each with the last of the summer's beans piled in the center crease to be strung and broken. Every couple of minutes a handful of bean pieces clattered into the bottom of the metal bucket on the floor between them.

"Betty sure raised up a fine patch of late beans," Pearl said.

"Did you watch *Oprah* yesterday?" Nell asked.

"I had a mind to, but my nap went long."

"There were two men on the show, and each of them had along their wife and their homosexual lover with them." Nell tossed another handful of broken beans into the bucket and took a sip of tea. "I swear I don't know where they find people like that." She picked up a few beans from her lap and began stringing and breaking them and then stopped. "Do you suppose they hire actors for such shows?"

"I used to wonder," Pearl said. "But I reckon the world is full of more low living than a person can think about, you know?"

This time the long black sedan passed in front of them without their noticing, and the snapping didn't stop until they realized the car had. They looked up and saw it sitting in the driveway of Betty's house.

A young man in a dark suit got out of the passenger side as the trunk popped open. He took out a red, white, and blue sign, attached a smaller white sign to the top of it, and started across the yard. On the other side of the walk that led to the front door, he tamped the sign into the ground with his foot. Then he returned to the car and got in. The unseen driver backed out of the driveway, and the sedan rolled past them again, its blackness gleaming in the mid-morning sunlight.

The two women on the porch watched until it turned left on Main and disappeared.

The snapping seemed louder when it resumed.

"Them fancy Asheville realtors'll sell Mill Street out from under us before long," Pearl said after a minute.

"It's a nice house," Nell said. "No reason for it to sit there empty." She tossed a handful of broken beans into the bucket. "Betty always was a good housekeeper, at least. And a good cook too, of course."

Pearl said nothing.

"But her cooking was too rich, good as it was. I think that was what brought on George's problems with his weight and his heart."

Pearl still said nothing.

Nell again stopped breaking beans.

"Do you think he caught them?" she said.

"What?"

"Do you think George caught them? Her and that man."

Pearl took a deep breath and blew it out through her nose.

"I reckon he must have, you know?" she said. "Else why was the gun in his hand when his heart give out? He weren't the kind to go and shoot himself on account of the mill tossing him off like they done. Why, he'd have took up residence on that couch with all them gadgets first thing next morning and shuffled Betty off to work at Whitson's Green Grocer or somewhere."

Nell sighed and started breaking beans again.

"I swear I don't know what gets into people."

"Why, Nell, I see what happened to Betty happen to folks on the TV all the time. It's strange as a dream, I'll warrant you, but I reckon I can sort of understand it, you know?"

"Well, I can't now nor ever will." After a few sharp snaps Nell threw another handful of broken beans into the bucket and looked again at the house. "I wonder who'll buy it," she said. "Wouldn't it be something if it was some young couple with a baby? It's been a good while since Mill Street had a baby on it."

Pearl looked past the new red, white, and blue sign in Betty's yard to the matching sign that had been in Carl Sanders's yard since the day of George's funeral.

For several long moments the snapping of the beans and the whistling of Nell's canary were the only sounds.

"I'll declare them signs make me want to get on the stick and buy the old Tweed place there," Pearl said. "I'd still like to rent it out to somebody nice." She dropped a handful of broken beans into the bucket. "Somebody local, you know?"

# A Poster of Marilyn Monroe

Troy Pate stood by the four-lane with his right foot propped up on the guard rail and his callused hands buried in the bib of his overalls. He scratched his belly and stared down the gradient into the tangle of blackberry bushes, wild rose, and other assorted brambles that choked the bottom land around Flat Creek. He rolled his unlit cigar from his right cheek across his tongue, into his left cheek and back again.

"Damn, I hate goin' down in there after her," he said and scratched his belly harder.

But he knew he would go. He'd invested the better part of the day in driving two and a half hours to Greenville so that he could pick her up in a place where there was a one in a million chance of running into anybody he knew. And that's not to mention the weeks the idea of getting her had burned a hole in his mind, night into day right up until this morning.

He'd arrived in Greenville at about eight-thirty, stopped at a Shoney's and treated himself to the breakfast buffet, and then found the mall right at ten o'clock. He walked around until he caught a whiff of some sweet burning drifting into the concourse—from a curio shop, he reckoned it was, exactly like the one his eleven-year-old grandson Dean always dragged him into at the Asheville Mall. Although the name of this store sounded unfamiliar, he walked past the same naughty gifts and the same naughty greeting cards and found the racks of posters in the same corner at the back. He stood there behind two young boys, who put him in mind of Dean—all but ignoring posters of women with hardly a stitch on, flipping quickly through the display to music groups he found it hard to look at and whose names he didn't like to say.

There she hung in black and white, in the paper flesh, not in the display racks but big as life on the wall. Even though the picture was cropped in such a way that the background did not make any sense, he knew it was from *The Seven Year Itch*. She stood very erect, in profile, on the bottom step of a stairway that curved up and to the left behind her. Her wavy hair, white and shining here, was fixed like that of a wife who spends at least three-quarters of an hour every Friday morning in the local beauty shop. Her gray eyes were cast slightly downward, but her face—her eyebrows, the corners of her mouth, her chin—was lifted in a faintly sarcastic smile. In her right hand she gripped the neck of a hammer. In her left she carried a cup of shaving things. The neckline of her short-sleeved nightgown—*More like a nightshirt*, he thought—was high and plain, not low and lacy like in some of the pictures he'd seen. From the buttoned collar the shirt sloped away until it fell from her bosom straight to her knees. The glowing calf of her left leg curved downward to a smooth foot nestled in a high-heeled slipper. The nightshirt would be white, he decided, but the slippers would be gold and the fuzzy-furry parts that almost hid her painted toenails would be a vivid pink.

He pulled off his hat and took a step forward and stood for a moment looking up at her.

A notecard with a number written on it was stapled to her upper right-hand corner. He knew from helping young Dean that the number should correspond with one on the end of some of the rolled-up posters all around him.

*Match the number and take her home*, he thought.

But he couldn't find a match. He rummaged first through the posters in wire baskets along the wall. When the two boys moved off, he looked all through the rack that held tightly wound, plastic-wrapped posters of models, country music singers, TV wrestlers, and rock groups. If his eyes weren't playing tricks on him, she simply wasn't there.

He again walked over close to the display poster. The blood throbbed in the sides of his throat and roared in his ears as he stood, hat in hand, before her. He looked at the corners and saw that she was held to the wall with ordinary thumb tacks and reached up with shaky hands to start freeing her.

"Can I help you?"

Troy jumped as if a gun had been jabbed into his soft ribs. He felt his face flush red as he turned around slowly, his hands still up in the air.

The girl stood with her left fist on her hip, her right knee at ease, her right hand hanging in front of her face. Strands of purple hair streaked through the yellow bangs that fell over eyes as green as a cat's. She glanced at him once but looked mainly at her fingernails.

"Uh, I was hoping to get this here poster," Troy said. "But I can't seem to find nary but this one." He put his hands down by his sides. "You see, it's for a joke on an old Air Force buddy of mine."

Pink chewing gum flashed as she flicked it from one side of her mouth to the other.

"All the posters we got are in these racks," she said.

"Would you mind looking real quick?" he said. "I done been through them and couldn't find a number to match with that one on the little card there. Maybe your young eyes might do better."

"I'll see," she said. She glanced through a couple of the wire baskets along the wall. "Nope. We're out of that poster."

"Well, can I get that one down off of the wall? I'll be glad to pay regular price for it."

"We don't sell those," she said. A small pink bubble erupted from her mouth, and she popped it with her lips. Then without a word she spun on her heel and walked back toward the front of the store.

He turned once more to the woman on the wall. His fingers worked the sweat-stained brim of the battered old fedora as he tried to think what to do next.

With another pink pop the girl was behind him again.

"The manager says you can buy that one," she said. "We aren't getting any more in."

Outside, he laid her—rolled and loosely bound with a rubber band—in the bed of his pickup, thinking that if anybody he knew discovered her before he reached home, he could say he'd been in town and some kid must have stolen the thing and nearly got caught and hid it in the back of his truck.

He'd been on the four-lane within a few minutes of Marshall when it happened. Some wind had come up, and he was driving too fast. He was passing the hollow of Flat Creek, on the hill at the end of which stood his daughter Jenny's beautiful new house, the fanciest one built near the four-lane so far. He was looking out the passenger-side of the windshield, up the hollow toward the house, examining particularly the south-facing wall of glass beneath the long sloping roof with the solar panels, when a sense of something moving tickled the corner of his left eye. He straightened up quickly, sure that there was something in the road ahead of him, but he found the movement framed in the rearview mirror.

*Marilyn.*

He watched her dip and rise again, saw her hover above the truck bed for a moment and then rocket out of the mirror's frame. He squirmed around in his seat just in time to see her shoot out over the guard rail, take a nosedive, and disappear into the hollow below.

He kept driving as if nothing had happened, just in case somebody might have been watching or coming up behind him, somebody he might know. He drove up the road and turned around, returned five miles back the way he'd come to the Red Dot where he bought a pint of chocolate milk and a honey bun.

When he came back to Flat Creek, he slowed down and eased the pickup to the side of the road and stopped as near as he could reckon to the point where she had disappeared.

Now he stood with his right foot propped up on the guard rail and looked once more at his daughter's house and then down into the creek bottom to see if he could spot the poster among the dark brambles.

Getting down the gradient wouldn't be that hard, he decided. But what if one of the boys who gathered nightly on the bench outside Johnson's stopped when he saw Troy Pate's truck parked on the side of the road? Or what if Clara Honeycutt stopped to see if he needed her help or if he wanted to come over for dinner after church one Sunday soon? He imagined her calling down to him as she stood by the guard rail, asking if he was all right. He saw himself struggling up out of the brambles at the sound of her voice, bits of brush and dirt on his shirt and overalls, tiny spots of blood welling up on the backs of his hands where he'd been pricked by briars.

Clara Honeycutt had a talent for catching him in moments like that. It seemed as if she had a sense of when he was down, when he might be most vulnerable to her effusive kindness. She wasn't an ugly woman. Far from it. Even at sixty-two her hair remained mostly blond and she retained a pleasant figure that, had her personality not so overrun him, he might have reached out to take hold of.

He looked long and hard at his daughter's house. But try as he might he couldn't come up with a story that would lower him down the gradient and onto the creek bed without putting him in a position of seeming to need help of one kind or another.

Then, after looking at the sky and deciding that it didn't seem to hold any rain, he got back in his truck and drove on to Runion.

\* \* \*

At home, he heated the leftovers of a meal Clara had brought him two nights earlier, squeezed down into one tiny chair at the tiny table, and ate his supper. As he sat there, he wondered if he shouldn't buy a full-sized kitchen now that Kitty was gone. He could get a normal refrigerator and range, a normal table and chairs. He could replace the low counter and sink and then raise the cabinet tops to the ceiling. After that he could go through the rest of the house, raising the mirrors and the light switches. It would do his old back a world of good, he decided, to raise the bathroom sink and the bed as well.

Later, during a commercial for microwavable fruit tarts that interrupted *Music City Tonight*, he thought of an excuse to go down that Flat Creek gradient after the poster of Marilyn Monroe. He would go back in the morning with a gallon bucket. If any shape of friend or foe loomed over him from the roadside, he would simply say that he'd been going through some of Kitty's old recipes and found one for her blackberry pie, that he thought he would try it and was looking for some late blackberries. No one would expect him to know that the blackberries had been gone well over a month. A man who has depended on a wife like Kitty for thirty years and more wouldn't likely know such practical things.

At eleven o'clock he turned to the Asheville station and flipped through the *TV Guide* while he waited for the weather. He wished there were more movies on late at night like there used to be. Years ago, on Fridays especially, when Jenny was out on a date, he and Kitty often sat up and watched old movies if they had nothing special to do the next morning.

She'd known from the beginning of his fascination with Marilyn Monroe. Sometimes she even told him when she noticed that *All About Eve* or *The Seven Year Itch* or *Some Like It Hot* would be coming on, lowering her face and glancing at him from the corner of her dark eyes and smiling devilishly. Then she would shake all over with quiet laughter, knowing, he thought, that when the movie was over he would be all over her in bed.

He'd fallen in love with Marilyn Monroe one Saturday afternoon in 1956 when he found himself at loose ends in Asheville, waiting for a family friend who was bringing a sewing machine for Mama Pate from the grand opening of a big department store in Charlotte. The train from Runion came in several hours before he was to pick up the machine at the station, so he ate downtown at Woolworth's lunch counter and then decided on a movie at the Imperial. It was *Bus Stop*. It didn't turn out to be one of his favorites of her movies after he saw them all—probably the only one he preferred it to was *The Misfits*—but when her character, a small-time lounge singer dressed in tight net and rather worn frills, sang a delicate and pain-filled version of "That Old Black Magic," he came away haunted.

He made up his mind as he took the train back to Runion

with the sewing machine in his lap that he would work through harvest and leave right after Christmas. He would make his way to Hollywood and marry Marilyn Monroe just like Bo Decker had done the lounge singer. And it would be the kiss he gave her that would do it, just like in the movie.

But then he met Kitty. She came with a group from Hot Springs Presbyterian to Runion's First Southern Missionary Church— the church he'd grown up in—to sing a Christmas cantata. She caught his attention because she was so small, a midget, and to him as strangely alluring as one of those plump cherubs in the Sunday School literature. She had a solo part during "In the Bleak Midwinter," and her voice was strong and clear. She mesmerized him. Being no tall man himself, he wasn't bothered by her size. He spoke to her across the punch bowl after the performance. She was jolly and witty, her dark eyes sparkled, and her laugh was as musical as her singing.

They slipped away from the little reception and walked up and down the cold streets of Runion. He soon found himself telling her about Marilyn Monroe and his plan to go to Hollywood to marry her.

"You don't follow the movie magazines, do you, Mr. Pate?" she said, lowering her face slightly and casting a sidelong glance up at him.

He stopped and looked at her.

"She's a married woman, you know," Kitty said. "She's married to Arthur Miller, that fellow in the Communist party."

Troy didn't say anything.

"He writes plays for Broadway," she said.

"Well," Troy said at last. "I reckon from what I do know about Hollywood that them sorts of marriages don't last too long."

He was about to resume his stroll with her when the small woman reached up and took the crook of his arm in her hand.

He stopped and looked at her again.

"I reckon it's likely that by the time I could get out there and figure a way to find her, she won't be married no more," he said.

"And meanwhile you'll be lonely and far away from home."

"Most likely."

"You deserve better than that, Mr. Pate," she said and sighed. "Perhaps we should plan this together, don't you think?"

"Together?"

"Oh, yes. I read all the Hollywood magazines. I could help you figure out when the best time to go would be. I could look for the names of people you might see to lead you around to her. Or I might be able to discover the place where she'll be filming her next movie. That might make it even easier for you to find her."

\*   \*   \*

After the weatherman recapped his prediction of another nice day for tomorrow, Troy turned off the television and the lights in the living room and the kitchen and moved through the darkness to his bedroom. He opened the door to Kitty's wardrobe and sat down heavily on the side of the low bed.

The amber-white glow of the nightlight that lit his way to the bathroom lit up the inside panel of the wardrobe door as well. That was where he planned to hang the poster of Marilyn Monroe. He would leave the door open when he came to bed and look at her until he fell asleep, and then in those moments that came to him every night when he suddenly awoke and lay there anxious and wakeful for very often an hour or two at a time, he would look at her again. And when he got out of bed in the morning, he would close the door on Marilyn Monroe and the tiny dresses that hung on the low bar, leaving it closed until the house was dark again that night and the dresses were lost in the shadowed recesses of the wardrobe and only the tall poster of the actress would be visible.

He lay awake and restless a long time. Sometimes he dreaded going to sleep so much that he fought it with every moment of consciousness. He preferred to make sleep wrestle him into submission instead of drifting toward it. If he allowed the drifting, he sometimes thought he could hear the soft whistle of Kitty's breathing. And if he let himself go that way, he almost always woke up with a start some few minutes later, sweating, having thought he heard her last sudden sharp breath as clearly as he'd heard it that night nearly six months ago. So he fought sleep with thoughts of things he needed to do around the house, with the arguments of candidates for elections still over a year away, with plans for trips he might take in the spring or next summer, with his old fantasies of Marilyn Monroe—of meeting her in the revolving door of some Hollywood hotel, of learning the Hollywood streets by heart and becoming the chauffeur who drove her to and from the courthouse for her divorce proceedings, of being Bo to her Chérie.

*  *  *

By mid-morning the next day, after breakfast in Runion with the crowd at the Stonehouse Café, he was moving down the steep gradient into the Flat Creek bottom. The metal bucket he carried swung and squeaked on its handle and now and again banged against his knee.

When he reached the edge of the narrow stream, he pulled a cigar from the bib pocket of his overalls and lit it. Keeping the bucket with him, he began to look earnestly for the poster. He carefully went over every inch of the area where he guessed it might have landed, but it wasn't there. He worked his way up along the near side of the creek, past the point where there was any possibility of the poster's having sailed, and then he carefully stepped on a stone in the middle of the stream and then stepped to the far side.

As he returned nearer to the culvert, he shook a thick bush to see if the poster fell out.

It didn't, but a small swarm of yellow jackets did.

He got the first sting on the back of his neck before he knew they were around him. The wasps were sluggish in the cool morning air, but they were persistent, stinging him twice on the right hand and once on the jaw as he swiped at them.

He ran towards the creek, aiming for another stepping stone in its middle, just a few feet above the mouth of the culvert. He missed and fell into the water with a splash.

The yellow jackets, apparently satisfied, left him alone.

He sat in the cold water, still smoking the cigar he had neither dropped nor gotten wet. He pulled another cigar from his pocket and began to bite off and chew pieces of it, applying little blobs of the saliva-soaked tobacco to the stings. But it was awkward. He couldn't get one to stick to his jaw, the sting that hurt the worst, and couldn't find the exact spot of the sting on the back of his neck. He wondered if perhaps he had two or three back there instead of just that first one.

Still sitting in the cold water, he stared through the culvert to the circle of light and shadowed brambles at the foot of another gradient across the four-lane. The world on the other side of that darkness was so like what surrounded him that it was as if he were looking into a smoky mirror. And it surprised him not to see himself in that image. He finally laid the remainder of both cigars in the water and watched them float like tiny logs into the darkness of the culvert. When he thought they'd probably floated out into the light on the other side, he stood up, poured the water out of his bucket, and waded to the bank.

At his truck, he took a piece of plastic from behind the seat and spread it out to sit on. Then he climbed in and started the motor.

In spite of the tobacco, the stings were aching.

He didn't like the idea of going home to nurse them alone, of then bending low over the counter beside the refrigerator to fix himself a sandwich for lunch. He sat there in his truck a few minutes, lightly revving the engine as he thought. Finally, he began to roll forward and eased the truck onto the four-lane.

\* \* \*

"Why, Troy Pate, you're soaking wet," Clara Honeycutt said when she answered his knock at her door. "Come in the house this minute."

After she doctored his stings, she washed and dried his clothes while he showered and then sat wrapped in a quilt in her easy chair. She fixed him a meal of pork chops, biscuits and gravy, and green beans, corn, and tomatoes from her own garden.

Within moments after his plate was wiped clean with the last of the biscuits, he stood with his hand on the handle of the screen door.

"I thank you, Clara," he said and cleared his throat.

She stood there, smoothing the flannel shirt over her breasts and

down her sides, fidgeting with the softly grayed hair above her ears
and at the back of her neck as if she didn't know what to do with
her hands now that the afternoon's fussing over him was finished.

"I'm much obliged," he said.

"I enjoyed doing for you." Her hands caught each other near
the front tails of her shirt. "I miss doing—" she started and then
stopped, fixing her eyes on his.

He held her gaze for a moment, pushed the door open a few
inches, and then looked out toward his truck.

He cleared his throat again and, without looking at her, said,
"I've been less than six months without her after more than thirty-
five years."

"And the six months seems longer than all those years," she
said. "I know." She put a hand to his arm and drew a decisive
breath. "I know exactly. It's been almost seven years since Caney
left me after our thirty-two."

He didn't say anything, nor did he move.

"We're both strong and healthy," she continued. "Young and
likely to live a good while yet." She dropped her hand from his arm
and let it fall to her side. "I would do all I did for you today and
more as long as I'm able."

He still didn't say anything, but now he pushed the screen door
open wide and one boot thudded on the board floor of the porch.

"I reckon I'll see you in church Sunday," he said and crossed
the porch and walked down the steps.

"Will you think about it, Troy?" she called from behind.

"Yeah," he said almost to himself as he opened the truck's door
and climbed in. He turned the key in the ignition and glanced at
her again for the first time since he'd given her his thanks.

She stood in the doorway, holding the screen door open with
her right hand, touching the door frame with her left in the same
way she'd touched his arm. She watched him, her face bright with
a parting smile, her eyes cast down at him as he ground the gears
and found reverse.

* * *

At home, a note from Jenny lay in his easy chair.

*Daddy,*

*Come to the new house Saturday afternoon at 4:30 and we'll christen the kitchen with mama's best recipes. I got her file out of the cupboard while I was here. Hope you don't mind. Bobby Jack wants you to watch some racing on the big TV he's put in the den. Dean's just dying for you to see his room. Bring a guest if you'd like.*

*Love, Jen*

\* \* \*

He arrived late on Saturday, and supper already lay waiting on the table.

"You came alone," Jenny said.

"I fell asleep on the couch, watching rassling," Troy Pate said. "Good thing you hollered to check on me. I might've woke up to Sunday morning preaching."

"I thought maybe you might bring Clara."

"No," he said.

Jenny turned toward a doorway and called, "Bobby Jack and Dean, Grandpa's here and supper's on the table."

Troy sat where his daughter told him to and waited for his son-in-law and grandson.

Dean came in like a whirlwind.

"Grandpa, come look at my room," he said.

"After supper, Dean," Jenny said. "Did you wash your hands?"

Dean went to the sink and turned on the water just as Bobby Jack walked into the dining room.

When they were all seated and Troy had offered thanks and added a blessing on the new house, the food was passed around the table.

Even in the unfamiliar kitchen and cookware, the meal was recognizably Kitty's. The potato casserole looked the same, smelled the same. The homemade crescent rolls looked as if they had been formed by her chubby little hands. The chicken was fried to the same shade of golden brown and showed the same black marks of a light burning on one side.

He filled his plate as the bowls and platters came around, and while Jenny, Bobby Jack, and Dean talked about this or that aspect of the new house, he ate.

The meal was like the memory of an old friend. Everything tasted almost the same, but there was that difference made by distance—as of a generation—in the preparation of it. He tasted less of the grease and batter of Kitty's fried chicken and more of the chicken itself. A mouthful of potato casserole held less of the tastes of butter, sour cream, and cream cheese, more of the diced potatoes and onions. And everything was less salty. When he finished eating he slid his chair back and rubbed his belly and wished for more of that old friend's company.

"Come on, Grandpa," Dean said when the chocolate cake was gone from his plate. "You got to see my room."

"Son, let's give him the whole tour on the way," Bobby Jack said, smiling. "Your room can be the grand finale."

"The what?" Dean said.

They left the dishes on the table and toured through the living room, which looked as if nobody had sat in it yet, and then the sunken den with its long windows and the skylights Bobby Jack said were between the solar panels. A 60" television sat in one corner, and on it Winston Cup cars circled mutely through the Mountain Dew 500. Attached to the den was a bedroom decorated in semi-precious twentieth-century antiques—an old iron bed frame, a spindly nightstand, a black rotary telephone.

"You can have this room whenever you want it, Daddy," Jenny said.

"Nice view," he said, looking out one large window toward the Flat Creek bottom and the four-lane highway beyond. He wondered if his daughter or son-in-law or grandson had watched him when he searched for Marilyn Monroe among those thickets and then got into the nest of yellow jackets.

Upstairs he glanced at another guest room and then, with a touch of heat on his cheeks, toured Jenny and Bobby Jack's large bedroom and their bath with its double shower. He noticed that Jenny kept her room as her mother had kept hers—no clothes on the floor but here and there a skirt or shirt draped neatly on the back of a chair or hung on a hook, a doorknob, or a bedpost.

"I've got to get back to the race," Bobby Jack said. "I'll be down in the den, Troy."

"I'll be there directly," the older man said, feeling a little less flushed in the face as his son-in-law disappeared downstairs.

"No, Grandpa, you've got to see my room," Dean said.

"We're going to your room right now, Dean," Jenny said.

"Mom, you go downstairs. I can show Grandpa my stuff by myself."

Jenny winked at her father and then left him alone with his grandson.

Once in his room, Dean sat on his bed and started playing a video game.

"Ain't you gonna show me around?" Troy Pate said.

"I want to show you this new racing game Daddy got me." Dean flashed through several screens too quickly for his grandfather to track. "My favorite car's this red Mustang."

He tried to follow the images on the screen but soon found himself studying the way his grandson's television and stereo equipment had been built into the wall, the way posters of Dale Earnhardt, Jeff Gordon, Luke Skywalker, and others had been hung. When Dean called his attention back to the replay of his race, he watched and then stood up to examine the items on the dresser top and then to check the closet space.

Marilyn Monroe was in that closet, hung with tacks on the inside of the door.

Startled, Troy Pate took a step backwards. Then he reached out to touch her, gently pushed her door wider open, and stepped back again until he felt the backs of his legs come up against Dean's bed. He swallowed hard and reached up to take off his hat, then realized it was still on the hook just inside the front door downstairs. He shoved his hands into the bib of his overalls and slowly scratched his belly.

"Dean?" he said.

"Hmm?" the boy mumbled over the volume of the Mustang's engine as he opened it up on a straightaway.

"What's this here?"

"Just a sec."

He stood and looked at her, forgetting his grandson for a moment, the roar of blood through his body drowning out the roar of the game's race cars.

She was none the worse for wear. She showed no signs of getting wet in the September morning dews, and no wrinkles showed in her skin or clothes. Hanging here in his eleven-year-old grandson's closet, she looked like a nice lady, very pretty and soft, but not alluring. She belonged to somebody else here. Here, it wasn't him she stood looking at and talking to, but some actor out of the frame. He couldn't remember who just now—maybe one of the names Kitty knew and he always tried to forget. Here, she could turn away up the stairs and be out of his reach forever.

"Grandpa?" Dean said.

Troy Pate tried to speak, but his voice stalled in a dry throat.

"Grandpa?" Dean said again. "You won't tell anybody about that, will you? I just kept it 'cause I found it."

The old man swallowed and turned.

"You don't—" he said and stopped. He cleared his throat and straightened his shoulders. "You don't want to keep a secret from your mom, do you, boy?"

"Oh, she knows about it," Dean said. "She even helped me hang it up there and told me her name was Mary Monroe."

"Marilyn," Troy Pate said slowly, and the word tasted warm and wet and sweet in his mouth, like one of Kitty's cinnamon rolls hot out of the oven. "Her name's Marilyn Monroe."

"Whatever," Dean said. "I just don't want Adam or Chase to find out about it."

The old man felt a slight smile play at the corners of his mouth.

"Why don't you want them to know? You reckon they don't like pretty ladies?"

"Sure, I guess," Dean said. "But they think black and white is stupid."

Troy Pate chuckled at his grandson's embarrassment and then stopped.

"Where'd you get her?" he asked.

"In the grass over by the road," Dean said. "I was playing an army game by the creek and found it when I climbed up the bank to shoot at enemy vehicles."

The old man shook his head and turned back to the poster of Marilyn Monroe. Once more he reached up to touch her, as if to smooth away a wrinkle or brush away a fly.

"Have you ever seen this movie?" he said.

"What movie?" Dean said.

\* \* \*

He left before the race was over and drove through the darkness back to the four-lane.

*You deserve better than that, Mr. Pate,* Kitty said. She cut her eyes up at him and smiled. *Better than a picture hanging in a closet.*

He sat at the stop sign in the early dark, lightly revving the engine and looking neither left nor right.

*She was a movie star,* Kitty said. *She wasn't real.* Her feet danced in the air above the floorboard as they'd always done. *For you in Runion, she was a movie star. Never real.*

He closed his eyes and leaned his head back against the headrest. He smelled the breeze that blew through the truck and carried the hint of autumn burning. But mixed with this the sweet scent of honeysuckle came up from the Flat Creek bottom. Breathing in the slight and familiar fragrance, he tried to remember seeing a stand of the flower among the brambles but couldn't.

*She's dead, Mr. Pate,* Kitty said. *You can go to California, if you want to, go to Brentwood or walk through the cemetery or sleep at the Roosevelt Hotel. But that's silly for a man your age.* Her voice was musical. *She was married back when you first wanted to go, and she's long dead now.*

*Found dead in her Brentwood home,* Troy Pate thought.

*That's right. But maybe you can see her ghost in that mirror in the*

*Roosevelt.* Kitty's musical laugh. *But that wouldn't even be as good as a poster in the closet, now would it, Mr. Pate?*

"And what about you, Kitty?" he said aloud as he finally pulled out onto the abandoned four-lane.

*Our life was real, and Jenny was real,* she went on. *And that grandbaby.*

He wondered who Dean would want to go find when he came of an age to leave his mother's home. He had the poster of Marilyn Monroe, but she was only a picture to him, a black and white draw for the hormones beginning to stir inside him. He would tear her down one day and hide her in the trash, maybe even burn her, to make room for the one that he would want. But who would he settle with? And would he be happy with somebody other than that body he held in his dreams?

*Our life was happy, and we were happy,* Kitty said, her voice sympathetic and reaffirming, not accusing. *And there's no call for your not being happy now.*

Once more he found he couldn't go home to the tiny things that reminded him of how he'd settled and what he'd lost. He had money in the bank, money enough to do what he wanted to. And if he wanted to he could keep driving until he pulled up to the Roosevelt Hotel and stood in front of the full-length mirror in the lobby, waiting for her. And he could talk with Kitty all the way there. And all the way back, if he chose to come back.

*You deserve better than that, Mr. Pate.*

And then a sudden light nearly blinded him, and as the door above opened, he wondered how he came to be standing at the foot of these steps.

Clara stepped out onto the porch, and, holding a coffee cup in her left hand, settled her robe over her nightshirt with her right. She moved to the top of the steps and stood there casting her shadow across him.

Troy Pate stood, hat in hand, looking up at her. He couldn't see her face clearly as she stood silhouetted against the bright porch light, and so, uncertain as to whether he was welcome or not at this time of night, he said nothing as he fingered the brim of his hat.

"Come in for a cup of coffee, Troy?"

Her voice was softer than he'd ever heard it.

"I've got vanilla ice cream and some blackberry cobbler too," she said. "I was just about to put on an old movie I rented today at Ingles."

He found his voice in the mist of his confusion.

"Is it Marilyn Monroe?"

"Heavens no," she said with a whispery laugh. "I used to get called by her name a lot when I was young, so I never really liked her. That's kind of silly of me, don't you think?" She let go her robe and reached her hand down towards him. "This has some actors in it that I don't know. It looked like it would be good, but we don't have to watch it if you don't want to."

"I'll give it a try, I reckon," he said and mounted the first step, slowly reaching up to take the hand she offered. "Anything ought to go good with coffee and cobbler and ice cream."

# A Fiddle and a Twilight Reel

Under cover of cool fog and predawn darkness, three men sat in a 1973 Ford pickup parked on an old logging road off Baylor Run. All smoked and waited. Two of the men—one riding shotgun and the other the middle—were young and round and heavy, sitting shoulder to shoulder and thigh to thigh in sleeveless t-shirts and blue jeans. The older man behind the wheel was neatly pressed and razor thin, narrow in both shoulder and hip, and this thinness created such a space around him that he couldn't have been less crowded if he'd been in the cab alone.

The young man in the middle leaned forward and flicked a cigarette butt through the open passenger-side window, and the spinning red-orange tip traced its arc into the dark woods.

"Benny, you keep an eye on where that butt landed," the older man said. "They's lots of trees done let loose of their leaves. We don't want to start no fires back in here."

"Yes, Daddy," Benny said. "If I see something start up, Billy can run out there and piss on it."

"The hell I will," Billy said.

"Watch your language, boy," the father said.

"Yes, Daddy," Billy said.

Two more cigarettes arced out into the darkness before anybody spoke again.

"Man, I can't believe the Nasty Boys lost to them pussies last night," Billy said.

"Billy."

"Sorry, Daddy."

"A faggot and a nigger," Benny said. "I can't hardly believe it neither."

"We oughta make us up a tag team and kick some ass," Billy said. "Sorry, Daddy." Then, "The NWA wouldn't never be the same."

"It's the WCW now," Benny said. "Man, I can't believe you're so stupid." He knuckled a punch hard into his brother's thigh and got an elbow to the rib meat in return.

"Boys," their father said, and the two sat still, their bodies putting out heat that began to fog the windshield.

Their father lit another cigarette, and first Benny and then Billy did the same.

"Rasslin' ain't real no how," their father said. "Most likely they's all queers or halfway so."

Neither of the young men spoke.

"Time to go," their father said then. "Careful of the door. And none of that chatter."

They stood beside the truck in the aborning twilight and listened to the waning night.

"Billy, you get the gas can and our friend there. And Benny, you get that bucket and the rope. Take care and don't slosh any out on the way." As his sons reached into the bed of the truck to take up their burdens, he took up the stakes and the hammer. "Let's go."

\* \* \*

Gabriel Tanner walked around the smoldering horror, now snapping pictures, the flash for which lit up the men and the yard and the bordering yellow-green woods, now scribbling in a notepad pulled from his shirt pocket. He was describing the straw effigy that hung above a smoking cross when Gene Fredericks, owner of the property, suddenly stood at his elbow.

"I don't want this in the paper, Gabe," he said.

Gabriel turned and looked at him.

Fredericks had aged in the months since his son had come home. Everything about him seemed thinner and grayer. The old sense of humor now and then still made a public appearance on

the streets of Runion, where he ran the oldest insurance and real
estate agency in town, but it wasn't evident in the weary slouch of
the man standing and staring at the spectacle staged in this lower
corner of his yard.

"I'll do what I can," Gabriel said. "But Mr. Shields has strong
feelings about getting stories like this out to the public. You never
know who might see it and come forward with something helpful."

"I understand that, and if the Sheriff thinks it'd be a good
idea—" Fredericks stopped and swallowed. "Mike's in a bad way
right now," he said. "Weak. He don't sleep much, and he was up
and saw it happening." He stopped again, and his jaws clenched
for a moment. "I don't know why he didn't call me when they were
out here."

"He saw them?"

Fredericks glanced down at the notepad, and Gabriel put it
back in his pocket.

"I'm telling you this because you and Mike were friends,"
Fredericks said.

"We still are," Gabriel said.

"Mike don't see too good in the dark. Never has. But especially
not now. He's pretty sure there was three of them out here. Deputy
Boyce found some footprints and thinks that might be right. Mike
said he couldn't tell who it was, but between you and me, I don't
think he'd say even if they'd walked up and gave him their business
cards."

"He didn't give you any kind of description apart from the
number?"

"No, that's all, except that they went off through the woods
when they finished."

"Who put out the fire on the cross?"

"I did."

"Well, I'll file your request along with my notes and pictures,
but Mr. Shields won't like not telling this story."

"I understand."

When Gene Fredericks walked back toward the house, Gabriel
went to his car, laid his notepad on the roof, and stood against the

car to transcribe this conversation with the distraught father of an old friend and finish recording his descriptions of the scene.

A cross had been stuck in the ground—hammered in with a couple of quick hard blows from the looks of it. That was probably done last—last, that is, except for the gasoline and the touch of fire. A length of rope had been thrown over a low branch of an old oak, and a straw-stuffed figure of a man wearing nothing but a fake beard had been raised up by the neck to hang over the cross. Apparently before it had been hoisted into the air, the areas around its mouth and crotch had been splashed with a red substance that was browning as it dried. The three suspects had most likely come and gone through the woods, into which the sheriff had sent a couple of deputies to track them.

Gabriel smelled Old Spice and looked up to find Deputy Davis Boyce watching him write.

"Mr. Fredericks asked you not to put this in the paper?" the deputy said.

"I'll do my best to keep it out," Gabriel said. "But you know old Shields."

Deputy Boyce grunted and looked off toward the spectacle and into the woods and rubbed his stubbled chin with his palm.

The other deputies, back from having found tire tracks on the logging road, were now taking the straw man down from the tree.

"Is that blood?" Gabriel said.

"Pretty sure it is," Deputy Boyce said. "And now I wonder what kind it might be."

"What do you mean?"

"Well, it might be a hog's blood, I reckon. It's getting close to time for slaughter."

"Seems like Granddaddy James always did that when it got colder. Late November."

"True," the deputy said. "That's true enough, I reckon. We'll get it tested and see." He started to walk toward the junior deputies, advice or admonition in his body language, but then he stopped and turned back to Gabriel. "You'll do your best with your boss, Gabe?"

"I'll do my best."

Gabriel put his notepad in his pocket and opened the car door. Just as he was about to sit down behind the wheel, he looked at the nearest window of the Fredericks house. He had the impression that Mike Fredericks was there watching the activity in the yard. Gabriel threw up his hand just in case and dropped into his car and backed out of the driveway.

*   *   *

Ben Frisby sorted nuts in Fricker's Hardware and Appliance, sifting through the various bins to find those pieces that careless customers had considered and then tossed back in with the wrong size. He held a few mismatched pieces in his open right palm and sorted them there with the tip of a finger. As he moved them from palm to bin, he noticed the blood dried in his lifeline. He slowly finished emptying his hand and turned it over. More dried blood crusted the channels around the edges of his fingernails. He looked at his left hand and found it the same. Standing there in front of the nut bin, he held up both hands and turned them over once and then again.

"You figuring you need a manicure, Ben?" Sam Fricker said from behind the counter.

Frisby let his hands fall to his sides.

"No, Mr. Fricker," he said without turning. "I was just noticing that I didn't do too good a job washing up this morning. Reckon I best take care of that."

"All right," Fricker said.

While Frisby was in the restroom, he heard the bell above the front door of the hardware ring, and when he came out drying his hands with a paper towel, Deputy Davis Boyce stood at the counter talking to Fricker. The two of them were leaning over a length of rope coiled on the countertop.

Deputy Boyce looked up.

"Morning, Ben," he said and turned back to his business.

"Deputy," Ben Frisby said and returned to sorting the hardware. He looked up and across the street at The Fredericks Agency and saw that the place remained dark and the CLOSED sign still hung on the inside of the glass front door. He pursed his lips and nodded slightly, turned his eyes to his work but bent his attention to what passed between his boss and the lawman.

"Well, that's just your basic twisted nylon rope, Davis," Sam Fricker said. "It looks like what we sell, but we sell a lot of it. I don't know that I can be much help to you in figuring out if it was bought here nor who bought it if it was."

"I just thought you might remember somebody buying some in the last week or so. It looks new to me."

"Ben?" Fricker said.

"Sir?" Frisby said, his eyes not leaving the shiny nuts in his palm.

"Do you remember cutting any of this half-inch nylon rope for a customer in the past week or so?"

"I did a couple of cuts. But I don't know who the people was. Sammy just asked me to get it, and I got it."

"Maybe my boy will know," Fricker said. "He'll be in—"

"I cut a length for myself too," Ben said. "Couple days ago. I marked it down in the book."

"Okay, Ben, thanks," Fricker said and turned back to the deputy. "Sammy'll be in after lunch, or you can get him at home this morning."

Deputy Boyce picked up the coil of rope.

"I appreciate it, Sam."

"I hate that for Gene," Fricker said, his voice almost a whisper. "I just can't think what it must be like for him."

"He's pretty well shook up," Deputy Boyce said.

"Added to a lot of other shocks he's got lately," Fricker said.

"Yes, there's that."

"I'll give him a shout later on today. Or I'll walk over and see him if he's in his office."

"You do that." The deputy turned to the door. "Ben," he said and stepped out onto the sidewalk.

"Deputy," Ben Frisby said without looking up.

* * *

When Gabriel Tanner returned to the Main Street office of the *Runion Record*, he sat at his desk for a moment, then picked up the telephone and dialed his wife.

Three rings and an answer—"Eliza's."

"Hi, Misty, it's Gabriel."

"Oh hey, Gabe," Misty said. "You know you don't have to tell me who you are every time. I recognize your voice."

"Sorry. Just old habit, I guess. Is Eliza busy?"

"Now, you know she's always busy, Gabe."

"Okay," Gabriel said with a short laugh. "Can I speak to Eliza?"

"I just got Pam Thorn shampooed and in her chair, so you called at a good time. They ain't got good and started yet."

Gabriel heard the music in the background grow louder and could picture Misty walking out into the main area of the salon— "It's your boss, boss," he heard her say.

"Well," Eliza's voice sounded in his ear. "Hello, boss."

"Her words, not mine," Gabriel said. "How's it going?"

"One just out the door and another in the chair."

"Sounds like normal."

"It's gonna be a long day."

"Listen, I just wanted to apologize for running out so quickly this morning. It was a pretty bad scene over at the Fredericks house."

"I was just gathering that."

"Misty said you've got Pamela Thorn there?"

"Yes, just started."

"Okay, I'll let you get to it," Gabriel said. "I hope you'll still be up for dinner and a movie tonight."

"As long as I don't get behind, I will be."

"I read you loud and clear," Gabriel said. "I love you."

"I love you too," Eliza said and hung up.

She stood the telephone among the combs, brushes, curling irons, and spray bottles on her station and returned to working the tangles out of Pamela Thorn's freshly washed hair. She hummed softly to the song playing on the salon's sound system but stopped when her throat tightened at an emotional swell in the music.

Pamela Thorn's blue eyes opened when Eliza's humming stopped.

"Amos told me he saw your husband out at the Fredericks house this morning," she said.

"Gabriel said it was a bad scene."

"Well, Amos was in the house most of the time, I think, so he didn't get too close to what was going on out in the yard. It sounds awful."

Eliza drew out a section of wet blond hair to its length so that the ends stood in a row between her fingers. She looked closely at it and let go, combed through the area again and drew out another section. This time she snipped twice with her scissors. She took a bottle from her station, sprayed and went back to work with the comb and scissors.

"Who do you think could've done such a thing?" Eliza said.

"Well, I know there's lots of meanness out there," Pamela said. "Amos has come across people that have that much hate in them. But to do this—" She stopped and, beneath the cape, shifted her hands from the arms of the styling chair to her lap. "That family is trying so hard to deal with this."

"I know what you mean," Eliza said. "They're not as easy in public as they used to be, but they're still out there." She made a snip with the scissors. "I don't know what I'd do."

"I don't either," Pamela Thorn said and stopped. Then quieter, "Did you know that Gene Fredericks subscribed to a gay men's magazine so that he could try to understand?"

Eliza didn't speak for a moment. With the heel of her scissors hand, she wiped the corner of first one eye then the other.

"Oh, that gave me a chill," she said at last. "I've gotta stop a minute." She sniffled and put comb and scissors into a pocket of her leather styling belt. "Can I get you some more coffee?"

\*　\*　\*

The Reverend Amos Thorn of the Runion Community Church sat in his office and stared at the cold mug between his hands. He breathed in deeply once and then let go the breath in a long exhalation. He set the coffee aside and leaned back in his chair, turning his head to stare at the window-framed images of a leaf-dappled lawn and cemetery and the October colors of Lonesome Mountain.

During his six years at the church, he'd met Mike Fredericks only a few times, either when he played his fiddle for a worship service or at impromptu gatherings at his parents' home—always last-minute events because Gene and Catherine never knew when their son was coming for a visit or how quickly after arriving he might suddenly leave for his home in Nashville or to go on tour. But in those brief moments when he gave himself back to the family and community in which he'd grown up, his talent amazed and his personality enchanted.

Vivid as they might now be in his memory, these occasions for contact had not allowed Thorn to know Mike Fredericks well enough to begin the task that this morning's events told him must be done soon. The room in which Catherine and Mike Fredericks and he had hidden themselves from the horrible scene taking place out in the yard was kept dark. Thorn thought the darkness must be easier on Mike's eyes as his vision seemed to be failing. Or perhaps it allowed him to pay less attention to the world as it—or he—faded. Then again, the darkness also distracted a visitor like Thorn, maybe his parents as well, from the ravages Mike's disease was inflicting on him. His body was wasted. Dark spots stood out on his face, even in the low light. Thorn hoped that the darkness also masked his own distress at witnessing Mike's condition, his body language that must be communicating to his suffering parishioners that he wanted to abandon them to their fear and grief.

And now he was away from them but not really removed from the illness and desperate sadness of that room. A drifting ache moved through his body, through his arms and chest and belly and thighs, coming and going like a ghost through the rooms of a house, as if searching for something only half remembered or perhaps wholly imagined. He shuddered and shifted in his chair and turned to his computer. He emailed Mrs. Ramsey, this morning's volunteer secretary, who sat at a desk outside his office door, not more than twenty feet away. He was supposed to go later in the morning to meet Granger Gosnell, another shut-in, also dying, but his email asked her to move that meeting to another time, maybe tomorrow or the next day.

He reached for the telephone, dialed the main number for Runion State University and asked for Jubal Kincaid. As his call was being transferred, he picked up a pencil and twirled it in his fingers.

"Dr. Kincaid," a voice answered.

"Hello, Dr. Kincaid," Thorn said. "This is Reverend Amos Thorn at the Runion Community Church. How are you today?"

"I'm fine, thanks," Kincaid said, his accent northern, Thorn thought, but not so much as to sound completely foreign to Runion. "I hope you are."

"Well, I am and I'm not," Thorn said. "I'd like to ask you a couple of things, but I'm afraid it might be too personal—" He stopped and cleared his throat.

"Okay, well, just go ahead, and I'll let you know," Kincaid said and chuckled. "How does that sound?"

"That sounds generous," Thorn said. "Thanks." He switched the receiver from his right to his left ear and held it there with his shoulder while he drew counterclockwise spirals on the pad in front of him. "Gene Fredericks told me this morning that you've been spending some time with his son, Mike. Did I understand him right?"

"You did."

"Well, sorry to be blunt, but my impression from this morning was that he doesn't have much longer—" He stopped again. "I wish I could find a better way to put it."

"I know what you're getting at, Reverend," Kincaid said. "I have indeed been spending some time with Mike. We were playing music together for a while, some Irish reels on fiddle and flute, and just talking. But recently he's been too weak for that."

"I would have liked to hear that music," Thorn said.

"It was fun. He's a great player." Kincaid stopped for a moment. Then, "Sad."

"Well, it's likely that his eulogy will fall to me when he's gone. Gene and Catherine are members of my congregation, you see." He paused and wrote Kincaid's name on the pad, while the other end of the line remained quiet. "So, I'm hoping that at some point, not necessarily now, we can sit down and talk. I don't know Mike well at all."

"Sure, we can do that," Kincaid said. "I can say that I know him a little bit."

For a moment neither spoke.

Then Thorn cleared his throat again.

"I'm guessing that you haven't heard what went on at the Fredericks' house early this morning."

"This morning?" Kincaid said. "No, I was practicing at home and then in class. What happened this morning?"

Thorn described the scene as well as he could, trying to be careful about what he said and how he said it to this man he had never met but about whom light community gossip had told him several things—where he came from and where he lived, that he didn't go to any of the churches in town, that he was gay, that his students and colleagues at RSU liked him very well so far, that the partner who moved here with him in July had left in early September and returned to Michigan.

"Mike saw it happen," Thorn said. "But the sun wasn't all the way up yet. He couldn't tell much about what was going on. Only that he thought there were three of them. There was fire involved, that much he knew."

"Dear God," Kincaid said.

"Dear God, indeed," Thorn said.

When they'd arranged a lunch meeting for the next day, Kincaid hung up the receiver and sat still at his desk, steadying his breathing and considering what was best to do. He should visit Mike, of course. Maybe he would call Catherine when he finished his afternoon lessons and ask if he might pick up carry-out somewhere and bring it to them for supper.

He could hear at least two pianos playing somewhere in the building—Gershwin's *Novelette in Fourths*, Chopin's posthumous

*Nocturne in C-Sharp Minor.* A talented soprano sang tritones, ascending by half steps. And a percussionist tapped out a syncopated rhythm on blocks. Danny Green, his flute student, played in a practice room not far away, working on Draeger's "Aubade" for later in the afternoon. Kincaid decided to wait until just before Danny arrived to call Catherine.

He left his studio and the music building and walked across campus toward downtown Runion, raising his face every few steps to the bright and perfectly blue October sky and wondering how such a horrible attack could happen to somebody like Mike at the beginning of such a beautiful day.

*Blue skies*, he thought, *are not always to be trusted.*

He quickly reached Main and stood at the corner just outside Rio Burrito. He'd eaten there twice in the past few days and might do so again with Reverend Thorn tomorrow. He crossed the street and from the deli in the back of Whitson's Green Grocer bought an old-fashioned bologna sandwich on white bread, with mayonnaise and tomato, and an RC Cola. He still knew very few people in the area, so with no interruptions, he finished lunch more quickly than he'd have liked. He left Whitson's and turned right and then stopped on the sidewalk, looking across the street at the Fredericks Agency.

The office was dark, and the CLOSED sign hung on the door. Nothing moved inside.

The darkness beyond the large front window caused him to shudder. He wondered why Hannah had not come in and then thought that maybe she was with the Fredericks family, helping around the house or in the yard. With that thought, the scene Reverend Thorn had described took sudden shape in his mind, and he lurched forward and entered Fricker's Hardware beneath a small bell that jingled when he opened the door and again when he closed it.

At first, he wondered if the store was empty, but then he saw a thin, hard-looking man standing partially hidden behind a tall revolving seed display and staring at him.

"Hi," Kincaid said.

The man neither spoke nor moved.

Kincaid had seen him a few times before, either sitting in his truck in front of Fricker's, usually with two younger men, in the mornings before the store opened or working somewhere among the aisles and bins inside the store when he had been in looking for something he needed for the house or the office. He couldn't recall ever having heard the man speak or ever having had the man look so directly at him.

"Okay," Kincaid said. "Do you sell motion-activated outdoor floodlights?"

Still, the man neither spoke nor moved.

The bell jingled behind him, and Kincaid turned and saw a tall young man closing the door.

"Howdy," Sammy Fricker said, looking at Kincaid as he closed the door. His direct and friendly gaze darted from Kincaid in the direction of the man beside the seed display and then back again. "Can I help you with something?"

Kincaid repeated what he wanted.

"Yeah, we have those," Sammy said. "They're right over here." He gestured for Kincaid to follow him. "You want battery-operated or hardwired?"

Kincaid thought for a moment. "Battery-operated, I suppose. I'm a renter, so I should stay away from changes like hardwiring."

"Fine," Sammy said. "They don't light up as big an area, but if you're not worried about a big space, then they work just as well. But you got to remember to change the batteries regular and pay a little attention to times when the light stays on a lot due to critters or wind."

"I'll remember that," Kincaid said. "Thanks." Then, "I think I'll take two of them."

Sammy Fricker rummaged briefly through the shelf in front of them, then raised the box he held in his hand. "Ben, go in the back and get three or four of these battery-operated lights. I'll take one at the register, and you can put the others on the shelf here."

Without a word, Ben Frisby moved toward the back of the store and disappeared through a swinging door.

"You work up at State?" Sammy said across the sales counter as they waited for Frisby to bring the second security light.

"I do," Kincaid said. "It's my first year here."

"What do you teach?"

"Music. Flute."

"So, you took Dr. Anderson's place?"

"I did," Kincaid said. "Although from what I've learned about him since I've been here, he doesn't seem like someone who's easily replaced."

"Well, I never took a class with him when I was going to State, but I'd known him most of my life from seeing him in the store and around town."

Ben Frisby suddenly stood beside Sammy Fricker and across the counter from Kincaid. He put down one box without a word and walked away with the rest that he'd carried from the back.

Sammy watched him for a moment, shook his head, and then began writing up the sale.

"You being a musician and all," he said, "do you know Mike Fredericks?"

"I do," Kincaid said. "Gene Fredericks is sort of my landlord, so I met Mike through him."

"Man, I hate what's happened to him, being sick and all."

"It's a sad thing."

"Did you hear what happened out at their place this morning?"

"I did."

"Man, that sucks," Sammy said. "They don't deserve that." He pressed some keys on the cash register and told Kincaid his total.

"There are a lot of evil pe—"

"I'm taking my lunch in the back," Frisby said.

Sammy and Kincaid both turned to watch the wiry man disappear through a curtained doorway.

"Sorry," Sammy said.

Kincaid handed the young man a credit card.

"Daddy said those guys might have bought the rope here," Sammy said. "I'm supposed to go through the receipts this afternoon to look for clues."

"I hope you find something that helps," Kincaid said as he signed the credit card slip.

Sammy bagged the security lights and handed them across the counter.

"Me too," he said. "Thank you now. Come see us again."

"I'm sure I will."

"And let us know if you have any problems with these lights or just have any questions about them."

"I'll do that," Kincaid said. "Thanks. And good luck with your sleuthing this afternoon."

The tall young man smiled and nodded.

Within an hour, Sammy Fricker had six names of people who had, in the last month, bought the kind of rope used in the attack on the Fredericks place. Two of the names he wasn't familiar with—new people in the area, he guessed, maybe campers or hikers. Three were locals and regulars, and the sixth was Ben Frisby, who at that moment was somewhere in the back of the store, eating the lunch he'd brought from home.

He remembered, as a child coming to work with his father, having been afraid of the rough-handed man, but as the boy grew older and taller, Frisby seemed to shrink and wrinkle. But Sammy still found himself unnerved in the man's presence, especially at times when the two of them were the only ones in the store. Sammy's father had tried to include Frisby and his family in Christmas parties and Fourth of July picnics, but the man, his rarely seen wife and even more rarely seen daughter, and the two sons, one older and one younger than Sammy—*the dumbasses*, he'd dubbed them as soon as he was old enough to think such things— never attended. Not that Frisby seemed to have others in the area that he preferred. Sammy had noticed for years, without giving any particular name to it, the way Frisby became rigid and stared at certain of the townsfolk, maybe even most of them, that came and went in the course of a business day. Yet he always appeared duly respectful of Sam Fricker—and of Sammy, as he became involved more and more in the running of the store. Frisby rarely spoke more than a few words during any given day and worked steadily and well from the time he clocked in until he clocked out, but Sammy had come to think him as most likely mean and ignorant, vicious in that vague and unpredictable backwoods way that only men like Frisby and his sons could be.

He scanned again the list of names lying on the countertop in front of him, and his gaze kept coming back to Ben Frisby's. His father had told him that Mike Fredericks thought three men had been in the yard, and Sammy could easily believe them to be Ben, Billy, and Benny Frisby.

The bell above the door jingled, and Sammy looked up to see his father come in and close the door behind him.

"Been busy?" Sam Fricker asked as he strode across the floor of the showroom, his gaze taking in the place, looking, Sammy knew, for customers and making sure that neither he nor Frisby was idle.

"Not too," Sammy said. "The new music professor up at State, the one that got Dr. Anderson's job, bought some outdoor security lights, but otherwise it's been quiet."

"Did you get those names for Deputy Boyce?"

"Just finished," Sammy said and handed the list to his father, who scanned the names.

"Well, I guess Davis can look into these two that I don't know," he said. "It couldn't have been any of the rest." He looked at the list again and shook his head. "Go over to the jail and see if you can find Davis." He returned the list to his son. "Give him this. I can't see it's gonna be much help, but you never can tell."

* * *

"Shit," Danny Green spit into his flute's embouchure hole when his fingers failed amidst the bustle of a thirty-second-note passage a little more than a minute into "Aubade."

"Relax, Danny," Dr. Kincaid said. "Your shoulders are hunched, and your wrists are tense." He looked down and scanned the score in his hand. "Okay, take a deep breath and let it go. Then try it again from the top."

"Goddamn it," Danny snarled when the low C at measure twelve did not speak.

"Hey, relax," Kincaid said again and waited.

Danny took a shallow breath and pushed it out through his nostrils, flaring them, and began once more. Measure twelve's low C sounded soft and rich, but the flurry of thirty-second notes came out as little more than key clicks and exasperated breath. Danny jerked the flute away from his lip.

"Fuck it."

"Okay, who are you," Kincaid said with a smile, "and what have you done with Danny Green?"

His student attempted a laugh but failed at that as well.

"Well, we can stop and talk, or we can just stop." Kincaid laid his score on the studio's baby grand piano. "You're obviously not up for this today."

"Sorry," Danny said. "I was doing fine in my rehearsal room."

"I overheard," Kincaid said. "You were playing well."

Danny sat down on the piano stool, pulled his flute apart, and settled each piece in the case. He kept his eyes on his work.

Kincaid leaned back on the front edge of his desk and cleared his throat.

"So, what's up?" he said. "Anything you want to talk about?"

"No, sir," Danny said, sounding a bit more like himself. He threaded a corner of a white bandana into the eye of his cleaning rod and swabbed the interior of the flute's head joint. He withdrew the rod, returned the head joint to the case, and picked up the midsection. He inserted cleaning rod and bandana swab into one end of the midsection, pushed it through, and pulled the whole out the other end. Then he stopped and looked directly at Kincaid. "Look, I know you're gay, okay?" he said.

Kincaid returned Danny's look, wondering where this was coming from and where it was going.

"Yes," he said slowly. "Sure, it's no secret, I guess." He paused. "Is that what's bothering you?"

"Maybe," Danny said. Then, "No, not really." He laid the midsection in the case and picked up the foot joint. "It's AIDS, I think."

Kincaid cocked his head and tried not to grin or grind his teeth.

"What about AIDS, Danny?"

"My cousin's a deputy, and he was out at the Fredericks place this morning. He saw what happened there, and he found out Mikey Fredericks is dying of AIDS. He said he knew you'd been out there a bunch and I ought to be careful 'cause you been with him. Been with Mikey Fredericks, I mean." Danny stopped and caught his breath and inserted the bandana swab into the foot joint.

"I see," Kincaid said after a moment. He fought a tightening in his throat, unable to tell if it were from anger or sadness. "Look, Danny, I see where you're coming from, and I understand how this might throw off your playing. Listen, you don't need to worry." He thought about saying something sharp against Danny's cousin or something sarcastic about ignorance regarding AIDS, but he took a deep breath and blew it out gently through his lips. "I haven't 'been with' Mike in the way your cousin might have implied." He dropped his gaze to the floor for a moment and then raised it again to meet the young man's. "Mike's a fellow human being," he said, as Danny's gaze broke toward the studio window. "He's a fellow musician and a damned good one. He's a fellow gay man, and he's dying. That's all you need to know and nothing you need to worry about, okay?"

He noticed that Danny slowly relaxed the grip he had on the cleaning rod of his flute. He saw the young man's jaw clench. His lips moved, not a tremble from withheld tears but as if speaking silently to himself. Then his jaw relaxed, and his mouth stilled to a firmness. He returned Kincaid's gaze and nodded.

"Okay," Danny said. He lay the foot joint in its place and snapped the case shut. Then, "Okay." He folded his silk polishing cloth and his bandana swab and lay them with the cleaning rod in his soft-shell case, put the hard case in on top of them, and zipped the soft-shell closed. "I'll play better next week," he said as he stood.

"I know you will," Kincaid said. "Why don't you work on the piece with your accompanist some and see if he can come in with you." He stood as well. "If we need to move things around a bit to accommodate his schedule, we can do that."

"Okay," Danny said. "I'll check with him." He extended his hand.

Kincaid took it.

"Okay," he echoed and saw the young man out as the studio telephone began to ring on the desk behind him. He closed the door, considered ignoring the ringing, but stepped to the window and reached down to pick up the receiver. "Dr. Kincaid."

"Hello, Jubal," Catherine Fredericks said. "Do you have a minute to talk?"

"Yes, of course. I actually meant to call you earlier and forgot." He paused. "Are you folks all right?"

"I guess you heard about our morning," she said. "It's been a difficult day, but yes, we're all right, I think."

"How's Mike?"

"Believe it or not, he's having one of his best days in a long time. The craziness seems like it's energized him somehow."

"I'm glad about that," he said. Beyond the kitchen clatter of whatever Catherine was doing, Mike played "Ashokan Farewell," and Kincaid could picture him sitting on the porch near the window open above the sink. "I can hear him."

Catherine fell quiet, and they listened together.

Then she drew a sharp breath and said, "Can you come by this evening? Mike has some adventure he wants you to help him with, and he says it just has to be tonight."

"Sure, Catherine. Can I bring you folks anything for supper?"

"That's sweet of you," she said. "But I feel like cooking tonight."

"Well, I look forward to that," Kincaid said, rubbing his left hand up and down his belly. "But do let me know if I can bring anything, okay?"

After they said their good-byes, Kincaid replaced the receiver and stood looking out the window.

The campus trees still retained much of their red and yellow foliage. Groundskeepers, growling blowers strapped to their backs, herded browning leaves into temporary berms alongside wide walkways and the one visible campus street. Hanging between two trees, a bright blue hammock cocooned at least one student, maybe two. A few others walked in the midafternoon sunshine, toward the dorms or toward the cafeteria. Across the small quad, a burly man in an unbuttoned blue-and-black flannel shirt, black t-shirt, and blue jeans appeared in the doorway of Mashburn Hall, came partway down the steps, and stopped. His thick shoulder-length hair and bushy beard shone white in the slanted light.

*Dr. Caldwell Rowe, Professor of History.*

Kincaid remembered noticing him at the reception that followed the fall faculty convocation. Dr. Rowe had stood in a circle of chatting and laughing people congregated near the punch bowl and cookies. Kincaid had first noticed the hair and beard, but then, with furtive glances at the eyes and face they framed, he realized that the man was not as old as all the white hair suggested. Maybe around fifty, he decided.

Dr. Rowe bent slightly back and lifted his face to the sun. His upper body expanded with deep breath.

Kincaid, standing in his unlighted office behind the east-facing window, breathed deeply with him and missed Chuck, missed him as he'd been in those Michigan days and nights. But the missing lasted only a moment. He didn't miss the Chuck who'd made a hell of the first few weeks in Runion before fleeing north. Chuck's constant and final badgering and bitterness broke the love Kincaid wanted to believe they'd shared but now knew they hadn't.

How little such pettiness and brokenness mattered in the face of greater realities—like that of Mike Fredericks.

Despite the energy surge Catherine reported, her son would die very soon. Kincaid knew—and Catherine probably did as well—that those close to death often experience a brief burst of something like vivacity just before the end. But a mother could hardly be expected to acknowledge this. And although Kincaid had never engaged in high-risk behaviors, he'd watched good friends—Bako ... Allen ... Warner ... Sergio ... Todd—sicken, fade, and die.

The telephone again began to ring as Dr. Rowe lumbered down the remaining steps and turned toward the library and disappeared.

"I should find out more about you," he said to the empty

window and reached for the telephone. "Dr. Kincaid," he said into the receiver.

"Jubal," Catherine Fredericks said, "I'm sorry to bother you again. Would you mind picking up some ground cinnamon before you come over? Gene doesn't want to run out to get it."

"That's all right," Kincaid said. "I'll be glad to. I might even have some in my spice rack that I can bring. Anything else you can think of?"

"No, that's it, I think," she said. "Thank you so much."

"Not a problem. See you in a bit."

"Bye," Catherine said, hung the receiver in its cradle on the wall, and returned to the sink and the window above it.

Gene still worked in the yard, as he'd done since he left the table at lunchtime. It had taken her almost to the end of the dishes to realize what he was doing—removing from that slope of yard every visible trace of the morning's horrors. He removed the scorched cross and carried it into the woods, where he could be heard breaking it into pieces, grunting and growling through the effort. She understood this, but she thought it might be some kind of sin to treat a cross that way and hoped that she could somehow ask Reverend Thorn about it without getting her husband in trouble with him, the church, or the Lord. Gene had returned emptyhanded from the woods and filled in the hole where the cross had been driven. Then he raked the slope twice and carried the rakings across the road, where he tossed them into the bramble. When she thought he must be finished, he raised a ladder to the limb where the monstrosity had hung and scraped or trimmed away every sign of the fire that had burned in the predawn darkness. She wanted to tell him to stop before he fell and broke something, but in a flash of insight that made her both sad and proud to have thought of it, she recognized that he was already broken and that all this activity was an attempt to heal himself. So, she'd held her tongue and watched. Now, with the ladder put away, he was raking the slope again.

From the shadow at the end of the porch, her Mikey provided a soundtrack to his father's work. She recognized improvisation when she heard it—after years of having asked, "What's that you're playing?" to which her son always responded with "I don't know" or "Nothing in particular," followed by "Just improvisation"—and wondered if he watched his father as he worked. What he played, she'd slowly realized, fit so well with the breaking and raking and erasing. She lost count of the snatches of reels and measures of hymns and phrases from Barber and Copland, to whose work her son had introduced her, music she'd surprisingly come to love in the years of his mysterious absences.

"He's playing to you, Gene," she whispered at the window above the sink. "Just listen."

* * *

Papa Lotta's voice crackled and boomed from the rusting horns that hung under the eaves of the pink-and-white cinder-block concessions building at the center of the Twilight Reel Drive-In. Strained nearly to the whine of a gnat, the same words and gruff Italian accent squeezed through the ancient metal speakers that hung inside the window of the Tanners' car.

"He sounds like one of those gangster movies," Eliza said. She dug into the paper tub in her lap and lifted loaded fingertips of buttered popcorn to her lips. "How did he come to be in Runion?"

"He married a woman from here," Gabriel said. "Mom told me she was a Bullman from over on Sodom. Either she was in the military and stationed in Italy or they met on a cruise ship. I can't remember which."

"Mama Lotta, she won't be happy if I bring all this candy home," Papa Lotta boomed. "So, come to the window and fill up your pockets like early Halloween." He coughed directly into the microphone, and the explosion of sound echoed against the hills that walled the Twilight Reel. "Everything's a-gotta go."

"I can't believe he's closing this place down," Gabriel said. "Mom and Dad used to pile Butler and me in the car and come down here every couple of weeks." He sat for a moment, looking toward the high white screen silhouetted against a still-bright-blue western sky dappled with pied cloud forms of golden yellow and tangerine with magenta edges and floating blue-gray tufts. "I remember *The Sound of Music* and *Butch Cassidy and the Sundance Kid* and *The Bible* and *Jaws*." He paused a moment, then smiled. "We came to see *Deliverance*, but Mom made us leave in the middle of that one."

"I guess if this many folks came out on a regular basis," Eliza said, "Papa Lotta wouldn't be shutting down."

"You're right, and we're among the guilty," Gabriel said and pulled on his straw. "When was the last time we were here?"

"Gosh, I guess it's been at least three or four years," Eliza said. "Was it *Forrest Gump* we saw?"

"I think so. Or it might have been *Interview with the Vampire*."

"I hope it was *Forrest Gump*," Eliza said. "That makes a better memory."

"Right again, my—"

The speaker crackled loudly once, and then a garbled mix of indistinct voices was followed by a sharp burst of feedback.

"Y'all's movie'll start in fifteen minuti," Mama Lotta announced in her mountain twang. Then said, in a more distant voice as she turned to her husband without turning off the microphone, "I reckon that's the last time I'll say that," and the speaker crackled loudly again and fell silent.

"That's her classic line," Gabriel said. "No telling how many times she's said it over the years."

He dipped into the tub of popcorn and then sat munching and looking at all the darkening vehicles parked around them. He recognized a few and knew who sat in them, and he could guess at the human contents of a few others, having seen somebody he recognized climb in or out, before or after visits to the concession stand or the restroom.

In the row ahead and a couple of spaces to the right sat a faded and rusted pick-up truck, out of which Billy Frisby had rolled a few minutes earlier and stood stretching in tattered and spattered blue jeans and black Nasty Boys t-shirt, cut off at the sleeves and midriff. He looked around for a moment and then clambered back into the truck and slammed the door.

"Lord, help," Eliza had said.

At that moment the passenger-side door screeched open, and Benny popped out. Dressed like his brother, he stretched as his brother had done and then stepped aside and held the door as a yellow-blond woman came trotting out of the dusk from the direction of the drive-in's fenced edge and ducked into the truck. Benny watched her in, then grinned and raised his head to look all round before climbing in behind her and slamming the door.

"Damn," Gabriel said. "Was that Loose Lucy?"

"Lucy Barnard," Eliza said. "You're not in high school anymore, Gabriel."

"Sorry, you're right." He sat a moment. Then, "Was it?"

"Yes, I believe it was."

"Damn," Gabriel said again. "She must be, what, twenty years older than the Frisby boys?"

"At least," Eliza said, still staring at the old pick-up truck. "Sad."

"I think their dad went with her for a little while back in high school."

A car passed between them and the truck.

"There's Cutter and Rendy," Eliza said. "Don't tell Cutter about Lucy and those guys, okay? You know he'll do something crazy."

Gabriel promised to say nothing as Cutter maneuvered into a space in the row ahead and to the left, a dozen doors from the pick-up in which the Frisby boys were holed up with Lucy Barnard. As soon as the Explorer's lights went dark, Cutter and Rendy climbed out and, hand-in-hand in the deepening dusk, headed toward Gabriel and Eliza, Cutter coming to Gabriel's window and Rendy to Eliza's. Gabriel and Cutter walked to the concessions building together, where they talked briefly with Mama and Papa Lotta before returning to the Tanners' car with their arms full of goodies. The four made plans to go to Johnson City the next afternoon for steaks at The Peerless, and then Cutter and Rendy returned hand-in-hand to their Explorer.

Darkness fell across the grounds of the Twilight Reel, and the grounds fell quiet in response. Cars and SUVs and pick-up trucks faded to grayscale shapes. The screen—toward which all were oriented—seemed to hang in midair, a ghostly monolith against the last blue-gold glow rimming the silhouette-black ridges behind it.

From the Frisby boys' pick-up, one cigarette glow and then another twirled in an arc through the darkness, each bursting into sparks upon impact, one in the dirt lane between rows and the other against the back bumper of a hulking SUV.

"I win, cocksucker," Billy laughed as he rolled up his window.

"Fuck you," Benny said as he rolled up his.

"Boys," Lucy Barnard said. "Is everything a competition between you two?"

"Sorry, Miss Lucy," they said together, and each dropped a meaty hand on one of her thighs.

She gently took each by its thick wrist and moved them to their own thighs.

"Stop it," she said. "Benny, honey, reach me another beer, would you?"

"Yes, Miss Lucy." He bent forward with a grunt and groped in the floorboard. He came up with a Pabst Blue Ribbon, popped the top, slurped at the foam, and handed it to her.

She looked at the top of the can for a moment, then at Benny.

"Just hand it to me, next time, child. I can suck my own foam."

Both boys snickered and fell quiet.

The atmosphere in the cab hung humid and overripe with the odors of Jovan White Musk and the natural musk of the Frisby brothers, of old truck and gasoline, of beer and breaths of beer and cigarettes.

Benny cleared his throat.

"I just didn't want you to break a n—"

"Something's fucked up," his brother interrupted.

"What?" Benny said.

"Hell, I don't know. The movie ain't starting, and there's some flashlights moving around in under yonder."

Flashlight beams moved spastically in the dark beneath the screen.

"Maybe somebody lost something," Lucy said.

Then one flashlight went out, and the other pointed upward and held steady.

"Nah, something's fucked up," Billy said. "Looks like somebody's climbing up to the screen."

"What the hell for, you reckon?" Benny said.

Billy swung his arm around, forcing Lucy to push back against the seat as he fisted his brother in the chest.

"How the fuck should I know what for?" Billy yelled, raising his right arm up to fend off his brother's counterattack.

"You boys, stop it," Lucy screamed, trying to spread her arms to hold each brother in his corner of the cab. "Just stop it!"

"You stay out of this," Billy growled.

"How the fuck can I stay out of it," Lucy laughed, "when I'm stuck right in the fucking middle of it?"

"You old wh—goddammit!" Billy yelled as Benny knuckled a punch into his thigh.

"I'll scratch y'all's fucking eyes out if you don't stop," Lucy hissed, spreading her arms again—a referee breaking up fighters. Holding them back for the moment, she took a breath. "And if you ever call me what you were just about to call me, Billy Frisby, you'll wake up from a drunk some night and find yourself tied and gagged and castrated. I swear to God you will."

Sudden light caught the three in this tableau, and they turned to face the source.

As if a film capturing a starless twilight sky had catastrophically broken, the screen held almost nothing but the projector's whitish light. Its supporting structure invisible in the darkness, it seemed a portal suddenly opened to the dingy radiance of another world, out of which three illuminated figures had materialized to sit side by side on the screen's catwalk, casting sharp shadows backwards into that radiant place.

The projection light beaming from the near side of the concession stand stunned Dr. Jubal Kincaid's eyes, and reflex brought up a hand to shade them. Mike and Gene Fredericks sat to his right, and six legs dangled a dozen feet above the ground. Below and in front of them some twenty yards, those cars and trucks in the front row caught enough of the reflected light to reveal Twilight Reel patrons on the other side of their windshields.

Beyond this row, a small sea of faceless and colorless vehicles spread out and faded into darkness. The low-roofed concession stand stood like an island in the midst of this sea, its projection beam like a lighthouse beacon.

Mike Fredericks sat slumped, his chin upon his chest, as if the effort to get this far in his plan had exhausted him. With hands that looked weak and pale in the projector's light, he held fiddle and bow in his lap.

Mike's father sat on his right, leaning back on straightened arms and splayed hands, just far enough away so that he was out of range of his son's bow elbow but close enough so that his left arm was at the ready for any need. His eyes never wandered from his son.

Jubal sat on Mike's left, his blackwood keyless piccolo dangling from his left hand. He reached out and touched the fiddler's shoulder.

"Hey," he said. "You okay?"

Mike Fredericks drew a deep breath as he raised his head and straightened up. With a flick of his left wrist, he held the rump of the fiddle against his chest. He released the breath slowly and evenly.

"Feeling a little otherworldly but all right," he said. "You ready?"

"Ready when you are."

Mike lifted his bow, and Jubal positioned the piccolo against his chin and lower lip. With little more than a nod from Fredericks, they leapt into "The Mossy Banks."

Jubal sat with his upper body gently torqued to his right so that, as the reel rushed forward through the light and into the darkness beyond, he kept his eyes mostly on Mike, watching for signs of unsteadiness, but every few measures his gaze swept along the lines of vehicles parked facing the screen. He saw one couple arguing, one making out—both oblivious. He saw confused looks on faces, read *What the?* and *That's Mike Fredericks* on lips. Doors opened, and people rose up out of their vehicles, their expressions unreadable.

Further back in the dark, beyond the reach of Jubal's vision, Gabriel and Eliza stood in their open doors and listened.

"Wow," Gabriel whispered, looking across the roof at the soft glow of Eliza's face.

"That is so cool," she whispered back.

The reel sounded strangely strong at this distance as it swirled and twirled through the air above them, the fiddle and piccolo intertwining through rapid repetitions and variations—a two-spirited, two-voiced deity passing overhead.

Both doors of the Frisbys' pickup screeched open at the same time, as Billy scrambled out the driver's side and Benny out the passenger's.

"What the fuck?" Benny yelled. "What the holy hell fuck?" He slammed his left fist down on the hood of the pickup.

Billy just stood, staring.

"Goddamn faggots!" Benny screamed. "Fucking abominations!"

"Hey, shut the hell up," somebody called from the darkness behind Billy, somewhere off to Gabriel and Eliza's right.

Benny whirled around.

"You shut the hell up, how 'bout it." He gestured back toward the screen, still screaming at the dark. "Them's goddamned faggots." He whirled back around to face the screen. "Fucking holy hell abominations," he yelled again and threw his head back and howled at the stars.

Lucy Barnard slid out of the cab of the truck and slipped behind Benny. In a running crouch, she faded into the darkness.

Billy still stood quiet and staring.

Benny howled again and shouted across the hood of the truck.

"Billy," he yelled and slammed both fists down on the hood. "Billy, let's go burn us some queer bitches."

Billy began stumbling forward as if entranced by a mixture of music and rage.

"That's what I'm fucking talking about," Benny yelled. "Let's go fu—"

An unopened can of beer exploded against Benny's head, and he crumpled to the ground beside the truck and lay still as the ruptured can hissed and spewed in the dark.

"Now, that's what the fuck," a voice said.

"Watch your language," another voice said.

"Nice throw," a third voice said as all were shushed from every direction.

Billy stomped forward toward the screen, passing between vehicles, between one row of them and then another, bumping or pushing Twilight Reel patrons out of his way with a continuous and menacing growl. And just as he veered left to round the projection end of the concessions stand, Papa Lotta stepped out the side door in the midst of swinging a thunderous right hook that caught the young man in the middle of his sneering growl. Billy seemed to convulse and levitate at once, hanging for a beat before crashing to the ground to lie as still as his brother.

The iconic photo of Ali standing over Liston leapt into Jubal Kincaid's mind, and the music-haunted air seemed to stutter. Jubal wondered if shock waves from Papa Lotta's punch startled him into dropping or adding a beat—he couldn't tell which.

The reel stuttered again.

With just a glance at the fiddling fingers, Jubal recognized that Mike Fredericks was losing control of the reel and his instrument. He almost felt Mike's imminent seizure like the approach of a dead-drop cliff may be felt in the landscape and atmosphere.

"Catch him," Jubal said as the music stopped and his right hand grabbed Mike's thin wrist and the thin neck of the fiddle in one grip.

At the same moment, the left arm of Gene Fredericks wrapped around his son's slumping back and held. He first pulled back away from the drop and then gently guided his son's head and shoulders onto his lap and hovered over him, whispering.

With the bow lost to the darkness below, Jubal laid the fiddle gently aside and secured his friend's thin legs across his own lap. Then the projection light went out, and he could see nothing at first. But then the lighted window in the near wall of the concession stand took shape and framed Mama Lotta, who spoke excitedly into the telephone.

\* \* \*

After the ambulances hurried through the gate of the Twilight Reel, lights ablaze and a-twirl, sirens awakening just as tires hit the blacktop, and after the dark firetruck lumbered that way as well, followed by Papa Lotta's terse and thickly accented announcement of the last show cancelled and refunds available, Gabriel and Eliza rolled slowly with the line of cars exiting the drive-in's grounds.

"Did you want to get our refund?" Gabriel asked.

Eliza chuckled and said, "I think we got our money's worth." Then, "I hope they're all all right."

Gabriel shifted in his seat but kept his hands on the steering wheel.

"I think the Frisby brothers will be. They're likely to be different for better or worse, but they'll be all right. Not too sure about Mike though."

He fell silent, and she reached out her left hand and rubbed his shoulder.

"So, nobody knew he was gay?" she asked. "All the time you were growing up with him?"

"Nobody I knew anyway. He seemed just like the rest of us."

Eliza dug in the nearly empty popcorn bag and came up with a couple of half-popped kernels, which she crunched and chased with ice-melt.

"I wonder who threw that beer can," she said and gurgled the bottom of her cup with the straw.

Gabriel grinned and shrugged and rolled their car a few feet forward.

They were nearly to the exit gate when she lightly touched his arm.

"Look, there's Lucy," she said. "Let's give her a ride."

When the line of cars stopped to wait for the vehicle in front to pull away, Eliza opened the door and got out. She hurried over to Lucy, who flinched and shied away at her approach. Then Eliza was talking with her and pointing back toward Gabriel. Almost reluctantly, Lucy nodded and followed Eliza back to the Tanner vehicle, where Lucy slipped into the back seat as Eliza returned to the front.

"Hey, Lucy," Gabriel said. "How are you?"

"Just dandy, Mr. Tanner," Lucy said in a grim voice. "Just goddamned dandy."

Gabriel glanced at Eliza, who managed to give him a weakly

reassuring look in return.

"We went to school together, remember?" he said. "Just call me Gabriel."

Lucy sucked her upper lip for a moment and then her cheeks.

"I don't like saying that," she said. "But I'll call you just Tanner, if that's okay."

Gabriel glanced at Eliza again.

"You don't like the name Gabriel?" she asked, turning halfway around in the passenger's seat.

"I ain't saying that," Lucy said. "I just don't like saying it. Tanner's okay, ain't it?"

"Sure," Gabriel said as they reached the front of the line and he stopped at the edge of the highway. "Which way, Lucy?"

"Take me to town, Tanner."

"You've got it," Gabriel said and turned left on Pump Gap Road.

They rode through the October darkness without speaking. The hums of engine and of tires on the blacktop beneath them and Lucy's clicking and sucking mouth noises were the only sounds until Pump Gap ended at Lonesome Mountain Drive and Gabriel turned right toward Runion.

Lucy's lip smacking and teeth sucking stopped, and she cleared her throat.

"Reckon them boys'll be okay, Elizy?" she asked, leaning up from the back seat, her face hovering near Eliza's left shoulder and her beer breath clouding almost visibly toward the windshield.

"I think so. Gabriel went over and talked to the EMTs and said they didn't seem overly concerned."

"I think Billy's nose is broken and a couple of teeth got knocked out," Gabriel said. "But he'll be all right." He rolled the window down half an inch. "They figured Benny might have a concussion, but they were mainly concerned with getting his head to stop bleeding."

"Precious Jesus," Lucy said. "Ben's gonna be madder than hell." She sat back again. "Lord, God, Elizy, I don't know what he'll do." She fell quiet again as they approached the first lights of Runion.

Then, "What about Mikey Fredericks?"

Eliza turned to Gabriel for a moment, but he kept his eyes on the road.

"Gabriel said they thought he was just exhausted."

"You mean from his queer sickness," Lucy said.

"From his AIDS, yes," Eliza said. "And from the day he's had, I'd imagine. He and his family had a bad experience early this morning."

"Yeah," Lucy said. "I heard."

Gabriel slowed down to just below the town's speed limit.

"Lucy, do you know why Benny and Billy reacted like that? I mean, nobody else seemed to mind."

"Search me," Lucy said. "I know their daddy thinks queers is an abomination. Rubbed off on them boys, I guess."

"You're probably right," Gabriel said. "It just seemed like they took Mike's presence there so personal." He paused. "You got a guess as to why that might be?"

"No, I don't. They hate queers. Reckon that's enough, ain't it?"

Eliza half turned in her seat.

"Lucy," she said softly. "Did they say anything to you before they jumped out of the truck and all the yelling started?"

Eliza looked at Gabriel, and he smiled slightly as he kept his eyes on the street.

Lucy leaned forward and said, "Drop me off there by the Pizzeria, Tanner."

"All right," Gabriel said. "Did they say anything?"

He pulled to the curb across from the Pizzeria and stopped.

Lucy Barnard immediately opened the door and, with a grunt, stood up out of the vehicle and steadied herself with a hand on the door frame. Then she turned, leaned down, and spoke without looking at either Gabriel or Eliza.

"They been up since before it was light, and they been drinking a lot. I guess they was a little on edge. I don't know. They got blood on their hands." She closed the door but then bent down to Eliza's window.

Eliza fumbled with the switch, found it, and the window opened.

"And Benny has it on his shoes." She straightened up and stepped back from the curb. "I'm pretty sure I seen some."

Eliza turned to look at Gabriel, and then both faced forward to watch Lucy Barnard walk away from the Pizzeria, past Fricker's Hardware, and on toward Stackhouse Park Riverwalk, looking around, one moment as if in fear and the next as if on the hunt, jiggling and shimmering like nothing else in Runion that night.

# Two Floors above the Dead

Gunther Gosnell stands by the span of windows that takes up much of the living room wall and looks over the moonlit rooftops of the buildings across Main Street, down to the dark gray French Broad River and up the black swells of Piney Ridge.

"On t'other side of Piney Ridge," he says.

He tries both to remember and to forget the dreams of the night. *Accepts all comers*, the man with the handlebar moustache said. *Stay in three minutes and win fifty dollars*. He didn't care about the money, thought only that it would be fun. But the monster lifted him until he felt on his face the heat of the big light that dangled overhead. Then he was flying above folding chairs, above laughing and screaming people.

"Them's dreams," he says and turns from the windows and pads across a floor cold with moonlight like snow.

A dim square of light floats just off-center the oval surface of water.

"Bulb out."

The image shatters and scatters in a frenzy until the trickle ends and the square trembles back together.

A sneeze and a fart. Another sneeze and a sniff.

He eats a banana with mayonnaise and peanut butter and drinks a glass of buttermilk.

At the windows again, he sips a cup of lukewarm instant coffee, watching the descending day and remembering the mobile home he lived in so long, over there, beyond the ridge line, in the trees above a deep cutback in the narrow two-lane.

His Christmas lights—lights in every room, lights on every outside edge, lights in the yard and in the trees. Lights everywhere. Lights from Halloween to Easter.

"Pretty!"

One New Year's Day when the lights lay dark beneath ash and snow, Granger brought him to live in this place, up two long flights of stairs ascending without a turn from Back Street to the third floor of Mr. Ramsey's funeral home, to two rooms with a bath and a kitchen and so many windows.

"Light."

And the dead people two floors below.

Granger is there now. So still and pale and thin that it doesn't look like Granger. Not like he was back in springtime.

"Gunther," Mr. Ramsey had said, "we need two holes dug tomorrow. One of them's for your brother, God rest him, and if you don't want to dig that one, I understand. I can get somebody else, no problem. You can just dig the one for the Fredericks boy."

As he dresses, he remembers March, not long after the blizzard. Two graves then too—an old woman, an old man. Another short day to dig. Snow still deep on the ground. When Mr. Ramsey buried the old woman who'd frozen to death in her house, Gunther returned to the cemetery and, as he always did, sat waiting on his machine at some distance from the hole as the graveside service proceeded. He remembers closing his eyes and thinking that the mild air and the bright sunshine, red through his eyelids, made it difficult to believe that the blizzard had happened. And he said so again and again to the light midday breeze. When he opened his eyes, he saw people looking in his direction, most of them he didn't know, and he thought they must be looking at his beautiful machine. A couple of faces that turned toward him he recognized and named to himself and to the breeze. When he saw Granger, he waved and called, "Hey, Granger!"—then giggled to himself when Granger put a finger to his lips and shook his head.

Those congregated around the grave were going away, and

Granger came to him. They shook hands, and without a word other than his name, "Gunther," Granger dropped heavily to one knee and tied Gunther's work boots.

Granger said some things that Gunther can't remember now as he tries to tie his boots for this day's work—a shorter day than the one in March to dig two graves. Only the last thing Granger said he remembers. Granger took his hand again and gripped it firmly without shaking.

"I love you, Gunther," he said and let go and began to turn away.

Gunther giggled again and nodded his head.

"Thank you," he said. "Thank you."

As he turned to mount his machine, he thought he wanted to say something else, but he couldn't at that moment think what it might be.

"I love you too, Granger," he said later, when it was almost dark above the grave of the old man from the college.

"I love you too, Granger," he says again, now, and bends to pick up his coat from the floor.

He pulls down his wool cap, tight over his ears, and grabs his lunchbox—"Porky's Lunch Wagon"—filled with Moon Pies and the old thermos of cold coffee. Then he goes out the door and descends the stairs past the living and the dead.

*   *   *

Before he died, Granger Gosnell requested that Mr. Ramsey not pressure or even encourage Gunther to attend his funeral.

"He won't understand," Granger said. "And he won't sit still for it." He also feared that if Gunther caught hold of the grief that would swell in the church or swirl around the gravesite, he might feel trapped by it—his understanding overwhelmed—and explode into a desperate and mindless violence likely to hurt himself and others. "He's a big boy," Granger wheezed. "A dangerous child. Let him watch from his machine. Like he does."

Mr. Ramsey agreed, and the two of them sat quietly, looking

through the picture window at the faded November fields and the blue-brown mountains beyond.

\*   \*   \*

Gunther lurched out of the large wooden shed atop his Kubota tractor and backhoe. He whipped left on Back Street and then bounced right on Mill, left again at the new Main Street traffic light, right again at the bottom of the hill and across the bridge to Piney Ridge. Wearing a bicycle helmet too small for his head, along with goggles and scarf, he pushed the Kubota as fast as it would go through the cutbacks that climbed up toward the ridgeline, his grin wide, his nose and cheeks reddening in the mid-November air.

At the cemetery he found the graves of his grandparents and parents and his sister-in-law Carrie and took into account the distance between his mother's grave and Carrie's. He stared at a certain spot on the ground and plotted the length and width, no longer needing either measuring tape or wooden form to see the eight-feet-by-three-feet area he would need. The two feet on each side would be close enough, he thought, for Granger to hold the hands of their mother and his wife until he got used to the dark.

Gunther grinned and took his sod spade from its rack on the Kubota and set to work, slicing cleanly beneath the grass and laying the sections neatly on the ground to the left, just at the foot of his mother's grave. When he finished, he had a rectangle of bare earth just the right size and exactly parallel with the graves on either side and in line with graves at its head and foot.

Then he walked into the woods, where a small shed stood among the trees. From this shed he carried back two thick sheets of plywood, which he put on the ground to protect both the tops of the graves and the vaults beneath from the wheels, stabilizers, and weight of the backhoe. Then he rolled it into position and anchored, reversed the seat and began to dig.

\*   \*   \*

Sky light gray and full of cold wind. A snow sky still refuses to release the beauty of the first flakes of the season. Faded and browned grass, stiff, trembles as the sky's breath moves across it. Naked trees. Their leaves lie on the ground at their feet, a few still bright with color.

His machine grabs scoopfuls of earth and lifts them, extends to the left, and unloads.

A mound grows atop the grave of his father.

"Don't drop dirt on Mama," he says to his machine.

In a day or two, Preacher Thorn will stand between the hole and Carrie's grave. People who come here will sit or stand on and around Carrie, but that can't be helped. Mr. Ramsey's boys will put down something to protect her from the tramping and poking feet of people and chairs.

Mama watches his work as he digs straight down from the outline he cut in the sod.

*Stay inside the lines, little man.*

"I will, Mama," he says and smiles at her.

Carrie neither speaks to him nor looks at him. She stands and stares into the deepening hole.

*Has Granger took good care of you?*

"Yes, Mama." He tells her again about the fire at his mobile home and how Granger found him a new place to live.

*Who's gonna look after you when Granger's here with us?*

"Little sister will," he says.

*O Lord, that Ollie.*

"Ollie'll help me, Mama, you'll see. Granger says so."

Carrie stands watching as her husband's grave grows deeper and darker.

\* \* \*

Gunther wanted to speak to Carrie, but he didn't. She'd been kind to him during all the time he'd known her. Kinder to him than anybody not in the family, maybe even kinder than anybody except his mother. When that big man he was playing with at the county fair had lifted him and thrown him into the fourth row and broken his body, hurting his mind, too, even more than it had been hurt when he was born, Carrie nursed him until he could be alone again. His mother had cared for everybody else and for him as she could, but Carrie took care of him more.

The grave was finished, and his mother was gone. Carrie had disappeared too, without word or look.

He removed his machine from the dig site and parked it by the cemetery entrance. Then he returned the plywood to the shed, brought back the grass-green tarpaulin with which to cover the naked earth raised from the grave and mounded over his father, sat down at the foot of the hole, his feet dangling inside, and ate three Moon Pies.

\* \* \*

The grave for the Fredericks boy was to be dug in the cemetery adjoining Reverend Thorn's church, so he bounced back toward Runion, waving, as he crossed the bridge, to Mr. Ramsey's two-man crew going to raise the tent top over the newly opened earth up on Piney Ridge.

He whipped into the Runion Community Church's parking lot, then slowed and maneuvered gently toward the plot Mr. Ramsey had marked sometime during the morning by planting a small red flag and leaving protective plywood and another tarpaulin. Gunther fixed his machine so that it was ready to dig and then filled the plastic thermos cup with cold coffee and drank it with another Moon Pie while he sighted the outlines of the grave.

\* \* \*

Graveyard of slanted light and air still cold but snowless. People from the graves not easy to see this time of day. They stand around and watch his beautiful machine work. Some faces are familiar to him, but he doesn't know names.

"Mama says I ain't got no common sense is why I don't know people," he says. "There's a boy to be buried here with y'all," he tells them as he digs. "I don't know how come him to die."

These silent townsfolk used to make him nervous when he dug here, shimmering like a sheet of water that isn't really there on a summer highway. Their silence neither mean nor sad. Nor like Carrie's.

"Y'all know my Granger, I bet," he says above the noise of digging. "I just dug him a place over to Piney Ridge."

His machine grabs a scoopful of dirt and lifts it as he watches.

A voice reaches him, and he looks up to see a living man among the dead.

\* \* \*

"I'm sorry about your brother," Reverend Amos Thorn said again when Gunther shut down the backhoe. "He was a good man."

Gunther removed his wool cap and began working it around and around with his thick fingers.

"Afternoon, Preacher Thorn," he said.

Thorn walked through the crowd of shades and stopped beside the Kubota and stood for a moment looking up at Gunther. Then he turned and surveyed the work.

"That's a fine looking grave, Gunther," Thorn said. "Gene Fredericks will appreciate it."

"Thank you. Thank you."

Thorn turned back to Gunther.

"How are you holding up?"

Gunther sat and looked at the barely visible ghosts.

"Are you all right?" Thorn said. "That's what I mean."

"I'm fine, thank you," Gunther said. "Fine, thank you."

"You can talk to me if you need to," Thorn said.

Gunther looked at the sky and figured a couple of hours of good light remained. He needed to finish before the boys arrived to put up the tent, and he needed to be out of the graveyard before sunset.

"Have you seen your sister Ollie?" Thorn asked. "Is she all right?"

Gunther looked directly at Thorn for the first time.

"Yes," he said. "I know Ollie all right. She'll take care of me now." He suppressed a giggle. "Mama don't think she'll be good at it, but she will."

Thorn stared a moment and then cleared his throat.

"She had her baby some weeks before Granger passed, didn't she?"

"Yes, yes," Gunther said. "She's got her a girl child name of Rose." He giggled out loud this time. "I call her Rosie, and she ain't no bigger than a nit!" Then he faced the sky and laughed out loud.

"Rose," Thorn said. He seemed ready to say something else but didn't.

Gunther moved to start the engine again.

"You can come to me, Gunther," Thorn said quickly. "If you or Ollie or the baby needs anything, you can come to me."

"Yes, sir," Gunther said. "Yes, sir, Ollie's a strong woman. Full grown." Then he started the engine, looked at the sky, looked at the grave, and resumed his work without further notice of Reverend Amos Thorn.

*  *  *

Just after sunset, he returned to the Back Street shed without the usual cleaning of the Kubota's bucket and teeth, its tires and stabilizer pads.

"Hey, Granger, I'm back," he said to the double doors at the foot of the wide stairs.

"Hey, Mr. Ramsey, I'm home," he said to the doors at the middle landing.

He turned on water for a bath and shed his clothes, rinsed his thermos at the tub spigot and set it on the back of the toilet. When the tub was half full he turned off the water and squeezed down into it, hips squawking against the sides as he settled. He sat still for a long time, thinking nothing.

When he felt the water cooling, he washed his face and hair with soap, rinsed by pouring soapy water from a big red plastic NC State cup he kept beside the tub, and pulled the plug.

On the stovetop in the kitchen, he found the soup beans and cornbread Mrs. Ramsey had brought sometime in the afternoon.

He stood naked by the table and ate these along with a glass of buttermilk, then went to his chair in the front room and watched the last light drain from the sky above Piney Ridge until he fell asleep.

\* \* \*

While Gunther slept two floors above the dead in Mr. Ramsey's funeral home, Ollie sat suckling Rose in the kitchen of the house Granger had left her and wondering if she could ever make it her home. She wished she could take the baby and go back to her cabin in Belva, but it had burned to the ground a few weeks after she'd moved here in midsummer, already several months pregnant, to take care of Granger. This was the homeplace. This her mother's kitchen and then Carrie's. She hadn't been here often when Carrie ruled, but she could remember her mother moving back and forth through this space, cooking—always cooking. They'd never gotten along, her mother and she. People had said many times within her hearing that the two of them were too much alike to get along. Ollie still couldn't see that. During slow, silent nights in her cabin, she'd come to believe that the chasm between them had opened when Gunther had come home so very wounded and her mother, Ollie believed, had rejected her—eleven years old at the time—in order to care for him.

She was never that close to Granger either, he being almost twenty years older. Even though Carrie and he never had children, he was the golden boy in both family and community, whose birthright seemed stamped on their mother's affection and everything in the house and everywhere in the fields. He'd tried to reclaim her as a Gosnell, as a dependent, after their mother died, but she snubbed every effort. They'd come to know one another better in his last few months but not really as brother and sister.

Granger had requested, at the end, that she take care of Gunther. She told him, of course, that she would, but she worried about how seriously to take such a deathbed promise. Gunther frightened her. Only three years younger than Granger but still nearly seventeen older than she was, he had, from her earliest memories, filled her mother's house with his big body and his giggling voice and his volatile energy. Then he was gone for a long time but returned at twenty-seven the kind of mammoth simpleton that often haunted the horror shows she later watched over the bony shoulders of boys at the Twilight Reel. Her mother welcomed him home as prodigal at the same time that she piecemeal banished Ollie as profligate. She dropped the notion of herself as daughter and little sister and became strong and independent, but now she felt her independence lost in the role of caretaker for first Granger and Rose, now Rose and Gunther. She hoped the strength that had kept her independent for so many years wouldn't abandon her but transform into more of her mother's kind, even though that thought turned her stomach.

The upstairs room Gunther had, she knew, shared with Granger during much of their boyhoods required some work in order to be made ready for him. He seemed to be managing well in his little apartment, so she need not rush to bring him here, she thought. For now, she could work out a schedule with Mrs. Ramsey so that a few nights every week she and Rose could take supper to Gunther and stay and get to know him better. She could carry in some groceries and maybe cook there from time to time.

The baby stirred and stopped feeding.

Ollie looked down to find Rose not asleep but staring up at her with an intense absence of expression. Once again she tried to discern the color toward which the eyes were tending, but they remained an infant's deep and impenetrable slate blue.

\* \* \*

Dark again. Ceiling patterned with foreshortened window shapes from streetlights below. Cold room. Cold skin.

*Gunther, get some clothes on. It ain't decent nor healthy to sit around naked like that.*

Two shades haunt the shadows in the corners of the room. Granger is one. The other must be the Fredericks boy.

*You'll catch your death, little brother.*

"No, I won't neither, Granger." He sits and looks at the second shade, a dark outline and two glittering eyes. "Mikey Fredericks, that's your name." He rubs his naked belly and leans forward suddenly. "He likes it! Hey, Mikey!" He giggles behind his hand.

*Don't be scared, Gunther.*

"I ain't scared. And don't you be scared neither, Granger. Mama and Carrie is waiting for you." He tells Granger about digging his grave and about seeing their women there, what they did and what he and their mother said, how Carrie hadn't said a word and how he wished she had. "I told Mama Ollie will help me."

Granger stares downward through a window.

*You need to get on your pajamas and get in the bed.*

"I don't have any pajamas."

*Ask Ollie to get you some. You can't parade around the house like that when she takes you home with her and Rose.*

"I will, Granger," he says and smiles at him. "I won't."

*I love you, Gunther.*

"Thank you," he says. "Thank you." Then, "I love you too, Granger."

He stands up and stretches, goes to the refrigerator for a few swallows of cold buttermilk, wipes his mouth with the back of his hand, and then disappears into his bedroom without a glance at the shades left lingering in the shadows.

\* \* \*

With Gunther pacing to and fro in front of the silent backhoe, Ollie was the only immediate family in attendance at the graveside. Mr. Ramsey's oldest son, a thin and serious young man and very much in control of the proceedings, seated her—Rose in arms—center of the first of two rows of folding chairs set up for mourners. Cousins she knew only by name and only because they'd visited Granger in his final weeks took seats on either side of her. Other elderly folks settled into the second row, and a few men stood at random behind.

The vault with its lowering device was positioned over the mouth of the grave, and when all were seated, the pallbearers came shuffling and stamping heavily with the casket between them and maneuvered it onto the lowering device. Then one by one these removed the flowers from their lapels and laid them on top of the casket.

Ollie paid close attention to Gunther, to his movements and the modulations of his mumbling voice, watching and listening for signs of distress. Even when Reverend Thorn took his place in front of her and looked down with a nervous smile, she didn't take her eyes from Gunther.

Thorn cleared his throat and, after a moment, began.

"We gather here in this beautiful glade on Five Finger Mountain to commit Granger Gosnell to his final rest between his mother, Sally, and his one true love, Carrie."

Ollie heard a louder but still inarticulate sound from Gunther, and she felt those around her start in their seats. Gunter had stopped pacing for the moment and stood staring open-mouthed toward graveside and mourners, and Ollie wondered what, if anything, was in his mind.

"Think of all the changes in the world Granger witnessed since his birth in 1939. My goodness, it's hard to imagine. But what's even harder to imagine are the changes he's experiencing now."

"Amen," from one of the standers.

"Although Granger and Carrie, who I'm sorry to say I never met, had no children, he will be long remembered in this community, in his church, and in the lives of his family, Ollie and her Rose and—"

\* \* \*

"—Gunther."

A name. His name. Beneath the cold gray sky, heavy with pendant snow. In the preacher's voice his name shivers among the winter-brown grass.

*Gunther. Gunther. Gunther.*

In more voices now—Mama's and others'—it rises to echo among the stones and scatter into the woods.

The shades of the dead stand all around in gradations toward invisible in the weak midday light. Over near Ollie stand Carrie and Mama and, yes, Granger, clearer than any.

"Carrie?" he calls.

She looks at him in the way that he remembers waking to see her looking at him as she nursed him through his bad time. Then she turns to Granger, and Granger turns to her.

"Granger, my boots need a tying!"

He lurches forward toward the hole he dug the day before. He sees Ollie looking at him, directly at him, eyes wide as she rises and thrusts Rose into the arms of Preacher Thorn, who looks down at the child as if afraid of such a tiny thing.

"Ain't no bigger than a nit!"

Ollie comes to meet him. Runs in her mother's black dress to meet him.

Then he is on the ground. On his back on the ground. Like when that big man threw him out of the ring and into the fourth row.

Ollie sprawls on top of him. Somehow holding him down.

"Carrie!"

Ollie says something. Says it again.

*Ollie'll take care of you now.*

*Granger's voice? No, Carrie's.*

And he begins to still. Facing a sky without expression.

Against the blank gray above his Ollie. Something. A grayer speck against the gray. Something descends. An angel. A dollop of cloud. Something descends and becomes strangely smaller as it falls. And whiter. Descends from the gray sky and past the tops of the naked gray trees. Without haste. It alights in Ollie's black hair, lingers there for a moment, perfect and white against her black hair, grows smaller, and then disappears into her.

# Witness Tree

On the top floor of the Peery-Lenburg Library at Runion State University, Carol Boyd-Boyd emptied the trash can by the entrance to the Archives of Southern Appalachia and then peeled off her yellow rubber gloves, stuffed them down in the front pocket of her smock, and sank into a plush golden chair. She liked to leave the vacuum in the closet in the stacks and take these late breaks in the ASA reading room, where she could sit in the quiet of the nearly deserted library, dreamily breathing in the history displayed around her and fantasizing about being witness to this or that event. She felt the past, felt the weight of it, sometimes warm and dense like she imagined the downward pull of summer fruit felt to green branches, sometimes cold and ponderous like encasing ice or wet snow on naked limbs. Tonight, with students gone after finals and the library prepared to close for the holidays, she found herself sinking deeper into the plush quiet, heavy with imagined pasts and the apprehension that when she came to the end of this shift the door of the library would lock behind and strand her in the cold present of husband Carroll and his family throughout Christmastide and its Y2K fears.

Directly in front of her comfy chair stood her favorite exhibit, the Runion White Oak Tree Ring Display—proud remnant of the fallen oaken god that had overseen all but the past ten years of the community's history. On the wall to the right of the display hung photographs of the tree as it appeared in the nineteenth century, when it witnessed—and had been, she imagined, an unwilling participant in—the meting out of capital punishment for a dark variety of local crime. The photographs portrayed men hanging from the tree's hefty lowest branch in the years before 1910, when North Carolina took unto itself—out of the hands of its counties and local governments—the power to put men to death.

She'd learned this three months before, on a Thursday morning in September, when she sat in this same chair and listened as RSU's Dr. Caldwell Rowe gave a public lecture on Runion history, a talk in which he featured the oak as the central figure around which the community grew. He'd shown slides that enlarged the sepia images for his audience and also provided a glimpse of the unseen yellowed backs of the photographs. In each, the oak and a hanged man figured prominently. Right of the oldest photo's center, beyond the crowd gathered to witness the execution, appeared evidence of the recent groundbreaking for the Methodist Episcopal Church, South, and on its back somebody had scribbled in pencil, "Death of James Boyd, for sodomy and murder, 20 March 1846."

Since that morning lecture she'd traced James Boyd through Madison County genealogical materials and local lore to learn he was one of Carroll's Boyds, not hers, a discovery she found both satisfying and disturbing.

In the second and next oldest photograph, part of the church building itself appeared alongside the beginning of its graveyard, and on the back the same hand had written, "Hanging of Jonah Roberts, for thieving, 7 July 1867." The third image revealed members of the church choir darkly dressed and standing on the church steps, songbooks open in their hands and mouths open to round Os. The grotesque image of the convict's lifeless body, Carol remembered, was made more haunting by the messages penciled on the back: "Hanging of E. Z. Godly, for rape, 29 December 1877," and in another hand below, "Mose Davis confessed to this crime on deathbed, April 1911."

While the tree stood its ground and continued to grow skyward, the world beneath it changed. A spur branched off of Runion's Main Street and angled toward Putnam's sawmill, separating the oak from the church building. The Township of Runion then created Back Street just beyond the rear lots of the businesses along the northwest side of Main, linking Lonesome Mountain Drive and Mill Street. The fact that the Methodist Episcopal Church, South, supported secession caused the denomination to fall into disfavor after the Civil War and Reconstruction. The congregations inhabiting the building over the next half century gave it a number of names, until it eventually became home to the First Southern Missionary Church, which was its name when she'd married Carroll there on the first of June in 1963. These changes in the human world left this mighty tree standing at the southeastern corner of the Runion State University campus, looming over a faculty parking lot, the intersection of Back and Mill Streets, and the First Southern Missionary's front yard and cemetery.

"Ten years ago today," Dr. Rowe had concluded, "on September 23, 1989, a Saturday, as many of you will remember, a stray gust from Hurricane Hugo toppled this old white oak onto Back Street, blocking traffic and the back doors and docks of Cowart's Department Store, Radio Shack, Ramsey's Funeral and Cremation, and The Fredericks Agency. By Tuesday the 26th, the tree was limbed and cut into several sections. By noon on Saturday the 30th, men from a coalition of Runion-area churches reduced the remaining limbs to cords of firewood and boxes of kindling for local poor, several of whom were known descendants of men who had, from those same limbs, hung by the neck until dead."

When Dr. Rowe thanked his small audience and asked if any had questions, Carol raised her hand with the intention of outing her husband's cousin Honey Boyd as a recipient of one of those cords of firewood and thus a descendant of the hanged James, implicating her husband in the process, but the history professor's gentle manner cowered her so that she asked about the physical display itself—a stupid question to which she already knew the answer.

According to a plaque mounted beside a fourth picture of the oak, this one in color as the tree lay, still whole, where it fell, all of the trunk sections but one went to Sunrise Sawmill in Asheville. The remaining section, a cookie ten inches thick and one hundred ninety-one inches in circumference, went to the dendrochronologist

in the Department of Geography and Planning at Appalachian
State University, and almost four years later, early in the summer
of 1993, this cookie, reduced to a thickness of five inches and
preserved with polyethylene glycol, returned to Runion State with
a certificate indicating an estimated age of three hundred fourteen
years. The package also included a map of its rings that identified
the approximate year in which each ring formed. The following
January, Dr. Jack Fleenor, curator of RSU's Archives of Southern
Appalachia, began supervising majors from the university's
Departments of History and Appalachian Studies in a semester-
long project that resulted in this permanent display in the reading
room of the Archives.

Pins with heads of Runion State blue and gold were inserted in
a number of rings sectioning the thirty-inch radius of the cross-
cut. In consultation with Dr. Fleenor and their departmental
mentors, the students researched and chose years based on local
historical interest, with some state, national, and world events
included for context. Threads of rainbow-colored yarn stretched
from pins stuck in the rings representing those years to pins that
bulleted twenty-one points of historical interest printed clockwise
in the margin around the cookie.

- c. 1675 – This White Oak sprouts in Province of Carolina,
  270 miles from Charles Towne (named as capital in 1691)
- 1712 – White Oak continues growth in new Province of
  North Carolina
- 1769 – Daniel Boone traveled through the North Carolina
  mountains en route to the Kentucky territory

Pins indicated 1776 and 1783, when the new government of
the United States of America opened land west of the Blue Ridge
region of the Appalachian Mountains, and 1789, for the U. S.
Constitution and North Carolina statehood.

- 1807 – Twenty-four British immigrants establish a Pantisocracy
  on a nearby trio of French Broad River islands they name
  Christabel, Inchcape, and Nether Stowey

- 1838 – Trail of Tears results from Indian Removal Act of 1830 and the New Echota Treaty of 1835
- 1844 – Concurrent founding of Laurels Institute (Presbyterian) and village of Runion
- 1851 – Madison County created from northern portion of Buncombe County and western portion of Yancey County and named after President James Madison
- 1856 – Secession first preached at Methodist Episcopal Church, South; Laurels Institute becomes Laurels Presbyterian College

*Now there's a true portrait of Runion,* Carol thought, and in her mind loomed an image of the white oak standing as witness tree between the properties of town, college, and church, dangling a once brutish, ignorant, and now dead man above their joining. *And him a Boyd, no less, and me a Boyd, too, and married into his line.*

- 1863 – Thirteen old men and young boys executed in Shelton Laurel Massacre, local event in American Civil War, 1861-1865
- 1897 – Laurels Presbyterian College becomes Runion College

A blue pin was stuck in a ring for 1903 in honor of the Wright Brothers and their first flight at Kitty Hawk on North Carolina's Outer Banks. A yellow pin for 1916 remembered World War I and an unnamed July hurricane that made landfall in Charleston, South Carolina, causing a record-breaking French Broad River flood that swept away the remainder of Runion's nearby island settlements. Pins in 1929, 1945, 1960, and 1969 memorialized events that devastated Wall Street and Japan and commemorated momentous first steps at a Woolworth lunch counter and on Earth's moon.

- 1972 – Runion College joins University of North Carolina System, chartered as Runion State University
- 1989 – Restoration of Nelson Hall, oldest building on RSU campus, completed; revolutions begin collapse of Soviet Union and end of Cold War; this White Oak falls on 23 September, less than two months before the Berlin Wall

The great tree had stood with its leaves singing way up in the winds of all that history, and below the people of Runion had often seemed joined like children dancing around a maypole. In its everyday life, it had served as witness to the joining point of property owned in the nineteenth century by men mostly lost to Runion history: Robert Johnson and a Henderson without a recorded Christian name and Mallie Reeves, who had donated the land upon which the Runion Methodist Episcopal Church, South, was built and its cemetery established. While this last bone of their witness tree stood encased in glass and bathed in the display's warm light, all three men lay deep in that cold burying ground this very night.

Carol shuddered.

A distorted electronic bell tone startled her almost to standing.

"May I have your attention please. The library will close in twenty-five minutes. Please bring materials to be checked out to the Circulation Desk now."

"Good, Lord," she muttered.

*Thirty minutes and then the last vacuuming of the year. . . . Of the century.*

She smiled at that and closed her eyes and nestled deeper into the chair.

*Let's see*, she thought. *1712.*

The tree stands at a little over thirty feet, like a child among elders in a church. The woods around it tumble away, loud with life and yet somehow quieter than the woods surrounding Carroll's zero-hour compound still two hundred eighty-seven years in the future. The recent change from Carolina to North Carolina changes nothing here beneath the lush canopy that shades this swell of nameless ridge. Bird People, Animal People, Insect People—all are here, unmolested as of yet by the English Crown's claim on them. The Human People, the Cherokee, are near but not too close, not in this moment when she is a black bear in green summer, feeling no fear of breeze-haunted ferns and scratching her back against an almost forty-year-old white oak.

Carol nuzzled against the patterned fabric of the chair and opened her eyes and looked at her watch and closed her eyes again.

*1769.*

Six men and their pack animals walk in single file along the ridge, bearing westward, about to pass within an arm's length of Carol, now dreaming she is the tree itself.

One hundred years old and over sixty feet tall, she towers above the travelers for a moment and then lets her consciousness descend the trunk—a sensation like going down in a glass-walled elevator—to get a better look at the scruffy faces as they go by.

Boone stops and reaches out and touches her.

She flinches—or tries to—as her sense of towering power crashes to the ground at the feet of the man. Rooted and mute, she realizes she is over sixty feet of powerless strength and natural beauty. The men could choose, she knows, to take her down and use her for any purpose—or for none. Unable to speak or smack him into her own time with a low-hanging limb, she launches her consciousness upward into her highest branches, where she peers out toward a lonesome mountain and attempts not to feel the touches below.

"Look here where a bear's wallowed up against her regular," Boone says. He leans in and sniffs where his fingers touch. "Not been here in a long, long while though."

"Perhaps 'twasn't a bear but one of them Yahoos," John Stewart says.

The men laugh—a bit nervously, she thinks—while Boone shakes his head and smiles.

"That's the foolishness comes from reading lies in novels," he says. "We'll finish Captain Gulliver's adventures before we're two nights into Tennessee and will then read more profitably from the Holy Scriptures."

"Amen," William Cooley says.

Cooley, Stewart, and Joseph Holder sit to rest, while John Findley and James Mooney walk away together farther along the ridge. Boone stands leaning against her, the flat of his palm warm on her trunk.

"Men," he says after a time, now turning and leaning his back against her, "If this river we've been following begins to tend toward the southwest, we'll have to turn away from it soon, as our destination is more to the northwest."

"Well, that's a flustration," Stewart says. "I've enjoyed the fishing and the sound of water." He pushes the earth end of his stick into the leaves and dirt in front of him, creating a small trench. "Speaking of which," he says and stands and pees a stream.

She wonders if her roots will yearn for that moisture and feels her stomach turn somewhere in the trunk above Boone's head.

"I've heard tell of a Broad River hereabouts," Stewart says. "Reckon this'n's it, Dan'l?"

"I reckon it to be."

"I've likewise heard tell of it," William Cooley says. "If that's it, we must be in the land of the Cherokee."

"Deep into it," Stewart says. "Although their principal towns lie a good ways to our southwest."

"Yet we don't have to be in their towns to get sculped," Cooley says.

"True enough," Boone says. "And since their recent tussle with the English they keep a more vigilant eye in this direction. A leader up from Settacoo come and led raids all the way past here to the Yadkin and Catawba—"

With a crackle and swish through dead leaves and sticks, Findley and Mooney return hurrying along the ridge, and Boone, Stewart, and Cooley step forward to meet them.

"We seen something just down from the end of the ridge," Findley says.

"Something or somebody," Mooney adds.

"Cherokee?" Cooley says, getting both hands on his long rifle.

"I think not," Findley says. "A devil, more like."

During the talk about the Cherokee, she'd lowered her consciousness to the level of the men and now studies the faces of Boone's friends and sees in them both the flush of excitement and the pallor of fear.

"A devil?" Boone says, a smile in his eyes.

The men shift in the leaves, situating themselves around Boone and her so that they can see him and each other and the pathless run of the short ridge.

Findley wipes palms on the front of his coat. Then, "We seen it from a distance—"

"It?" Cooley asks.

"I reckon I don't know how else to call what we seen," Findley says. "'Twas about fifty yards from us, I reckon."

"Stood on two legs, it did," Mooney adds. "Just stood there looking at us."

"'Twas about five feet high, I reckon. And covered all in black hair."

"Black bears'll stand on hind legs."

"I know that, Cooley, of course I do. But 'tweren't no black bear and, before you say it, 'tweren't no Cherokee Indian nor negro neither."

"Could you make out its face at that distance?" Boone asks.

"No more than the whites of eyes and teeth," Mooney says.

"Sharp teeth?" Holder asks, his voice dry and tinged with fear.

"Couldn't tell," Findley says.

"Don't it seem like a Yahoo, Dan'l?" Stewart asks.

"It does," Boone says.

She hears a smile in his voice.

"Maybe you conjured it with your joke about the tree rubbing."

"'T weren't no conjuration nor imagination," Findley says.

She feels something drop quietly onto one of her branches. She can't look at it but knows it to be a black thing and a stillness, sitting twenty feet above the heads of the men. She wonders if, in that far future of Carroll's compound, something black like this might sit in a tree and watch the paranoid Boyd boys tend and stock their fortress. She wonders if it enters the place when they are away and have left the door open, if it touches and sniffs the narrow cot intended to be hers. She wonders if it has seen her there, and she shudders.

"Quiet," Boone whispers.

All stop and stand still until Boone releases his breath.

"I thought I felt movement," he says. He closes his eyes, takes a deep breath, holds it for a moment, and then releases again. "All seems still now."

"Anybody ever heard or seen something like this in the woods before?" Holder asks. "Excepting Yahoos, of course."

Stewart, Cooley, Findley, and Mooney shake their heads.

"As a boy in Pennsylvania," Boone says, "I recollect hearing stories of such a novelty as this in the woods around Northumberland. 'Twas described as James and John have described what they saw. Those who testified to having seen it confirm that 'twas strongly formed in the shape of a man and said that it had the face of an old negro. Several who seen it agreed in this description. Those that got too near it said it showed its teeth at them but 'twasn't remarkably shy. It allowed a man named Abraham Miller to get within a few yards, but then it run away on two legs and when the chance come it vaulted up into the trees. I heard that a party of men, mounted and on foot, set out to capture it and got close enough that one of them attacted it with a whip, at which it turned and returned the favor with its hand and struck the offender senseless with a single blow. Then it outrun 'em all, horse and man alike, and went up into the trees again and was lost."

John Stewart laughs.

"That's as good a tale as Master Gulliver's," he says.

"I remember my pa," Boone continues, "talking with a fellow by the name of Cope who said 'twas a natural point of curiosity as to whence this solitary creature came. Old Cope reckoned it may be a negro lost in the woods in infancy, or a rascal of some sort escaped from a showman." He paused. "He likewise reckoned the description of it, except for the blackness, didn't materially differ from that given by naturalists of the ouran outang."

The men stir. Findley and Mooney pick up their packs.

"Don't know how such a beast as that would find its way into them woods or these," Holder says. "Reckon they ever found out what it was?"

"Not to my knowledge," Boone says. "Pa moved us to Carolina, and this is the first time I've come across anything resembling those stories."

"Ain't them mountains in Pennsylvania connected to these?" Mooney asks.

"Very like," Findley says.

Boone looks at the sky, and she is surprised that he doesn't see the black thing above him.

"I think we ought to continue more directly north from here." Without another word he turns, touching her again as he steps away. "There's the mouth of a smaller stream coming into this one just down yonder. Haply it tends more northerly." He sets out through the trees.

The five others and their animals follow.

*Now they're in the faculty lot, over which part of me will fall in two hundred twenty years.*

*Now they're crossing campus quad, walking through the steps of the library, and traversing the first floor like men fording a belly-deep stream.*

She felt a presence in the room—a shift in the air, something static or magnetic—but slowly opened her eyes to find herself alone.

She knew Daniel Boone hadn't passed close enough to touch the young white oak around which Runion would one day grow. Far away to the east, he and his band would have turned north toward the Iron Mountains and the Great Warriors' Path. But Boone had become her favorite historical figure when she'd seen Fess Parker play him on TV just two weeks into her twenty-first year, and she liked to imagine that he'd come so close. And even if he hadn't trekked across these ancient hills and through their river valleys, he'd served as a herald into this unsuspecting highland wilderness, where, within twenty-one years of his 1769 expedition, some one thousand white people had settled—hungry for land, hard-working, afflicted with violence, sweet-natured, bedeviled by religion, Old-Testament pioneers.

She held her watch up before her eyes, then let her arm drop into her lap.

*Eleven minutes.*

From a hillside dappled with the yellows and wine-reds of October and overlooking Drover's Trail and the French Broad River, this time as the black thing up in the tree again, she watches the man, the men with him, their wagon, and their animals coming along the Trail from the direction of the hot springs. The horses blow with their work, and the men with him chatter without pause. All smell of sweat and mud and male.

Body rocking with the gait of his horse, the man tilts back his head, and—from beneath the broad brim of a low-crowned black hat—speaking eyes seem to petition the pale blue sky. Then his gaze lowers and appears to fasten on her where she crouches on a broad limb and hugs the trunk.

She feels as if, unafraid of her blackness, he would communicate something to her as he did to the sky. She shudders and shies and utters a low growl that rumbles under her breath until his gaze releases and disappears beneath his hat's broad brim.

At the lip of Laurel River's mouth, they stop and clamber down from horseback and wagon and begin shedding and stowing their heavy coats.

"Brother O'Haver," the man says, as he cinches a saddle bag closed. "Your company and the use of your wagon make the miles easier." Free of his cloak of fulled wool, he rolls his shoulders to adjust the drab frock coat buttoned up to his neck and straight collar. "I thank God you and Old Gray agreed to keep us company to Brother Killian's."

"I ain't been upriver from Warm Springs in several year," the wagoner says. "I'll continue and renew an old acquaintance with Brother Killian and others thereabouts." He climbs onto the seat of the wagon. "And if the people should gather at Brother Killian's, I should be glad to hear you give them a sermon and an exhortation."

"Lord willing," the man says. "Lord willing." He rises to his saddle. "If you tarry 'til the morrow, I intend to visit the Buncombe courthouse and speak from the seventh chapter of Second Kings."

She watches the wagon venture into the Laurel behind Old Gray, watches the horse feeling its way through the clear water and the wagon bumping across the rocky bottom as the water level rises to the middle of its wheels. She watches them pass the midpoint of the crossing, but then the wagon's right front wheel rises, jolts down, and sticks fast. Old Gray strains forward once, twice, a third time, but the wheel lifts only slightly and for only a moment, then settles again.

"How now, Old Gray?" O'Haver says. "We ain't mired, so let's onward march." He makes sharp sounds with his mouth, and the horse pulls so that the wheel rises higher this time but then rolls back down. O'Haver turns in the seat and says, "Bishop Asbury, if you gentlemen will ride singly along the left side of the wagon, I believe we can rise out of this trouble."

"We rise by prayer," Asbury says.

"Of course, sir, yes, Bishop," O'Haver says. "And our helping ourselves will petition the Lord to help us as well, I believe."

"Amen."

"Now, again, ride singly by my left, and if you see something in the wagon bed you can reach and lift with one hand, then carry it to t'other side."

When the first rider splashes into the Laurel, O'Haver rises and lunges lightly from the wagon to Old Gray's back. He leans down over the horse's neck and speaks softly and continually near its ear as his companions pass one by one. When Asbury, the last rider, passes, picks up a bundle from the bed, and then for a moment smooths Old Gray's forelock, O'Haver speaks sharp words of encouragement, and Old Gray lurches toward the rest of its kind and their riders.

The wagon rises and rolls forward, and Old Gray stumbles at the release but recovers and then makes it safely through to join the others.

"Amen," Asbury says again. "Brothers, there's a sermon in this, if I can find the words for it."

"Amen, Bishop," the men answer and then laugh as each tosses his burden back into the wagon's bed.

O'Haver swings his right leg over Old Gray's neck and slides down to the ground, then moves along the side of the wagon, reaching in to resettle the bundles to order.

One of the youngest and largest among the men removes his hat and wipes his face with a brown and red spot'd kerchief drawn from around his neck.

"Now, friends, how is it that 'twas freezing on t'other side yonder and burning up on this?"

"You ought to work that up into a sermon of your own,

Brother Carroll," O'Haver says as he steps up to the wagon's seat.

She shudders and growls on her limb.

While the men laugh and the water drips from their boots, Bishop Asbury sits his horse with his gaze again seemingly fastened on her tree.

"Lord," he says so sharply and suddenly that the landscape seems startled. "I had too mean an opinion of Carolina." His gaze sweeps across the river to the pine-dappled ridge on the far side and back. "It is a much better country than I expected or understood before now."

She wants to tell him of the people and the town, the churches and the university to come, but she knows that she is a black thing with a wild and unimaginable voice. She hears messages of wonder and dread passing between the trees, and she wants to tell him that when he reached this side of the Laurel, she felt the wilderness roil deep inside her, felt the roiling become a wild sound trapped in her belly.

"The country, maybe," O'Haver says. "But the men are notorious eye gougers." He lifts the reins from the hitch.

The wild sound within her begins to swell upward.

Old Gray suddenly shies backwards in the traces, neck elevated, eyes wide and nostrils flared.

O'Haver tightens his grip on the reins, leans slightly to his left, but continues talking.

"Now, I've heard tell that many a North Carolinian cannot salute you without putting a finger in your eye—"

The wild sound moves, upward and unstoppable, into her throat and ears before breaching her lips.

She sat up on the edge of the plush golden chair, hearing her shriek reverberate around the reading room. She felt her face redden and craned sideways to look down the hall toward the elevators.

Nobody appeared.

She leaned back in the chair again and was shaking her watch into place, but the distorted bell tone sounded before she had a chance to look at the time.

"May I have your attention please. The library will close in three minutes. Please make your way toward the front exit."

She knew she should get up and start with the quieter tasks of finishing her work.

*Not that there's anybody around for the vacuum to bother.*

But she felt herself settling into the chair again and began to see—along the wooded ridge of her semiconsciousness—a figure approaching.

A Cherokee, she knows, moving through woods his people can no longer enter as their own. She notices the signs of settlement and the height of the tree—over eighty feet tall, she guesses—and knows also that this is probably a young man who has fled, Tsali-like, into the mountains to avoid removal. He will likely subsist on roots and groundnuts and berries until captured by General Scott's troops or starved to death or, if he escapes these fates, perhaps impressed into service in Thomas's Legion some few years hence.

"You okay in here?"

The reading room again popped into place around her, and she saw Tammy Garcia standing in the doorway.

"What?"

"Are you okay? We thought we heard something like a shout or a scream from up here."

"I'm fine." Carol pushed herself up from the chair to her feet. "Just dozing on my break and waiting—"

The bell tone sounded, and the voice said, "May I have your attention please. The library is now closed."

"For that," she said. She smoothed the front of her smock and the seat of her pants.

"Well, maybe it was just one of our ghosts."

Carol walked toward Tammy and the doorway.

"I thought I felt one of them in here a few minutes ago, so thanks so much for the reminder," she said. "And now you're just going to head back down to your second floor and leave me up here all alone."

Tammy smiled and pulled rubber gloves from the front pocket of her smock, and Carol did the same.

"And if I don't see you, have a merry Christmas."

"You too."

"See you on Tuesday the fourth," Tammy said and headed for the stairwell.

"If computers don't end the world for us," Carol said to herself as she entered the PN – Z stacks. "Like they could." She took the vacuum from her closet and startled when it roared to life the moment she plugged it in.

*  *  *

The library doors sighed shut and left her standing in the haunting honeyed light of Leininger Plaza at just after two o'clock in the morning on the eve of Christmas Eve. The air was cold, but not quite freezing, and moving in stuttering gusts. The sky hung clear, radiant with the glow of the full moon hanging somewhere above the library. Campus lay mostly dark and quiet around her— luster of ghostly moonlight, pockets of safety lighting along the walkways and in the entrances to buildings, trills of the campus screech owl, scratches of a brittle brown leaf skittering across the plaza like a ghost crab.

Instead of turning toward the lot behind the library where she'd parked that afternoon, she walked toward the area where the oak had stood, thinking maybe she would offer up some kind of prayer to any witnessing spirit that lingered there. She would look at the Christmas tree in the yard of the Runion Community Church and wander along Main Street to see the winking and blinking of holiday and traffic lights. Then she would follow Lonesome Mountain Drive back to her car.

Where from there, she didn't yet know.

Only loosely tethered to time and place, she saw Boone and his men hurry across the walkway in front of her and heard Asbury and his struggle to ford the mouth of the Laurel. The mighty white oak seemed to rise and spread above them all, and beyond it she glimpsed the lonely Cherokee fugitive hunkered down in the graveyard of the RCC. On the ground this side of the ghostly trunk, impassioned lovers wrestled as one in lush green grass now long gone.

She waved her hand, as if fending off some flying fiend, and these images scattered to reveal the southeast corner of campus, where the ground—open and manicured or covered with cracked asphalt—still seemed to ache for the absent white oak.

*Like a body missing a limb,* she thought.

No matter the season or the time of day or night, the faculty parking lot the tree once shaded reminded her of a barren patch of ruined ground in the middle of Carroll's woods.

*Our own Devil's Tramping Ground,* she thought. *And right about there—that third parking space—is where life started going the way it's gone.*

Instead of raising a prayer, she waved her hand once more, and these things of the night—remembered or imagined—faded in the dazzling white, green, red, and blue lights that embodied the darkness of the neatly trimmed Fraser fir growing in the Runion Community Church's yard. She turned aside, to the right, and as she approached the intersection of Mill and Main Streets, a single car passed beneath the blinking traffic light, heading south on Main toward Barnard, Marshall, Asheville.

At the light, she turned right again and strolled the gently inclining sidewalk toward the intersection of Main Street and Lonesome Mountain Drive, lingering along the way to take in the Cowart's Department Store window, with its glowing plastic village set up on yards of glittery cotton, and the antique nativity scene in the window of Aslan's Wardrobe & Christian Thrift. She stood for a moment at the corner of Main and Lonesome Mountain, looking across at the Runion Pizzeria and realizing she was hungry. But then, instead of turning right toward her car, she turned left and drifted down the other side of the street, likewise lingering over the classic Christmas stories and CDs in the window of Two Rivers Books & Music, the small Santa's Sleigh filled with hiking boots and hunting vests, maps and knives, in the window of Lonesome Mountain Outfitters, and Whitson's Green Grocer's papier-mâché replica of Scrooge's "prize Turkey."

She walked slowly, wondering if the scenes and sentiments brought to life in window displays up and down Main Street would disappear into the mist of myth and legend if the world descended into darkness in eight days. She found it hard to imagine that historical waves of renaissance and enlightenment could be swallowed up in revenant dark ages and fanaticism. She shuddered to realize that it wasn't difficult to imagine Carroll as a backwoods warlord—to imagine him good at it.

The future was a black thing.

She shuddered again and hurried into the garden alley between the town's branch of the Madison County Public Library and Reeves Dental, where Runion's Christmas tree stood, a cut tree and not so spectacularly lit as the RCC's, decorated with only a few well-placed white lights but laden with local ornaments—stars and trees and angels, hand-painted or wrapped in crinkly aluminum foil at the elementary school and the nursing home.

She stepped over the drooping strand of chain to look closer at these in the available light of tree and street, but she almost tipped face-first into the display when a dizzying swirl of blue and red suddenly played along the library wall and among the ornaments. She grabbed a branch to steady herself, and two ornaments fell to the ground at her feet. When she was sure of her balance, she turned to see Deputy Davis Boyce rising up out of his squad car.

"Morning, Mrs. Boyd-Boyd," he said with a smile. "You okay?"

"Yes, I'm okay, Davis," she said, now holding another branch. She picked up the two ornaments and hung the star back in the tree. "But you scared me to death with those lights."

"I thought they'd add to the seasonal feel." He leaned into the car, turned off the lights, and stood up again. "I guess it's good I didn't goose you with the siren."

"I'd've jumped out of my skin." She rehung the fallen angel and kept a hold on the branch.

He chuckled and stepped toward her, smiling, but she could see that he was taking in the scene of which she was the centerpiece, scrutinizing her body language and countenance.

"I'm all right, Davis," she said, letting go of the branch. "Really I am." She saw him relax somewhat and reach out his hand, which she took, to steady her over the drooping chain. "I just finished at the library and wanted a little walk before I headed home."

"Well, it's a mite chilly, but for December, I reckon it ain't too bad for a walk." He put his hands on his hips and looked up Main and then back at her. "Your choice of time is questionable."

She laughed and said, "I know, but's the only time I had." She raised her eyes to the full moon above Aslan's and the Fredricks Agency, then let her gaze follow the rooflines to the empty sky above Main St. Theater and Rio Burrito. "I was just up in the Archives Reading Room spending some time with our white oak. Made me want to visit its old home. And then take a look at these other witness trees and the Christmas lights."

Deputy Boyce turned and took a step back to stand beside her, likewise looking up at the empty sky.

"It's strange, Carol," he said. "This town somehow hasn't looked nor felt the same these past ten years." He ran a palm across his mouth. "We're more and more in pieces since it fell, seems like to me." He jingled his keys, twirled the ring once around his right index finger, and snapped the jingling quiet in a fist. "There's the college folk that don't like the business folk—and t'other way around. There's church folk from town and holler that can't get together on what the hell they believe." He dropped the keys into his jacket pocket and slid his fingers into the back pockets of his khaki uniform pants. "There's kids making out in back seats and stealing cigarettes, like always, but then there's others doing God knows what manner of shit up their noses and on their computers." He stopped. "Pardon my French."

"You ought to write that down, Davis. Send it to Gabe for the paper." She smiled up at him with a sidewise glance. "Bad French and all."

He pulled his hands from his pockets and crossed his arms over his chest.

"I might do that if I knew where it was all tending or could say how to stop it." He looked at his watch. "Now, won't Mr. Boyd-Boyd be worried?"

She smiled again, then laughed.

"Oh, my gosh, I hope you never call him that to his face." She watched a hardness develop in the deputy's eyes and understood that he didn't like Carroll Boyd or his brothers. She looked away from him, and her gaze rose again to the full moon. "Anyway, he's dead to the world when he's asleep."

He seemed about to say something but didn't. Then his face softened.

"Can I give you a lift to your car?"

She dropped her gaze from the moon but couldn't meet his, focusing instead on the Fredericks Agency's dark and undecorated window across the street.

"I'll walk, Davis, if that's all right."

He nodded and turned, and they stepped together from the garden alley to the sidewalk.

"Sure, that's all right, as long as you go directly there and don't wander about anymore tonight." He opened the door of his car and set his right foot inside. "I'll be watching." He grinned and dropped into the seat.

"Now, don't go all pervy on me, Davis."

"Can't help it," he said. "It's my most precious character flaw."

They laughed together as he closed the door, and both headed, at their different speeds, up Main toward Lonesome Mountain Drive.

\* \* \*

Carol turned right off Sandy Bottoms and onto Candler's Stand. She slowed the car as she approached her driveway but then rolled past it, leaning over the steering wheel—careful not to press the horn with her breasts—and looking across the little unnamed creek at the ghosted house on the small knoll above the road.

As usual, Carroll hadn't left on even a glimmer of light for her.

She imagined him asleep in their overheated, pitch-black bedroom, pictured him by the greenish glow of his night vision goggles. Lying on his back. Left leg covered, right leg not. Quilt and sheet bunched at his naked waist. Broad and black-haired belly and chest swelling upwards in the dark, then collapsing to swell upwards again. Mouth agape, innocent as a child's with its beautiful lips but discharging roaring snores.

She continued slowly along Carter's Stand, past Marion's house and Francis's. Then she veered right onto a worn dirt track that looped a quarter mile into the woods behind the brothers' properties.

She didn't know when Carroll first heard about the catastrophic possibilities looming over the turn of the century, but he and his younger twin brothers seemed to have been planning for years—since the Reagan Administration, at least—to build a three-bedroom fortress beneath the witness tree that stood where their properties joined in the backwoods. And for months now, Carroll had brought a few extra items home from Whitson's Green Grocer in Runion or Ingles in Marshall—gallons of water, multi-packs of Dial soap bars, cans of Del Monte vegetables and fruits, bags of rice, tins of Chicken of the Sea, bottles of cranberry juice, and more. She'd reluctantly helped transport these through the woods to the stronghold, which, she had to admit, was an impressive structure to be the work of three bumpkin brothers.

The Boyd witness tree was also a white oak, although, she guessed, no more than half the age of the one on display at the library. Its summer canopy easily shaded their compound and the work going on inside it. But at this time of year, the tree stood bare, and the light of days rapidly descending toward last night's solstice had sifted down through its branches and touched the fort like something akin to snow.

A bright, motion-activated light lit her way inside, where she closed the door behind her, bolted it, and made her way to the cold and quiet kitchen.

Digging around in the refrigerator, she rejected the bread and sandwich meat, choosing milk, butter, and an egg instead and setting them on the counter. From the pantry she took flour, baking powder, salt, sugar, and Mrs. Butterworth's.

A few minutes later, with her stack of pancakes smothered in buttery syrup, she returned to the refrigerator, grabbed and popped a can of Natural Light, and sat down at the table.

\* \* \*

By half past four in the morning, she'd cleared away all signs of her being there and gone from light switch to light switch until she sat on her cot in a darkness that seemed absolute. She knew—barring something more dramatic than her absence—Carroll would be oblivious to her empty side of the bed for at least two more hours, so she had only that long to decide what to do and get started.

To go away was fraught with uncertainties, from where to go—DC? Charleston? New Orleans?—to how to live there and who to be there. To go home was just as problematic. Her mind flitted back and forth between these without finding any stable place to land, but then it seized up and she lay down.

She didn't know she'd fallen asleep until she awoke, suddenly remembering the black thing in the tree of her historical reveries, the creature that had spooked Boone and his men and spied on Asbury and his. But she knew those visions to be of her own making out of reading she'd done, which meant the black thing was hers, too, and she wondered if she'd read somewhere about some such apparition.

Then she remembered her passing thought that a descendant of the creature—or the long-lived creature itself—might have been here in this place, sniffing and pawing her cot. She shuddered and lay frozen, holding her breath and listening for a long moment. Then she slowly released the air in her lungs, and inhaled again, slowly, seeking any smell.

*Nothing*, she thought.

She didn't release the breath immediately but held it and listened again.

*All quiet.*

Body and mind relaxed a bit as she slowly exhaled and closed her eyes in the dark.

*1962. Early May.*

The French conduct underground nuclear tests in the Algerian Sahara, while the Americans conduct atmospheric tests near Christmas Island. The Civil Rights Movement is progressing from the Woolworth Counter in Greensboro to the University of Alabama. NASA has flown John Glenn three times around Earth and now runs headlong toward a future imagined as defined by spaceflight.

Beneath a waxing crescent moon, beneath the newly greening

overstory of Runion's oak, atop the tender new grass of a lawn that will soon give way to a parking lot for faculty, she rides the bucking pelvis of Carroll Boyd. She is four months shy of eighteen but already finishing her freshman year at Runion College, and this is his twenty-first birthday.

The campus carillon chimes a quarter past two o'clock.

She feels the chill of the night on her scalp and upper lip, between her breasts, and at the small of her back. These mix with internal chills just as physical—but also emotional, perhaps even spiritual and moral. She digs her fingers into the mat of dark hair on his chest and looks into his half-lidded eyes, unable to tell if he sees her or not. Then she arches her back and looks up past the heavy limbs of the tree to the moon winking through new leaves that dance and sing in a light breeze.

She feels welling up within her a shout or a scream that will go out from beneath the oak to echo among the tombstones across Mill Street and between the buildings on Main, to wake the sleepers within earshot, draw the campus cops and maybe even Deputy Boyce to where—she almost laughs to think it—Carol Boyd and Carroll Boyd—no relation—wrestle and sweat in the cool grass.

He grunts and clenches to stillness beneath her as his breath catches, holds for a long moment, and then his chest deflates. His eyes close.

Not finished, she rides harder but loses rhythm, feeling him already going soft inside her. She stutters to stillness, and the scream caught in her lungs vaporizes to a sighed "No."

She awoke again, overwarm in the chilly bunker, almost hearing the exasperated word trail off in the dark, her fear of the black thing gone. She rose and stumbled to the entrance, where she unbolted the door and pulled it open and drew in a deep breath of December morning darkness.

She hadn't thought of that night in a long time. Nor of what followed it. Within the next twenty-four hours after they rose and dressed in the shadows beneath the oak, she aced her history exam and failed biology, and he went on a drunk that totaled his '58 Chevy Delray, broke his right leg, and killed his best friend. The following spring semester, she flunked out of Runion College and miscarried a child. Somehow they'd still found the heart to marry on the third of June, 1963.

*Thirty-six years*, she thought as she pulled the bunker door closed behind her and looked upward into the twilight nakedness of the Boyd witness tree.

She passed the twin houses of Francis and Marion again, still undecided if she would go or stay. At the last moment she decided to go and pressed the gas just as she then decided to stay and turned too late, missed the narrow log bridge, and dropped the nose of her car over the lip of the creek bank.

"Well shit."

Rather than risk waking Carroll trying to back out of the predicament, she set the brake, killed the engine, and got out. She stood in the cold air, looking from the car to the overcast sky, to the house, to the blacktop that led down to the intersection with Sandy Bottoms Road.

Glad that the morning was still on the darker side of twilight, she let herself in the house. She pulled off her shoes and walked quietly through the kitchen, wondering if in a few days they'd have to abandon this place for the fort.

Carroll lay just as she'd pictured him earlier, the hair on his chest and belly black as that night beneath the oak, although his beard looked nearly white in the weak predawn light and the hair on his head was either gray or gone. His snoring sounded more like a growl than a roar, which meant that he would be waking soon.

She quickly stripped in the master bathroom and, on a whim she couldn't fathom, put on a musky flannel shirt that he'd thrown over the shower rod either last night or the night before. She carefully stretched out on the bed, took the covers he'd tossed off, pulled them up to her neck, and rolled onto her side with her back to him.

She would wait, she decided, to see how this Y2K panic panned out. If the world fell apart at the millennial midnight, she could either find protection and survival with the bumpkin brothers in their fortress or find it easier to disappear into the chaos of reconstruction. She even thought it possible that in the midst of such a catastrophe, she and Carroll might rediscover the love that helped them survive those calamitous times in which they married.

In the meantime, her own Boyds having all disappeared or died, she would have to suffer Carroll's Boyds through the holidays, at least until New Year's Eve. Staying for now meant that she needed to get Carroll something for Christmas. On trips to Gatlinburg and Pigeon Forge during last summer and fall, she'd already bought what he would give to his mother and father, his brothers and their families. But she'd easily resisted buying anything for him. She hoped now that Lonesome Mountain Outfitters would have some decent stuff left, maybe a wonderfully powerful flashlight or a water purifier that would allow him to drink his own piss.

In that last thought she felt the rise of the feeling that had nearly sent her to the intersection with Sandy Bottoms and to wherever from there. Given that she was in his bed rather than on the road to that wherever, she tamped down the feeling.

The growl stopped. His breathing caught for a moment and then released in an almost vocal sigh.

She held still and shifted her thoughts toward cooking and the groceries needed for it. She had jars of green beans that she and her sisters-in-law had canned with their mother-in-law the previous summer. She would need chicken and ham, maybe a couple of steaks, russet potatoes, new potatoes, sweet potatoes, and maybe some broccoli or asparagus. She thought a meatloaf might be a nice New Year's Eve surprise—so, ground beef, too.

The bed shook, and she knew Carroll had swung his feet to the floor and sat up.

"Goddamn," he groaned, beginning his morning liturgy.

She concentrated on what she did and didn't already have for meatloaf. She would need onions. At the thought of mincing them, she could feel the tears well.

Carroll cleared his throat and scratched his beard.

"Shit," he sighed.

She thought of New Year's Day, of collard greens, cornmeal, maybe some cabbage for boiling instead of potlikker soup, black-eyed peas and other ingredients for Hoppin' John—those onions again.

But what if New Year's Day dawned on a world gone dark? What if it began a frantic attempt to recover the memory of how to live without money and grocery stores and electricity and law and so much more? What if suddenly the Carroll Boyds of the world took charge because they were prepared to do so? Because it was their moment?

She felt the bed shake once more and go still as Carroll left it with a popping of knees and a grunted "Fuck." She decided she'd better leave planning of the New Year's Day meal until later. Or, better yet, leave it to her mother-in-law.

When he flipped on the bright bathroom light, she made sure not to let her closed eyes flinch, in case he looked back at her, and when the toilet seat banged against the flush box, she didn't startle. She eased her eyes barely open and watched through her lashes for a moment as he stood with his back to her and dribbled pee into the bowl and onto the floor. Then she glanced quickly at the bedside clock.

6:16.

She closed her eyes before he turned and quietly—slowly—released a breath she hadn't been aware of holding.

She eased down into darkness.

* * *

*Rooted and mute, she realizes she is over fifty, too old to be climbing trees. And yet she stands at the foot of this mighty white oak and feels in herself the strength to vault up the massive trunk. Without another thought, she rises past three men hanging—Godly and Roberts twisting and swinging in the breeze that inspires the singing leaves overhead, Boyd dangling still and watching her with half-lidded eyes. She passes beyond his vision and continues to rise. She seats herself on a high branch among the choir of wine-red leaves as the tree begins to walk with slow steps away from the point where it has shaded councils and stood witness for over three hundred years, walks toward the moist, dark earth at the river's edge, to drink deep of upstream places, lives, and memories. And then she is falling, not out of the tree but with it, into the river, to splash and roll and spin her way slowly downstream to whatever snag or sea might come.*

❧ ☙

# ACKNOWLEDGMENTS

My thanks go, first and always, to Leesa, for her love and support, and to our sons, Lane and Raleigh, for their love and energy. I'd also like to thank my extended Cody and Reeves families, particularly the Reeves side, for living and telling stories that I've often borrowed, stolen, adapted, and willfully—or not—misquoted for these pages. My colleagues, friends, and students in the Department of Literature and Language at East Tennessee State University provide a creative and supportive community for teaching and writing, and I appreciate it.

The creation of the cover art for *A Twilight Reel* was largely a family affair, a collaboration of blood kin: my son Raleigh Cody came up with the photo concept; my cousin Joey Plemmons was the photographer; and another cousin, Jamie Reeves, put it all together for the cover design.

The following stories would not be what they are without the input of those connected to them below:

- Early versions of "The Wine of Astonishment," "Overwinter," and "Grist for the Mill" were developed under the guidance of Rick Boyer, Jim Addison, and Jim Byer, my M.A. thesis committee at Western Carolina University.

- Jeff Mann provided important feedback for this trilogy of stories: "The Flutist," "The Invisible World Around Them," and "A Fiddle and a Twilight Reel."

- Friend and colleague Dr. Alan Holmes offered invaluable suggestions for a working ending to "The Loves of Misty Sprinkle."

- "Conversion" received a lot of help from my colleague and friend Dr. Yousif Elhindi, who guided my representation of Muslim culture and provided Arabic phrasing; Denton Loving's Orchard Keeper's Writer's Retreat, where significant work on the story took place; Ann Pancake and the participants in her fiction class that was part of the Appalachian Writer's Workshop at Hindman in Summer 2020; and Silas House for further editing suggestions.

- Friend and colleague Dr. Mark Baumgartner offered invaluable suggestions for a workable beginning to "Two Floors Above the Dead."

- Last but not least, my east Tennessee writing group—Tamara Baxter, Bob Kottage, Tess Lloyd, and Cate Strain—read all these stories over the course of a year and improved them with their feedback.

I am eternally grateful to A. D. Reed of Pisgah Press for his faith in me as a writer and his tireless work in support of my writing; the management of a small press is not for the faint of heart, but his is up to the task.

# About the Author

Michael Amos Cody grew up in the village of Walnut, jewel of Madison County, North Carolina, not far from the ruins of Runion, a place he has reimagined for stories appearing in *Yemassee, Tampa Review, Still,* and other publications, as well as in his first novel *Gabriel's Songbook* (Pisgah Press 2017). He lives with his wife Leesa in Jonesborough, Tennessee, and teaches in the Department of Literature and Language at East Tennessee State University.

# Also available from Pisgah Press

*Letting Go: Collected Poems 1983-2003*                              Donna Lisle Burton
$14.95
*Way Past Time for Reflecting*
$17.95

*Letters of the Lost Children: Japan—WWII*                       Reinhod C. Ferster
$34.95                                                           & Jan Atchley Bevan

*Musical Morphine: Transforming Pain One Note at a Time*         Robin Russell Gaiser
$17.95
*Open for Lunch*
$17.95

*MacTiernan's Bottle*                                              Michael Hopping
$14.95
*rhythms on a flaming drum*
$16.95

LANKY TALES                                    C. Robert Jones
*Lanky Tales, Vol. I: The Bird Man & other stories*
$9.00
*Lanky Tales, Vol. II: Billy Red Wing & other stories*
$9.00
*Lanky Tales, Vol. III: A Good and Faithful Friend & other stories*
$9.00
*The Mystery of Claggett Cove*
$9.00

*Homo Sapiens: A Violent Gene?*                                     Mort Malkin
$22.95

*Reed's Homophones: A Comprehensive Book of Sound-alike Words*        A.D. Reed
$17.95

*Swords in their Hands: George Washington and the Newburgh Conspiracy*
$24.95                                                             Dave Richards
Finalist in the USA Book Awards for History, 2014

*Trang Sen: A Novel of Vietnam*                                 Sarah-Ann Smith
$19.50

*Invasive Procedures: Earthqukes, Calamities, & poems from the midst of life*   Nan Socolow
$17.95

*Deadly Dancing*              THE RICK RYDER MYSTERY SERIES            RF Wilson
$15.95
*Killer Weed*
$14.95
*The Pot Professor*
$17.95

## To order:

Pisgah Press, LLC
PO Box 9663, Asheville, NC 28815
www.pisgahpress.com